Kleos Prime

P.W. Schuler

Published by P.W. Schuler, 2023.

KLEOS PRIME

First edition. October 17, 2023.

ISBN: 979-8223500100

Written by P.W. Schuler.

Table of Contents

"What is history, but a fable agreed upon?"

- Napoleon Bonaparte

For Craig, gone but not forgotten.

Part One A Surprise Encounter

Introduction

FOLLOWING THE ADVENT of interstellar travel nearly four centuries ago, the human race quickly spread to the nearest star systems in the galaxy. Masters of terraforming, humans were able to colonize dozens of planets that would normally have been inhospitable. Consequently, the human population expanded rapidly and now numbers in the hundreds of billions.

Newly established human colonies were legally designated as 'Freeholds,' thereby establishing the rights of the new owners to the planet, the solar system and its accompanying resources.

However, humanity's insatiable quest for additional planets caused tension with several alien species also seeking new worlds to colonize. Inevitably, several planetary systems claimed by human colonists as freeholds were also claimed by alien species.

These escalating tensions led to numerous atrocities against civilian populations. Once hostilities erupted, humanity found itself at war with a number of competing races simultaneously. These conflicts, when referred to collectively, became known as the 'Freehold Wars.' This devastating series of wars lasted nearly 80 human standard years.

Following a string of grievous defeats suffered by military expeditions sponsored by individual planets, the vast majority of human colonized planets decided to pool their resources and band together for common defense. This confederation was established as the 'Telluric Alliance,' drawing its name from the term 'telluric,' meaning 'of Earth.' A Council of Governors, comprised of representatives from all the various

Telluric planets, was appointed to formulate strategy and direct the war effort.

The formidable war machine known as the 'Combined Telluric Fleet' emerged from the alliance's efforts. Eventually, this force triumphed over their alien adversaries, but at a staggering cost: Billions of lives lost and devastation across many planetary systems. Presently, this so-called Telluric Alliance reigns as the dominant power within their quadrant of the Milky Way. But, whether this reign will prove benevolent or lead to unforeseen, sinister consequences remains a question to be answered by time alone......

It is the 388th year since the advent of interstellar travel, the 17th day of the 6th month according to the Telluric Standard Calendar.

Location: On Board the Interstellar Starship Archeron

"HEY, SWEET THING," I heard from over my shoulder. "Can I buy you a drink?" The stench of cheap aftershave assaulted me like a trash bin on a hot day. I turned to see a skinny young man had approached and was, indeed, speaking to me.

I'd walked to the crowded, noisy pub from my cabin a few hours before, and since then I'd heard many versions of that same, dumb joke. The men obviously thought they were being clever, since drinks were included with our 2nd class tickets. Most everything was included on board the Archeron. Unfortunately for me, that seemed to include annoying creeps like this one. He looked like a genuine dirtbag, with his hair slicked back, his shirt unbuttoned to his navel and a sleezy grin on his rodent-like face.

"I already have one, thanks." I answered from my seat at the bar, holding up my drink. "But if you go take a shower and brush your teeth, you can come back and ask me again."

"Frigid hag" he mumbled as he walked away.

The crowd in the pub was an eclectic mix of middle-aged couples casually enjoying cocktails and singles aggressively on the prowl. Venturing from my cabin in order to do a bit of 'people watching,' I'd randomly stumbled upon this establishment. Soulless electronic music permeated the smokey place, the sound of clinking glasses and bleating laughter threatened me with an impending headache. I was seriously thinking of returning to my cabin when my attention was drawn toward the pub's entrance.

Two men had entered bellowing loudly and causing a stir. I assumed they were males, but they certainly weren't human. The two pale-skinned hulks were each over two meters in height, their broad shoulders and muscular arms displayed in sleeveless tunics. Prominent suborbital ridges marked them as Caladrians, a feature which might lead you to believe they're of low intelligence. But that'd be a mistake; they're well known to be devilishly clever.

Caladrians are near neighbors of the Telluric Alliance, and had been allied with us during the wars. Still, I hadn't seen many in person before, just a few students at the Academy.

These two caused a fuss among the pub staff, as two waitresses had quickly attended them when they squeezed into a booth. One of the men even grabbed a handful of a waitress's ample bottom and gave it a good squeeze, laughing loudly as he did it. The girl good-naturedly slapped his arm and appeared not to be offended. I think she even giggled.

A managerial type approached them; I expected him to confront the Caladrians about their raucous entrance and inappropriate groping, but instead he acted differential toward them. The waitresses returned quickly with two large flagons of something frothy as the manager tried hard to make the men feel special. Hmm, *alien big shots*. My people watching excursion had finally gotten interesting.

Staring indiscreetly at the scene, I was startled when a well-dressed man slid in next to me at the bar. Surprisingly, he didn't sit in the unoccupied stool, instead choosing to remain standing.

"Well now, why is a striking young woman like yourself drinking all alone?"

At least this one seemed fairly harmless. He was a bit older than me, tall, handsome, and carried a snifter in his left hand. I guessed he was probably well on his way to being drunk, like everyone else in the pub. But if he was seeking a conquest he'd be sorely disappointed.

"As you can see," I answered, "I'm hardly alone, there's hundreds of people in this place."

"True, but none of them interested you; at least until now." He grinned, as he nodded toward the Caladrians.

I cursed myself for my lack of subtlety. "You mean those two? They don't interest me in the least."

"I don't blame you; pirates are normally more interesting than the average hoi polloi."

"Pirates? You think they're pirates?"

"It's a logical assumption; Caladrians gravitate toward nefarious pursuits, generally speaking. However, in this case I happen to know them. They're regulars on board the Archeron, I hear. They come here to blow off steam."

"You know them?"

"Know *of them*, I should say."

"If they're pirates, aren't they dangerous?"

"Extremely."

"Then why're they allowed on board?"

"Same reason as you and I, my dear: coin. They come here to gamble; and for the human females, of course. This ship is one of the few places non-humans can mingle with humans openly without causing trouble. Everyone's welcome on the Archeron; everyone with coin, that is."

"Well," I said, my eyes drifting back in the Caladrians' direction, "The staff in this pub treats them like royalty, they must have plenty."

"Pirates' fortunes rise and fall, but when they have it they don't mind spending it. Those two own their own ship, believe it or not. A sleek little vessel with a loyal crew. They're quite successful, in a small-time way." He paused, a sly grin creasing his face, "But, I wouldn't trust them alone with my sister... or my wallet."

"You say they come here for human females?" My incessant curiosity often got the better of me. Plus, the visual in my mind was luridly fascinating. It'd have to be a courageous woman to take on one of those 210cm alien brutes.

"Many aliens find human females desirable, not just Caladrians. And, if you'd ever seen a Caladrian female you'd understand completely. But, it'd be unwise to encourage them."

"Oh, I wasn't, I mean, I didn't." I explained, flustered by his insinuation. "I was just watching when they came in; they were being very loud."

"A habit they are rightfully famous for. Allow me to introduce myself, my name is Bradley, Theodore J. Bradley. Most people just call me Teddy. And what's your name, my dear?"

"My father always warned me never to talk to strange men, especially in a pub. Just because this pub is in a giant star liner is no reason to eschew good advice."

"A sound philosophy, to be sure. But, in case you didn't notice, you're already talking to me."

"Perhaps that was a mistake."

"I doubt you make many. Besides, if you never speak to strangers, you'll limit your horizons. You never know when a golden opportunity might come from a strange place." He said with a grin, clearly enjoying the banter.

He seemed interesting, but I'd been fending off drunk morons trying to get 'more acquainted' for over two hours and I was thinking of calling it an evening. There were several nightclubs, pubs and hostess lounges aboard the Archeron. Normally, a lowly professor like me could never afford an all-inclusive, 2nd class ticket. Luckily, I was traveling on the Academy's coin, so I was trying to take advantage of the perks while I could.

"And, here you are, my white knight; bestowing that golden opportunity on me. There's plenty of women in this place, Mr. Bradley, why am I so lucky?"

"I was simply wondering why you're drinking alone. You know, most people say it's a sign of alcohol abuse. I, however, see it as a sign of good sense and strong moral fiber. I do it all the time myself." He raised his glass, "I'd offer to buy you another, but... "

"They're free." I finished his sentence.

"Included. I was going to say included." He smiled.

Even though I was enjoying the banter too, I didn't want to encourage the man any further. I'd be wasting his time if I kept dragging it on.

"Well, it's been nice talking to you Mr. Bradley, but I feel like I'm wasting your time. I'm not interested in anything more than conversation, and I should be heading back to my cabin, anyway." I turned to leave.

"Come now, don't be so hasty, Professor Thornwell. It just so happens conversation is *exactly* what I'm here for." He responded.

"Perhaps we can converse about something other than the nocturnal habits of Caladrian privateers."

I stopped and turned, examining him with a more critical eye.

"How do you know my name?" I asked, the playful tone had left my voice.

"You *are* Abigail Thornwell, correct?"

He paused as I searched for something to say. Sensing my loss for words he continued, "No need to worry, I simply asked one of the stewards earlier. A little coin loosens their lips quite effectively." He smiled charmingly again, displaying straight, white teeth and dimples a matinee star would envy. "Is this your first time aboard the Archeron?"

"This is my first interstellar trip." I said with a bit of embarrassment, my lack of travel experience making me self-conscious.

"Ah, a first timer. Well, you actually *are* lucky; Aries is quite reputable and this ship is their finest. My 2nd class suite on this ship is nicer than most of the 1st class berths I've had. I have to say I've never been on a more luxurious spacecraft." he smiled again; dimples exposed. "What do you think of it, so far?"

"I haven't seen much of it yet, just this pub; and my cabin. I spent yesterday in my cabin working; I'm on business."

"What a shame, a *working holiday*. One of my least favorite oxymorons. You know Abby... may I call you Abby?" he continued without waiting for an answer, "I'm actually a fan of yours. Your book, *Expansion*, about the early colonial period, was fascinating."

"Uhm, thank you. I actually wasn't aware anyone had ever read it." I joked; my standard self-deprecating quip.

I was wrong earlier assuming he was on the way to being drunk. He wasn't slurring his speech in the slightest, and his blue eyes were crystal clear and piercing. Bradley appeared to be hovering around the age of fifty, though he carried his years with grace and charisma.

In addition to being undeniably handsome, I realized he was wearing a status-invoking, mind-numbingly expensive Peter Chambord suit. Chambord was a famous label from Darlington Circle, the even more famous garment district on the planet Titus. The tailored clothing spoke of wealth and privilege and I decided I didn't like him, even if he did say he liked my book.

The glint in Bradley's piercing eyes, however, hinted at more than just material wealth. He was clearly a man who was accustomed to getting what he desired, as if the universe itself conspired with him.

"I understand you teach at the Amporan Academy of Sciences. It so happens archeology is a hobby of mine and the fact is, I must confess, I booked this passage on the Archeron for the purpose of meeting *you*."

"That's hard to believe. My book was informative, but it wasn't exciting enough to create groupies. Exactly who are you, and what do you want?" I asked.

"Ah, right to business. Very well, my dear; the fact is I was a friend of your father's, Henry Thornwell."

I paused, speechless. The invocation of my father's name had stunned me. My father had passed away nearly ten years before.

However, before I was able to formulate a response, I was startled by a deep, gravelly voice coming from my right. This time, to my alarm, the voice had emanated from one of the Caladrians I'd seen entering the pub earlier.

"Hey babe, where've *you* been hiding all week? I don't remember seeing you before." he slurred. He'd obviously had a flagon too many.

He towered above me as I turned, like a ghostly giant. I quailed, my earlier bravado with ferret-face a distant memory.

"I wasn't... hiding. I just boarded yesterday." I squeaked awkwardly.

"That explains it, then. I'd never miss a fiery little thing like you; I like the little ones. Let's you and I go somewhere private and get to know each other, eh? Come with me and I'll show you a good time, doll." He propositioned me boldly.

"No, thank you. I'm not interested." My panic had quickly turned to resolve. There's no way I was going anywhere with *him*.

He began to reply, as he grabbed my wrist "Oh, don't be that way darlin', I can... " but then he pulled his hand back with a surprised grunt.

"That's quite enough," said Teddy Bradley, his voice cutting through the tension. "Do all Caladrian mothers teach their sons such appalling manners?"

He'd seized the pirate's other hand and was bending it backward awkwardly. The Caladrian's face had transformed into a grimace as he reached for Bradley's arm. Bradley increased the pressure, and the massive alien went to his knees in obvious pain.

"Release me, human!" the Caladrian demanded through clenched teeth, his voice a strained growl. Beads of sweat erupted from his huge brow as Bradley stood above him, pressing a thumb into the bewildered Caladrian's palm.

"Just as soon as you apologize to the lady; and me, of course. It was plainly clear she and I were in the midst of conversation when you approached. Uncouth behavior is a pet peeve of mine."

"You know *not* who you insult, human. I'm... " he began through gritted teeth, but as Bradley twisted his arm the Caladrian was silenced, his face a rictus of agony.

"I know exactly who you are, *Magnus*. You can apologize to the lady, or I can break your wrist; it's your choice."

The Caladrian's companion appeared beside us suddenly. My heart leaped in my chest, and I instinctively dropped from my stool, poised for a swift escape. Several patrons had cleared a space around us, and I heard someone call for security, but I doubted they could arrive in time to make a difference. Bradley still had the first man in his painful hold, but the second Caladrian had arrived with a drawn dagger and fire in his eyes.

Expecting violence, I was stunned as the newcomer halted abruptly, and momentarily gawked at Bradley as if he'd seen a Benoan Gorka Beast in rut. His violent demeaner vanished, and he quickly sheathed his blade.

"Taki Ruhbar" he whispered; then, "Magnus, you fool!"

Bradley, displaying remarkable composure, said, "Your brother forgets himself, Captain."

"He's a fool, but he's my brother. I assure you; he meant no disrespect. He obviously didn't recognize you in his drunkenness. Please, accept our apologies, Taki Ruhbar."

"Ruhbar?" mumbled the man on his knees. The look of consternation on his face was quickly replaced by a look of recognition. "Oh, fuuuck... please accept my apology, sir; I'm clearly at fault."

"That, you are. But, I accept your apology." Bradley stated, but continued his painful hold on the man. "But you owe this woman an apology as well. You were quite rude to her, and presumptuous. She's no trollop, you idiot. She's a lady; and human as well. I should post your names with the syndicate."

Panicked, the Caladrian in Bradley's grip sputtered, "I'm sorry, miss. Truly. Please forgive me. I'm not myself, too much drink. Please, miss, I'm very sorry."

Confused and not knowing what else to do, I simply said, "You're forgiven."

Bradley released his hold on the man's hand. The Caladrian gasped in relief, and lurched to his feet. His brother put his arm around him to steady him and turned to Bradley.

"Please, Taki, if there is ever anything you require, let me know; Captain Numinus of the ship Krestor Ka is at your disposal. It would be my privilege to make it up to you in some way." He forced a half-hearted laugh, "My brother is sometimes impetuous and lacks discretion, and I am indulgent to a fault. But I assure you this will never happen again."

"That's gracious of you, Captain. The syndicate values discretion, as you know. Perhaps I'll find some use for the Krestor Ka in the future, I'll keep you in mind. For now, I think you should leave this establishment. Goodbye, Captain Numinus." Bradley dismissed him.

"Goodbye." The Caladrian captain said, "Thank you. Thank you, Taki."

The two Caladrians left the pub quickly, never looking back. Bradley simply turned toward me, pulled my stool out so I could sit again, and took a sip from his drink. I don't believe he'd spilled a drop.

"Well, my dear, where were we?" he asked as if nothing had occurred.

"Thanks for your help. I wasn't sure how to deal with that guy, I appreciate it. But, I don't understand what happened. What was it they kept calling you: Taki?" I sat again, shaken but relieved.

"It's a Caladrian word, I believe."

"But, what does it mean? They acted like they were scared of you. What are you, a gangster or something? Or secret police?"

He chuckled, "I'm about as far from a secret policeman as you can get."

"That's exactly what a secret policeman might say. What's Taki mean?"

"I don't speak the language, but I believe Taki could be loosely translated into the common tongue as 'uncle.' Though it doesn't necessarily indicate a familial connection; it's more of a term of respect for someone with higher status."

"What was that you said; post their names with the syndicate? What's that supposed mean?"

"It would mean they'd no longer be able to do business with my syndicate; a serious threat to a privateer."

"Exactly what sort of business are you in?" I asked, skeptically.

He produced a silver case from the inside pocket of his suit and handed me a card. It read: 'Bradley & Associates Import, Export and Cartage' and gave a comms code followed by several registration and license numbers.

"Satisfied, my dear?"

"I suppose. But, what was that hold you used on him? I've never seen anything like it before."

"There's a nerve cluster at the base of Caladrians' thumbs. The right amount of pressure applied renders them as docile as a kitten." He smiled. "Sometimes a bit of knowledge can be as useful as a plasma rifle."

"Well, thanks. I guess I owe you."

"Think nothing of it. Now, where was I? Oh yes, I was telling you I was a friend of your father's, and that I'd boarded this ship in order to meet you. The truth is, I have something tremendously important to discuss with you, my dear."

"Mr. Bradley..."

"Please, call me Teddy."

"Alright Teddy, thanks for the help, but I find it doubtful you knew my father. He would've been at least 20 years older than you and never, to my knowledge, left the Ampora system. I don't know where you're from, but you don't sound like you're from Ampora."

"Whoever said I was from Ampora?" then, in a shockingly perfect Amporan accent he said, "And you might be surprised what your father got up to back in the day. Your father and I traveled together extensively. And I personally accompanied him on several archeological digs."

That was an outlandish claim. However, I was thrown into confusion by the accent and the bewildering statement, so I couldn't come up with a witty reply.

"Digs? My father was never on any digs." I stammered. "The Alliance all but banned digs during the wars. He was purely an academic researcher as far as I know; like I am." I was mentally backpedaling though; *My father went on archeological digs?*

He continued in his original, unrecognizable accent, "Yes, I'm aware. You're a professor of History at the Academy. You have a PHD in History, and hold a senior research chair in Archeology. Henry was a Doctor of Archeology and was also a professor at the Academy. It appears the apple doesn't fall far from the tree."

"Seriously, how do you know so much about me?"

Bradley ignored my question, "Purely a researcher you may *have been*," He leaned in close and whispered into my ear, "And yet here you are, my dear, on the way to a dig in the Kleos system."

Again, I was caught by surprise; this time alarmingly so. It seemed impossible Bradley could know that. *Nobody* was supposed to know that.

"Uhm, well, you are misinformed, Teddy. I've never heard of... what'd you call it?... the Kevro system?" I said, "Anyway, it's my business where I'm going, I don't see how it could interest you."

"It interests me a great deal, my dear, a *great deal*. And like it or not, I know your destination; try as you might to deny it. Information is the most valuable commodity I know of, and I devote a great deal of my considerable resources to acquiring it. At times it can be easily obtained, *if* you possess the means, of course." Bradley casually asserted.

Disturbingly, I was, *in fact*, heading to the Kleos system to participate in an archeological dig on an uninhabited planet known as Kleos Prime. That information was supposed to be confidential. I was warned strongly not to tell anyone.

"What'd you do, bribe someone at the Academy to spy on me? Who?" I asked, beginning to worry. Who in the hell would be so interested in what *I was doing* they'd bribe someone to find out? I was just a history professor for Gods' sake.

"Bribed has such a negative connotation; I have a paid informant at your Academy I regularly check in with. He's an employee, that's all. However, Abby," he glanced around the room subtly. "Perhaps this is a conversation best suited to a more private environment. There's informants everywhere these days, and that small tussle might've drawn too much attention. Should we continue this discussion in my cabin, perhaps? Or would you prefer yours? Home court advantage, as it were."

"Informants?" I whispered instinctively, "Why should I worry about that? They shouldn't care about anything I have to say."

It was common knowledge the secret police employed civilian informants on a massive scale. Even at home on Ampora you could never be sure who might be working for them. Everyone, as a matter of habit, was careful what they said in public; always being sure not to criticize the government or the Alliance too vehemently.

"One can never be sure what the Ministry of Security might find interesting, my dear. It's better not to tempt fate. Shall we adjourn to my quarters? I promise you'll find what I have to say quite compelling."

Spending any more time with this Bradley character seemed like a bad idea, especially after he'd bested two huge Caladrians with nothing more than his reputation. He was obviously dangerous, but I needed to find out why he knew where I was going; and why he *cared*. I'd never be able to sleep until I had some answers. Plus, he said he'd known my father. I couldn't just leave it at that.

"Are you going to explain to me how you knew my father and why you know so much about me?"

"Of course."

"Then lead the way, Teddy. I prefer your place; that way I can leave any time I want. And don't you try anything funny, I can take care of myself." I may be small in stature, but I worked out regularly, studied martial arts, and was no pushover.

"Of that, I have no doubt." he said with a big grin. I couldn't tell, but he was probably patronizing me. We left the pub and headed for the lift, Bradley checking behind us several times to make sure we weren't followed.

In retrospect, it was pretty foolish of me to follow him not knowing what I was getting into. But, as the famous Old Earth, 20th century philosopher, Yogi Berra, so eloquently put it: When you come to a fork in the road, take it.

Part Two A Father's Secrets

Interstellar Date : 388-06-17
On Board the Archeron

ALRIGHT, SO I KNOW Yogi Berra wasn't actually known as a philosopher, technically speaking. My father had gifted me with a book full of famous quotes when I was young. Pop wanted me to memorize quotes from Aristotle, Albert Einstein or Winston Churchill, but Berra's deceptively thoughtful, homespun wisdom always struck a chord with me.

Walking beside Bradley, the Berra quote had leaped unbidden into my mind, and nostalgic memories of my father followed. But, like always happens, the nostalgia was followed by melancholic memories of my father's death. He'd died, relatively young, from a rare disease as I sat a vigil at his bedside. I still missed him terribly after all this time, so Bradley's claim of knowing Pop created an irresistible urge to know more. Even though I realized it might be foolish, I couldn't resist going with him.

The massive cruise ship we were racing across the galaxy in, the Archeron, had been in service for less than two years, and was ridiculously luxurious. Every amenity you can imagine was packed into the thing. From fine dining, luxury spas and shopping to virtual reality theaters and live shows. Plays and concerts were available around the clock. The ship had an art museum, a 24-hour casino, a petting zoo with cuddly creatures from all over the galaxy, 12 swimming pools, a waterpark, a zero-gravity exercise dome, and perhaps the star attraction: an enormous arboretum with trees from all over the known galaxy.

Supposedly there was even a red-light district on board, complete with union organized entertainers.

It would only take eight days to travel a fourth of the way across the quadrant, a journey of several thousand light years. With REL drive and a fusion/antimatter reactor reportedly powerful enough to supply several large cities with energy, bending space/time was easy for the Archeron.

The corridors in 2nd class were unexpectedly wide, painted cream with subtle gold and blue accents, and had plush carpeted floors which silenced our footfalls as we progressed. We passed several groups of fellow passengers along the way, and when I tried to continue our conversation Bradley shushed me.

"These walls have ears, my dear, and voices carry along the corridor. We'll soon be in my suite, where we can speak freely. I routinely do a thorough sweep for listening devices."

Great, I was following a *paranoid* martial arts expert to his room, *alone*. It was even money which one of us was the craziest.

When we arrived at Bradley's suite, which was lavish and much larger than my more basic cabin, the lighting was low as I furtively scanned the room. Out of the murky depths at the back of the suite I detected a presence. The hair at the back of my neck stood erect, and a chill ran down my spine. A pair of large eyes approached, glowing out of the darkness like those of a jungle cat. I felt an instinctual urge to flee that I was barely able to suppress.

A tall, striking woman stepped forward into the better illuminated part of the room. She had exceptionally large eyes as black as obsidian. A narrow nose with wide nostrils sat above her full lips, and her chin had just a hint of a dimple. However, her elven facial features contrasted starkly with her tall, muscular body.

She had golden brown skin, dark hair and large strangely shaped ears like the leaves of a giant tapinga tree. Her eyes and ears alone left no doubt in my mind she wasn't human. She had to be close to 190cm, but moved gracefully as she approached.

Her imposing presence was compounded by her attire. She wore a dark, body-hugging leotard, with armored shin guards over her boots, a breastplate, gauntlets and a wide metallic belt holding at least a couple of edged weapons I could see. I felt underdressed; my cocktail dress didn't include armor.

"Abigail Thornwell, allow me to introduce my companion, Ka'rra Corda Az-Mur Az-Codor, Pont-Jar of Az-Codor, Protector of the Weak, Keeper of Secrets and rightful heir to the Keep of Ran-Butra. Better known as Kara the Demon, or simply Kara for short. Kara, this is my new friend, Abby."

"Nice to meet you, Abby, I hope we can become good friends." she said in an unfamiliar accent with a deep, lustrous voice. Looking up at her I was certainly hoping we'd be friends.

"Uhm, yah, glad to meet you too, Kara. Bradley, you didn't tell me you had an Amazonian warrior for a bodyguard." I was more than a little flustered. My life as an academy professor hadn't prepared me for her.

"Not Amazonian, Az-Codorian. Funny you should say that though, because that's just what she is. Kara *is* my bodyguard, among other things. I literally trust her with my life. We can safely speak in front of her, she's also extremely discreet." Bradley explained, ignoring my lack of composure.

"Yes, I heard the part about 'keeper of secrets." I said. As well as 'protector of the weak.' I was hoping I qualified under that category.

"We've been together for many years and she's saved my life more times than I care to count. I want you to feel completely comfortable with her." His reassurance was of little help though, I was still feeling that unfamiliar impulse to flee.

"Uhm, good. I mean, I'm sorry, you just surprised me is all. I thought it'd just be the two of us. Kara the Demon, was it? That's certainly an impressive moniker." I stammered, "But, what exactly do you need a bodyguard for? Does it have something to do with this syndicate you were talking about? Are you in danger, or more importantly, am *I* in danger?"

"Syndicate?" Kara asked him. "How's she know about the syndicate?"

"Now, don't get upset," He told her. "We met two Caladrians in the pub and it might've been mentioned. Don't fret over it."

"I *knew* I should've come with you; next time I'll insist." She said, clearly agitated.

Bradley addressed me, "Have no fear my dear, we are quite safe here, I believe. Sometimes though, my travels take me to less secure environs. Having a traveling companion like Kara helps me remain calm, you see. I don't usually travel commercially like this, but sometimes it's necessary."

Kara spoke up in that deep silky voice "I won't allow anything to happen to you, Abby Thornwell; you can be sure of that."

Her voice gave me goosebumps. Just who or *what* was this woman? She was humanoid, but not *human*. That had become an important distinction under Telluric law.

Under our laws, if you weren't human, you couldn't be a full citizen, hold a government job, vote, own property, marry a citizen, travel freely and dozens of other restrictions. You also weren't eligible for government assistance of any kind. Everyone needed some kind of assistance; even I couldn't pay my rent without my government housing allowance and I held a full-time position at the Academy.

"Would you like a drink, my dear?" Bradley offered. "I brought a case of my favorite Kyntavan brandy on board with me. I realize that seems a bit eccentric, since spirits are gratis here, but I really can't do without a few creature comforts from home when I travel. We have some fine cheeses as well, or wine if you prefer."

"No thanks, I'm not here to socialize. How do you know so much about me?"

"Professor, social conventions are the glue that holds civilization together." He smiled.

"Don't worry, Ms. Thornwell, sometimes he takes a while but eventually he'll get to his point." The bodyguard said.

"Alright, Kara. While you tease me, Abby's getting annoyed. Professor, archeology is a hobby of mine, so I maintain sources at many of the major Universities and Academies that might be allowed to dig. Sadly, there's few of them nowadays; the permits are devilishly hard to obtain. My source on Ampora informed me of the expedition the Academy was undertaking and your invitation to join it. Subsequently, I did some research on you before we boarded; I hope you don't mind. Tell me, Abby, do you have any idea what your colleagues are looking for at Kleos?"

"First, I haven't agreed with your assertion about my destination. Second, you must know I couldn't tell you even if I knew."

The fact was I hadn't been told exactly what the aim of the expedition was. The whole thing was curiously last-minute and mysterious for some reason.

The last dig my Academy had conducted was over 11 years before on Pithra 4, a planet devastated during the Freehold Wars. As the last refugees were being evacuated, a number of ancient ruins were discovered there; exposed by the Combined Telluric Fleet (or CTF as everyone referred to them) when they bombarded the planet from orbit. I hadn't been invited to participate in that dig because at the time I was finishing up my PHD and was told doctoral candidates weren't being considered.

"Please sit Abby, I may be able to fill in some blanks for you. In return I'm hoping you can help me." Bradley gestured to an area with a small couch, a couple of comfortable looking chairs and a table; a living area my smaller cabin lacked. I made my way to one of the chairs and was happy to get off my feet. Bradley handed me a bottle of water and I took a drink.

"Thanks, I didn't realize how thirsty I was."

"Space travel takes some getting used to," said Kara, "I'm almost always thirsty in space."

"Me too." Bradley added as he took a generous sip of his Kyntavan brandy.

"Ha, ha. He thinks he's quite witty." Kara said, "Please don't encourage him by laughing."

"I'll try not to."

She continued, "Many people find it hard to adjust to the atmosphere on spacecraft, especially the first time. There are separate environmental controls in your cabin which can be customized if you want. But there's nothing to be done about the common areas. Many people stay in their cabins for much of the time for that reason. But staying in your cabin would be boring on your first trip in space, Abby."

"Thanks, Kara, that's good to know."

It was good information, but I wasn't there to talk about air conditioning. I'd told Bradley it was my first trip in space when we were in the pub. I wondered how she could've known that. My guess was they knew because of the research he'd done on me. It was disconcerting they'd even done 'research' on me.

Bradley made himself comfortable on the small couch, but Kara, armed and armored, remained standing; seemingly on alert as if we might be assaulted by Pentoffian storm troopers.

"Now, Bradley, I want to hear how you knew my father."

"Of course, my dear. Well, I guess I should start at the beginning. I met your father when I was a student at the Amporan Academy. In fact, he was my favorite professor."

"You said you weren't from Ampora."

"In point of fact, I actually asked *you* 'who said I was from Ampora?' But no, I'm not from there. I'm from another planet that's almost as boring." He laughed. "I'm a citizen of the galaxy now. No roots anywhere special, though I maintain residences on several different planets."

"Several different planets? Just how wealthy are you?"

"Well, there's well off, and then there's *wealthy*. I suppose I could be considered well off; there's family coin and my import business has done quite well over the years. But those I'd consider *wealthy* are several orders of magnitude better off than I am. Does that make sense?"

"Not all academy professors are dim, I know what an order of magnitude is."

"I'm sorry, my dear, I didn't mean it that way. What I meant is not everyone knows about the enormous wealth some people amassed during the wars. There's a cadre of ultra-wealthy businessmen who wield tremendous power and influence in Telluric space. I deal with these sorts of people constantly in my business, but there's no reason an academy professor should even know such tycoons exist."

"I see. So you're rich, but not so rich I should hate you for it."

"Exactly. Well said." He smiled.

"Alright. So, when was this? When did you live on Ampora?" I asked.

"I wouldn't say I lived there, I was just there for school and only for a short time. I guess it was almost 30 years ago now. Anyway, your Father taught one of my favorite classes in my 2nd semester, Archeology and Interstellar History. I guess that's when I first got interested in archeology. I remember he had this old skull on his desk he'd named 'Vincent.' He'd sometimes talk to Vincent as if he expected a response. I always got a kick from that."

"I remember Vincent. I asked Pop once how he knew the man's name had been Vincent; I was probably 8 or 10. He said he didn't, but he certainly looked like a Vincent."

Bradley chuckled and continued, "I wanted to be noticed by him, which was difficult because he was immensely popular with all his students; many wanted to be noticed by him and get assigned to one of his research projects. Eventually I won him over, and Henry added me to his team working on deciphering the codex of Huru Bastar, the ancient Lord of Galbrod in the Kafo system."

He'd successfully piqued my interest with the mention of that codex. The Kafo Codex had made my father's name in Archeology; you might say it'd made his career. Academics still study it to this day. The text is a sort of epic poem, strangely formatted and filled with allusions and metaphors in the ancient language of Galbrodi. Deciphering it was considered an astounding accomplishment. My father asserted it held the secrets of galactic history, as well as predictions of the future. He'd deciphered it, but interpreting the meaning of the obscure passages was an ongoing and inexact science.

"I'm familiar with that codex, my father made me study it when I was young. He'd make me copy passages and give my interpretation. At the time I hated it, but now it's the sort of thing I do for fun. Did you really help decipher it?"

"Well, yes, I suppose I did my part. Several other research assistants and me. But it was your father who was responsible for most of the breakthroughs, we were just along for the ride." He admitted.

I was starting to believe Bradley actually *could* have been my father's student. "But you told me you went with him on archeological digs. When and where?"

"That came later, after we became friends. I dropped out, you see. The life I wanted to lead didn't require a fancy degree. Even though Henry didn't approve of my decision to quit school, he soon grew to appreciate my abilities in other pursuits. We began to collaborate, and then... "

"Master, excuse me, but there is movement in the corridor." Kara interjected. "I think perhaps we have company."

Master? What the hell? Was she Bradley's slave or something? I didn't think that sort of thing was allowed anymore in Telluric space.

"Are you sure it isn't passengers simply passing by, minding their own business?" Bradley asked, though he'd lowered his voice considerably. Kara shook her head subtly.

As for me, I hadn't heard a thing. Admittedly, I was listening closely to Bradley's story. It seemed more than possible he knew my father, and perhaps even worked on the codex that was one of my father's great accomplishments. He even knew about Vincent. If he was telling the truth it'd be strange though, because my father had never mentioned Theodore J Bradley to me. Ever.

Kara the Demon placed a long, slim finger against her lips and crept silently to the door. She leaned her head and pressed her ear to it. There followed a few moments of halting silence during which I could hear myself breathing.

The cabin doors on the Archeron slid into the wall when opened. A sensor on the wall, programmed to the cabin occupant's thumbprint, was used to open it. Theoretically it was quite secure, provided you didn't leave your thumb laying around where thieves might find it.

Bradley's bodyguard drew one of her weapons, a long thin dagger with a needle-like point. It was vicious looking, and I began to worry she'd skewer an innocent passer-by accidentally. She raised her thumb and placed it on the sensor. The door slid open like a breath of wind and the woman leapt through. I heard a gasp, a muffled expletive (I think) and a thud.

Kara reemerged into the suite, but this time with a prisoner. A short, green fellow with orange-yellow hair, stubby legs and arms (four arms in fact) and a look of abject terror on his ugly little face. Kara had a hand full of his wiry hair and he whimpered pathetically as she pressed her dagger to his throat.

It was my first musculux. I'd heard of them and seen pictures, but of course had never seen one in person. Ampora was notoriously xenophobic, and aliens (non-humans) needed special permission to visit, which they almost never got it.

He had leathery skin and bulbous eyes reminiscent of an insect. He was only about half as tall as Kara and somewhat corpulent. The fingers on his four hands were thick and stubby like little sausages and he was unshod. His feet(?) were round and blunt like an Old Earth pachyderm, with two grotesque, off-colored toenails the size of shot glasses on each; though no toes were discernable. Improbably, he was dressed in a well-tailored, three-piece suit. The effect was nothing short of comical.

But, Gods grace us; an odor, *his* odor, part rancid meat, part rotten fruit, part sickeningly aggressive cologne wafted from him in waves. I gagged involuntarily when it hit me, and took a sip of water to hide my embarrassment.

"Well, well, well. Wa' Keeny, my old friend. How nice of you to drop by." Bradley said with undisguised sarcasm. "You little toad, how dare you spy on me again? I should have Kara tear your arms off. They might grow back eventually; maybe we should try it and see? I think I'll talk to the Archeron's security to see if they know about you harassing their paying passengers."

The situation was quite uncomfortable; these people clearly all knew each other. I, on the other hand, knew nothing and no one. Not only did Bradley and his bodyguard know this... this weird little man, but they obviously didn't like him much. I had another pang of sympathy for the musculux; the look on Kara's face was somewhere between disgust and murderous hatred.

"Captain Bradley, tell your *fiend* to unhand me, I'm under the protection of the Trade Guild, as you know. Go ahead and call security, they may be interested to know the two of you used false identities to board this vessel."

Kara said, "How would you know *that*, Wa' Keeny, you little worm?"

"I'm not a fool. And stop calling me that name. My name is Wa' L'kyne Tubau, as you well know. I was just coming to let you know I was on board, and possibly to join you for a nightcap, if you had the good manners to offer. It's of no consequence to me what names you travel under." He put up a good front, but I could tell he was mortified to have been caught out. Kara seemed to terrify him; I empathized whole-heartedly.

"You see Abby, as I said, sometimes information is easy to get if you know how." Bradley explained. "Wa' Keeny here somehow found out where we were; he must've followed us on board."

The little guy was beside himself, "I said stop calling me that!"

It turned out 'keeny' is a word in his language, meaning something akin to vomit or spittle. Wa' is an honorific similar to 'Sir,' hence Bradley was calling him Sir Vomit, or Sir Spit. Kara pulled one of his arms behind his back and he squealed.

Bradley continued "This time you've annoyed me beyond tolerance, Wa' Keeny. Give me one good reason I shouldn't have Kara take you down to the cargo hold and split you from lips to giblets. Assuming you have giblets. I doubt you'd be missed."

"No, please," the little man begged. Apparently, Tubau was genuinely worried they might murder him. "I meant no harm. I was only doing my job; the Guild orders and I obey." he whimpered.

"Wait," I began, "Please, don't hurt him. I'm having a strange enough day already without becoming an accomplice to murder. Bradley, just who is this guy and why is he following you?"

The green fellow responded before Bradley could, "I'm not following him at all. As an agent of the Trade Guild, my employer, I was sent here to ask a few polite questions, that's all. I'm a customs inspector. Oww!"

Kara must've twisted his arm behind his back. I was beginning to think the threat of her tearing off limbs wasn't that far-fetched.

"Customs inspector? Ha! That's like calling a garbage man a terraforming engineer." Kara said.

Bradley turned to me "You see, my dear, from time to time I'm able to acquire various rare and valuable commodities for select friends of mine. This brandy is an example. Hard to get fruits and cheeses, wine, liquor, clothes, tobacco, tech, all sorts of things. I have trading vessels of different registries so it's only natural for me to be the one to deliver these things to my many friends."

"Friends? You have no friends, Captain Bradley." Tubau argued. "You only have customers; ones that pay handsomely for your rare commodities."

Ignoring Tubau's criticism, Bradley continued, "The Trade Guild has rather unreasonably labeled me a smuggler. Wa' Keeny here probably thinks I'm smuggling a Grovian apple up my bum as we speak."

"I wouldn't put it past you! You forgot to mention weapons, plus every other sort of illegal contraband one can imagine." He turned to Kara, "Please turn me loose, you devil! I can't harm you, so it's unnecessary for you to handle me so roughly."

"But I enjoy it." Kara responded.

Maybe I'm soft hearted, but I was sort of feeling sorry for the little guy. What if he really was only doing his job? I wasn't very familiar with the Trade Guild, having lived my whole life on Ampora. They dealt with interstellar trade, I assumed. It did seem like Bradley and Kara were being pretty rough on him.

"Very well, Kara, let him loose." Bradley said. She did, clearly reluctant, and Tubau breathed an audible sigh of relief. "Alright, Mr. Trade Guild, you have the floor. Let's hear your excuse for sneaking around outside our cabin."

"I wasn't trying to spy, I swear. I fully intended to knock; I was just working up the nerve. I know how you feel about me, and I don't relish the way your female villain treats me. Quite frankly, she scares me and I don't trust her. I'm sure I'm not the only one. As to why I followed you aboard, that's simple. The Guild is curious why one of the most notorious *smugglers* in the quadrant is traveling on a commercial liner when he has his own ships. I'd hoped you might be able to set my mind at ease, preferably over brandy and a cigar." Tubau explained.

Bradley wasn't mollified. "First, I don't believe you weren't trying to spy, I've caught you at it before. Second, the Guild had no idea we were aboard the Archeron unless *you* told them. Third, if I catch you spying on me again you're likely to have an outrageously horrible accident. When they scrape what's left of you off the floor and send it home, your family will faint from sheer horror."

"There's no need for such threats, Captain Bradley. I shall leave you be, for now."

"Then good day, you little scoundrel. Shall I have my lady friend escort you to your room?" Bradley asked teasingly.

"*No*, thank you very much, I can manage without *her* assistance." He puffed up his diminutive chest, "You know Bradley, one of these days your high-handed way of dealing with people is going to be the end of you. I'm just a small man from a small planet and have no power, not here. But someday you'll meet the wrong chap and it'll be a whole different situation."

Bradley responded coldly, "There's several of those 'wrong chaps' you're talking about buried in holes all over the quadrant, Wa' Keeny. You'd be wise to remember that."

Tubau turned to me. "I'm sorry we didn't get a chance to be introduced, miss. I would've liked to have made your acquaintance; perhaps another time under better circumstances? If I were you, I'd be careful." He said the last part with a glance toward my host, and he left.

"The bloody Trade Guild; harassing me again. Thank the light we hadn't actually said anything worth repeating yet." Bradley seemed calm enough now. "I must apologize, Abby, that was an unexpected and most unwelcome intrusion. But only a minor annoyance, as it turns out."

"Just what is the Trade Guild anyway? I've heard of it, but I guess I don't know exactly what they do. And why'd he call you *Captain* Bradley?" I asked.

Bradley explained, "The Trade Guild is a consortium of large and powerful corporations that own a virtual monopoly on interstellar trade. They enjoy the support of the Alliance, and pay hefty fees into the Alliance's coffers. Corrupt buggers, all of them."

Kara added, "Because of the power their monopoly gives them, they're able to control supply and therefore control prices. They strangle small competitors right out of business."

Bradley continued, "You see, my dear, I'm what you might call a minor shipping tycoon in my own right. I own several cargo vessels, barges mostly but also a few swift little ships that are capable of avoiding the authorities. The Guild calls me a smuggler, but I'm simply an entrepreneur trying to avoid the Alliance's unfair taxes and tariffs. My ships operate under local licensing agreements and therefore usually avoid legal entanglements with Alliance authorities."

These two were *outlaws*, Bradley and his demon bodyguard. "So, you actually are a smuggler?" I asked.

"It's a matter of perspective, my dear. Why should I pay fees to the Alliance in order to ship my goods from here to there in open space? It's preposterous. The Alliance does next to nothing to protect the shipping routes, and pirates abound. My little ships must travel heavily armed, which is expensive, make no mistake."

"What about putting people in holes all over the quadrant, like you told that guy Tubau? Is that true?"

"An exaggeration for effect, my dear. I find a reputation for violence often prevents the need for it."

That sounded logical, but I wasn't sure I believed him. I'd obviously placed myself in danger by even speaking with Bradley. He was a criminal who had enough enemies he needed a bodyguard. Bradley's claim of knowing my father had lured me and my curious nature right in. My problem was my curiosity had only grown since arriving at his suite. I needed to get the discussion back on topic.

"So, you were telling me about when you were my father's student."

"I was never the scholar you are, my dear. No, I was much more interested in practical matters, like stacking coin as high as I could." He laughed. "Your father had volumes of knowledge about where archeological treasures might be found, but he never understood the practical benefits of the knowledge he possessed. I was aware of the thriving black market for artifacts, you see. I knew Henry was my golden goose; his knowledge joined with my savvy and skill would make a great team."

"Black market? You teamed up with Pop to sell artifacts on the black market? I don't believe you."

"He resisted at first, of course. But, I finally convinced him I could deliver him to destinations which were forbidden by the Alliance. My skills as a smuggler can come in handy, you see."

"Don't you mean shipping tycoon?" Kara asked.

"Yes, that's what I meant, smartass. Anyway, Henry never approved of my black-market business, but he tolerated it as my fee for smuggling him to places he wasn't supposed to be. He kept the artifacts he thought were important, and I took the ones I thought I could sell. Often, we'd have animated discussions about who got what." Bradley chuckled at this.

"You're saying my father knew you were selling artifacts on the black market? My father? My stuffy old, straight-laced father? I still don't believe it." Two hours before, I would've thrown a drink in his face for suggesting it, but I wasn't so sure anymore.

"Well, Henry never actually sold the stuff, I took care of that. You see, he wasn't interested in coin, he was interested in the archeology. He thought it was an outrage the Alliance had all but halted active archeology. He often said in class an archeologist wasn't a real archeologist unless they were adept with a trowel."

That actually sounded like something my father would say. He'd mentioned to me on quite a few occasions he wished there was more active archeology being done. According to Bradley, my father *himself* had been actively digging in secret. Words cannot express my shock at that revelation.

"What happened to the artifacts my father kept?"

"I presume he added them to the Academy's collection. You've probably seen some of them in the archives. I believe Henry simply falsified the provenance."

"Falsified the records?" I asked, incredulously.

"Of course, out of necessity. Those artifacts were obtained in places no one was allowed to go. Henry had an inexhaustible appetite for going places he wasn't supposed to. At the beginning we were just using each other, but eventually we became friends."

"So, what types of things did you look for?"

I have to admit I was intrigued. My father jaunting around the galaxy searching for buried treasure (of a sort) was something I'd never pictured in my mind. My father the daring adventurer? If you'd known him, you'd know why I was bemused by the idea. He was sickly, wore glasses, dressed in old fashioned tweed, and walked with a cane. I never saw him move quickly in my life.

"At first we collaborated, Henry would name a place he wanted to go, and I'd agree if I thought we might find something valuable to sell. There's an endless number of collectors hungry for artifacts. Especially artifacts from alien worlds and ancient civilizations. Eventually, Henry became obsessed with artifacts having to do with the supposed Reges Scientia Empire."

"Reges Scientia? But that's a myth. Are you telling me the two of you went looking for Reges Scientia artifacts?" The story was getting good now; I am an archeologist after all.

"That's exactly what I'm saying. Not only that, but we *found* unexplainable items we both believed could belong to an incredibly ancient civilization, much older than anything that's been established. Items which led us to believe this ancient civilization was technologically advanced. Anyway, isn't that what the theory of Reges Scientia describes? An ancient, super-advanced society?" he asked.

"Yes, that's it. I've always thought it was more science fiction than science."

The Reges Scientia, literally 'Kings of Science,' is a theory proposed by some historians, scientists and let's face it, *fiction writers*. Basically, it theorizes an ancient civilization, ancient in the extreme, hundreds of thousands, possibly millions of years old. This civilization possessed incredibly advanced technology, and with it either conquered or colonized much of the galaxy.

The seductive aspect of the theory, to some, was the possibility that finding artifacts left behind by this civilization might lead to unlocking their super-advanced technologies. Imagine being able to skip all the research and development for centuries of technological advancements, and acquiring those technologies overnight? It'd be sort of like having the golden goose dropped right in your lap.

"Teddy, are you saying you and my father actually found Reges Scientia artifacts?"

"Well, why don't you tell me?" He gestured toward my neck. "I'm curious, do you still wear your amulet everywhere you go?"

"How do you know about my amulet?"

"I was there, Abby. When your father found your amulet, *I was there*. It's one of the many artifacts we collected together, and by far the most valuable, most *important*. Later, he told me he'd given it to you as a gift, and that you wore it all the time, everywhere you went. Is that still the case?"

I reached up and removed my necklace, a simple leather string supporting the amulet my father had given me on my 16th birthday: My favorite possession. It was roughly rectangular, about 4x7cm and was covered in strange, alien symbols. I offered it to Bradley, but he didn't accept it.

He said, "This was found on one of our last expeditions, near a 100,000-year-old ruined city. The planet was barren, but we dug where it appeared possible water had flowed in the ancient past. We found ruins a few meters below the surface. On a lark, and since we had the equipment with us, we decided to drill some core samples near the ruins."

"To see if there was anything deeper." I said automatically, caught up in the tale.

"Exactly." He continued, "The amulet was discovered in a sample taken a few hundred meters below the ruined city. I was surprised and curious, but Henry's face turned ashen when he saw it. He instantly recognized it as a major find; possibly universe altering. We couldn't identify the alloy, laser ablation was useless because the material was impervious, seemingly indestructible; literally like nothing we know of." Bradley paused and gathered himself.

"Henry believed those markings were most likely an example of the aliens' language. We both concluded we were in possession of something new, never discovered before, and, if more complete artifacts could be found, with similar markings, we might be able to decipher the language. So, tell me Abby, how does it feel to have been wearing one of the most valuable artifacts ever discovered around your neck for most of your life?"

The nerve endings in my fingertips were firing around the small piece of metal. The tingling ran up my arm and straight to my brain. I was stunned, to put it mildly. What was I to make of this? The assertion by a man I'd just met a few hours ago that my father wasn't who I thought he was, and I was apparently the worst archeologist in history; having walked around for years with the discovery of a lifetime hanging around my neck and never realizing it. A relic from an ancient, technologically advanced civilization? The possibility gave me goosebumps.

I took a long look at the relic for the thousandth time and the first time. It was a strange color, almost bronze but a shade lighter, and not as heavy as it appeared. It was unlike any alloy I could name. Yet, I'd never thought to have it analyzed by a metallurgist. I'd always thought the thing was nothing but a curious trinket, it's value to me being the fact it was a gift from my father.

The markings Bradley had mentioned were rows of tiny unfamiliar symbols. I'd searched the Academy archives many times, trying to find references to anything similar, and had no luck. I'd once even taken it to a professor of ancient languages to have the markings translated. The professor told me he couldn't help me. I'd just assumed the old fellow was too lazy to try, or simply not interested.

Bradley interrupted my thoughts "Abby, can you guess where your amulet was found?"

"Kleos Prime?"

"You see Kara, I told you she'd be brilliant."

Part Three The Secret Police Aren't Much of a Secret

Interstellar Date: 388-06-18
On Board the Archeron

AFTER WE CALLED IT an evening, I'd staggered back to my room with my head swimming. The implications of Bradley's story shook me. The image of my father being some sort of deep-space adventurer was intoxicating for some reason. I found I wanted it to be true; more than I could easily explain.

Why? I'd always been rightfully proud of my father. In my mind, I pictured him as this stout, very correct, and honest man. His stern gaze, framed by silver-streaked temples, had been my compass of morality. What if he wasn't who I thought he was? If what Bradley told me was true, my father had been a criminal, of a sort.

My mind traveled back to my childhood. My mother died when I was an infant, so I'd been raised by nannies as a small child. Was it possible my father had been absent, rocketing off into space gathering artifacts to pawn while my nanny fed me kelp noodles in between games of hide-and-seek? I didn't remember him being gone, but what'd that prove? I was a child. My childhood memories were hazy and elusive, like most people's. I remembered waking up and my father was gone; going to bed before he got home. I thought he was at work at the Academy; was he even on Ampora?

Later, I'd been at boarding schools for great stretches of time. He certainly could've been 'scavenging' then and I never would've noticed. Could it be possible my father was on some distant planet with Teddy Bradley digging for ancient artifacts? The notion was preposterous, like

33

a scene from a cheap, dime store adventure novel. But I couldn't deny the secret thrill the possibility gave me, the idea that beneath the facade of my father's stoic respectability lay a secret life filled with daring exploits and adventures.

I slipped into the comfy bed in my small cabin, but sleep was elusive. It could've been because it was only my second night in space and my body hadn't adjusted to the artificial gravity. Or, it could've simply been the unfamiliar surroundings; I'd rarely traveled, even on Ampora. I could count on one hand the times I'd spent a night away from home except for school. But in my heart, I knew the reason: My view of the Universe had been radically shaken and I just couldn't wrap my mind around it.

When I finally surrendered to exhaustion it was a restless sleep, filled with fragmented dreams that taunted me. In one snippet, I was a child again, and my father stood above me, his face etched with concern. Beside him was an unfamiliar, shadowy silhouette. My father was saying something, his words lost in the murky depths of memory. The dark figure, an ominous presence, uttered a single phrase, "not her," before I was jolted awake.

Waking in a sweat, sheets soaked, and not sure where I was had me disoriented. The ceiling and walls were unfamiliar and when the ship's computer interface spoke, saying "Good morning, Dr. Thornwell," I just about jumped out of my skin.

Strange dreams notwithstanding, I hadn't slept well. The shower, an unexpected luxury in deep space, had a steam setting. Billowing clouds of piping hot steam melted away my disorientation and erased the lingering effects of my dreams.

Mornings I'm hopeless without coffee. A holographic map of the ship magically appeared when I asked the computer for information. Seeing the promenade deck was a reasonable distance from my cabin, I decided to walk there instead of ordering room service like I had the day before.

The promenade on the Archeron is a wide concourse over half a kilometer long, lined on both sides with shops and restaurants. Down the center are dozens of kiosks selling every manner of goods and services.

"Meat pies! Custard tarts! Citrus Punch!" and similar calls carried up and down the concourse. Hundreds of passengers milled about between the stands, some heeding the barkers' calls.

Blue sky, wispy clouds and a mid-morning sun shone high above me; all computer generated of course, and ultra-realistic. The artificial sun, somehow, was as warm and bright as the midday sun on Ampora. Incredibly, a soft breeze also blew in my face and moved the flags and banners atop the myriad kiosks. If I didn't know better I would've sworn I was in downtown Pelios, my home city on Ampora. I saw humans and humanoids of every description, but no non-humanoids like the musculux in Bradley's suite.

One stand was selling baked treats from various cultures around the quadrant; placards identified the planets of origin of the various confections. I was reminded of the corner bakery down the block from my apartment at home. The currant cakes from there were one of my favorite, guilty indulgences.

Of course, there were a number of souvenir shops. Shirts, hats, statuettes, ashtrays, bobbles and paraphernalia so diverse it made my head swim. One shirt read: 'I toured the Milky Way aboard the fabulous Archeron, and all I got was this crappy shirt.'

Finally, the rich, unmistakable aroma of roasted coffee beans made its way to me. A coffee shop had appeared, nestled between retailers on the far side of the concourse. I headed that way in happy anticipation. Coffee was an important crop, and was cultivated throughout the quadrant; at least anywhere suitable. Thank the gods for that!

I chose a breakfast roll to go with my large coffee, took a seat, and to my delight the roll was delicious, with perhaps just a hint of honey. Real honey is extravagantly expensive, but the synthetic stuff is almost as good. Honestly, I couldn't tell which was used to create the soft, warm treat I was eating.

I saw a group of passengers at a table in a nearby restaurant who were enjoying a sumptuous looking banquet. A round of applause erupted from the ten or so diners when servers in pressed uniforms carried a huge platter supporting three large, roasted birds of some kind to their tableside. A Matre'd appeared and began to carve grand slices of the succulent meat; his underlings scurrying to serve the patrons with panache. It was well-known that roasted meats, seafood, fruits and vegetables from all over the known galaxy were available on the Archeron; it's famous for it. Gastronomes, at least the wealthy ones, flock to the giant ship to sample the legendary fare.

One of the many oddities of space travel aboard a vessel like the Archeron was on full display: Though my internal clock told me it was morning, fellow passengers weren't necessarily in sync. Some slumbered peacefully, while others stirred from their slumber, and yet others were fully immersed in their day's activities; all simultaneously. This constant bustle demanded round-the-clock operation of the ship's amenities, a feat requiring an army of crew members.

My curiosity was piqued as I watched the diverse crowd mill about. I wanted to mingle and ask people about their origins, but hesitated. Would it be considered impolite? I had no idea; I'd never travelled before. The Archeron welcomed both destination travelers like me and pleasure-seeking vacationers. Most aboard were there for a 14 to 28-day escape, enjoying the ship's luxuries and attractions. There were also several ports of call offering simple pleasures or exotic adventures depending on your tastes.

The boutiques along the promenade catered to an upscale clientele. I recognized a few prestigious brands, far beyond my modest means. I resisted the urge to window shop, contenting myself with the exceptional cup of coffee.

This ship, and others like it, was basically an extravagant playground for the wealthy elite. The cost of a 30-day cruise on the Archeron was more coin than I earned in a year. It was incredible to me that so many people could afford such luxury. What'd they all do for a living; where'd all their coin come from?

I was contemplating attending a concert advertised on the holographic display in my cabin. Numerous options were available, but my preference leaned toward symphonic music. I briefly wondered if my new friends might share my interest. Impatience nagged at me; I was eager to hear more about my father's exploits with Teddy Bradley. To be honest, Bradley and his formidable bodyguard intrigued me greatly. They were characters I'd never encounter back on Ampora.

I was just finishing my respite and considering another large coffee when I felt a hand on my shoulder. I've never liked my personal space violated, so I turned my head abruptly to see who was being so rude.

"Sorry miss, I didn't mean to startle you. Please excuse me, but would it be possible to have a few moments of your time?" said a solidly built man in a neatly pressed military style uniform. My neighbors in the coffee shop avoided my eyes, discreetly hunching over their mugs.

"Well... " I began, but he cut me off before I could continue.

"Please. It'll only take a few moments; it's important." He insisted.

"I suppose I can spare some time." I said half-heartedly as I stood.

The other patrons parted to make way, clearly intimidated. I still didn't understand what was happening, but as we emerged from the little shop I saw another uniformed officer waiting and it struck me... I was being arrested!

They wore the uniforms of CTF security, minions of the Ministry of Security. Most people at home referred to them as the 'secret police,' but officially they were simply the fleet's military police. The Ministry of Security was a name that struck fear into the hearts of everyone I knew. The paranoia ran deep; neighbors, colleagues, literally *anyone* could be a Ministry informant. At home, dark-humored jokes circulated, like, 'How many secret policemen does it take to get a confession? Come with me, sir, and you'll find out.'

Their authority, unchallenged and limitless, spanned the Telluric sphere of influence. Rumors spoke of coercion, blackmail, and even torture to extract confessions. Citizens everywhere lived in dread of finding themselves in the very situation I suddenly found myself in.

Officer #1 took me firmly by the arm and ushered me briskly along the promenade deck. Other passengers either stared at us or averted their eyes nervously. I might've imagined it, but the concourse seemed to hush as we passed. Officer #2 followed a few steps behind us, but said nothing.

I'd never encountered Telluric security forces of any kind before; I'd only ever heard stories. Ampora wasn't exactly a hot bed of subversive activity. But some of the stories were decidedly scary; people abducted never to be seen again. I'd never taken any of those stories seriously before, but on the promenade that day I found myself desperately trying not to panic.

My frayed nerves wouldn't allow me to remain silent, "Am I under arrest or something?"

"Arrest? No, of course not. We just want to have a discreet word with you, that's all. Nothing to be worried about. We'll have you back to your planned activities in no time, trust me." the one with an uncomfortably firm grip on my arm said. There had to be hundreds of witnesses to my abduction at the coffee shop and the march down the promenade; that hardly qualified as discreet in my opinion.

Passengers kept parting like the Red Sea as I was marched. "What'd she do?" a young boy asked my escort as we passed. Officer #1 ignored the boy, but the child's mother admonished, "Mind your own business, Alfy. That lady did something she shouldn't have, that's all."

I wanted to argue, but I held my tongue. I wasn't at all sure the boy's mom was wrong.

"Here we are Ms. Thornwell, just this way." My captor said, pointing toward a narrow corridor to our right. The use of my name was the first indication they even knew who I was. Until then I was sort of hoping it was a case of mistaken identity.

He asked me for my comms device, "Just a precaution. I'll give it back to you when we're done." he said as I turned it over. Just like anyone, the loss of my comms was akin to losing my right hand; I was on it constantly, checking news, browsing the I-web or messaging.

We made our way to a nondescript door at the end of the corridor. There was nothing to let one know it was the lair of the secret police, but then again there wouldn't be, would there? We entered a small, brightly lit office that contained only sparce furnishings; just a plain, ordinary metal desk with two matching metal chairs. The walls were completely bare and painted an ugly, institutional beige. It felt like a halfway house for an insane asylum.

Behind the desk, a much more inviting stuffed, leather chair awaited, but it was already occupied by another one of the Ministry's minions. He was older than the first two; I'd say close to my own age. Officer

#1, still gripping my arm uncomfortably, guided me towards one of the uninviting metal chairs, while Officer #2 exited the room, leaving me envious.

The seated officer sat quietly, checking his comms device. He was clean shaven with close-cropped, blond hair and gray eyes. But, his most prominent feature was a jagged, gnarled and purplish scar from the corner of his left eye down his cheek to the neckline of his starched collar. As a consequence, the lid of the eye was only open about half mast, lending him an air of menace.

There were several pins and ribbons on his uniform, and epaulettes with stripes on his shoulders. I could tell you exactly what the uniform of a Marshall in Napoleon's La Grande Armee looked like, but I didn't know anything about modern military ranks and insignias. However, with all that hardware on his jacket I figured this guy must be in charge. He ignored me as he seemed to be reading messages on his comms, and responding. Finally, he put the device down and addressed me.

"Sorry about that; official correspondence. If I ignore it for an hour it becomes an unmanageable mess; I have to stay on top of it."

Battling my nerves, I blurted "No worries."; a phrase which I'd never used before in my life.

"Professor Thornwell, is it ok if I call you Abigail?"

"I suppose so. I prefer Abby, though." I said, cautiously.

"Abby it is then. My name is Gordon. Commander Gordon, Combined Telluric Fleet. You can simply call me Gordon if you want and ignore the rank, it's of no significance here."

On his collar I noticed a small, silver silhouette of a bird of prey, and a pin that read MoS. Ministry of Security, presumably.

"I wasn't aware the CTF stationed soldiers on civilian ships." I said.

"Of course. After all, the CTF's primary mission is to protect our citizens. There's normally a company of marines on board the Archeron at all times; as a deterrent to pirates, mostly. Although it'd have to be a pretty desperate pirate to take on this ship. But, CTF Security doesn't always have officers on board. This is a *special* circumstance."

"What's special about it?"

"That may become evident as we speak. However, I didn't bring you here to answer *your* questions, Abby. You're here to answer *mine*."

"Of course, how can I help you Commander?" Damn, he was touchy.

"First, I must warn you, this is an official interview. Therefore, you're required to answer my questions truthfully and completely. We're being recorded, and everything you say will be part of the official record. Not to put too fine a point on it, but in your own best interest try not to dissemble. Understood?"

"Yes." I croaked. The tension had ratcheted up significantly. My palms were sweating; an embarrassing symptom of my nervous nature. I had no idea what was going on; no idea why I was there. I felt like a lobster thrown into the middle of a Spikeball match.

"So, you're on the way to join an officially sanctioned archeological expedition. Isn't that correct?" he asked.

"That's true. Is there something wrong?" I fidgeted in my uncomfortable seat. That non-descript little room was inexplicably intimidating.

"Not at all. You should know, Abby, your expedition is under the protection of CTF security. *Me*, in fact. I've decided all participants must be thoroughly screened. The others were screened previously, but since you've just recently been added to the expedition, *this* is your official screening."

Why the Academy's expedition would be under the protection of the Ministry of Security, I couldn't imagine. It made no sense; the Academy is a civilian institution; we have nothing to do with the military.

"I filled out a questionnaire last week and submitted it to the Academy." I offered. "Why would the CTF be involved? The Academy's a civilian institution."

"Yes, I've had the chance to review your questionnaire and you'll be happy to know I saw no obvious red flags. But, those forms are never entirely comprehensive. We have a saying at the Ministry, 'there's always another question to ask.' That's why I'm here, so let me do my job, ok?"

"I'm sorry, I'll try to curb my curiosity."

"Thank you. But, since you asked, the CTF is involved because the Kleos system is outside Telluric space and unsecured. It could very well be dangerous, don't you think?" he said with a touch of sarcasm.

"I see. I didn't think of that, I suppose."

"That's what I'm here for: to think of things no one else does. The Academy being a civilian institution has no relevance either, the Ministry has authority over *all* Telluric citizens."

"Yes, of course." A lump the size of a Talvian Ghost Spider had formed in my throat.

"A place like Kleos Prime could be a haven for terrorists or pirates; enemies of the Alliance. We wouldn't want to endanger the lives of innocent academy professors, now would we?" he said with obvious sarcasm. I hate to be spoken to condescendingly, it's one of my pet peeves. Gordon was laying it on thick.

Fidgeting, I said, "I didn't know pirates or terrorists would care about a bunch of professors digging around in the dirt. Thanks for watching over us, I guess." I said, lamely.

"Think nothing of it, it's our job. Now, since you were told you'd be joining us at Kleos Prime, have you shared that information with anyone?"

"No, of course not." I answered truthfully. I didn't tell him Bradley already knew when I met him. That's not what he asked.

"Did you share your travel plans with anyone? A neighbor, a colleague, your cleaning lady?"

"Why would I do that?" I fidgeted again.

"Just answer the question, Abby, or we'll be here all day. Did you share your travel plans with anyone, or not?"

"No."

"Since learning you were to join us, have you been contacted by any other members of the expedition?"

"No, I haven't. Should I have been?"

"Absolutely not. Just checking." He smiled and his gruesome scar made it seem like a parody.

"Oh."

"You seem nervous, Abby. Why is that?"

"I guess it's because I've never spoken to a CTF security officer before."

"That you know of. We have many operatives that don't wear uniforms; you might've spoken to a dozen of them and not even known it. Relax, Abby. Try to forget I work for the Ministry of Security. There's nothing to be nervous about."

"I'll try."

"In my experience, nervous people often have something to hide. If you have nothing to hide, you should be able to relax. Now, I saw in your file you hold a senior research chair in archeology at the Academy. Forgive me, I'm not familiar with highbrow institutions like yours. What, exactly, does a senior research chair do?"

"It's nothing glamorous." I said, ignoring his sarcasm, "I spend a lot of my time poking around in the Academy's archives, doing research on ancient civilizations. Every once in a while I fill in for one of the regular archeology professors and teach a class or two for them. I normally teach history."

I was a little shocked to learn the secret police had a 'file' on me.

"Does your boss give you assignments? Or can you research anything you like?"

"Sometimes I assist colleagues with their research, but mostly I'm on my own and I can research whatever I want."

"That must be nice." More sarcasm. "I understand from your colleagues on Kleos Prime you're considered the preeminent expert on the contents of the Academy's archives. Other faculty even seek you out to help with their research, correct?"

"I'm as familiar as anyone, I guess. I don't know about preeminent."

"That's their word, not mine, Professor; false modesty is just another form of vanity. The Amporan Academy's archives are famous. Artifacts and manuscripts from hundreds of cultures can be found there. You're one of the main curators, and that's why you're here. We're in need of all the knowledge stored in your mighty brain. Things haven't progressed as well as expected with the expedition."

"Whatever I can do to help."

"Good. You must've researched Kleos Prime thoroughly; you've had more than two weeks since learning you were going. Tell me, did you see anything in the archives about previous archeological expeditions to the Kleos system?"

"No, I didn't. I was under the impression Kleos was an unexplored system. I thought the Academy was the first to dig there."

"Just because professors believe something, doesn't make it true. Did someone tell you the Academy would be the first to dig there?"

"Nobody told me, exactly. I guess I assumed."

"Abby, you know what happens when you assume?" His awkward smile made me cringe.

"Yah, I've heard that one before."

Gordon was a weird character. There was something seriously *off* about the man. Like the guys you read about who're good neighbors, go to church regularly and volunteer at the soup kitchen, but then you find out later they were secretly killing little old ladies and putting their livers in the soup.

"Alright, let's return to my question about previous digs at Kleos. Have you ever heard anyone talk about it? Rumors? Gossip? Anything at all?"

"Not that I can recall. Perhaps, if I could speak with Dr. Hughes I could help you more. How's he and the rest of the Academy crew at Kleos doing?" I asked, attempting to change the subject.

"Another question, Professor? They're all fine, but I'm afraid it won't be possible for you to speak with them. For security, I've instituted a communications blackout at Kleos Prime. I don't want anyone *unauthorized* to know what's going on there. Loose lips sink ships, as the saying goes."

"Oh. I see."

But I didn't. I couldn't, for the life of me, think of a reason why our dig should be a secret. I shifted in my horribly uncomfortable chair, fidgeted again and looked over my shoulder toward the door, showing my impatience.

Gordon leaned forward in his chair, "Abby, forget about the door. You aren't going anywhere until I'm satisfied. Are you positive you've never read about or heard about previous activity on Kleos Prime? Archeological or not."

"I'm positive."

"Alright. What, then, can you tell me about the planetary system? Since you're the expert, go-to researcher at the Academy, you must've done some research on it in the last two weeks."

"Well, of course I did some research on the planet and the system. There's not much information available, only a few old survey reports. The system was first surveyed 65 years ago by a military navigational survey ship. Kleos Prime is a barren planet in a barren system; no life, no water and no evidence of previous habitation. I wasn't sure why the Academy chose it as a target for an expedition, but Dr. Hughes knows better than I do."

"Your description of the place is accurate; I just came from there. It's a desolate rock. Cold, ugly, and lifeless. But we aren't the first ones there."

"We aren't? Did the expedition find something? Is that why Dr. Hughes sent for me?" I asked excitedly.

"He didn't send for you; *I did*."

"*You* did? Why?"

"Again, that will become evident as we speak. You just can't help asking questions, can you? I suppose I should make allowances, that's probably what makes you such a *genius* researcher." Again with the sarcasm.

"I'm no genius."

"Uh huh. I also saw in your file the esteemed Professor Henry Thornwell was your father; do we have that correct?"

"Yes, he was. He passed away some time ago."

"I know; my condolences." He said, offhandedly.

"Thank you." I said automatically.

Gordon wasn't *acting* like an asshole; he was the genuine article. He paused for a few moments, studying me with his unblinking eyes.

"Before he died, did your father ever mention the Kleos system? Even in passing? Think hard, it could be important."

"I don't remember him ever mentioning it. Why would he?"

"I'm simply being curious; it's in my nature and a byproduct of years of training. I imagine your father was quite knowledgeable about archeology. He's the foremost archeologist ever from Ampora, it's he?"

"I suppose that's true. But, he would've probably argued, he was always humble to a fault."

"Like his daughter, it seems. Abby, I thought it'd be a good idea for us to meet, seeing as we're going to be spending a great deal of time together in the next few weeks. You see, after EV765, you'll be a passenger on my frigate, the CTS George Upton, enroute to the Kleos system. Then we'll be together on the planet for quite some time. I was hoping you and I could become friends, or at least become friendly."

"I'm going to Kleos Prime on your ship?"

This tidbit was news to me, and unwelcome news at that. My paperwork said I'd be met at EV765, the Archeron's next port of call, and transported to Kleos Prime on a vessel privately contracted by the Academy. There'd been no mention of the CTF. I was attempting, and most likely failing, to keep the alarm off my face. The prospect of being Gordon's friend made me nauseous, and the prospect of spending the next few weeks with him was too repulsive to contemplate.

"I thought it best, since we're both going to the same place. The George Upton is at Kleos as we speak, but will meet us at EV765; I took the liberty of cancelling your contracted shuttle. Security is my primary concern; I didn't want some random private vessel showing up in the Kleos system." He grinned. He could tell how I felt about this turn of events, and he was taking sadistic delight in his maneuver.

"Thank you, that's thoughtful of you." I couldn't think of a better retort. The depressing news didn't help my nerves. I was hoping Gordon was about done with me, I wanted to go back to my cabin and shower to wash the grimy caress of that bleak little room from me.

"It's my pleasure." He said. "Now, please wait here, and I'll return shortly. I have something to show you that you may find interesting." Please wait? Did I have a choice?

Gordon stood without saying anything more, and left the room. The same officer still stood guard by the door. Why'd they need to guard the

door? Did they think I was going to make a break for it, jump overboard
and try to swim home? Good Gods.

I waited with the officer whose name I didn't know for what seemed
like hours, but it was probably only a few minutes. He said nothing, just
stared straight ahead, never looking at me. I had no way of knowing how
long Gordon was gone. I don't normally carry a chronograph at home,
and carrying one in space seemed silly. They'd confiscated my comms,
as I said before, leaving me without a tether to the outside world. I
had a new-found understanding of the anxiety my students felt when I
demanded their comms before a test.

Finally, the door opened, and Gordon returned. He made his way to
his *comfortable* chair and sat. He studied me for a minute, as if deciding
how to proceed.

"I confess, Abby, I wasn't sure how to handle this meeting. To be
honest, in the old days standard procedure would've been to simply
throw you in a cell for a week with nothing but bread and water, and
no one to talk to. Then, and only then, they'd have brought you out for
questioning. It's a tried-and-true method."

"I don't understand, what are you talking about?"

"I'm talking about our meeting; this *interrogation*. I'm sure you've
realized by now that's what this is."

"I have no idea; I've never been interrogated before. What's going on,
why am I being interrogated?"

Gordon slammed his fist on the table. "I'll get you to stop asking
questions, one way or another, Professor. My first instinct was to go old
school and throw you in the brig. But, this being the new kinder, gentler
Ministry of Security, I decided to bring you in for a friendly chat instead.
However, you're not being as cooperative as I'd hoped, so I'm forced to
abandon my friendly demeaner."

He paused for a few moments, possibly letting me have a chance to
remark. I wanted to ask, 'what friendly demeanor,' but I remained quiet.
Also, I honestly thought I *was* being cooperative.

"Your father died after a long battle with a rare type of viral
meningitis, correct?"

"Yes, I was told it was viral meningitis. I don't know if it was all that rare." Where the hell was this going?

"Trust me, it was pretty fucking rare, thank God. It was a very potent, bioengineered strain; developed during the war by the demented scum on Pentoff, and quite deadly to humans. Pentoffians reportedly only have minor symptoms, similar to a common cold. Sanguinem Cerebrum it's called; Bleeding Brain. It killed thousands of marines and CTF crewmen before drugs were developed to counteract it."

"It was a bioweapon? None of my father's doctors told me that."

"Of course not; that information is highly classified. Few civilians even know the disease exists. The virus was never able to spread to Telluric home worlds. It's a good thing too; it would've killed billions of civilians and possibly changed the outcome of the war. It was mostly contracted in combat zones, but less frequently on ships that had inadequate medical-grade air filters. So, it's curious a professor from Ampora died from it, don't you think?"

"As I said, nobody told me it was a bioweapon. I was just concerned with getting him the best care available."

"Highly commendable, Abby. It was just bad luck the bug spread into your father's spinal fluid; that's an almost certain death sentence."

"Why is my father's death relevant, Commander? And how do you know so much about it?"

I was getting tired of the topic, and annoyed by how much Gordon knew about my father's illness and death. It struck me as inappropriate and creepy.

"I told you; *I'll ask the questions*; and I'll decide what's relevant, Professor. Cases of Bleeding Brain are closely tracked by the CTF medical corps. I have access to any of the records I wish to see. Professor, your father was never near a combat zone during the war with the Pentoffian Empire. How do you think he contracted it?"

"I honestly don't care, but you seem to think it's important, so why don't you tell me how he got it?" I challenged.

I'd asked yet another question, and it momentarily looked as if he'd like to slap me. There was obvious anger in his eyes, but he restrained himself.

"*Obviously*, it came from a faulty air filter on some old spacecraft he was on. It came from *space*, Professor. He couldn't have contracted it on Ampora." Gordon threw a plastic baggie on the desk, and it landed in front of me.

"What's that?" I asked.

"You tell me, you're the intellectual. Look inside the baggie and tell me what you see."

"It looks like an old derma patch. What's that have to do with me?"

"One of your Academy colleagues found that patch on Kleos Prime. That brand didn't exist 30 years ago. What do you make of that?"

I was at a loss for something to say, so I just stayed quiet. It was clear, after my conversation with Teddy Bradley, the derma patch must've accidently been left behind when Teddy and my father left Kleos.

"Cat got your tongue, Professor? You *do* know what those things are used for, don't you?"

"Normally, they're used to administer pharmaceuticals. The drugs are absorbed through the skin."

"I knew you couldn't be as thick as you let on. We tested it in our lab, and here's the kicker: they found organic residue. Guess who's DNA was on it?" he asked smugly. I was getting tired of his game of 20 rhetorical questions.

"I give up."

"Henry Thornwell."

The name hung in the air for several moments. Of course the thing belonged to my father. His health problems were a long, drawn-out affair, and he was always on some new drug or another. My mind was scrambling for something to say, but it was drawing blanks. I wasn't even sure what he was accusing me of, if anything. I stared at the thing stupidly, but finally found my voice.

"But, how's that possible?"

My secondary school drama teacher, Mr. Haig, would attest I'm not much of an actor. But I believe I pulled off a decent performance. My mock stunned expression spitting out that pretend question seemed pretty convincing to me. But the only thing that mattered was if Gordon bought it.

"Actually, I was hoping you could tell me that. Obviously, Henry Thornwell visited Kleos Prime within the last 30 years. Since he's been dead for 8 ½ years and was sick and hospitalized for most of the 3 years prior to that, he was there between 30 and 11 ½ years ago. I checked, he never had permission to go there. Now, let's try this again: what'd your father tell you about his *illegal* trip to Kleos Prime?" Gordon demanded.

"Nothing, I swear. My father never once mentioned Kleos Prime. The word *Kleos* never even crossed his lips that I remember. I'm as shocked as you are, Commander."

I *was* telling the truth; it was Bradley who'd told me about them going to Kleos. In retrospect, I can't honestly say why I didn't tell Gordon all about my father, Teddy Bradley and my amulet. I was tempted to, out of fear, of course. The whole scenario with an angry secret police Commander questioning me in that bare, ugly room was frightening.

The only thing I can say is my instincts told me not to tell Gordon anything, mostly because I didn't like him; he was an asshole. And my heart was screaming not to betray my father. I didn't know *why* Pop didn't tell me about Kleos, but I had to assume there was a good reason. If he didn't tell *me*, he sure as hell wouldn't have told Gordon. So, I wasn't going to tell him anything either.

"Well, that's disappointing, to say the least. I find it hard to believe you're as ignorant as you claim. Withholding information is just as incriminating as giving false information. Frankly, I have enough reason to doubt you I should probably hold you in custody." He threatened. "A few days in the brig might jog your memory."

"I've told you the truth, and I haven't withheld anything. I don't see what reason you have to doubt me."

"My profession teaches you things; like the fact people are terrible at keeping secrets. They tend to unburden themselves by telling someone close to them. Fathers and daughters are often quite close, as I imagine you were with your father. My instincts and experience tell me he probably told you all about his trip to Kleos."

"Well, he didn't. You'll just have to take my word for it."

Gordon chuckled, "I don't have to take your word for anything. In my opinion you're withholding information. What I can't figure out is *why*."

"I wouldn't. If he'd told me anything about Kleos I'd tell you. Why wouldn't I?"

"That's exactly what I'd like to know. You see, this is where, in the old days, they would've thrown you *back* in a cell, with *no* food or water, until you begged to talk. Or, depending on the urgency of the situation, things might not have been *that* pleasant."

I sat there, sweating, as a secret police commander contemplated whether to throw me in a cell, and 'hold me in custody.' I couldn't believe my day had taken such a turn; never in a million years would I have imagined such a scenario. I wanted to protest, make a case to let me go, but I couldn't formulate an argument against such a non-sensical point. He wanted to imprison me simply because he had a *hard time believing me*.

"You can't detain me; I haven't done anything wrong." I challenged.

"I wouldn't bet your last coin on it, Professor. You might be surprised what authority I possess. Section 11, subsection C of the Ministry's operational guidelines states that an officer, *that's me*, may detain a subject, *that's you*, for further questioning if he has a reasonable suspicion of wrong doing." The bastard chuckled again. "Withholding information *is* wrong doing."

"But, you don't have a *reasonable* suspicion." I was getting angry, and that was probably a bad thing. I needed to calm down before I said something to *really* piss him off.

The creep chuckled again and said, "Relax, Abby. When I said I'd like us to be friends *I meant it*. Plus, it's a long way to the Kleos system, we have lots of time to continue this discussion, and we certainly will. I have a feeling you're not telling me everything you know, probably in an effort to protect your father, since he didn't have permission to go to Kleos. If so, you're being foolish. Your father's dead; I'd have a hard time throwing *him* in the brig."

"Commander... " I began, but Gordon cut me off.

"However, out of respect for our new friendship, I'm not inclined to ruin your time aboard this ship by making you sit in the brig needlessly. So, I'm going to let you go, *for now*. Besides, you're not going anywhere." He said, as he produced a passport from his jacket pocket and held it up for me to see. It was mine.

"Gordon, you stole that from my cabin! How'd you get in?"

"Please." He scoffed, "We're the Ministry of Security, we go where we like. I'm going to hold onto this. There's ships docking with the Archeron daily, transports, cargo ships, private yachts and everything in between. But, you need a passport to disembark to another ship. So, go enjoy yourself. Get a spa treatment, eat some gourmet food, take Zero-G lessons, live it up. I'll give you some time to think; try to remember anything your father might have told you about Kleos Prime. Maybe he hinted, or left you a clue; search your memory. We'll resume this conversation in a few days."

"You don't have to hold my passport; I'm not going anywhere. I have no place to go."

"The galaxy is a big place, Abby, there's always *someplace* to go. I'll sleep better knowing you can't leave the Archeron. We'll have plenty of time to get better acquainted traveling together to Kleos. I'm sorry to say the George Upton isn't as luxurious as the Archeron, but we make do."

"I'm sure it'll be fine. I'm not accustomed to luxury, so don't worry about me. Can I go now?" I couldn't wait to get the hell out of there, passport or no.

"In a moment. First, I must caution you, everything said here today between us is confidential. You are **not** at liberty to divulge any of it. In fact, you aren't at liberty to divulge this meeting even took place. I've programmed my code into your comms device for your convenience, just in case you want to get in touch with me. You may leave now. I hope you enjoy the remainder of your trip on the Archeron, and I'll see you later."

I left alright, just as quickly as I possibly could without actually breaking into a run. The guard that had stood by the door had to chase me down to give me back my comms device. No kidding, I actually did go back to my room to shower. I'd survived my first run in with the

Ministry of Security and had a whopper of a story for the next faculty mixer. I'd come out of it unscathed, so to speak, but minus my passport.

AFTER I SHOWERED AND changed clothes I poured myself a drink from the mini bar; some very good whisky I'd never heard of before. As I've said, I'm not a drinker usually, but I needed to calm my nerves. I poured a second whisky and sat down to think.

I wasn't happy about the turn of events. Having the secret police watching our every move at Kleos Prime would be stressful, but the question eating at me was *why?* Why was the Ministry of Security even there? I couldn't make any sense of it. I didn't buy Gordon's account, that they were simply there to provide security. There was something more to it, there had to be.

And the fact they'd found my father's DNA there complicated the situation in ways I couldn't yet grasp. Gordon obviously didn't believe my father had never mentioned Kleos to me. I'm not sure I'd believe it if I was in his place. Hell, I was having a hard time believing it just thinking about it; it was actually kind of ridiculous. Why *hadn't* he told me about it? I was stumped. I poured another whisky and downed it in a single gulp.

I had a few hours to kill before the concert I wanted to attend. I was already feeling tipsy, so I thought I might as well find a bar and continue drinking. My colleague at the Academy, Dr. Payne, always joked there's no problem a few drinks can't solve.

So, I left my cabin and headed toward another bar. I tried a different one this time, more of a hostess lounge. The sign read Tasha's, and as I entered, a lovely young blond woman greeted me. She was wearing a cocktail dress that revealed an abundance of cleavage. According to her name tag, she was called Arrella.

"Good evening, madam, welcome to Tasha's. We offer fine spirits and premium tobacco products. Would you like a table? Is there just one or are you meeting someone?" Arrella asked.

"It's just me. A quiet table please, if that's possible." These tobacco clubs had become quite popular; there were two within walking distance from my apartment at home.

"Certainly, madam. I know just the one, follow me please. Would you like a menu?" she asked with a pretty smile. I shook my head. I just wanted to sit quietly, drink and think.

Tobacco was another important crop and was cultivated everywhere it could be. I wasn't a regular smoker, but from time to time I partook. It was hard to believe the crop had almost disappeared several centuries ago. The health effects were to blame. It was said tobacco caused cancer. But the crop made a big comeback after cancer was eradicated. And besides, one puff from a pulmo inhaler before you sleep makes your lungs just like new.

Tasha's was multi-leveled, each level had its own tables and chairs, all pointed toward a semi-circular stage. And on the far side of the stage, there was a grand piano that wasn't just collecting dust. It was attended by a young man, coaxing out a pleasing, jazzy tune. Center stage stood a woman in a long evening gown holding a microphone. She joined in with a gorgeous voice, softly singing an old-fashioned ballad.

You couldn't miss the long bar, a real classic, against one of the walls. Two bartenders were holding court, whipping up drinks and adding to the buzz of the place.

The vibe was cozy, with a bit of smoky charm lingering in the air. You could actually hear yourself think in there, which was a rarity nowadays. It was like the perfect spot for folks looking to unwind and enjoy some good music. To be honest, it was right up my alley.

Arrella led me up to the top tier and to a tucked-away table that should give me some privacy. It was small, with only two chairs, and surrounded by partitions that promised much-needed seclusion. The table was already set with a lighter and an ashtray, a perfect setup. I expressed my gratitude with a polite nod, and Arrella left me to my own devices.

In the blink of an eye, another young woman appeared, her name tag read 'Bridget.' She had a head of long, wavy brunette hair and curves in all the right places, just like Arrella. Her outfit left little to the imagination: a black corset that highlighted her generous bosom, and a maroon skirt that was scandalously short. The skirt revealed the tops of her stockings and a hint of creamy thigh. Bridget's heels and lipstick matched her skirt, telling me she was meticulous about her appearance. It took some effort, but I managed to tear my gaze away from her figure and meet her eyes, which sparkled with a mischievous twinkle, accompanied by a winning smile. In a nutshell, Bridget was a knockout.

"Can I bring you a drink, madam? Or perhaps something to smoke?" Bridget's voice was silky and flirty.

"Yes, thank you. Whisky, please. Do you have the brand they stock in my cabin's mini bar? Corson's or something like that." I asked.

"Certainly, Cordson's is wonderful. Aged 16 years in lightly charred barrels made of stimetta wood from Nemea 2. Many of our patrons ask for it. I'll bring you a double. Rocks or neat?"

"Rocks, please."

"Anything to smoke?" Bridget's sweet tone lured me in. Her accent was enchanting, and her beauty was undeniable. As I looked around the place it seemed all the girls working there possessed such beauty, though I couldn't help but wonder if perhaps a surgeon had played a role in their charms. After all, cosmetic surgery had become as common as getting a simple dental procedure.

"Can you recommend anything, Bridget?"

"We have hundreds of premium tobacco products from all over," Bridget leaned closer, displaying her charms. In her seductive accent, she whispered, "Or, if you'd like something to help you relax even more, I can bring you a cheroot of caffarra leaves from Vitrallum. The smoke's mild, tastes delicious, and will make you feel oh, so yummy," she playfully licked her lips and let out a giggle.

"That sounds nice, bring me two." I laughed. "Are the cheroots included, or are they extra?"

What the hell, I was on vacation, sort of. At least while I was on this giant pleasure liner. I might as well try to enjoy myself. After my run in with the secret police I could use some relaxation.

"The cheroots are 125 Telluric coin apiece, but for two I only ask 200."

"Two it is then."

No wonder she was smiling. She was making a fortune on the side selling those cheroots. I didn't begrudge her enterprising, trying to make a little extra coin. I'd assumed the whisky was included because the other pub hadn't charged anything. I'm glad I asked about the cheroots though; it could've been embarrassing not having enough coin.

As Bridget returned to my table, she had a sly grin on her face. She casually placed my drink and the cheroots down, and her dimples made an appearance once more. I tried to be inconspicuous about reaching for my comms, not wanting to land her in hot water. It was clear she was bending the rules, selling caffarra on the side.

When I first came aboard, I declined to create a deposit account since everything was supposedly included. But, to my annoyance, the promenade shops weren't part of the package. So, earlier, I had to bring out my comms to pay for my coffee and roll, accessing my account back on Ampora. Thankfully, they accepted it. But with Bridget, I wasn't so sure.

"Is this alright? I'm afraid I don't have a deposit account," I apologized.

"No problem, love. I can take it straight from your comms. But you know, your bank at home will charge you a fee. Life would be easier aboard the Archeron if you had a deposit account; no extra charges. Then, I could just scan your thumbprint with my comms," she said, giggling.

She leaned in closer and said softly. "You know, I'm off in a couple of hours. For 1500, I could swing by your cabin and share one of those cheroots with you."

Naïve me, I almost asked why it would cost 1500 to share a cheroot, but then it dawned on me: Gods, she's a prostitute! I stammered, "Ah, well... uhm... thanks, Bridget, but I don't know. I was just... maybe some other time?" I cringed inwardly at my awkwardness. Attractive women turn me into a fool.

She laughed, and I joined in, my cheeks surely on fire. Of all the things I imagined might happen on my trip, being propositioned by a beautiful young prostitute wasn't among them. I'd never encountered a situation like this before, and it was a bit shocking. She was about the same age as my students back home, maybe even younger.

"Don't worry, love. I just thought you looked nice. If you change your mind, you know where to find me," she giggled and blew me a playful kiss as she departed. She was undeniably beautiful, and I won't lie, I was tempted. But paying for sex was something I'd never even imagined. Plus, 1500? That was a hefty sum for me, more than a week's pay.

Tasha's oozed nostalgia, like stepping into a time machine. The smooth jazz was slow and soothing, and the singer could melt your troubles away. The décor was old-school charm, but it all fit perfectly with the vibe. Even the lingering haze of smoke was strangely comforting; it reminded me of my father's pipe in his home office, a smell I'd always loved.

I couldn't help but wonder about the gorgeous women gliding around the room. Were they all working some unofficial side gig? I figured many probably were, one hustle or another. I'm sure the entertainers' union would want them to work in the onboard brothels, keeping tabs and taking their cut. So, Bridget and maybe a few others were doing it on the downlow.

I took a slow sip of my whisky, mulling over my impending trip with Gordon. Traveling with him after EV765 was about as appealing as a tooth extraction, maybe several. So, I decided to light up one of my little caffarra cheroots.

Bridget was right, the smoke was sweet, fruity, and as smooth as it gets. My body gave in to relaxation almost immediately, every muscle melting.

After a few puffs, I felt like I was on cloud nine. If Gordon showed up, I might even have hugged the asshole. I was feeling just like Bridget promised: *yummy*. So, I leaned back, closed my eyes, and soaked in the sensation and the music. Maybe I should just stay at Tasha's and skip that concert.

The feeling brought me back to my student days and memories of Daniel Bimmel, the guy who had a huge crush on me. We'd shared a few puffs of local cannabis back then, but this caffarra was on a whole different level. No wonder it was used medicinally.

Daniel and I had been friends and study buddies, but he wanted more. I tried for a while, even lost my virginity to him. But my heart wasn't in it. Breaking it off was tough, he was a nice guy. Here I was, still single, still alone with no prospects. Last I heard, Daniel was a successful litigator, married with kids. I had no regrets, though. My Pop always said, live without regrets, and truthfully I didn't regret that decision.

I opened my eyes, mostly to find the cheroot and put it out; I'd smoked less than half, and didn't want to waste it. But then, a jolt of surprise hit me. There was a woman in the other chair at my table. I had no clue how long she'd been there; I'd lost track of time with my eyes closed.

She wasn't one of the hostesses, that was obvious. She had an air of sophistication, older and dressed more conservatively; an ankle-length silk dress, vibrant and intricate in design. Her dark skin and hair framed her strikingly, and she puffed on her own cheroot elegantly with an old-fashioned cigarette holder. She flashed a pleasant smile as she noticed my eyes open.

"Hello, darling," she said, her voice low and conspiratorial. She'd caught me in such a relaxed state I couldn't formulate a response. "How're you feeling?"

"Wonderful." I guessed she knew what I'd been smoking wasn't tobacco. Still under the influence of the caffarra and a few too many whiskys, it took me a moment to process that a stranger was sitting with me.

"Who're you?"

"Right, let's start with introductions. I'm Tasha Ving, the owner of this club," she said, her tone reassuring. "And you're Abigail Thornwell, aren't you?"

"Yes, I'm Abby. Why are you sitting here?" I replied, a little rudely without meaning to be. I was struggling to clear my head.

"Abby, listen, you're not supposed to be here. That is, we need to get you out of here. There are men coming and they can't be allowed to see you." Tasha told me.

"Tasha, I'm sorry about the caffarra. Please don't fire Bridget; I asked her to get me some."

She waved that off with a laugh. "Don't worry about that, darling. Bridget and I have an arrangement. This is about something else. Kara asked me to sneak you out of here. Grab your stuff, and let's go."

So, I quickly downed my drink, collected my cheroots and comms, and followed Tasha through the dimly lit club. Being intoxicated isn't as much fun when you're trying to follow someone through a dark nightclub. I must've banged my knee half a dozen times. I also knocked over a man's drink, eliciting an angry snort. But, I eventually made it to a door behind the bar, where Tasha had disappeared moments before.

That's when, out of the corner of my eye, I spotted Teddy Bradley, dressed in another Chambord suit, sitting at a table with two imposing men. Kara was nowhere to be seen. I couldn't hear them, but the men seemed to be having an animated discussion with Teddy. One of the men was gesturing emphatically with his hands, the other slammed a fist on their table, knocking over a drink. Teddy, for his part, appeared to calmly be listening to them berate him. At least that's how it appeared until Teddy abruptly stood. His face displaying anger and annoyance, he said something that immediately put an end to the discussion. Oh, how I wished I could hear what was being said.

The two men stood and turned just enough so I could see their faces. They both wore beards, and had elaborate tattoos covering their bald heads. In fact, it appeared in the low light they had tattoos covering most of the skin exposed by the casual clothes they wore. To say they looked unhappy would be an understatement. Whatever Teddy had told them obviously hadn't gone down well, but they'd stopped their ranting. The argument had garnered the attention of many nearby patrons, and some of them had alarm written on their faces. I leaned back a bit behind a partition so Teddy couldn't see me, at least I didn't think he could.

Just then, Tasha opened the door behind me, grabbed my sleeve, and pulled me into a brightly lit office I assumed was hers. The stark contrast in lighting snapped me back to reality.

"Tasha, who were those men with Teddy Bradley? Is that who you were trying to hide me from? What's going on?" my nosiness was unchecked because of my intoxication.

"You weren't supposed to see that. Those men are trying to make a deal with Captain Bradley. Or perhaps they've already made a deal, I don't know. They aren't the kind of men respectable people deal with, if you know what I mean. Although, I've made deals with them from time to time." She laughed. "Rare things, hard to come by, they seem to have a knack for acquiring. But they scare me, so I've been dealing more with Captain Bradley lately. He's more my style, and much more handsome." She winked. "Would you like a drink?"

"No, thanks. How'd you know who I was?"

"We have a mutual friend, darling: Kara Az-Codor. She pointed you out to me and asked if I'd sneak you out before anyone at that table could see you. I've known Kara for a long time, she's helped me on numerous occasions. It seemed a simple thing to do for all I owe her."

"So, Kara was out there in the club too? I didn't see her. Is Teddy in danger?"

"You'd only see her if she wanted you to, and Teddy has nothing to fear with Kara nearby, I can promise you that. Kara spotted you and asked me to help; I hope you don't mind. How exactly do you know Kara?" Tasha asked.

"I don't, not really. We just met yesterday, she and Bradley. What kind of deal was going on out there?" I asked. "Those men looked like criminals."

"Oh, darling, I couldn't tell you that even if I knew. I know those men however, and they're the type it's unwise to cross."

"Kara thought I might be in danger if those men saw me?"

"Something like that, I'm not entirely sure. But, when Kara asks for a favor, she has a good reason, that much I know." Tasha explained.

"Thanks for helping me out. Please tell Kara thanks as well, if you see her. And let her know I'm going to a concert on deck 8 before turning in. Thanks again."

"You're welcome, darling. Come back and see us sometime, alright? I'll make sure Bridget scares up something even better for you to smoke," she said with a mischievous laugh. "Or maybe I'll just scare up Bridget for you."

So, Tasha knew about Bridget's second side hustle. And she saw right through me. Using her private exit, I returned to the corridor and headed to deck 8. The rest of the evening passed in a hazy blur. Being both drunk and high made the concert an unforgettable experience. I promised myself I'd do this again before leaving the Archeron.

After the concert, I couldn't wait to get back to my cabin. I ordered an excessive amount of gourmet food and drank some more whisky, but saved my cheroots for another time. 200 coin had put a dent in my account, I was only a lowly professor and perhaps the poorest person on the ship. I planned to sleep for a solid 12 hours and hopefully forget all about Commander Gordon.

I went overboard with room service, ordering two entrees and a dessert. I ate and drank until I felt sick. I didn't fall asleep so much as pass out. I didn't remember my dreams, I usually don't. But, I knew my waking dreams would be haunted by a rendezvous that never occurred, over a small matter of 1500 Telluric coin.

Part Four A Day with Kara Az-Codor

Interstellar Date: 388-06-19
On Board the Archeron

I WOKE WITH A MONSTROUS hangover, an upset stomach and little awareness of where I was. It took several moments to realize I wasn't at home in my cozy little apartment on Tyndall Avenue. My room was a mess, a veritable disgrace. In my drunkenness I'd spilled a good portion of my late dinner on my innocent floor. I spilled Cordson's as well, which was a crime.

I drank two large glasses of water and searched the cabin for any kind of headache remedy. There was none, so I called room service again. The boy arrived with my pills and a large, heated carafe of coffee. He took one look at my cabin and gave me the most disapproving look I've ever received. Properly chastised, I took the medicine and headed for the shower.

I took a nice, long soak with the water as hot as I could stand it. When I emerged, my skin was bright pink, my headache was completely gone, and I felt almost as good as new. Those pills were miraculous.

After drinking the coffee and cleaning up some of my mess (I didn't want the cleaning staff to see it the way it was), I sat thinking about what I should do next. There were literally hundreds of things to do on board the Archeron, but what I wanted to do most was look up Teddy Bradley and his lady friend again.

As I stood, intending to find some breakfast, I heard a knock on *my* door. I opened it not knowing what to expect. It could be Bradley and Kara, or jack-booted goons, or even housekeeping for all I knew. To my great relief it was Bradley with a wide smile on his face. My relief was immense, if illogical; I wasn't even sure I liked him that much.

"Good day, Professor, I hope you slept well." he said cheerily.

"Well actually, I guess I did. I had far too much to drink last night so I sort of collapsed in bed. Would you like to come in?" I scanned the corridor and saw no sign of Kara.

"Sorry to hear it; it happens to me all the time." he laughed, "I can't stay, thank you. I must run, people to see, you understand. I only dropped by to ask a small favor of you."

"A favor? I guess, if it's something I can do."

"Well, I have some appointments today, and it's hellishly awkward, but I'm afraid I'm not at liberty to bring Kara with me. She makes these people uneasy you see, and it's just simpler all around if I go alone. I don't feel the need for a bodyguard anyway."

"So, what's the favor?" I asked, trying not to show my disappointment. I was looking forward to continuing our previous conversation.

"Well, it just so happens Kara is dying to see the remarkable arboretum on board. It's supposed to be quite spectacular, trees from all over they say. I wondered if you might accompany her? Afterward the two of you can avail yourselves of the fine shopping on the promenade, my treat; no limit. I understand there is a reputable clothier specializing in safari wear. You could outfit yourself with new clothes for your dig."

Hmm, he wanted to buy me clothes, no limit. That seemed extravagantly generous for a person I'd known for two days.

"You want me to babysit your demon?" I giggled. "Do you have special instructions for something like that? When's her nap time?"

I thought my little joke was quite funny until Kara appeared from around a bend in the corridor walking in our direction. I had no idea if she'd heard, but I was mortified, nonetheless. Foot-in-mouth is a frequent failing of mine.

"After shopping, you ladies can visit one of the many fine restaurants as well, also my treat. I'm afraid my appointments may run quite long." Teddy ignored my joke, thankfully.

If he was attempting to win me over with his coin... well... it might just work. Actually, the day he described sounded like fun, and that's exactly what I needed. I was planning on seeing the rest of the ship anyway. Being awkward socially, I'm normally most comfortable alone, but to my surprise I found I was in the mood for company.

"Hello Kara, you look amazing." I told her as she approached. It was a massive understatement.

"Hello Abby Thornwell, so do you." It felt almost like we were going on a date.

"Teddy here says we can empty his account today. What do you say bodyguard, sound like fun?"

I was staring at her outfit in awe. She wore the same type of form-fitting, full body suit as the other day, but this one was a different color. It was dark rose with golden threads laced through it in intricate patterns. Today, instead of armor, Kara was adorned with bangles on her arms and long, slim boots of supple leather all the way to her knees. In her hair were more of the golden threads, woven to match her outfit. At her waist was a similar belt as before but slimmer and only one blade was evident, the needle pointed dagger she'd used to threaten the ugly, little Tubau. She literally looked like a goddess descended from heaven.

"I say it sounds like a wonderful time. My master has generously given me access to his deposit account and my thumb is loaded and ready. But first, I'm absolutely starving. Would you mind if we find something to eat?" She smiled warmly at me; her perfectly white, perfectly straight teeth (including prominent canines) were on full display.

"Why not? I could eat." I agreed.

My stomach had settled, and I was starting to get hungry. I didn't know what in Orah's hat was in those pills room service had delivered, but they fixed me right up.

The two of us set out toward the promenade deck, she dressed as a goddess, me dressed in my normal, frumpy shirt and slacks. I blended in with the predominantly human crowds we encountered, but I had a hard time imagining Kara blending in anywhere.

Also, as we passed through the teaming crowd, I noticed Kara wasn't the only one armed. I saw plenty of knives and cudgels evident in the crowds of passengers; something strictly outlawed at home. I didn't notice anyone sporting projectile or energy weapons though, so they were probably banned on the Archeron. I knew there were many places that allowed people to go around armed any way they liked. Still, for me, it was a little disconcerting strolling by a group of men, all with small clubs and large knives hanging from their belts. I was glad to have Kara with me.

As we looked for a place to eat, our presence didn't go unnoticed. We attracted curious glances and more than a few stares. I soon realized that some of the stares weren't solely due to Kara's beauty or our unconventional pairing. There was an undercurrent of disapproval in those accusatory looks, mostly directed at me.

"See anything that looks good?" I asked.

"You choose, Ms. Thornwell, I'm not particular. And I'm hungry enough to eat anything." Kara replied. She seemed to have become tense as we walked. I couldn't be sure why.

"Please, call me Abby." I told her, "We're spending the day together. It's going to get old calling me Ms. Thornwell all the time. How about that place?" I pointed to a restaurant across the concourse from us that appeared busy; always a good sign when choosing a restaurant, in my opinion.

"Fine with me," Kara responded.

We neared the entrance of the upscale establishment, and a tuxedo-clad man stepped in our way, blocking entrance. His disapproving gaze suggested I didn't meet their dress code. Beyond him, elegantly dressed diners could be seen enjoying their meals. Kara, as I said, resembled a deity. The idea of returning after a wardrobe upgrade crossed my mind. Before I could propose it, he singled me out, ignoring Kara completely.

"We'd be delighted to seat you, miss, but I'm afraid we won't be able to seat your *friend*." He uttered 'friend' with derision in his voice; almost as if the word itself offended his taste buds.

"Why not?" I asked, slow to comprehend.

"We're a *human only* establishment, miss. We don't serve *non-humans*."

I was shocked, and embarrassed. "My friend is a 2nd class passenger. I can't..."

Kara interrupted with a tight smile, "It's fine, Abby, I'm quite used to this sort of thing. We'll just find another place to eat. They probably have rats in the kitchen anyway." She turned and walked away leisurely as the tuxedoed maître d' stared at her with obvious contempt.

I followed Kara, absorbing disapproving looks from several humans seated along the way. The in-your-face racism was quite shocking to me. On Ampora I'd never had such an experience, but then again Ampora had few non-humans. I had no non-human acquaintances there, and therefore had never had an opportunity to be denied entry like that. My heart sank as I imagined the crushing humiliation she must've experienced.

"Kara, is that something that happens often?" I asked, in my naivety.

"Of course. This is the domain of the mighty Telluric Alliance. That sort of thing happens all over the galaxy now, anywhere the Tellurians rule. And it's getting more blatant all the time." She must've sensed my unease, "Don't worry, little human, you're not to blame."

We returned to the wide concourse and made our way further along. We were quiet as we walked. I confess I didn't know what to say. I'm awkward at the best of times, and I was at a loss for a way to alleviate the tension. The situation called for a change of topic, but my mind failed me.

Finally, Kara broke the silence "You worry too much, Abby. I'm not some fragile child, unable to take care of myself. I'm made of stronger metal than that, you needn't protect me." She teased me, breaking the sour mood.

We approached a small stand where an old woman was grilling some greasy chunks of meat over a charcoal brazier. The aroma was mouthwatering and I could've sworn I heard Kara's stomach growl as we approached.

"Hey, ho, ladies!" the woman yelled in our direction. "This is the best food stand on the whole ship! I guarantee it!"

The old woman looked human and appeared to be manning the small stand by herself. I had to admit, the sound of the grilling meat and the smoky steam rising from her stand were inviting.

"I've got some lovely grilled suppett filets here, just past bloody." the old woman called to us. "It's my secret recipe, passed down from my great grandsire. He operated a stall in the Teblesco Square on Cerante Minta. Come on, aren't you hungry?"

"Yes, starved." said Kara. 'We'll take 2 orders. And two mugs of ale too."

"What's a suppett?" I asked tentatively, not entirely convinced. It smelled delightful, spicy and rich, but I'd honestly never heard of a suppett before.

"Ha, never, ever ask. If you have to ask, just walk on girl. My name's Evetta, and suppett is my specialty. I guarantee you've never had better." The old woman declared. "It's seasoned with over a dozen spices and herbs, then I grill it to golden perfection. Just wait! You'll be telling your friends to come here!"

There was a counter in front of the woman's grill and stools to sit on. We slid onto the two least filthy stools. The woman slapped a platter down in front of us with several cubes of meat sizzling upon it, and a bowl of what I supposed were disks of unleavened bread. Evetta slapped down two huge pewter mugs of ale as well.

"This ale is from Astraea, the very finest. I guarantee it's the best on the ship!" Evetta was quite a saleswoman.

Kara tucked in first, grabbing a piece of bread and using it to liberate a few chunks of meat from the platter. The platter was awash with blood and fat, but it certainly did smell good. As Kara reached for a second helping I steeled my nerves and tucked in as well.

The meat was amazingly tender and delicious. The spices were exotic to my palate but blended wonderfully with the medium-rare chunks of meat. Red meat is an extravagance on Ampora, and I rarely indulged, so this was a real treat. As advertised, I'd never had better 'suppett.'

"More." Kara agreed with my assessment.

The woman cackled as she put together a second platter for us. She relished our obvious appreciation. And the strong ale was excellent as well, just as she'd promised. I ate until I couldn't hold another bite. I must've polished off a gaggle of suppetts, and Kara, a herd.

The wonderful meal put us in a great mood. We thanked Evetta profusely as Kara paid by pressing her thumb to the scanner, tipping extravagantly. What the hell, it was Bradley's coin anyway.

"So, Kara, what exactly is a suppett?" I asked as we walked away full of the stuff.

She laughed. "There is no such thing. These vendors never know what sort of supplies will be available at the next stop. So, whatever meat they can procure is what they serve. It's much easier to have 'suppett' on your menu than to change your menu constantly."

I thought I'd be ill. "Are you telling me I just feasted on *mystery meat*?"

Kara laughed uproariously and said, "In space, even eating lunch can be an adventure."

We strolled along the promenade, pointing out oddities and joking like we'd known each other for years. I was having a fine time. There were clothiers, jewelers, furriers, cafes and restaurants. One particular furrier's stall caught my eye, displaying an intergalactic tapestry of colors and styles. This was a stark contrast to the restrictions back home where furs were forbidden. But there were no such proscriptions here aboard the Archeron, in open space.

In a dimly lit shop filled with gleaming blades and military gear, we browsed for a while. Kara's dagger, with its intricate design, caught the shopkeeper's eye. He asked to examine it and Kara, her pride evident, unsheathed it and placed it on the counter. He leaned forward, his curiosity palpable.

"I've never seen its equal, madam," he said, admiration in his voice. "I'd love to have it. If I put it on display in my window, it'd increase my foot traffic substantially. What'll you take for it?"

Kara's response was firm, "My Sur-rok is not for sale."

The shopkeeper persisted, "Oh, come now. Everything has a price. I'll give you 7,000 Telluric coin, or 7,500 in store credit."

"The scabbard is worth more than that." Kara replied. As we left the man was still calling out offers.

We started toward the center of the giant ship, where many of the attractions were clustered. At one point we approached a group of young men, 5 of them, loitering along a wall near a pub. A couple of them held half empty glasses of ale. They were talking loudly amongst themselves, and laughing the way men sometimes do in a group. It never fails, when a group of more than two males gather they revert to juvenile behavior. These boys weren't too far from being juveniles, by appearances.

The tallest of them, a cocky, rugged looking, dark-haired boy of perhaps twenty, called to us as we neared, "Hey, ladies. Where're two such beautiful ritas heading all by yourselves?"

The term 'rita' was a common one used when referring to attractive young women. I think it was derived from one or another Old Earth language. It wasn't necessarily a derogatory term, but it depended on how it was used.

We attempted to ignore him, but he persisted. "You should have a *man* to escort you, to keep you safe." His companions all chortled and egged him on.

"Let us know if you see any." Kara responded sarcastically.

Affronted, he asked, "What did you say, you *trash-breed*?"

I supposed he didn't want to lose face with his comrades. Trash-breed *was* a derogatory term, however. It was commonly used as a catchall insult for humanoids who weren't human. The implication being they were a lower form of life.

He might've been fine, Kara might've ignored him and kept walking. But he made the mistake of stepping toward her aggressively. He raised his finger to point at her and began to say something more, but before he could utter a sound Kara stepped towards him. She'd made a fist, and with speed rivaling a pit viper, shot it toward his solar plexus. He stopped abruptly and doubled over in pain; the air gone from his lungs.

"When he regains his breath, you children might teach your friend some manners. Next time, if he doesn't mind his tongue, I shall remove it." She told the others as she unsheathed her viscous dagger and showed it to them.

They'd seen her speed and strength humble the biggest one of them, and when they saw the blade they all shrank back over toward the wall, properly intimidated.

We walked away and after a few moments I said, "That was the first fight I've ever witnessed. That was awesome, you took the guy down with one blow."

"That was no fight. That was more akin to swatting an insect."

Eventually we made our way to the famous Arboretum. The entry was a long corridor, its transparent walls and ceiling revealed a breathtaking scene. To the right, a tropical rainforest unfolded, adorned with vibrant, broad-leaved trees and a profusion of flowering vines. The dizzying array of color was astonishing.

On the left, as we continued down the tunnel, we encountered a diverse forest of deciduous trees. While some seemed vaguely familiar, I couldn't identify any. The sheer scale of the place was awe-inspiring, with hundreds of trees in view, it was only a small glimpse of the vast arboretum. We were still in the entryway.

Emerging from the tunnel, we found ourselves in the midst of a huge forest, surrounded by trees so colossal it defied belief. This section featured alien versions of conifers, pines, spruces, and their kin. Some trunks were a staggering 5or 6 meters thick. The forest canopy soared to a height of at least two hundred meters. We wondered how deep the ground must be to accommodate the enormous roots required to support these massive trees. Or what sort of technological wizardry was employed. The forest floor was carpeted with detritus, scattered pine needles, and an assortment of seed pods.

Kara confessed with wonder in her voice, "I'm such a fool. I've been aboard the Archeron many times, but this is the first time I've set foot inside this arboretum. I can't believe I've been missing *this* the whole time."

We continued deeper into the arboretum and stumbled upon a vast orchard. Towering apple trees dwarfed anything we had back home, their branches heavy with huge, fist-sized apples ripening in clusters. Nearby, Baloto trees from Ixion stood with their robust trunks and stubby branches bearing impressive clusters of their renowned tangy-sweet fruit.

And further down the path, the Tatanga trees from Elatus 6 stretched skyward, their slim frames crowned with fruit the size of my head, the flesh of which was famously spicy and pungent.

A few passengers were gathering fallen fruit, I supposed to take back to their cabins. I looked around for a sign forbidding it, but couldn't find one. I strolled over and retrieved an apple, wiped it off on my shirt and took a bite. I didn't spit it out, but I was tempted to. The flesh was crisp and sweet at first, but there was a noticeable chemical after-taste that put me off. I dropped the thing and hurried to catch up with my companion who was striding away down a cobbled path between the trees.

The domed, transparent roof must've been over three hundred meters high. Clouds even appeared to drift in the treetops. The artificial light provided inside the dome seemed incongruous with the mass of stars beyond it. But the overall effect was stunning, nevertheless.

I caught up with Kara, who'd paused amid a stand of mighty conifers, "This reminds me of my home." she said, not without a touch of sadness in her voice. "The mountains there are often shrouded in clouds. The forests are vast and teaming with game. The high valleys hold streams as cold as ice. When you swim in them your skin turns blue, but your heart soars."

"Where *are* you from, Kara?"

"Later, Abby, I'll tell you about it. For now though, I want to enjoy this."

There were paths through the trees for hiking. So, we set off, curious to see what other secrets would be revealed. Along the way we paused to read the small signs that identified the origins of unfamiliar trees. Surprisingly, I'd never even heard of a few of the places. The science behind this wonder was far beyond my understanding. How could they possibly keep all these trees from different worlds, different climates and even different atmospheres alive? Aries Starlines had done it, though.

We came upon a clearing in the forest awash in brilliant colors. It was a flower strewn meadow, with a small playground at the center. There, several children played while their parents looked on; it was a lovely scene. Birds and flying insects abounded as well, most of types I'd never seen before. I spied a small songbird with a pretty blue crest. It was a bird I recognized from home, from Ampora. But, for my life, I couldn't remember its name. I vowed to find one when I returned and learn what it was called.

We lingered there in the arboretum for quite some time, enjoying the stunning beauty of it. I struggled to remember when or if I'd ever been so moved by a place. Whomever was responsible for this should be celebrated as a genius. Eventually we made our way out and back toward the promenade.

"Do you still wish to shop, Abby?"

"To be honest, I could use some new clothes but I'm not sure it's appropriate to take Teddy's coin. It'd be like I was his mistress or something."

"Teddy has a lot of coin, some of it is even earned honestly." Kara laughed with me, "Trust me, little human, he can spare it. And I guarantee there will be no 'strings attached,' as they say. Think of it as a reward for *babysitting his demon.*"

Oh gods, Kara had heard what I'd said that morning. I wanted to crawl in a hole.

"Oh. I'm so sorry Kara... it was an awful joke. Please don't be angry." My face had to be the color of a Jijian fire melon.

"I may forgive you, *in time*, as long as you help me purchase a dress. My master wishes me to have a change of clothes; one that doesn't make me look so threatening. Can you help with that? You could hold my hand so I don't get lost." She teased me. I guess that meant she wasn't angry.

We strolled the promenade scrutinizing the many retailers, trying to decide which looked promising. Thank the gods there were no more awkward incidents of merchants trying to keep Kara out. On Bradley's advice we entered a shop called 'Safari Adventures.' There, I picked up hiking attire, a sleek jacket, and a pair of stunning titanium-toed hiking boots that slid onto my feet like they were custom-made. The stuff was outrageously expensive and I felt guilty as hell, but Kara just scoffed when I said so.

"My master is a generous man. He constantly buys me gifts I don't need, and I always accept because it makes him happy. I truly enjoy making him happy. He'll be happy to see you wearing these new clothes, and he'd be unhappy if you hadn't accepted his generosity. So, you see, you're doing *me* a favor. You're an excellent babysitter."

We ran in to difficulty finding a dress for my Az-Codorian companion, though. None of the merchants had anything her size in stock. They all offered to order or custom make something, but Kara said Bradley wanted her to have it right away. There was one rude clothier who made a remark about the difficulty of finding a dress 'for a creature her size.' We exited that establishment quickly after the remark.

Kara was philosophical about it. "It's of little consequence what an ignorant fool says or thinks. If I were to attribute more importance to it than it deserves, I'd be as big a fool as he."

Eventually, we found a shop whose proprietor assured us he could fabricate a dress in only a few minutes. It seemed he had equipment that could produce custom clothing quickly. Kara and I debated a long while about the color. I thought blue looked good on her, with her dark features. Kara preferred black. I was afraid she'd look like she was going to a funeral, so thankfully she deferred to me in the end.

The shopkeeper was as good as his word. When we left, we took with us a pretty, cobalt blue frock dress that looked wonderful on Kara.

She said, "I've never worn a dress before; I'll probably look ridiculous."

"I don't think so, it looked great on you in the shop. You've really never worn a dress before?"

"Once, when I was a child, my mother tried to get me to wear a taava to my cousin's wedding. A taava is a long, flowing garment women wear for formal occasions. I tore it to shreds. My father laughed, but my nurse beat me with a stick." Kara laughed. I couldn't help but laugh with her, even though I was a little appalled. No one beats children on Ampora.

Because of our suppett feast, neither of us was hungry yet, so we made our way back toward our rooms. The 2nd class accommodations seemed to stretch on endlessly through long corridors. I couldn't even guess how many rooms there were. So, we had a nice walk ahead of us, carrying our packages.

I have to admit, I couldn't remember a time I'd enjoyed myself so much, and the company was most of the reason. I'd never had so much fun with anyone before, ever. Unexpectedly, Kara had turned out to be a delightful companion. Even the humiliating incident at the restaurant hadn't dampened her mood more than a few moments.

"Thank you for keeping me company today, Abby, and for helping me pick out a dress. I couldn't have done it without you, you know *so* much about fashion."

I was pretty sure Kara was teasing me again. Obviously, I was no more informed about fashion than she was. What could I say? I kind of liked her teasing.

"You're welcome. And thank you for keeping me safe today. I know Teddy only wanted us to spend the day together so you could watch over me. I appreciate it. Yesterday, at Tasha's, were you watching over me then?"

"I was surprised to see you there. I thought if Teddy saw you, it'd throw him off and foul up his negotiations. That's why I asked Tasha to intervene, that's all. So, I was actually trying to protect him, that's my job after all. And, in truth, if you'd unknowingly went up to Teddy at the table and made yourself known to those men, it's possible they might've tried to use you to make Teddy do as they wish. They are quite unscrupulous and dangerous."

"So, you were protecting both of us. Thank you, Kara. But who were those men?"

"I shouldn't say; It has nothing to do with your business with my master. Is it enough to tell you they're dangerous criminals?" she asked.

"Dangerous criminals? Are they part of the syndicate I heard about?"

"Ok, Abby. I guess it won't hurt to tell you." She said, with an exasperated sigh. My curiosity was beyond my control sometimes.

She continued, "The Karmarinski brothers are the heads of their own syndicate based on New Britain. They'd make vicious enemies. My master has cleverly made them partners in some of our enterprises. In this way they are becoming dependent on our shared profits and have less reason to become enemies. He is gregarious and generous to a fault at times, but when it comes to business my master is clever and resourceful. Have I answered satisfactorily?"

"Of course, I'm sorry for asking. I guess I'm a bit nosey sometimes." I confessed.

"Nosey? What's that?"

"It means I stick my nose in other people's business too much."

"Ahh, I'm guilty of this as well, sometimes. Teddy doesn't know you were there at Tasha's, so it'd be awkward if you brought it up. He has enough on his mind without worrying about your safety. I can do that better than he can anyway." She asserted.

"I won't say a thing. You don't have to continue watching over me anymore, you know. Your cabin is that way," I pointed left down the corridor, "And mine is this way. I can get home from here unharmed."

"Ah, ah, Abby Thornwell, I must see you all the way to your castle. I'm a knight, and that's the chivalric code. You might be eaten by a Graf-tuk if I left you alone." Kara argued.

I knew she was still teasing me, but what was I supposed to do? I had visions of being thrown over her shoulder and being carried to my cabin. That might be embarrassing and thrilling in equal measure.

"My master was a little worried yesterday when we couldn't locate you. I even went to your cabin and knocked."

"I'm sorry about that. I was just out exploring the ship. I went to a concert last night, after Tasha's. It was nice. I would've invited you, but I didn't know how to contact you. We didn't trade comms codes the other day." We stopped for a few moments to do just that.

I wanted to ask her what time she'd knocked; was it during my 'interview' with the secret police, or while I was drunk and dosed with caffarra at the concert? I didn't ask because, obviously, I didn't want to answer her inevitable follow up questions. I let it drop. As Falstaff said, the better part of valor is discretion.

We strolled casually down the corridor, without apparent urgency. Kara's legs were considerably longer than mine, yet I found myself having to slow my pace to stay slightly behind her. She'd gone quiet and seemed to be in silent contemplation. I wondered what she was thinking; though I doubted it was the same thing I was thinking.

She paced just ahead of me, allowing me a chance to steal glances at her. If I were to be honest, "ogle" might be the most appropriate word. Perfect, that's what she was. Sculpted. It didn't help that her outfit left little to the imagination, especially from my perspective.

Come off it Abby, I thought, don't torture yourself. I began to feel self-conscious about my own body, of which I was normally proud. But compared to Kara I had love handles, saddle bags, flabby arms, and little definition. I seemed inadequate by comparison. I was being foolish.

Yet, it wasn't simply her natural beauty, and perfect body that captivated me. It was her self-assured attitude. It was obvious she possessed tremendous confidence and poise, traits I knew I lacked. It was safe to say I'd never known anyone like her, human or not, and I wanted to know everything there was to know about her.

"I know you have questions my pretty, little human. This would be an excellent time to ask." Kara was reading my mind again. Plus, she'd called me pretty, giving me a momentary thrill.

"Well, alright, since you brought it up, I actually do have some questions. I'm a little confused; Teddy called you his companion and bodyguard, but a few times you've called him master. What's that about?" Well, she *said* I could ask.

"I'm not his slave if that's what you're asking." She smiled, "Slavery is outlawed in Telluric space, as you know. Though I've seen instances of it before. But don't worry, Abby, that's not what's going on. It's much more complicated than that. You see, I've made a strong commitment to my Gal-vek, Bradley. I owe him a *life debt*, and I've ritualistically bound myself to him."

"Ritualistically? What's that mean?"

"Many years ago, he was able to save the lives of my mother, younger brother and little sister. They were in terrible danger after my father's treacherous death at the hands of his brother, my uncle. I was powerless to protect them, and Bradley used his spacecraft to take them away from danger to my maternal uncle's fiefdom. Afterward, in appreciation, I offered to pledge fealty to Bradley as his vassal."

"How'd Bradley happen to be there, on your planet?"

"On my planet he was known as a wine merchant. His trade often brought him there. The fruit we make wine from is only grown on my home planet. Our wine is renowned far and wide now, partly because of my master. He just happened to be in my homeland at the time of the coup. A stroke of luck for my family, and me."

There was a pause in her story, as Kara considered how to continue. I realized the recounting of her tale was taking an emotional toll on her. Her father had been murdered by his brother? How awful.

"At first I couldn't convince Bradley to accept me. But, after some pleading on my part, and assurances, he agreed. We scaled a small mountain to a shrine I knew, and there performed the traditional ceremony. We recited the incantations together, co-mingled our blood and drank wine together from a sacred chalice. As I said, ritualistically joined. At the end, he pronounced me his Dartok-tgur, or 'Demon Protector' in your common tongue."

"I see; but didn't he say you'd saved his life many times? Doesn't that make you even?"

"He exaggerated." she smiled, "But that doesn't matter, the debt I owe can never be paid in that way. He is my Gal-vek, similar to a liege lord. I've sworn fealty to him until he frees me from my vow. When I called him master that was simply your common tongue's nearest equivalent to Gal-vek. Another way would be to call him lord. He doesn't like me to call him lord or master, it embarrasses him."

She laughed at this, "Of course, sometimes I do it anyway, not to annoy him but because I like it; it feels correct. The honor is deserved, he has been very good to me. I had nothing, no place in my world. He gave me purpose, acceptance and eventually satisfaction. Now we are inseparable."

Kara paused and stopped walking. She turned to me and asked, "Abby, you don't fear me, do you?"

"No, of course not." What an odd question.

"I'm used to humans fearing me, they can't help it. My ancestors were predators. Humans can sometimes sense it and become afraid even if they don't understand why. It's instinct. But it would sadden me if you feared me."

"I don't fear you, we're friends." I wondered if she'd sensed my fear when we'd first met, my instinctual urge to flee.

"Good. It's taken ages for me to master the common tongue you speak so easily, how am I doing? Should I continue my story?" she asked, as she started to walk again.

She seemed to speak it pretty well in my opinion. "Oh, yes please. I'm enjoying your story. I'd like to hear all about your home, it sounds amazing."

"Yes, amazing and beautiful. But also, savage and dangerous. Wars rage constantly, and often power shifts from one faction to the next. It'd be a dangerous place for a pretty professor to visit." Again, she called me pretty. I was beginning to crave the way she teased me.

"I wouldn't be worried; I'd have you to protect me." I was sure I was blushing, "Demon Protector is a pretty awesome nickname. Why demon though, aren't demons supposed to be evil?"

"In my culture a Dartok is a supernatural being of immense power and ferocity. There are people who worship their local Dartoks, and all are revered. They live in the mountains and only visit the realms of the Tovolek, my people, when vengeance and retribution are requested by a powerless innocent. Or, if some deserving person is greatly in need and a wandering Dartok takes notice."

"What happens then?"

"Then, the Dartok sweeps down with all their power and punishes those deserving; laying waste to their land, destroying their homes, even killing their families. But, they aren't evil, they are more akin to an avenging Angel in human culture."

We arrived at my door, and I pressed my thumb to the sensor. I was rewarded with a swish and an open doorway. Kara entered first, set our bags down and did a quick sweep around my small room.

Kara explained "Apologies, I needed to reconnoiter your room, just to make sure no villains lurked." She smiled and I knew she was teasing me again. I didn't mind.

I was enjoying Kara's story immensely. I wanted her to keep going, "Where is this Az-Codor place Teddy talked about?"

"Az-Codor is my father's fiefdom, in the northern hemisphere of my home world of Nir-Kvek. Or, it *was* my father's fiefdom before the usurper stole it. My planet lies far outside the realm of the human alliance in which we now find ourselves. My family is safe though, and I'll forever be grateful to my master. The last time I visited home my brother had become a knight in the service of my mother's brother, and my sister had been married to a minor noble and had three children. A happy ending, I think you call it."

"It's awful what happened to your father, your uncle must've been a horrible person."

"*Is* a horrible person. He still rules the fiefdom he stole. He's ruthless and cruel, and rules through fear. It saddens me to think about it." Kara declared. "My father once told me that when the brothers were young, my uncle became jealous of him. My father was the heir to Az-Codor, he was better at most things like hunting, and soldiering, my father was even a renowned poet. But the final straw, the one which forever broke any bonds between them, was when my mother was betrothed to my father."

"Let me guess, your uncle was also in love with her?"

"No, my uncle cannot love; his heart is foul and dark. It was his greed that drove him. My mother's family is one of the wealthiest in the empire. Her father was a great Lord and ruled his own fiefdom, Az-Furat."

"That's where your family lives now?" Kara's story was like an adventure novel. I couldn't get enough of it.

"Exactly, yes. My uncle had set his sights on my mother as a bride. He'd been to their city several times trying to ingratiate himself. My mother was also considered a great beauty, but that didn't matter to him. My uncle knew if they married he'd gain control of a large estate and great wealth. That's what he was interested in." Kara paused again.

"What happened, did she refuse him?"

"No, on Nir-Kvek high-born ladies marry who their father wishes them to marry. Before he could finalize the betrothal, my Lord Grandfather negotiated a marriage between my father and my mother. It was a better arrangement for my mothers' family; she'd be married to the

Lord of Az-Codor, instead of the Lord's younger brother. I believe now that my uncle began plotting his treachery that very day."

"He waited many years for his revenge. I can't imagine plotting against your own brother that way."

"He's evil, and a vile pretender, full of hate, but also quite clever in his way. He fomented rebellion among the minor nobles and eventually acquired allies in nearby fiefdoms. In the end though, there were no battles, no war. My uncle breached the Citadel with a few hired mercenaries in a surprise attack. Probably with help from inside. They dispatched my father's household guard and murdered him before most of the fiefdom knew what was happening."

"Where were you when this happened?" I asked, indelicately. I was too absorbed in the tail to curb my curiosity.

"My father assigned me to escort the rest of my family to a celebration in a neighboring fiefdom. The young lord-to-be was coming of age and there was a banquet and festivities. My little sister was almost marrying age and my mother, ever the diplomat, wanted to meet the young man and assess his potential. We were gone from home for 13 days. We took many of the household guard with us, and I believe that's why my uncle chose then to strike."

"Our caravan had just returned across our border when the news of my father's death arrived. That's where Teddy the wine merchant came into the story. My uncle had offered a price for all of our heads, mine most of all as the rightful heir. We could trust no one, and it was a long, perilous journey to Az-Furat. My master agreed to fly us there in his spacecraft, saving all of our lives."

After a few moments of silence, I tried to console her, "I can't imagine such treachery. But I'm glad the rest of your family escaped."

"Thank you, Abby. It was thanks to my master."

I'd begun to feel a real kinship with this strange, wonderful woman. Her life seemed so much more interesting than mine. Interesting didn't nearly cover it, her life was simply more exciting than mine. I imagined what it must be like to be her, to be a bad-ass warrior that no one wanted to mess with. It must be thrilling to have that sort of power. It must be thrilling to be her.

"Abby, would you like to see my Sur-rok?" She pulled the dagger from its scabbard and offered it to me.

I'm no warrior, but in the archives I'd handled dozens of knives and swords before. I took it with reverence and studied it. The blade was perhaps 40 cm and tapered to a wicked point. The handle was ornate, inlaid with gold and even a few precious stones. There was a crest on the base, and writing etched into the blade in what I assumed must be Kara's native language. It was beautiful and deadly, a blade befitting a Demon Protector, or an Avenging Angel.

"Kara, it's absolutely beautiful. I've never seen anything like it. I wouldn't want to guess at its value the way that merchant did. And it must be incredibly precious to you. What's the etching say, if you don't mind my asking?"

My appreciation of her blade had given her a huge smile. I think I'd made her day. It made me unaccountably thrilled to think so. I was probably smiling as big as she was.

"Sur-rok is a family heirloom, hundreds of years old, passed down to the oldest child generation after generation. The etching is our family motto, in your tongue it reads 'Within Our Blood Resides Our Power,' blood refers to family." she recited proudly. "One day the usurper will pay for his outrages."

Apparently, the irony wasn't lost on her. It was family that'd murdered her father.

"I'm so impressed and jealous, Kara. The only family heirlooms I have are my amulet and my father's old pipe that smells like stale tobacco. So, what's Sur-rok mean?" I was asking so many questions I was sure she'd get tired of me soon.

"It means 'Little Tooth.' I'll always carry it; until I'm dead. Now hand it back to me Abby, little humans shouldn't play with such dangerous toys." There she was, teasing me again. I should hate being called 'little human,' but instead every time she said it I could feel myself blushing.

I handed the dagger back thinking it seemed more like a large tooth to me. I wanted to hear more about Nir-Kvek, the mountainous, forested, mysterious home of my friend. I wanted to hear more about

Kara's life. I wanted more of Kara. I was wondering how I could keep her there talking with me because I didn't want the wonderful day to end.

Kara woke me from my thoughts, "Come now, Abby Thornwell, you avoid the one question I know is foremost in your mind."

I thought I *might* know what she meant, but I couldn't make my mouth form the words. If only I wasn't so damn awkward. My pulse was quickened, my damn palms were even sweating again. How embarrassing.

"Uhmm, well, this might be too personal. I mean, we just met and you've been very nice to me. I don't want to offend you."

"Offend me? Abby, my sweet little human, go ahead and ask. I promise not to rip any limbs off." Very reassuring. I wasn't sure about her sense of humor; it must be an acquired taste.

"Well, when Bradley referred to you as his companion, did he mean... uhm, what I mean is, are you and he, well... there was only one bed in your room."

I must've been ten different shades of red at that point. I couldn't believe I'd had the nerve to say that. Wow, Abby; where's that nerve been your whole life?

"You are so cute, sweetling. I just want to eat you up. Hey, that's an idea, don't you think? I've never tasted human before. Is it considered a delicacy? Is it as good as suppett?" Her teasing made my knees weak. Why did it affect me so?

"No... I..."

"You want to know if Bradley and I are lovers. Very bold of you, little human." But she smiled again. Her smile affected me as much as her teasing. "The answer is yes, and no. Have I taken pleasure with him before? Yes, but not as often now as I once did. He's my lord and master, and when we met, he was quite attractive. I still find him attractive. But, do I love him, does he love me?"

She took my hand in hers. "My mother told me once; how'd she put it?... 'When you're with someone you love completely, and they return your love completely, it's like time borrowed from heaven'... Teddy and I were never like that."

Kara leaned down, so our eyes were much closer, and said, "We're very close though, and trust each other implicitly. We're more akin to comrades, and we're used to each other's quirks like an old couple that've been together for a long time. We *have* been together for nearly 19 of your years. However, he doesn't begrudge me having fun, he's not at all jealous." I had to be blushing even deeper.

Kara's eyes seemed to penetrate my thoughts, again. She was a perceptive woman. Well, Demon.

"Now, Abby Thornwell, I'm going to ask *you* a question. Would you like me to kiss you?" That voice. That silky voice.

Oh, Gods yes! All my life I'd fantasized about a dark, mysterious stranger seducing me. No Prince Charming for me, or *Princess* Charming in my case. Here, right in front of me, was the ultimate dark, mysterious stranger. Not Princess Charming, but instead: Princess *Terrifying*.

She didn't wait for an answer, she just leaned down, enveloping me in her powerful arms and placed her luscious lips against mine. Softly and sweetly, defying all reason the powerful female warrior kissed me. Her lips were warm and soft, her tongue hot and insistent. It was just what I needed to set my mind at ease, let my fear drift away and my body relax into her. How could I be afraid of someone who kissed like *that*?

She reached down and lifted me as one might lift a feather. I leaned my face against her shoulder as she carried me to my bed and gently placed me on it.

It seemed impossible this incredible beauty would have any interest in me, an ordinary professor from the history department. I was thrilled beyond reason. I realized why I'd felt so fearful when I'd first met her, even though my attraction to her had been instantaneous and powerful. It wasn't because my instincts were telling me to flee. Well, it wasn't *only* that.

No, it was more than that, much more. Because of my awkward shyness around women, I'd endured a virtual lack of a love life. So, I'd curled myself into a metaphorical shell, a protection against failure and frustration. My real fear arose from the terrifying possibility my attraction might be reciprocated, and I wouldn't know how to handle it. I *didn't* know how to handle it.

"I never, I mean, I don't usually do... things like this," I whispered, "Oh gods, I've only ever been with a few girls when I was younger. I'm not sure I know what to do." I was stammering, "I don't have much... experience."

Kara began to slowly undress, "Well then, let's get you some... little human."

Part Five The One Where the PHD Gets Educated

Interstellar Date: 388-06-20
On Board the Archeron

AFTER I WOKE, MY OPINION of space travel had drastically improved. I don't think I'd ever had such a wonderful night's sleep. That is, after our exertions, of course. My dreams were vivid and full of ancient relics, interstellar adventures and a certain beautiful female bodyguard. Kara had slipped out of my room at some point, and I wondered what exactly she'd told Bradley.

I showered, had a modest breakfast delivered by room service, and set out for Teddy and Kara's suite. When I turned the corner nearest their room I realized we hadn't made any definite plans the night before; events had sort of taken their own course. I worried I'd arrive at the room and they wouldn't be there, or worse, that I'd dreamt everything. I'd exchanged comm codes with Kara, but I was still too insecure to call her. I decided the best course was to drop by unannounced. That way at least she couldn't hang up on me. A lifetime of insecurities still haunted me, it'd take a bit of time to overcome them completely.

However, the fact was, the encounter with Kara had been nothing short of a revelation. I found I'd gained an enormous amount of confidence, literally overnight. I'd always known my preference for women, a fact I'd never tried to hide. But I hadn't necessarily advertised it either, because of my crippling lack of self-assurance with the fairer sex. Drop me in a room full of intellectuals and I could be a force of nature, but a room full of debutantes would reduce me to a stammering, cringing mess.

I'd never had an official 'lover' before, no enduring connection. A few fumbling teenage encounters, and even fewer, mostly unsatisfying attempts as an adult. The grand result of it all was simply to reinforce my lack of confidence. So, I'd devoted myself to my studies and then to teaching.

As I reached the door I was seized by apprehension; what if I said something awkward and off-putting? I knew through bitter experience I was entirely capable of ruining what should be a cheerful reunion.

Bucking up my courage, I knocked. To my delight Kara answered my second knock and greeted me with a huge grin. She looked amazing, with no armor on, just the lovely blue dress we'd purchased the day before. The hem of her dress fell just below her knees, loose and flowing, showing just enough of her amazing legs. Strappy sandals and even a bit of makeup were evident. The transformation was remarkable.

"Good morning, Abby, I'm happy to see you." Kara said cheerily with a smile that immediately made me feel everything was fine. I relaxed considerably.

"No armor, huh?"

"We're going to visit 1st class today. Teddy didn't think the full battle armor would go over so well. I feel a bit naked though." She complained.

"Trust me, you look gorgeous. Naked might cause a riot in 1st class." I was flirting; I *never* flirt.

I wish I'd have known about a 1st class field trip; I was dressed for comfort in slacks, long sleeved shirt and sensible shoes: my usual weekday, teaching attire.

"Ah, well, I guess I can come back later. When do you think you'll be back?" I asked, not sure if I was invited.

Bradley emerged from the ensuite, with wet hair and a towel around his waist. I guessed I was too early, though I'd been awake for quite a while. I was thinking they must not be early risers, but it struck me: I was still on Ampora time. At home it'd be early afternoon right now. Space travel: I couldn't imagine how people do it all the time.

"Good morning, Professor, how'd you sleep?" Bradley seemed cheerful.

"Like a baby, thank you. I had wonderful dreams; I wish I could remember them better." I replied.

Bradley smiled wickedly, "I'll bet."

The cheeky bastard. I hate it when people know my personal business, but I imagined they didn't keep many secrets from each other. I surely turned bright red. I always blush when I'm embarrassed, and knowing it makes it even worse.

He said, "It's good you're here. I was just gonna have Kara try to comm you."

"Kara says you're going to 1st class today?" I asked.

Bradley corrected, "*We're* going to 1st class. You're coming with us. We have a meeting with someone important."

"I didn't realize; should I change?"

"No, you look fine as you are; professors are supposed to be eccentric."

He dropped his towel and started dressing right there in front of me. I think I led a sheltered life back home; casual nudity wasn't something I was used to, or comfortable with. I had to be blushing again as he casually dug in a drawer searching for, finding, then donning a pair of what appeared to be silk boxers.

I was a little shocked by Bradley's physique. After he'd bested that Caladrian in the pub I knew he was skilled in martial arts, but I didn't realize he was so fit. Out of his clothes he could pass for a body builder half his age. I guessed the tailored suits he wore hid it well, as if he wanted to surprise foes if they challenged him. He certainly didn't look like a fellow in need of a bodyguard. I thought of Kara and had a small pang of jealousy. And, what'd he mean eccentric?

I turned to Kara, "Do you think this outfit is eccentric? These are my normal clothes; I teach like this. I think maybe I should change."

"No sweetling, you look like an academy professor. That's what you are, you're dressed appropriately. I'm the one in a costume."

I asked, "What about your weapons, are they out as well?"

Kara leaned over and whispered conspiratorially "I've got a few things up my sleeve." She unfolded a crease at her hip and revealed 'little tooth' in its scabbard, neatly concealed.

Immediately, I was reassured. Two days before I was scared to be in the same room with her, but now, after our day together, I was thinking of her as my very own demon, protector of the weak. I had no idea if that was normal or not, and I didn't much care.

Bradley began, "I talked with a few of my sources while the two of you were busy reducing my net worth. I've discovered there's a contingent of green shirts aboard the Archeron."

I interrupted, "Green shirts? What's a green shirt? I've never heard of that."

"No reason you should've, my dear. You see, practically everyone in the Combined Fleet wears a blue uniform, or sometimes white for formal occasions. Marines wear camouflage of differing types, depending on the terrain in which they're deployed. But the ones who work for the Ministry of Security wear olive drab uniforms, hence 'green shirts.' They're also known as the secret police, though that moniker is belied by the fact they're hardly a secret." Teddy explained.

Kara added, "They themselves aren't secret, but anyone you meet could be one of their informants."

"The green shirts have unchecked authority, and act accordingly. They bully and badger their way around the quadrant. They're thoroughly detestable, to a man. We need to avoid them." Bradley warned.

I wasn't sure how to react to Bradley's 'news.' Of course, I already knew there were CTF security officers on board; I'd been abducted by them. But if I told my new friends that, it'd raise too many questions for comfort. Besides, my issues with Gordon were *my* issues. It had nothing to do with Teddy and Kara.

However, I was no poker player, and I was fearful Bradley, or more worrisome to me, the mind-reading Kara, would sense something from me. She always seemed to know what I was thinking. I wasn't ready to share the story of my encounter with Commander Gordon, so I attempted to change the subject.

"What else did your sources say, Bradley?" I asked.

"Please Abby, my friends call me Teddy. We *are* friends, aren't we?" He asked with a smile.

"Alright, Teddy. So, anything else I'd like to know?" I asked, desperate to change the subject away from the secret police.

"Nothing good I'm afraid. It seems the CTF has at least two frigates patrolling the sector in which Kleos lies, which certainly complicates our plans." Teddy said.

"Plans?" I asked.

Teddy said, "That's right, I haven't told you yet. Kara and I plan to go to Kleos Prime ourselves. The CTF activity is a large wrench thrown into our works."

Kara said, "I trust the CTF about as much as I trust a rampaging Targa Monster. Everything they do is laced with venom."

"Now, now, no need to jump to conclusions, my love. Kleos is just beyond the borders of Telluric space. Normal CTF operations are to patrol the border regions. It most likely has nothing to do with Abby's expedition."

Teddy tried to set Kara's mind at ease. I glanced her way, and her face told the story; she obviously hated the CTF. And Teddy had referred to her as 'my love.' Another pang of jealousy hit; this might become tiresome. I had to remember she wasn't mine; we'd only spent one night together. One *glorious* night.

"I'd planned for Kara and I to take one of my better crews to the Kleos system in one of my small, swift ships. Probably the Tito, but I haven't decided yet. But now, considering these revelations, we might need something to help us. Therefore, I've arranged for the three of us to meet with someone who can help: A man named Cyrus Baaqir. He's a wealthy and powerful man, with access to unique and useful technology." Bradley explained.

"Maybe we should back up a bit. Last time I was here your story ended with you finding my amulet. What happened after that?" I wanted the whole story, damn it. Cyrus Baaqir, whoever the hell he was, could wait.

"Ok, what happened next... Your father and I found ourselves in a sort of Santorian Trap. If we announced our discovery publicly there would've been an immediate investigation into our activities. No one had permission to dig on Kleos Prime, you see. The investigation would most likely lead back to our on-going, illicit operation, and we'd have been in serious legal trouble. It was, and still is, quite illegal to sell cultural artifacts on the black market. I certainly didn't want to go to prison, and Henry didn't want his reputation destroyed. I'm clearly *far* too handsome for prison." He smiled.

"Clearly." Kara agreed sarcastically.

The reference to a Santorian trap gave me some insight into the mind of Teddy Bradley. Santor was a deity within the mythology of an ancient civilization on Dekstra Minor. To me, the reference signified Bradley was well read and knowledgeable far beyond being a simple smuggler, or even a criminal syndicate member. Santor was lord of the dark, and he'd been forced to keep a secret in order to retain his powers as a deity. In exchange he could never again enjoy the light of day, for the rest of eternity.

"It was the discovery of a lifetime, but we didn't dare tell anyone about it." Bradley told me. "That amulet is quite possibly a Reges Scientia artifact, there'd be no way to keep it under wraps once the story emerged. So, we did what we had to do, we kept it to ourselves."

"But why didn't my father ever tell me about it? I don't see why he'd keep it a secret from me."

Something still wasn't adding up in my mind. Bradley said my father was *obsessed* with finding Reges Scientia artifacts. If that was true, he would've insisted on a full expedition to Kleos Prime.

"Come on Teddy, there had to be another reason you kept it a secret." I said.

Kara said to Teddy, "You have to tell her eventually. The plan depends on her, she needs to know what it's all about."

She turned to me, "Abby, after our first meeting, Teddy and I decided we should take you into our confidence. I'm sure you're not an informant for the secret police, and we need you to understand our situation. Please, just be patient and listen for a while, everything will become clear; I promise."

I sat down to listen, as she'd told me. I probably had a bewildered look on my face; that was certainly the way I felt. And I was surprised they'd even considered the possibility I was an informant.

"You're correct, my dear, there *was* another reason Henry wanted it kept secret; and it had nothing to do with his reputation or my criminal status. It was simple, you see; he didn't trust the Telluric authorities. My dear, have you ever heard of Dectus Artiga?" Teddy had stood and poured himself a drink as he posed the question.

"Brandy?"

"No, thanks. Dectus Artiga rings a bell. They were terrorists or something, right?"

I remembered reading about them several years before. The way I remembered it they were a dangerous and violent terrorist organization that was taken down by the Ministry of Security.

"They weren't terrorists, that was just the way they were portrayed in the media. Dectus Artiga means 'Freedom Through Truth' in Lirannian. They were a group of Telluric citizens who were committed to exposing corruption and lies by the Alliance." Bradley said, seemingly in their defense. "They weren't the only ones either. There were many such groups back when I was young. But Dectus was the most prominent."

"But, what does a group of terrorists," I began, but Teddy cleared his throat, "excuse me, 'political activists,' have to do with you and my father?"

"Well, my dear," Teddy looked abashed, "Your father and I were members of Dectus Artiga."

"What?! My father belonged to a terrorist organization? I don't believe you."

"Abby, I told you, Dectus weren't terrorists; far from it. We were just concerned citizens trying to find and expose the truth. Henry was the one who recruited me to the cause; he was passionate about it."

"Why, in the name of all the Gods?" I asked. "He was just an archeology professor."

"Trust me, he was far more than that. He and his Dectus friends believed the Alliance had been co-opted by a cadre of racist, human-centric politicians and oligarchs; along with several huge, faceless corporations. This group of power brokers, led by the Council of Governors, has used the Ministry of Security to ruthlessly suppress free speech throughout the entire Telluric realm. The members of Dectus Artiga were fed up with it, and were dedicated to exposing the truth."

"What truth?"

"Ah, you've asked the million-coin question, my dear. Make yourself comfortable, Professor, class is about to begin." Teddy told me. "I'm sorry to lay all of this on you at once, but we have some time now before our meeting with Baaqir, and it's clear I need to catch you up on current events before we can proceed."

"I'm all ears." I couldn't wait to hear this. *My father the terrorist?*

"Ok, the Magrids were wiped out, the Pentoffian Empire surrendered and the Alliance declared the Freehold Wars over; we won. Right?"

"That's right." But I could tell from their faces it wasn't. "Isn't it?"

"Abby, after the Pentoffians surrendered, the CTF didn't stop." He told me, "They kept right on conquering planets and expanding Telluric dominion. Strategically it makes sense; the Council of Governors has adopted a strategy of expanding their borders as far away from the core of Telluric space as possible, in order to create a buffer against invasion. They're trying to protect themselves against a repeat of what happened 100 years ago. It's not a bad strategy, theoretically, but unfortunately there are planets full of innocent people in the way; and they suffer the consequences. I should say, you and I might consider them innocent people, *but they aren't human*; so they don't get the same consideration from the Alliance."

Kara spoke now, "Abby, think about this: the Freehold Wars have supposedly been over for close to thirty years, right? If that's true, why are Alliance planets still contributing such massive amounts of coin and materials to the CTF? Not to mention tens of thousands of recruits every year? Where are all of those resources going? What's the CTF need millions of marines for, if they're at peace?"

That was actually a good question, I had to admit. The simple fact was I realized Ampora was still contributing huge sums of coin and recruits to the CTF, I just hadn't stopped to consider why. Embarrassingly, I'd never even thought about it. Like all good citizens I just assumed the fleet was keeping us safe.

"I suppose I never thought about it." I confessed.

"Exactly." Teddy said. "*Most* citizens never think about it. It's so far removed from our daily lives it never enters our thoughts. And, that's exactly how the authorities like it. The Council of Governors created the Ministry of Security specifically to suppress dissent. They don't want us questioning how they spend our taxes, so the Ministry cracks down on anyone who does."

Kara spoke again, "Abby, the Ministry strictly controls information within Telluric space. Over the years they've systematically taken control of all sources of news and information. Any news outlet that has the courage to question the government or the CTF is quickly shut down. All the management and owners are arrested for sedition and imprisoned. The news is censored and tightly controlled, and if you search Dectus Artiga on the I-web now, all that will come up is stories about them being violent terrorists. What citizens know is what the Ministry of Security allows them to know. I'm sorry to be the one to tell you, Abby, but you've been lied to all your life."

I supposed what Teddy and Kara were telling me could be true. I remembered an I-web news service I subscribed to for a few years. Once, they published an exposé about the shoddy government housing in Pelios, Ampora's capital city. A few days later I stopped receiving the feed, and I eventually learned they'd gone out of business. The whole thing seemed fishy at the time.

"That may be true, but it doesn't prove the Alliance is still conquering planets. What makes you so sure they are?"

Teddy shook his head subtly and produced a small device from his pocket. It was shaped like a hexagon, about 3cm in diameter. He placed the thing on the table and pressed a button on the side. A three-dimensional, holographic map of the galaxy materialized above it.

"This map is a depiction of the quadrant, as accurate as we can make it with the information we have. I told you before, Abby, information is *the* most valuable commodity I know of. This map is compiled and updated using intelligence gathered by multiple sources. My syndicate, my own personal sources, which are extensive and carefully cultivated;

as well as data leaked from within the CTF, and even official documents stolen by a few brave individuals inside the Telluric government."

"Needless to say, you must keep the existence of this map to yourself. If I were caught with this, I'd be thrown into the deepest, darkest dungeon the Ministry of Security has, never to be heard from again. Or, simply taken out and shot. I tell you honestly, not to scare you, but if the Ministry found out you'd *seen* this map they'd throw you in the dungeon with me. Normally I keep this well-hidden, but I felt I needed to share it with you, to show you what we're up against."

"I'm not good with maps. Tell me what I'm looking at." I said.

Kara took over, "These blue dots represent Alliance planets; here's Ampora." She pointed to my home. "The light blue ones are Telluric colonial worlds. You see these white dots here, and here.....and all of these over here? They represent planets the Alliance has recently conquered and occupied."

Teddy continued, "They call them 'client' worlds. There's a system for it: They invent some crises there, then send marines to help keep the 'peace.' Sometimes there's not even a fight, but if the inhabitants resist it gets ugly quickly. The CTF is brutal; they won't shy away from genocide. Afterward, the Tellurians send in bureaucrats and administrators to 'straighten things out,' and pretty soon it's a client world. Kara and I have friends it's happened to."

"We have several." Kara told me. "There are refugees right here on the Archeron that've been forced to leave their home worlds for one reason or another. Even that little toad Tubau comes from a 'client' world called Hovenop. In his case though, he left his home to work for the Trade Guild, so he's no refugee. He's more like a collaborator."

I said, "I know about client worlds. They asked to come under the protection of the Alliance."

Kara argued, "Lies. Told to you by your media, which is controlled by the Ministry of Security. Think about it logically, why would they ask to come under the Alliance's protection? The only thing they need protection from *is* the Alliance. People don't just *ask* to have their freedom taken away."

"I guess that makes sense." I admitted. "But, why keep this all a secret? Why not just admit what they're doing? Telluric citizens might not care."

Teddy said, "Citizens put up with the CTF during the Freehold Wars because we'd been attacked and threatened with extinction. The Council of Governors doesn't know *for sure* if the billions of citizens will put up with their current military exploits. So, why take the chance? They keep everyone in the dark and do as they please. They like it this way."

Kara took over again, "The thing is, Abby, these client worlds depicted here have all been conquered in the last twenty years or so, after the Freehold Wars were supposedly over. You can see, there's almost twenty of them. We don't think they're done, either. All of these dozens of green dots are 'free' planets. They might as well be little targets instead of green dots."

"I had no idea. The people on Ampora don't know anything about this." I confessed. "What are these red marks next to these dots?" I indicated several marks spread around the map.

"Those planets are currently in the midst of rebellions against the Telluric occupation." Kara explained. "Those insurgents fight for their freedom against incredible odds. They're outmanned, outgunned and face terrible reprisals from the CTF, but they keep fighting."

I was shocked at the number of red marks on Teddy's map. If what they were telling me was true, the CTF actually *was* still fighting wars; a great many of them. I couldn't wrap my mind around it. The Alliance authorities keeping this all a secret was fraud on an incredible scale.

Teddy added, "Abby, we travel all over for business. There's little CTF presence here in Telluric space. Why? I mean, pirates are numerous, they're everywhere. I know half of them on a first name basis." he laughed. "I believe the CTF just has better things to do than chase pirates."

Kara continued, "The Council gave the Ministry of Security control of the CTF military police. The Ministry turned them into their own private army, and what people now call the secret police was born."

"I don't get it, why's the Ministry of Security need an army? Who are they going to fight?" I asked.

Teddy answered me, "That's *exactly* the right question, Abby. The Ministry needs their secret police to control *us*, the citizens of the Alliance. Henry was a member of Dectus Artiga because they were at least trying to *do* something about the Ministry's monopoly on information. I joined because I was devoted to Henry, but I soon came to believe in them. Dectus weren't terrorists, they never hurt a soul. Our only goal was freedom of information, that's it."

"So, what happened to Dectus Artiga? I don't remember the details about it." I asked.

Teddy explained, "Dectus came into the spotlight, and therefore into serious trouble, when a group of them tried hacking into Alliance data bases. The idea was to release all the data into the public domain so the billions of citizens could see what was really going on."

"Sadly, it didn't work." Kara said, "The hacking attempts failed and eventually lead to the capture, imprisonment or execution of the members of Dectus Artiga. Most of the members." She nodded at Teddy. "The authorities labeled them a terrorist organization, as well as all the other groups like them. They were hunted down and wiped out. The Ministry is terrifyingly efficient, and utterly ruthless."

I apparently *did* lead a sheltered life. I'd heard very little of any of this, and I had a damn *PHD in History*.

"But you and my father escaped capture. How?"

"We weren't part of the hacker plot." he said. "We laid low and waited to be arrested, but we got lucky, no one gave them our names. There were a few tense months though, that's for sure."

"You and my father were subversives." I said, trying to come to terms with the fact. "I can't imagine being wanted by the secret police; it must've been frightening." Gordon wanting to be my friend was bad enough.

"Literally terrifying. We had no illusions about what would happen to us if we were arrested. Many of our friends were tortured to death." said Teddy.

"My Gods." I said, envisioning my father being tortured.

"You see, Abby, after all of *that* went down, Henry refused to reveal what we'd found at Kleos Prime. He was convinced the Alliance would immediately seize the planet and claim it for themselves. And, of course, that's the last thing we wanted."

"You thought the Alliance would use what they found at Kleos to do terrible things."

"Exactly." Teddy told me. "Henry was a man of deep conviction, as you know. He believed our discoveries belonged to everyone, not just humans. The whole galaxy should benefit from the discovery of Regis Scientia artifacts. But we knew if the Alliance seized Kleos Prime, they'd keep anything they discovered all to themselves. Can you imagine what the CTF could do with even more devastating weapons than they already have? Or, a source of unlimited power? Or a form of interstellar travel faster and more efficient than REL drive?"

"I see your point. That's why you kept your discovery secret." I said.

"Since his passing, I have to say, I've not seen much to suggest Henry and his Dectus friends were wrong about the Alliance." Teddy explained.

"They weren't wrong." This came from Kara the Demon again. "The Telluric Alliance: the very name is racist. Abby, imagine you wanted to bring me back to Ampora to visit your home, give me a tour of the Academy where you teach, meet your friends and so forth. What do you imagine would happen? First, it'd be highly unlikely for me to receive permission to visit. But, if I did, I'd be treated as a second-class person. I wouldn't be allowed on public transport, in government buildings, restaurants and shops. I'd be denied medical treatment if I were injured, I could go on."

"You're familiar with Amporan laws?" I asked her. I was feeling embarrassed. Embarrassed by Ampora, something I never thought I could be. Four days in space and I was questioning everything I thought I knew.

Kara continued, "My home world hasn't yet been conquered and dominated by the Tellurians, and I will do anything within my power to prevent that from happening."

I was at a loss, unable to formulate a defense of my home. "You're right, of course. I'm sorry, I guess I never considered these things and I feel ashamed. Kara, can you forgive me?"

"Sweetling, you don't need to apologize for something out of your control. You've never been in space, never visited other worlds, you had no way of knowing."

Kara forgave me, but she was my friend. Now that I knew what the Telluric Alliance was doing, I wondered what a non-human who wasn't my friend would think of me, a citizen of Ampora?

It was surprising how quickly I'd become friends with these two people I had so little in common with. They knew things about the galaxy I was entirely ignorant of, and that was distressing. I hated the feeling of being uninformed, so I was grateful to my new friends for educating me.

It was sobering, also, that these new friends of mine were actually *against* the Telluric Alliance. They were actual *subversives*. That was a dirty, dangerous word even on Ampora. I was putting myself in jeopardy even being here with these two. Astoundingly, I didn't care. I wasn't leaving, and I didn't intend to.

But, there was something that gnawed at the back of my mind: It was the possibility the couple was taking advantage of my naivety. It was clear they'd planned to recruit me to their subversive cause. Bradley obviously needed me for some reason, he just hadn't revealed what it was yet. They seemed to know everything about me, what if they knew what an introvert I was and planned to exploit it to their advantage? Had Kara seduced me the night before because she found me attractive, or had Bradley ordered her to seduce me to make me more sympathetic to their cause? It pained me to think that was possible; I liked Kara, perhaps too much.

Kara was beautiful, strong and capable in all the ways I wished I was. Was it all an act to draw me in? No! I couldn't believe that, I couldn't! That'd be too horrible, too cruel to contemplate. I had to move forward based on my instincts, and my instincts told me Kara was genuine.

I wanted to believe Teddy too, if for no other reason than his version of my father had captivated my imagination. And their assertions about the CTF's activities were compelling, to put it mildly.

"Alright," I said. "You've convinced me. But, what'd you do after Dectus Artiga was wiped out?"

"Well, after spending time in hiding, I wanted to sell some more of our artifacts. Your amulet wasn't the only thing we'd discovered on Kleos Prime. We'd found several small fragments made of the same inexplicable alloy as your amulet. I wanted to sell them to raise some coin, but Henry and I had a terrible argument. Henry thought revealing the lesser fragments would raise too many questions about where they came from. After we fought, he made me swear on my life never to reveal the existence of *any* of the artifacts we'd found at Kleos. He was adamant."

"You kept it a secret this whole time. And now you've told me. Why?" I asked.

"It just so happens I need you, my dear." he told me with a charming smile. "After learning of your Academy's dig, I knew something had to be done. I came to see you hoping I could trust you, after all you are Henry's daughter. I haven't seen you since you were just a tyke, but I knew if you were anything like Henry you'd be as trustworthy as they come."

I thought maybe I'd heard wrong, "You knew me as a tyke?"

He nodded, "I met you a few times. You were the most beautiful child, my dear. You were this tiny little thing, with long, straight red hair and gigantic blue eyes. I always told Henry you'd make a wonderful child model. He'd get annoyed and say you were going to be a brilliant scientific mind and how would it look if the chief magistrate of the Academy was also on the label of a baby food container." Kara and I both chuckled.

"Later, I saw you once when you were a teen. The beautiful child had transformed into a striking woman. I'm sorry Abby, I should've come back for Henry's memorial. That was abominable of me. After the Dectus fiasco, and our argument, Henry and I had gone our separate ways. We stayed in touch, but I never saw him again."

"It doesn't matter." I said. "He wouldn't have known, and I'd never have recognized you." Teddy's compliments touched me, though. More than I was prepared to admit.

I have to say, my feelings were a bit hurt because my father had chosen to keep his discovery at Kleos Prime a secret from me. How could he not trust me with something like that? My face must have given away my thoughts.

Teddy said, "Abby, you're thinking about it all wrong. Your father was protecting you. He believed the authorities were ruthless and would stop at nothing if they discovered the existence of Reges Scientia artifacts. But, don't you see, he also trusted you implicitly, leaving what he believed to be the most valuable archeological find in history hanging around your neck. He knew you'd always keep it safe, and you have."

That actually *was* a little reassuring to me. My father knew I recognized the amulet as a rare and valuable artifact, even if he never told me exactly *how* rare and how valuable, or where it came from. He also knew I'd never part with it because he gave it to me as a gift. Smart man.

My sheltered existence on Ampora had been more like a coma. The rest of the 14.5 billion residents were the same, and I realized *that* was exactly what the Council of Governors wanted, just as Teddy said. The Ministry of Security was keeping the residents of over thirty Alliance worlds in the dark. Plus, dozens of colonial worlds. Billions upon billions of people had no idea what the Alliance was up to. It was a totalitarian nightmare.

I'd only heard the truth about current events here, on board the Archeron, and only because Teddy Bradley had come up to me and introduced himself. Space travel was prohibitively expensive for 99.9% of citizens. The rich could board the Archeron and frolic amidst the luxuries, but everyone else was planet-bound for the most part. Thus, there was no end in sight to the Ministry's monopoly on information; the implications were chilling.

"You said you need me, Teddy." I said. "What, exactly, do you want from me?"

"Whether by coincidence or not, your Academy has stumbled upon Kleos Prime as a target for exploration. The danger of this Academy dig should be evident, and it prompted me to come and find you, my dear. If only we knew what your Academy is looking for." He said.

Kara cut to the chase, "The fact is, it doesn't matter. We can't allow them to find *anything* there. Whatever discoveries they make will end up in the possession of the Tellurians eventually. And that would spell disaster for the non-human residents of the quadrant, maybe the entire galaxy. Who knows what technologies those bastards could unlock if they actually find ancient artifacts from an advanced civilization?"

I still didn't understand where I fit in. "Again, though, what can I do?"

Teddy explained, "Abby, we plan to go to Kleos Prime and if artifacts are to be found there, we intend to be the ones who find them. The Alliance can't be allowed to have them; we must prevent that at all cost."

Kara spoke up, "And, we want you with *us*, Abby. We want you to come to Kleos Prime with us instead of the Academy. We need someone to help us evaluate artifacts if we find any. Neither one of us could tell an ancient artifact from a beggar's coin cup. We need your help; will you help us?"

Teddy laughed, "Well, that might be a slight exaggeration, although I've never actually seen a beggar's coin cup. But a brilliant archeologist like you, Abby, certainly couldn't hurt our chances. It may be a bit presumptuous of me, but I imagined you'd help me because of Henry. He would've done anything to prevent high-tech relics from falling into the hands of the Alliance. I simply hoped his daughter would feel the same way."

"You want me to ditch the Academy dig and go with you instead?" I asked. "Simply because you claim you were friends with my father?"

"Henry *was* my friend." Teddy declared. "Our falling out still haunts me. I need your help, Abby. I'm no archeologist. Henry was the expert; he's the one who found things. I just sold them on the black market. What we need is an expert. That's you."

"I'm flattered." I said. "So, your plan is to go and snatch artifacts, from right under their noses? What happens to the artifacts if we find them?" I asked.

"The important thing is to keep the Alliance from getting their hands on them. We can figure out what to do with them later." Teddy said. "We have a huge advantage over the Academy, in my opinion. I know where your amulet was found; they have no idea where to look. We're ahead of them already."

"We're not there yet, and they are." Kara cautioned. "The Academy expedition has been there for a while already. We won't know if we have an advantage or not until we get there."

"Come now, love. Let's try to stay positive." Teddy told her.

I asked the obvious question "What if they found out about you and my father, and they already know where the two of you dug? What if that's the whole reason they're there?"

"That's highly unlikely. Henry and I never divulged a thing about Kleos to anyone. I must believe this current Academy dig is simply a coincidence. They picked Kleos for some reason that has nothing to do with us. Coincidence, it has to be." It sounded like he was trying to convince himself, not me.

"Abandoning my Academy colleagues without explanation would make going back to my job a bit awkward. The Academy might just terminate me. And there's no guarantee I can find anything once we get there, don't forget I've never been on a dig before." I couldn't believe I was seriously contemplating it.

"That's easy, tell them you were sick. Tell them you got food poisoning from eating too much suppett." Kara smiled.

"I *have* been on digs before." said Teddy, "I know what I'm doing when it comes to the dig. The real challenge is getting there without being detected by those CTF frigates."

"How do we do that?" I asked. Only after I'd asked it did I realize I'd used the word 'we.' I wasn't just contemplating it; I was thinking of myself as committed. I must've been crazy.

"It just so happens I have a plan, which involves the enigmatic Mr. Baaqir. He's the key, you see. He has something we could use." Brady asserted. "So, Abby, will you come with us to Kleos?"

"Maybe, I haven't decided yet. I'll think about it." I said.

But, in my heart I'd already decided I wanted to go with Teddy and Kara. They'd convinced me the Alliance was doing horrible things, and I was enamored by the idea my father was a sort of rebel. My father had told me on numerous occasions to live my life without regrets. Well, I hope you're happy, Pop.

However, I had an obvious problem: I had to find a way to ditch Commander Gordon, not just the Academy. He expected me to go with him to Kleos, and I didn't think he'd take being sick as an excuse. I needed to brainstorm a solution, and I didn't have much time to come up with one; we'd be at EV765 in only a few days.

"It's time master, we should be going." Kara announced.

Teddy agreed, "Right, we're getting up against it, we better make our way upstairs. Now, Abby, this fellow we have an appointment with is no one to be trifled with. If there really is a secret cadre of extremely wealthy and powerful people running the quadrant like Dectus Artiga believed, he's certainly one of them. He's a member of the Trade Guild as well, which makes him an enemy of the syndicates. I imagine he doesn't like me very much. However, we've done business in the past, and he's above all a businessman. Hopefully, we can partner again."

"Great." I said with a bit of sarcasm. "This syndicate of yours, just how illegitimate is it? What are we walking into here?"

"You remember when I explained to you what the Trade Guild was? Well, the syndicates are basically the same thing, except we aren't recognized and sanctioned by the Alliance the way the Guild is."

"That's too simple, Teddy. Remember, not all academy professors are dim." I said.

Kara jumped in, "Abby, we used to lose a lot cargo and sometimes even ships to pirates. My master has created a syndicate of those same pirates and several other smuggling organizations. He made them partners, shared profits with them, and now we lose a fraction of what we used to lose. I told you he's clever when it comes to business."

"So, you're partners with pirates and other smugglers. Great; I'm hanging out with criminals. That's why those Caladrians recognized you in the pub; do they belong to your syndicate?" I asked.

"Not yet, but they'd certainly like to." Teddy said. "The galaxy is fueled by coin, my dear, not fusion. And you're not just hanging out with us, you're going to be our partner too, in this Kleos Prime business. Why, you're practically a member of the syndicate." He laughed. Nice.

With that, we left the confines of their suite and began our journey to the first-class section of the ship, and our meeting with some big shot named Baaqir.

Part Six The Enigmatic Cyrus Baaqir

Interstellar Date: 388-06-20
On Board the Archeron

AS WE WALKED DOWN THE corridor, Teddy began, "Now, let's get our story straight. I'm Captain Theodore Bradley, handsome, charming, roguish smuggler and I have information about some startling, ancient artifacts." He smiled. "Kara is my co-pilot and partner. You, Abby, are our archaeology expert. The best cover is always a hair from the truth. Hopefully, our subterfuge will fool him."

"What cover? That's exactly who we are." Kara said.

"Exactly, my love. Our subterfuge isn't our identities, it's our intentions." Teddy explained.

"This might sound dumb, but why do you need me to meet this Baaqir person?" I asked.

"Abby, my dear, this fellow is no fool. If he starts asking archeology questions we're far better off having you answer than me. As I said before, on Henry's expeditions I was more of a highly skilled chauffeur than an archeologist." He grinned, "I can snake-charm your average collector, but as you'll learn, Baaqir is not an *average* anything. He's an industrialist, banker, political broker, patron of the arts and a founding member of the Trade Guild. He's tremendously powerful, incredibly intelligent, and as dangerous as a Benoan viper."

"Alright, so what are we trying to get from him, why do we need him so badly? I mean, if he's that dangerous, can't we just do without him?" I was starting to hate this situation.

"I wish we could, my dear, but I'm afraid we actually need him. You see, he has access to hardware capable of rendering a spacecraft difficult to detect. As long as it's a small craft it's supposedly quite effective. It's a kind of stealth technology, but much easier to actualize than the more conventional hull plating and sensor damping. It's not available on the open market, only to his friends. His *particular* friends." Bradley explained.

"So, how are we supposed to *become* his particular friends?" I asked. My palms were sweating again.

Kara asked "Yes, master. How do we go about that?"

Bradley answered, "Don't worry, the wealthier they get, the greedier they get. So, Cyrus Baaqir is pure greed. We'll tempt him with something he's never seen before and believe me that's saying something. I don't think he'll be able to resist. But we have to be careful, he's enormously paranoid; gaining his trust will be tricky."

"What do you have he's never seen before?" I asked.

"Why, genuine Reges Scientia artifacts, of course." Bradley produced two small pieces of metal from his pocket and held them up, then handed them to me. "The man will be captivated the instant he sees these. He's an avid collector of rare artifacts, and I believe he'll see the significance right off. If he doesn't, we have the eminent Abigail Thornwell, Doctor of Archeology with us to convince him."

"I'm not a doctor of archeology, Teddy. I have a PHD in History, only a masters in archeology." I corrected him.

"Baaqir won't know that." Teddy laughed.

One of the chunks of metal was a few centimeters long and narrow. It was twisted and appeared discolored on one end, almost as if it'd been burned. The other was in the shape of a disk, about 8cm or so across, with rough edges. It also had a faint design on one side. Three circles of different sizes, lined up in a row. It might represent three planets, or it could be a type of rune or hieroglyphic, there was no way of knowing.

"Master, no. That's too dangerous. We can't let him know those exist!" Kara warned.

"As I said, the best cover is always a hair from the truth. When he sees these, he'll give us what we want." Bradley seemed sure of himself.

It dawned on me what the pieces of metal were. They were the other fragments Bradley and my father had discovered over 20 years before. I had to agree with Kara, it seemed foolish to expose their existence. After all, they'd gone to great lengths to keep them a secret all that time, what sense did it make to reveal them to Baaqir?

"Teddy, if this Baaqir fellow is some sort of oligarch, he's part of the system. After you reveal the fragments to him, what's to prevent him from telling the Alliance authorities all about it? This seems like a terrible risk." I agreed with Kara.

"Human nature, my dear, human nature. I'm counting on his avarice to carry the day. He'll want the find all to himself. Exclusivity, as it were. He'll be like a small child with a bar of chocolate, not willing to share with his friends. Trust me. Come, or we'll be late." Trust him? I hate it when people say that.

Kara led the way, I followed, and Teddy walked next to me. Kara was nicely dressed as I've said, and Teddy was wearing a silk shirt, beautiful blazer, slacks and leather shoes of a fashion I hadn't seen before. It all looked expensive and well made; probably from Darlington Circle. It must be nice to be wealthy, I mused. I was dressed like an underpaid civil servant, which of course, I was.

After a long trek, we eventually came to the 1st class lift. To gain access to the 1st class section of the ship you were required to submit to a retinal scan. We, of course, had no official access to 1st class. So, Teddy told the security guard stationed at the lift, Jorgensen, according to his name tag, that we had an appointment to see Mr. Cyrus Baaqir.

Jorgensen was average height, but stocky, wearing a black suit jacket, tan slacks, and carrying a sidearm. I guessed the ship's security were allowed projectile weapons. I wondered to myself if firing a handgun in a spaceship was a good idea.

"What's the meeting about?" The guard asked gruffly, looking at a tablet which glowed slightly.

"I suppose that's between the three of us and Mr. Baaqir." Teddy answered with a polite smile.

Jorgensen scowled, "Your names aren't on the list. You'll have to wait while I call to check you out." He waved us away; I guessed we were standing too close for his comfort. We wandered a few meters away and stood like school children waiting to be scolded by our headmaster. Our excursion was off to a less than promising beginning.

A wait ensued. I was already a nervous wreck, and standing there waiting put me even further on edge. I passed the time by imagining my demon dismembering the decidedly rude guard. The thought gave me a secret thrill.

After several uncomfortable minutes the Guard's comm device discreetly bleeped, he turned away and spoke a few barely audible phrases. I couldn't be sure, but I thought he whispered, 'they have a primitive with them.' Kara stepped toward the guard in a menacing way, my senses flared and for a split second I thought there'd be blood all over Bradley's fancy shoes.

But, with an almost imperceptible gesture, Teddy signaled Kara, and she resisted the urge to teach Jorgensen a lesson. 'Primitive' was a derogatory term used for an alien from a planet considered to have a backward society and limited technologically. He'd obviously meant Kara, and I got the feeling the guard had narrowly avoided a well-deserved and humiliating beating.

He turned back toward us and said, "You may proceed. Mr. Baaqir is in suite 13. Just follow the ramp down to the end and turn left, the suite is at the end of the corridor. I have it entered in the log as a one-hour meeting. The hour starts now. If you haven't returned by the time one hour has expired, I'm required to come expel you."

Kara said, "I would relish that."

The guard glared, apparently angry but unsure what to say or do. It's possible he was surprised by the thinly veiled threat, or maybe he was taking a moment to assess his chances in a confrontation. Thankfully, he stepped aside to let us pass.

But, as we walked away the guard said, "And keep that thing under control" in obvious reference to Kara. The fool was pressing his luck. I might've detected just a hint of pinkish color around her throat to indicate her anger, but all things considered I think Kara admirably restrained herself. At that point I was positive the guard was a lucky man.

We continued as the guard had directed us, down the ramp and to the left. The surface we tread upon was a beautiful, dark, polished wood, and the decor was opulent. Paintings and sculptures lined the walls, muted lighting and low symphonic music set the mood. It was more reminiscent of a museum than a cruise ship. And we saw no passengers wandering about. I guessed 1st class passengers didn't 'wander' around, they had servants for that.

Teddy spoke in a hushed voice "You may be shocked at first when you meet Baaqir. He's been augmented, at least he was the last time I saw him more than two years ago. It's probable he's had even more implants since."

Augmentation was all the rage two or three centuries ago but had since been outlawed by the Council of Governors. During the wars, the Council had quickly become the political embodiment of the Telluric Alliance. They'd ceased being simply the administrators of the CTF, they'd become a sort of default legislative body as well. They began passing laws that applied to all allied planets, in the name of Telluric security. Eventually the Council of Governors had supplanted much of the individual planets' self-rule, as Telluric law was deemed to supersede planetary law. Telluric law extended to all Alliance member planets, all colonial planets, all conquered planets and everywhere the CTF held sway. In short, the Council of Governors made the rules we all were obliged to live by.

"Augmented how, exactly?" I asked, "I thought that was illegal."

"You'll find men like Baaqir do as they wish, my dear. At our last meeting he had several cerebral implants, as well as some sort of device embedded in his left forearm. There may be more now. Also, he's a bit hard to look at. He was born with a type of genetic defect. His right arm is withered, and his right hip is malformed. His face is misshapen and elongated like a cubist painting; don't stare if you can help it. He's never met either of you, so he may try to test you in some way for his amusement. I can't say how, so just do the best you can, I have every confidence in each of you. Ready?" Bradley asked as we stood at the door of suite 13.

I was battling my nerves and my palms were sweating again, even though the temperature was much cooler than in 2nd class. I searched my memory for what I knew about augmentation, and it wasn't much.

One thing I did remember was cerebral implants were specifically forbidden before other types. Cerebral implants, supposedly, could greatly increase memory and intelligence. They also supposedly caused psychosis over time. I'll admit to a great deal of apprehension as the wide door slid open.

We were immediately faced with a cadre of security minions, all well-armed and sporting prerequisite scowls. They carried large, intimidating rifles as well as sidearms. I counted six guards, but there were almost certainly more we couldn't see. I glanced at Kara who looked unbothered and nonchalant. Oh, I wish I had her confidence; I was a wreck, and we hadn't even met Baaqir yet.

The suite stretched around us, impossibly large, a realm of opulence reserved for the privileged few who traveled 1stclass. The ceiling was at least five meters above us, and on it was painted a giant mural depicting a planet with four moons. It was quite spectacular, the colors vivid and vibrant. I couldn't help but wonder who'd painted it and how.

The floor beneath our feet, made of sumptuous wood, differed in color and grain from the corridor outside, but if anything it was even more beautiful. Its beauty was accentuated by hand-woven rugs scattered in haphazard elegance.

Every wall was adorned with art, and several intriguing artifacts were on display. I would've loved some time to peruse and attempt to identify them and the civilizations they represented. Gold trim adorned every fixture and a crystal chandelier hung from the lofty ceiling but provided no direct light; it was simply for show. The furniture, covered in exotic leathers, exuded an air of luxury that bordered on ridiculous. Above a giant, marble fireplace, some magnificent creature's head was mounted, its origins a mystery to me. A fireplace on a spaceship? The sheer excess of it all left me in awe, struggling to imagine who could possibly live this way.

We moved toward the center of the space we were in, which included a gorgeous fountain about four meters across with purple tinted water and frolicking fish. The fountain appeared to be carved from a single piece of beautiful, red-hued stone. The monstrous thing must've been installed in the suite as the Archeron was being constructed, it had to weigh thousands of kilos. It occurred to me the water was actually blue, it only appeared purple because of the red stone. The effect was absolutely stunning.

I approached the fountain and observed one of the fish leap above the water. It was beautiful, its back a sparkling, shamrock green and it's belly was shining gold. I bent to touch the rock at the edge of the water, and suddenly a fish leaped *at me*, its mouth agape and razor-sharp teeth bared. I gasped and jumped backward as the alien barracuda was halted mid-leap by an invisible force field which apparently surrounded the fountain. Thank the Gods for that! I very nearly lost a hand!

"Please don't tease the fish, ma'am." One of the security guards said with a grin..

I quickly rejoined the others. Then one of the guards stepped in front of Bradley and began to frisk him, another approached me and laid his hands on my shoulders, but that's as far as his search progressed. As fast as a bolt of lightning Kara leapt to my rescue. She grabbed the man by his arm and neatly wrenched it backward, spinning him into a heap on the floor, disarming him and twisting his arm up high all in one movement.

"Hands off." she said.

I realized, then, the purpose of Kara's costume (as she called it) was camouflage. Bradley had wanted them to underestimate her. It'd worked wonderfully because the guard had certainly been surprised, but her cover was blown now because she'd leaped to protect me. Now, they all realized she was quite dangerous. I guessed that could be good or bad.

Several of the minions pointed their weapons at Kara and I noticed I hadn't taken a breath for several seconds. The guard that had run afoul of Kara had a look of pain and surprise on his face. She was holding his wrist at a strange angle, similar to the hold Teddy had used on the Caladrian, and his weapon was dangling from her other hand.

A burly looking guard said to Kara in a calm voice, "Let him go." He didn't seem angry, but he did point his rifle at her. I realized, then, what the rifle was. It was known as a Z-gun. A Zymtal rifle, named after the inventor, a man named Yosef Zymtal. It was a laser enhanced, non-lethal(usually) stun gun police and militia used on many planets, including Ampora. I'd never seen one up close before, but supposedly it

generated a blinding laser burst while simultaneously hitting the victim
with a paralyzing bolt of energy. It rendered the target both paralyzed
and blind for an hour or two. Reportedly, a hit from a Z-gun was
intensely unpleasant.

"My love, please unhand the poor man. Everything is quite alright;
he was just doing his job." Teddy said smoothly, attempting to defuse the
situation. "I assure you gentlemen we are all unarmed."

I wondered if Teddy knew Kara had brought her dagger with her.
Probably not.

Kara released the fellow's arm and he doubled over in pain. I began
to breathe normally again, and the minions lowered their weapons. They
seemed pretty calm considering, and none of them attempted to frisk me
again. They must've decided it wasn't worth the hassle. I wanted to tell
Kara she needn't have reacted so aggressively; I surely would've survived
a thorough frisking. But secretly I was unaccountably pleased with the
whole thing. She'd defended me; I wanted to kiss her.

I was also relieved they hadn't attempted to frisk Kara herself. After
her outburst I'm sure none of them wanted to, but I knew they would've
discovered 'little tooth' if they had. That might've been disastrous.
Knowing what I knew, I was sure she wouldn't have surrendered the
weapon without a fight. She nonchalantly handed the guard his weapon
back, and he took it with a look of amazement.

The burly one, who seemed to be in charge, said, "My name is
Sebastien Fowler. I'm the head of security. You will wait here, please.
Do not attempt to leave this room until you are sent for. Do not touch
anything. Do not attempt any more physical altercations." as he looked
at Kara. "You've been warned."

"And please remain quiet, Mr. Baaqir is currently in a virtual meeting
with the prime minister of Astraea." he finished. This was directed
towards Kara also, but I wasn't about to disobey him. He gave me the
impression of a serious fellow. While the guard at the lift had seemed
nothing more than a bully, Fowler gave off a different vibe. He wasn't
somebody to mess with. He walked away toward another large door in
the far wall and assumed station there. Kara looked at me and smiled,

trying to reassure me. I appreciated her attempt, but I noticed she didn't speak either.

We waited, Bradley checking his chronograph to see how much of our allotted hour was passing there cooling our heels. He was clearly annoyed and impatient, which was making my nerves worse.

An extraordinarily petite, stunningly gorgeous young girl emerged from a hallway wearing a sheer lavender wrap. Long, lustrous, wavy auburn hair cascaded down her back. The beauty of her alabaster complexion was interrupted by a smattering of freckles, not ruining but enhancing her beauty.

However, as she neared, it was her eyes that captivated me. I'd never before seen eyes of such incredible rarity; they were the most strikingly beautiful shade of violet, like two sparkling amethysts backlit with heavenly radiance. I wondered briefly if she could possibly be human with such eyes. Shockingly, the sheer fabric of her wrap revealed she was nude beneath it, and her charms were clearly visible. Describing her as tantalizing would be a monumental understatement; her beauty was almost supernatural.

"Welcome, esteemed visitors. My name is Leanna Callicenna; I am my master's body servant." Her voice was soft and pleasant, just above a whisper. Her accent was subtle, unfamiliar and exotic.

"My master, his excellency Cyrus Baaqir, Lord of the Kress, wishes to apologize for the delay. My master's time is not always his own. He will see you now and wishes you to know he has arranged with the Archeron's security for a longer interview."

I was distracted by this beautiful girl when Kara nudged me forward, with a good-natured sigh. She'd noticed my preoccupation. I was slow on the up take as the door in the wall behind Sebastien, the chief of security, had slid open and Leanna had motioned us in that direction.

I followed Bradley and Kara. Leanna had stepped aside to let us pass, and as I slipped by her she gave me a bright smile and a little head tilt. The girl was several centimeters shorter than my modest height: I doubt she'd measure 150cm. She followed us all into the next room. I smiled back thinking this Baaqir fellow can't be that awful, Leanna appears happy enough.

We stepped into Baaqir's private quarters, not a conference room or office as I'd expected. Again, the decor was opulent, but this space was thickly carpeted. Three huge windows dominated the far wall offering a magnificent view of space. As someone unaccustomed to space, the sight overwhelmed me. In the distance, a nebula cast its ethereal glow, while millions of stars sparkled, leaving me to wonder what it must be like to have that incredible view from one's bedchamber.

Commanding the room's center was an enormous, circular bed draped in plush golden fabric. It looked as if it could easily accommodate ten people. The size of the thing and what it implied was lewd. Above the bed, a large painting drew my eye, its vivid colors swirling outward from a central focal point. It was encased in a transparent protective case. Scattered throughout the room, several more paintings and sculptures attested to Baaqir's profound appreciation for art; he was obviously a connoisseur.

We were directed to the near side of the room where what could only be Baaqir lounged on a giant sofa, smoking a hookah and being stroked and massaged by two scantily clad young girls. We approached and sat opposite him; there were only two chairs so Kara was forced to stand. It wasn't lost on me that none of Baaqir's minions offered to retrieve another chair for her.

My attention was immediately drawn to his augmentations. A cluster of small, metallic knobs adorned his bald scalp, their polished surfaces catching the ambient light, numbering six, maybe eight. A discreet tech device lay embedded in his left forearm, its details obscured from me by my poor vantage point. On his chest, a rectangular prominence jutted above his left breast, a similar one could be seen on the right side of his abdomen. The purpose of these augments eluded me; a heart and liver modification, perhaps? I couldn't venture a guess.

His deformities, as Bradley had warned, were impossible to miss. His right arm was twisted and malformed, his right hip and leg seemingly replaced with mechanical counterparts. But it was his face that was the true horror. His left eye sagged significantly lower than its counterpart, while his mouth and jaw drooped leftward as well creating the appearance half his face had melted. An attempt at direct eye contact was an arduous task. My initial, overpowering reaction was one of sympathy: 'Oh, that poor man.' Naturally, I couldn't and wouldn't voice such a thought. I looked over at Leanna remembering she had told us she was Baaqir's *body servant*. What duties did that entail?

Baaqir relaxed on the sofa, his twisted body on display; he wore little more than the diminutive Leanna did. His garment, a robe of silk like fabric, wasn't as sheer as hers was, thank the Gods. And, as I've said, he was being attended to by two young girls wearing garments similar to Leanna's, leaving little to the imagination. They lounged against him on the sofa, stroking his torso like two kittens snuggling their owner.

However, the most embarrassing and disquieting of all were the two young people kneeling reverently on the plush carpet in front of Baaqir. They wore only loin cloths, their exposed, almost translucent skin had a strange, unsettling bluish tint, and their long, flowing hair was ghostly-white. Each held one of his feet, and appeared to have his toes between their lips; like a bizarre form of worship. The whole scene was repulsive, I think I gagged, but hoped I was discreet enough not to be noticed. I wanted to slap Teddy's face for bringing me there.

"Good day, Mr. Baaqir, Theodore Bradley at your service. I hoped you'd remember me. We conducted some successful business a few years ago." Bradley said, his voice confident and full of rehearsed charm.

"Hello, Bradley, of course I remember. You acquired an Alabrian church altar for me; a beautiful piece, and still in my collection." Baaqir paused as he scrutinized Kara and me. "Well, it looks as though you've brought two slaves with you. Nice, very nice. I like the little redhead. How much would you take for her?" He paused again after he spoke. My stomach was turning: I was the redhead.

"They aren't slaves, but acquaintances; friends of mine." Bradley said pleasantly. I guess he was unaffected by the disgusting man implying Kara and I were slaves. Or he was able to hide his disgust well. Was Leanna a slave? Were these poor souls debasing themselves at his feet slaves as well? How horrid.

"These two," Baaqir indicated the poor unfortunates kneeling before him, "are my newest acquisitions. A boy and girl, twins actually. They come from a place called Hollora. It's quite primitive." His speech was a bit slurred because of his deformed mouth, but it was fairly easy to understand him.

"I don't think I'm familiar with that system." Bradley said.

"No reason you should be, it was only discovered 16 months ago." Baaqir reached for his hookah and drew a huge lungful of some greenish smoke from it. He regarded Teddy closely, trying to gauge the reaction to his revelation of a newly discovered world. And, I think, enjoying the fact he knew of it and Teddy didn't.

My mind was churning on what he'd said. Slaves from a system only discovered 16 months ago; that could be evidence the CTF was still actively conquering planets as Teddy had asserted. I'd certainly never heard of a place called Hollora, and my annoyance at how ignorant we all were on Ampora struck me once more.

Baaqir was obviously referring to 16 standard Telluric months. In Telluric space, the calendar had been standardized long ago: 13 months comprised of 28 days each. Each day comprised of 24 hours, based on the rotation of Old Earth. Some planets kept to their own calendars, but for the most part governments, businesses, the military and anyone involved in interstellar commerce or communication uses the standard Telluric calendar.

Teddy didn't react to the revelation that I could tell. He simply said, "I see."

"You know, Bradley, you were quite fortunate I had an open spot in my schedule. My itinerary is normally filled weeks in advance. But, I happened to have an appointment with Garrius Jelks scheduled for now. Tragically, that fell through." Said Baaqir. "It was a shame what happened to the man, don't you think? Garri was a friend of mine."

"Yes, that *was* too bad. Space travel can be quite perilous." Teddy responded guardedly. "I hope they catch the villains responsible. But, alas, those corsairs can be elusive."

I had no idea who this Jelks fellow was, or what happened to him, but I got the feeling something significant was being discussed. Corsairs were pirates, so I thought the topic might be Teddy's syndicate, but I wasn't sure.

Baaqir said, "True. Elusive and clever, but not invulnerable. And *certainly not* above the law. Often, their own *friends* will turn on them, I understand. The Trade Guild has posted a substantial reward for information."

"So I've heard."

"To be blunt, Bradley, I'd appreciate it if you, yourself, made inquiries."

"I'm not sure what good I could do."

"You're too modest. I'm well aware you employ one of the most extensive networks of informants in the galaxy. Next to the Security Minister himself, I'd say you're one of the best-informed persons I know of. Let's not play games."

Teddy started, "I try to stay informed, but... " then Baaqir raised his hand and cut him off.

"Captain Bradley, don't be unduly concerned; I realize the perpetrators weren't part of your *particular* syndicate. However, I'm positive a man like you, with your many and varied sources, has a good idea which syndicate *is* responsible."

"I could make inquiries. It may take time."

"In matters of importance, I'm afraid I possess very little patience. Jelks' unsolved murder has plagued me these last few weeks and I wish to bring the culprits to justice as promptly as possible. So, as the saying goes, let us get down to brass tacks. You have a friend named Stepik, I hear." Teddy nodded.

"Your friend has amassed a cumbersome gambling debt at one of my resort casinos. My people seriously doubt his ability to pay."

"That's unfortunate, for *him*, but what's it to me?" Teddy asked.

"I'll make you an offer: You provide information about those responsible for the death of Mr. Jelks. In exchange you'll be able to claim the Guild's reward, erase your friend's gambling debt and continue this meeting. A fair offer, I believe."

Teddy hesitated, considering the offer. Then said, "They're no friends of mine, but I wouldn't want to become their enemy either."

"Anything you say to me is said in the utmost confidence." Baaqir assured, "There is no more secure place to speak in the entire universe than this, my home. And, I assure you, you'll be able to claim the reward anonymously."

"Very well then, I accept your offer. My sources tell me the culprits are part of the Yun syndicate from Dekstra Minor. I don't know the people involved specifically, but the leader of the Yun syndicate is a man named Tropev Warnalow. He'll know, and I imagine he can be *persuaded* to give up the killers."

"Excellent. Thank you, Bradley. That's been a sore spot for the Guild, and me, as you can imagine."

"I'm glad I can be of assistance." Teddy said.

"So, where were we?" Baaqir asked, "You say these two work for you?"

"Not *for* me, *with* me. Let me introduce you. This is my assistant Kara Az-Codor, from the planet Nir-Kvek. She is indispensable to me. And also," He gestured in my direction "My artifact expert, Professor of Archeology, Doctor Abigail Thornwell. The most brilliant archeologist I know." Well, I could be the *only* archeologist he knows.

"Brilliant archeologist, eh?" Baaqir chuckled condescendingly, "Well then, tell me *girly*, what do you make of the display behind me?"

Girly? I hadn't heard that one since 3rd form. But, this was probably the test Bradley had warned me about.

"Well, it appears to be..." I began.

"No, red," Baaqir interrupted me loudly, sweeping his hand to indicate the display behind him. "I want you to give me a detailed analysis of that piece. Imagine I'm your master, and I'm thinking of buying it. Take a closer look and tell me what you'd advise me to do."

He pointed to the twins at his feet and snapped his fingers "You two go over there and stand against the wall. Be still, be quiet." then to me again "What are you waiting for, red? Go take a closer look... go on. I want a detailed analysis."

Imagine he's my master? Really? With trepidation I moved around Baaqir's perch and to the wall display behind him. On a slim stand was mounted a beautiful ceremonial, wooden headdress with brightly colored feathers of an unfamiliar type. The feathers glimmered and shone in the subtle light from what I presumed was a hidden spotlight.

It was tastefully and professionally arranged, just like in a museum. I took a few minutes to examine it without touching it, of course. It was a beautiful piece, with an unusual aesthetic composition. It looked similar to a few headdresses we had in the archives. But, there was something strange about the shape, making it unique in my experience. I decided I had a good idea what it was. As I started back to my spot to the left of Teddy, the two men were in the midst of a conversation I'd tuned out.

"Your women are lovely, Bradley, even the tall beast. Those two over there" he indicated his blue skinned, white-haired twins "cost me only seventeen aurics. Can you believe that? For the price of that lamp over there, I bought myself two sweet little foot servants."

"That does seem reasonable, if you're into that sort of thing." Teddy commented.

An auric is a gold coin, minted by the Telluric Alliance. Each auric contained 50g of pure gold. I believed an auric was worth nearly 2000 Telluric coin. I couldn't help myself, I mentally calculated that Baaqir's lamp cost more than I earned in half a year.

"They don't speak much of the common tongue yet, but they seem to be adaptive people for primitives." Baaqir said.

The man was a raging racist against non-humans, even keeping slaves. Again, I wondered if Leanna was human. She appeared at least part human, but appearances could deceive.

After another puff from the hookah he continued, "I don't blame you when it comes to the redhead, Bradley, she looks like a bit of fun. But, the other one you can keep, I'm not as fond of primitive beasts, and she doesn't appear all that docile, like my twins. Although, she is attractive in the way they sometimes are."

A chill ran down my back as I heard it. Baaqir had just called Kara a 'primitive beast.' What would Kara do? There were six or seven well-armed security men in the room with us. Well-armed as in those viscous Zymtal rifles as well as handguns. I was scared she'd be disabled or even killed if she reacted. Meanwhile, I scrambled to think of something I could do to defuse the tension.

"Mr. Baaqir? I'm ready to give you my analysis now." I volunteered.

But there was no need to worry, Kara was still in the same spot, she hadn't flinched. She appeared cool and calm, but the pinkish hue on her neck had returned. It was obvious Baaqir was intentionally being rude, insulting and provocative, but I couldn't imagine why.

"You're in a hurry, red? In due time you may *dazzle* me with your insight. However, I can see by the way you're eyeing my augmentations you don't approve of me, do you?" Baaqir asked, catching me off guard.

"It's only that I've never seen any before. No one has them where I'm from." He was openly studying me, making my skin crawl. After a few uncomfortable moments he addressed me.

"There's a good reason you don't see augmentations where you're from, red. They aren't allowed anymore. Do you mind if I tell you a story? That is, if Captain Bradley can spare the time." Baaqir asked.

"I have plenty of time." Teddy agreed.

"I don't mind; what's the story about?" I asked.

"Why, *me*, of course. All my favorite stories are about me." His misshapen mouth formed a grotesque parody of a grin. "You see, when I was a child, I was wheelchair bound. I was born with this crippled body because of a genetic disorder. We visited surgeons and specialists, but they all agreed there was nothing that could be done, I'd never walk. All my sainted mother could do was go to prayer groups, donate lavish amounts of coin to the sycophantic priests, and feel sorry for herself; mostly feel sorry for herself. My father couldn't even stand to look at me, and therefore I spent most of my childhood in isolation, hidden away from his sight."

"That's awful." I said, honestly. "That must've been hard, growing up that way."

"Yes, my father was a total bastard, and my mother a religious fanatic, but that's not the point of my story. And please, don't feel sorry for me because of the way I grew up. Our home had 55 rooms and I was hounded, day and night, by nurses and nannies catering to my every whim." He smiled. "My *every* whim."

"Now, where was I? Oh, yes, other children, of course, were horrified by me. Because of this, I had no friends. Physical activities were impossible, so I read everything I could get my hands on. Every subject, every author, it didn't matter. I was determined to develop my mind to compensate for my disabilities." he pointed to his head, which just happened to contain cerebral augmentations. The irony was palpable. "As a result, I graduated university at the age of 14." He paused again to enjoy the hookah.

"That's very impressive, I've only known... " I started. But Baaqir held up his hand to stop me.

"I know what you're thinking. What does this have to do with my augmentations? Let me continue. When I was 19 summers my father died of a stroke. I took control of his considerable corporate empire, as well as his considerable personal fortune. I was finally free to travel to a distant planet, far outside of Telluric space, and there I received my first augmentations."

"Pardon me, but why couldn't you have gone to a distant planet before your father died?" I asked.

"Are you familiar with 'The Followers,' the dominant religion on my home planet, Dressida?" he asked me.

"Only vaguely."

"They exhort purity of the human race above all else. My mother was a devotee, so there was never any question of *sacrilegiously* helping her only son to walk."

"I'm sorry I asked."

"Don't be. It wasn't only my parents' close-mindedness, the Council of Governors themselves outlawed augmentations. I was forced to travel thousands of light years to get help."

"That seems ridiculous," Teddy said.

"My thought exactly, Captain Bradley. The alien surgeons replaced my lumbar vertebrae with augmented titanium. They augmented my legs as well, rebuilding my crippled right leg completely. My hip joint was rebuilt and augmented. As a result, I could stand and walk for the first time in my life. You cannot possibly fathom the thrill of walking for the first time after a lifetime of being an invalid. So, you see, my original augmentations were medical in nature, but they would still have been *illegal* within Telluric space." He paused again. No one spoke, we weren't sure if he was finished.

He wasn't, "Don't you see? Because some misguided zealots on the Council of Governors insisted on keeping humanity *pure*, I was supposed to remain a cripple for the rest of my life!? Today, if a child is born blind but could be cured with a simple synthetic retinal implant, Telluric law forbids it. Can you imagine the arrogance of that? Two hundred years ago, that same child could've led a normal, sighted life with an implant. But now, because of these outlandishly arbitrary laws against augmentation, that same child is sentenced to life in the dark. It's shameful; it's an outrage. *That* is why I have no qualms about my augmentations. Who are the Council of Governors to decide if someone has the right to walk, or see?" He paused again, enjoying the pipe. "Tell me, red, what do you think of my augmentations now?"

"I'm very sorry if I've offended you, Mr. Baaqir. I wasn't aware of the consequences of the laws. I think I see augmentation in a whole new light now. Your story has opened my eyes."

"Rubbish," he laughed "There is no need to patronize me, young lady. Take a good look at me, I'm well acquainted with the harshness of reality. You still disapprove of me. But, perhaps my story will make you think more about it. In time, I hope, you may see me as less of a monster."

Despite my irritation with his calling me 'red' constantly, I could actually see his point. The Council of Governors seemed to have over-legislated when it came to augmentations. However, I noticed his story never actually addressed his cerebral implants. Those weren't intended to fix his crippled body, but to give him an unfair advantage over the rest of humanity. Also, I was under the impression Baaqir was some sort of oligarch, entrenched within the power structures of the Telluric Alliance. But he'd just passionately criticized Telluric laws. That was quite interesting.

"Ok, my lecture on cultish fanaticism and medical ethics has ended. Now, I want to know what the Captain has to propose." He took yet another puff from the hookah, making me curious about what was in that thing.

"Of course," said Teddy. "Mr. Baaqir, I believe I have a golden opportunity, for the both of us. As you'll remember, I have an interest in archeology. It's a hobby of mine, and I recently happened across a couple of interesting pieces in an outlying system. When I saw them, I immediately thought of you."

"Which outlying system?" Baaqir interrupted.

"Well, if I told you that, you'd have no need for us, my friend." Bradley replied good naturedly.

"Let's make something clear; I'm *not* your friend, Bradley. We've done business before, that's all. I agreed to meet you because I believed a man with your connections could help bring Garri Jelks' killers to justice, that's all. He *was* my friend for over twenty years. Don't presume, or you can take your little expert and your trained alien beast, and go." Rude bastard.

"It was only a manner of speaking." Teddy said. "I obviously can't divulge where I found them."

Baaqir whispered something to one of his slave girls who proceeded to lay herself across his lap. Even though her outfit left nothing to the imagination, he nevertheless pulled the hem of her wrap up to the small of her back so his fingers were unimpeded. He began to fondle and stroke her shapely, upturned little bottom. The lewd display was performed casually, as if it was nothing out of the ordinary.

The man was a shameless degenerate. This latest outrage was simply to demonstrate his disdain for what our little group thought of him, I was convinced. I looked to Kara and my eyes must've given away my disgust. She walked over and stood behind me, placing her hand on my shoulder. I felt better, but I couldn't wait to leave that place.

"I'm afraid I'll require more information, Bradley. If only to verify you're not wasting my time."

Teddy relented, and forged ahead with his proposal, "It's a system far out on the galactic rim, beyond Telluric space, past the Cersares system. That's all I can say. It's a barren planet. I found these in my first survey." Bradley stood and handed the two small metallic fragments to Baaqir. This was the critical moment.

Baaqir produced a jeweler's glass from a pocket in the sofa (he didn't have any pockets in his clothes). He rolled one fragment around in his fingers and examined it closely as his brow furrowed. He snapped his fingers, and the girl arose from his lap and sat beside him again.

She must've been disturbing his concentration. Another snap and both girls stood with practiced grace. They retreated single file toward his grand bed, climbed on it and made themselves comfortable; presumably awaiting further instructions.

The peep show was over, I supposed, and I was incredibly grateful. My sheltered existence had officially come to an end, at least when it came to the sex lives of shameless oligarchs.

Baaqir took several minutes examining the metal fragments. He scrutinized each piece as if it might hold the secrets of the universe. He positioned his left arm up toward his face and a holographic interface appeared before him, glowing softly. I silently speculated the mysterious device embedded in his forearm must allow access to a quantum computer, or perhaps gave him access to an interstellar web relay, or both. There was no way of knowing how the synaptic spaces of his augmented mind worked.

The display before him was a chaotic dance of images and symbols that defied comprehension. Petabytes of data rippled before him, Baaqir's once steady gaze had transformed into something otherworldly, his pupils dilated and his irises were pulsing and vibrating. Because of his cerebral augmentations, Baaqir's brain had transcended even the most advanced supercomputers. The term cyborg flashed in my mind as I watched; the boundary between human and technology was blurred.

A subtle beam of light extended from his arm to one of the fragments he held; some sort of scanner, I imagined. The beam flickered and danced with the holographic display, changing too rapidly for me to discern what was there. Then, as abruptly as it had begun, the display vanished, and Baaqir's eyes returned to their natural state. He'd rejoined our world, no longer a cyborg but a man once more.

"Quite astonishing, I must admit. You obviously believe there's more where this came from, correct?"

"I do. My hope is the planet will yield more complete artifacts than those small fragments." Teddy said.

"So, what is it you want from me, Bradley?" Baaqir's interest was evident.

"The sector seems to have come to the attention of the CTF. My sources tell me it's being heavily patrolled. That makes reaching the system again a bit complicated. But I believe you have something that would help us: your newest stealth technology. I'm sure, using your device, we could slip in there and slip out without trouble. And, of course, once we've obtained more artifacts you'd have exclusive rights to them, for a price." Bradley was smooth and convincing. I began to think he might pull this off.

"Just exactly what do you know about my QSDM technology, Bradley?" Baaqir asked, "That technology is highly classified."

"I know only of its existence and have heard rumors about its capability." Teddy replied, guardedly. "I was told it can render a small ship virtually untraceable. I honestly have no idea how it works, though. A new type of stealth technology is the rumor."

"Your sources are disturbingly well informed. It's referred to as stealth tech only because no one has come up with a better name for it. It's been in development at KV42 for over three years. We call it a Quantum State Disruption Manipulator, and technically it bears no resemblance to past stealth technology. It's something completely new." Baaqir explained.

"Is it something that could be installed on one of my ships? If so, it might be the answer to our dilemma. To get to the artifacts we must get past the CTF." Teddy said.

"Theoretically, it could be installed on one of your ships. It would take technical expertise, and a little engineering. The actual device is relatively small but requires a great deal of power to function. The ship would need an excellent reactor."

"All of my ships have highly rated reactors; I make it a point. They compare favorably in output with the reactors on CTF warships."

Baaqir said, "That technology is extremely sensitive. I guard it closely, not wanting it to be copied. I need assurances, Captain, you won't pass the tech off to a third party once it's in your possession. It represents a tremendous amount of R&D at the Dressida Research Group's KV42 facility. Which means, of course, a great deal of *capital* as well. If I were to agree with your proposal, I'd need some sort of collateral to ensure its safe return."

"What sort of collateral did you have in mind?"

"I believe there's a vessel undergoing a refit at an overhaul facility on Kyntava. The Pruitt belongs to you, does it not?" Baaqir inquired. Teddy was clearly agitated.

"It does, but how'd you know that? Your sources are also disturbingly well informed. The registration is under an alias of mine."

"You will find there is little I don't know about your operation, Bradley, or your syndicate. Information is a commodity like any other, to be acquired and traded for profit. You'd need to sign the ship over to me and I'd return it when the QSDM device is safely back in my possession, *if I agree*. That's not an unreasonable stipulation, in my opinion. And a deal-breaker in any event."

"Leave it to a banker." Teddy half mumbled. "But, no, it's not unreasonable. The Pruitt is my best ship, and that refit is costing a fortune. Still, you have a deal, Baaqir. A hard bargain, but a good one."

"Excellent. The QSDM hasn't been fully tested, and therefore hasn't been offered for sale to the military yet. It should be a surprise to our friends in the Combined Fleet. It was clever of you to come to me, Bradley. I believe I may have underestimated you."

"I simply have tremendous confidence in the DRG corporation's skunkworks on KV42. With the device, I believe we have an excellent chance of success."

"Confident and cocky are very different attributes, Bradley." Baaqir responded. His attention turned back toward me. "So red, what was your verdict? What's the significance of that headdress?"

This caught me completely by surprise. I'd actually forgotten about the headdress, being distracted by the live peep show, Baaqir's life story and a crash course in Quantum State Disruption.

I had to mentally change gears, but I was ready, "It's a ceremonial headdress from Vindiac 4, I believe. Authentic, in my opinion. I've never seen one before, but I've read extensively about that civilization, and the Vindiac system. My Academy's archives are quite impressive, as you can imagine. This one seems to be in exquisite condition. It also appears to be quite unusual."

"Go on. Unusual in what way?"

"Well, I'm almost positive it belonged to an important warlord of the Hafta tribe, possibly even a minor potentate. The feathers have been treated to prevent decomposition, but I'd estimate it to be between four hundred and five hundred years old by the type and arrangement of the plumage, as well as the symbology along the base. Although I'm just guessing the age, if I had access to my lab back home I could give a more precise estimate. If I were your expert, I'd say it's pretty valuable, a beautiful piece indeed."

"*Almost* positive?" He challenged.

"No, I misspoke, I'm certain."

Baaqir pressed me further, "And the significance? What is the particular significance of it? How would you say it's *unique*?"

"It almost... no, it certainly belonged to a woman. And, as you probably know, it was extremely rare for a woman to ascend so high in that society. She must've been quite remarkable."

I was extremely proud of myself. Of course, the headdress was within my area of expertise. But still, I hadn't wilted under pressure. It was one thing to stand in front of a room full of students and explain archaic rituals and ceremonies, quite another to be put on the spot by a dangerous, misogynistic, possibly psychotic billionaire. And I came through.

"Very impressive, yes... very impressive. You have knowledge of alien anthropology as well. I like you, Abigail Thornwell. Any relation?"

"Relation?" At least he hadn't called me girly, or red. Maybe I'd passed his test.

"To Henry, the famous archeologist. Your father, I presume? He was also from Ampora."

"Well, yes, actually. He was my father. Though I wouldn't call him famous." Teddy had warned me the guy was smart.

"You have an Amporan accent, and I recognized the name, right off. Your father was a brilliant man. I've studied his codex for years." Baaqir turned from me and toward Teddy again.

"I also need to know what exactly you intend to find out there before I can, with good conscience, say yes to your proposal." He turned to me. "So, Professor Abigail Thornwell, artifact expert, tell me what these are."

With that he stood, slightly favoring his good side, and walked to where I was sitting. I stood as well, not wanting to seem rude. His appearance still unnerved me as he handed me the fragments Teddy had handed to him earlier.

Once again he'd put me on the spot. Baaqir returned to his seat and looked to me for my answer. I was still worried about revealing our secret to Baaqir. He might've deduced what the fragments were, or what we *thought* they might be. He was no fool. Then it came to me, Teddy had planned on this, the fragments were bait, Baaqir the fish. I needed to land him.

"Well sir, I've studied those pieces extensively," a small fib, "As you can see, they appear to be metal, but of an alloy we couldn't identify. Analysis was inconclusive as the material seems impervious to our equipment. In fact, the pieces are, by all indications, virtually indestructible."

Baaqir simply nodded thoughtfully, so I kept going, "I've examined artifacts from hundreds of cultures in my work, and I can honestly say I've never encountered this metal alloy before. If that's even what it is, for all we know it could be some sort of synthetic material."

"They do seem to be an alloy of some sort. And, like you Professor, I've never encountered anything like it. I can find no reference to it on the I-web, or in the planetary institute's archives on Dressida." Baaqir added. "My own scan was inconclusive; my personal database holds no record of this material. Keep going, I'm fascinated."

"Physical examination being so difficult, we have to look at the circumstances around the discovery. They were found at great depth on a desert planet, but one that'd previously hosted life. In fact, ruins belonging to an ancient, pre-industrial culture were discovered nearby, at a shallower depth. That culture was also previously unknown."

"Could these pieces be attributed to that culture?"

"I don't believe so, no. There were no artifacts found in those ruins similar to these. Especially the unknown alloy. But those ruins were dated at over 100,000 years old. Possibly even older. These metallic fragments were discovered at a greater depth than those ruins. Therefore, we can assume these fragments are even older based on stratigraphy and the law of superposition."

"And your conclusion? What are we looking at here?" he asked.

"It's my professional opinion that these fragments of unknown metal constitute a major archeological find. It's quite possible they belonged to an ancient civilization, extremely ancient in fact. A civilization that was clearly possessed of metallurgic technology we aren't currently in possession of." I had to let him make the final leap.

"You're implying pretty heavily you believe these are evidence of a Reges Scientia type civilization. A culture which was more scientifically advanced than our own. Isn't that correct?" Baaqir had reached the conclusion we were hoping he'd reach. "Surely you're aware that's science fiction, aren't you, Professor?"

"I am. Perhaps we can change the theory from science fiction into science fact. More evidence is needed, and that's why we need to go back." I explained. "Even if they don't belong to a Reges Scientia civilization, these fragments are almost certainly ancient in the extreme. I believe they are from a never before discovered civilization, and if we could find more complete artifacts they'd be extremely valuable. Museums would compete to have them."

"Or collectors, to complete your inference. How valuable, do you think?"

"At least from a scientific perspective, they'd be priceless. I'm not an expert on the coinage value of artifacts, I'm afraid."

"Priceless artifacts, how's that for a payoff, Baaqir?" Teddy asked.

"Very interesting." Baaqir paused for several seconds before continuing. "And what do you think of this symbol, or symbols, on the flat piece? What does it mean?" He was referring to the set of three circles on the roundish fragment.

"I couldn't say. Not without more context. It might be part of the language or a religious reference. It might just be part of a grocery list." I laughed. He smiled too, and I took it as a good sign.

"Professor Thornwell, if nothing else comes from this meeting, I must say you've impressed me greatly. Henry Thornwell was a brilliant man, and it appears his daughter is equally insightful." He complimented me.

Baaqir turned toward Teddy again, "So, Captain Bradley, you're proceeding on the recommendation of your expert, is that it?"

"Exactly. I showed those pieces to her not knowing what they were. She's convinced me I might've found something truly amazing. Wouldn't you agree?" Teddy asked.

"Indeed. Forgive me, Abigail, but I have something else to discuss with you before we proceed with this business about the artifacts. I can see Captain Bradley is getting impatient. I hope you can bear with me for a few more moments, Captain. I promise to give you an answer to your proposal shortly." Baaqir said.

"Not at all, I'm at your disposal, Baaqir. I'm actually enjoying myself." Teddy played along; he didn't have any choice.

Baaqir, who'd progressed from calling me girly, to red, then Professor Thornwell, to now addressing me as Abigail, continued.

"A man in my position has many requests made of his time, and time is the one thing I don't have in abundance. There are many tests of my patience daily; everyone wants something from me. I have meetings all day long almost every day." He paused to take another puff from the hookah pipe. "As a matter of fact, I have a virtual conference with the foreign minister of Dulose scheduled for now; but he can wait."

He now spoke to me directly "As you might imagine, 99 out of 100 proposals I hear I'm forced to decline. I simply don't have time for them all. What I expected today was just another waste of my time."

"I'm sorry Captain," he looked at Bradley, "but our previous business wasn't all that memorable."

"However, Abigail, you've surprised me. I've had at least a dozen so called experts evaluate that headdress since I've owned it. Not *one* of them ever told me it belonged to a woman. That is, of course, what I thought, and why I acquired it. It's extremely rare if not completely unique. That's why I wanted it. You see, it amuses me to own things no one else owns. As a collector, that's all that matters." He confessed.

"Do you know I once met your father? No, of course not, how could you? I happened to be at Ampora on Trade Guild business. While orbiting in my yacht, I remembered it was the home of the man who deciphered the Codex of Kafo. An excellent opportunity for me." He'd met my father. Small galaxy, I supposed.

Baaqir had changed demeanor completely at that point. The suspicion and paranoia had gone, replaced by a world weary, responsibility laden man. He was still a vile creature in my opinion, but appeared to be more than that as well. I wondered where he was going with his story.

"So, I arranged to have him taken up to my yacht. We had lunch and visited amiably for an hour or two. At the end of the meeting, I told him to let me know if there was anything I could do for him. Abigail, you must understand, I was at that time already a seriously wealthy and powerful person. Captains of industry and leaders of planets regularly asked me for favors. I could've done him any number of favors, yet your father never asked for a thing. A genius *and* a gentleman." He paused again, thinking of what, I couldn't tell.

"I'm glad you thought so. I'm pretty proud of him." I said.

"I must apologize to you; my behavior today has been atrocious. Leanna, would you bring Professor Thornwell some of that lovely Grovian fruit juice you enjoy so much?" Baaqir summoned the girl.

"Can my friends have some also?" I asked. I didn't want to seem rude, but shouldn't a host offer *all* of his guests refreshment?

"Of course, how thoughtless of me. Bradley, would you prefer fruit juice or something stronger?"

"Anything with alcohol is fine with me," Bradley chuckled.

"And for your tall beast, does she take juice? Or, does she require something a little more bloody?" Baaqir was infuriatingly rude to Kara. He obviously didn't care for non-humans, except as slaves, but he didn't have to be so rude and insulting.

Kara spoke up, "Fruit juice sounds lovely, thank you. I always appreciate a true gentleman." This of course was sarcasm; I mean, a person can only take so much. But my breath caught in my throat, waiting to see how Baaqir would react.

To my great relief, he actually laughed. *That* must've been Kara's test. "Very good. Leanna," he called, "bring two more glasses of juice, one with Dressidian grog, one without. She'll be right here, she's supremely efficient. In the meantime, what can you tell me about that painting over there, Abigail?" he asked me as he indicated the oil painting hanging above his enormous bed.

"Another test?" I asked. He didn't reply, simply shrugged and grinned his crooked grin. I accepted the challenge. "Well, I'm no art expert, but let me see." I stood and walked a part of the way toward the painting, just to get a closer look. The two girls perched upon the bed smiled salaciously at me as I examined the beautiful painting. "It looks aged, and there's a bit of damage to the canvas on the lower left, perhaps water damage?"

"Perhaps." He grinned, clearly enjoying himself.

It was an enormous canvas, well over three meters square. The background was dark, like an abyss. Then vivid colors swirled, progressively lighter and brighter, out from a central point, reminiscent of a tempest. But it was the texture that truly brought the masterpiece to life. The artist's skill had shaped the paint into peaks and valleys, creating an almost tangible depth, making it appear three dimensional. It was mesmerizingly beautiful.

"The composition is stunning. I've never seen one like it before in a museum on Ampora. I'm afraid what I know of art is mostly from books. It looks a bit like a painting I read about a few years ago while preparing for a lecture. We were studying the series of disasters... but... no, it can't be."

"Can't be what, Professor? Go on, you're doing fine." I think I preferred professor to him calling me Abigail, but I couldn't complain about either after 'girly.'

"Well, I was thinking it reminded me of a painting by..." I was interrupted as Leanna had shown up with our juice. I took a sip, and my face must've lit up because Leanna gave me a big smile. Kara let out an indiscreet "aaah" after a sip. It was excellent.

"But no. It's impossible. All of his works except two were destroyed. Those two hang in a museum on Theta Barriso. It couldn't be a Luewer Mahad, could it?" I ventured.

Baaqir nodded thoughtfully and said, "Quite impressive, Professor. You really do surprise me."

"But that's impossible, there're only two Mahads known to exist. The planet suffered a catastrophic volcanic event, the civilization was wiped out three hundred years ago." I said, realizing the painting must be priceless if it was an authentic Mahad.

"Three hundred twenty-four, to be exact. A lost Mahad; a masterwork. The third one ever discovered. I purchased it from a dealer who had no idea of its value. I paid two hundred thousand for it; however, today it's worth is incalculable. Honestly, If someone offered me two hundred million I'd decline. It is simply not for sale."

I thought I was beginning to understand him. "I don't blame you, it's beautiful. I'd never part with it either. Besides, what would I do with two hundred million coin, anyway?"

"Exactly." He smiled, enjoying my jest. "This is what I do Abigail, I collect rare and beautiful things. The rarer, the more unique, the better. The coinage value is meaningless to me. I already have more coin than I could ever spend. I collect rarities because it amuses me. After all, what good is it to be fabulously wealthy if I can't amuse myself. Look around you, everything you see in this place I collected because I find it beautiful, and it amuses me." Baaqir gazed at me with palpable intensity. "*You* amuse me, Abigail Thornwell. So, I have a proposition."

Uh oh, warning bells were ringing in my head. I had nightmarish visions of myself on my knees with Baaqir's toes in my mouth, gross! Or greeting guests in see-through clothing the way Leanna had. I needed to leave his lair while I was still able.

"Ahhh, I don't think so Mr. Baaqir, I'm not interested." I said.

"Yes, Baaqir, we have business at hand." Bradley came to my defense.

Kara stepped closer to me, implying she'd protect me. I was hoping *that* wouldn't be necessary.

"Don't be so hasty, Professor, hear me out. I want to hire you as *my* archeology expert. You're far too intelligent to work for this pirate." he chuckled again. "I can give you a cabin here on the Archeron, near this one in 1st class. After all, I own Aries Starlines; at least my investment group, DFH, has controlling interest. This art you see around us is but a tiny portion of my collection. The vast majority is in my palace on Dressida. Personally, I prefer space, so I rarely leave the Archeron. However, when we travel home you could curate my collection there." He smiled his hideous smile.

"I'm not sure I could live in space full time." I interjected, attempting to derail the conversation.

"It's incredibly liberating, think of all the places you could visit. I can pay you two hundred, no, make it three hundred thousand per annum. You'll never want for anything. I could even give you Leanna as your own servant to take care of you. I've noticed the way you look at her. What do you say, have I piqued your interest?"

Gods, three hundred thousand? That was nearly five times my current income. I'd be able to live in luxury in a 1st class suite on the Archeron, surrounded by beautiful art, eating the finest foods, drinking the finest wine and doing nothing but evaluating rare and beautiful collectables for Baaqir. It might be the most extravagant gilded cage ever. And Leanna, don't forget Leanna. I could set her free if she actually was a slave.

"Why? That's what I'd like to know. You don't need me, Mr. Baaqir. You seem to be doing fine without me."

"Need? Need has nothing to do with it. I *want* you. I want to be able to tell my peers and competitors I have Henry Thornwell's very own daughter as my *personal* artifact expert. They'd be green with envy, and *that* would amuse me. After all, what good is wealth if I can't amuse myself? I'll give you until we reach EV765 to decide. I may even be persuaded to pay four hundred thousand per annum. Will you at least think about it?"

"I'll think about it, and I thank you for the offer, it's extremely generous." I'd rather drink bilge water, but I had to humor him, didn't I? We hadn't finalized our deal yet.

Sebastien Fowler approached with a concerned look on his face. Baaqir said, "Please excuse me for a moment, something urgent has obviously come up. Perhaps the foreign minister is anxious, he clearly wants something from me. I will be with you again shortly." He left with his security chief and left us with his servants and a few guards.

Bradley said to me, "Well, well, my dear, congratulations! You made a marvelous impression. You were splendid, just splendid. The man even offered you a job! If he agrees to my terms, I'll have you to thank for it. Well done."

"Yes Abby, you were wonderful. I'm so proud of you." This was Kara, and I'm sure I blushed after she said it. It was surprisingly meaningful that she said she was proud of me. I realized no one had ever said that to me except my father, and he on only a few occasions. I felt a burst of happiness practically overwhelm me. Sadly, it was something I was remarkably unfamiliar with.

Unexpectedly, a soft voice came from near Baaqir's empty sofa, "Yes, my master was certainly impressed with you, madam. I've never known him to react that way to anyone before. You are quite special."

It was Leanna of course, smiling sweetly as she said it. The one part of Baaqir's offer I'd regret turning down was his gift of Leanna. I'd do anything to set her free. Well, except work for Baaqir, of course.

Baaqir reappeared and returned to his sofa. Leanna brought him a drink of some dark liquid; I assumed it must be liquor. We were all at the edge of our seats waiting for his response to Bradley's proposition. He was silent and thoughtful. He smoked his hookah and examined one of the fragments again with the jeweler's glass. No one spoke for several tense minutes.

Finally, "Alright, Captain Bradley, you'll have what you need. I agree to your terms. The possibility of acquiring ancient artifacts so incredibly rare is impossible for me to resist, as I'm sure you were counting on. But I must be assured that I, and I alone will have the rights to anything you discover." the collector of rarities declared. "As well as the absolute security of the QSDM technology."

"Absolutely, Baaqir. One hundred percent exclusivity, that's the bargain. We can haggle over coin later when we know what we've found." I could tell Bradley was both relieved and excited he'd succeeded. *We'd* succeeded. "As for the stealth tech, you have nothing to worry about."

Baaqir nodded subtly and ended the meeting, "I want any artifacts you find. But I warn you, do not betray me, Bradley. That would displease me tremendously." He added ominously. "I'm quite capable of making your life extremely unpleasant, as you must certainly know."

"Never fear, I will return with something amazing, I know it." Teddy declared.

"We shall see. But for now, a toast to our joint enterprise." Baaqir stood as he raised his glass and we all followed suit, "Here's to a well-defined purpose, a worthy adversary, a long life, and a quick death. Prost!"

"Here, here." Bradley exclaimed as we all drank.

Baaqir finished, "I must confess, I'd love to add Reges Scientia artifacts to my collection. It would amuse me greatly."

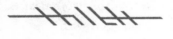

Part Seven Livva

Interstellar Dates: 388-06-20, 21
On Board the Archeron

AS WE DEPARTED THE suite of Cyrus Baaqir, I gave a subtle wave to Leanna. I couldn't shake the feeling I was abandoning her to an unsavory fate. Slavery is an abomination and had been outlawed long before, when the Telluric Alliance was in it's infancy. Until then it'd been a matter of local planetary law, and a disgraceful number of planets had allowed it.

The oligarch, Baaqir, considered himself above the law, flaunting his augmentations and keeping slaves. Teddy was correct, I didn't have any idea men like Baaqir existed. I felt a brief longing for my previous sheltered existence, but it passed quickly; I'd never wish for such ignorance again.

We walked quickly back to Teddy and Kara's suite; an air of excitement propelled us. They seemed in fine spirits, apparently unaffected by Baaqir's flamboyantly abhorrent lifestyle, or his rude behavior. But his antics had certainly made an impression on me.

"Well, my dear, you are a wonder, make no mistake. You had the man eating from your proverbial hand. Congratulations are in order; and gratitude. Thank you, Abigail." Teddy was exuberant.

"Did you two notice Baaqir's security men were carrying projectile weapons? Aren't those dangerous on a spaceship?" I asked.

Kara responded, "They can be dangerous anywhere, Abby, but only as dangerous as the people wielding them."

I tried to ignore Kara's sarcasm, "That's not what I meant. Isn't it possible to create a hole in the hull if you shoot a gun on a spaceship?"

"Ah, I see. Abby, those pistols they carry could never breach the hull of this ship." Teddy explained. "The hull of the Archeron is made of many overlapping layers of armor consisting of various materials, such as polyethylene, graphene, graphene paper, palladium alloy and several others. It's designed to withstand missile strikes, plasma bursts, high energy laser cannons and projectiles created specifically to pierce armor."

"Not to mention salvos from Rail Cannons and the like." Kara kept going, "Even the domes on the Archeron, like the one above the Arboretum, are made of materials that can withstand bombardment from an enemy ship. Those handguns couldn't possibly penetrate the hull."

"Sorry, I guess that's good to know. But I'm pretty sure they could penetrate me, so I still don't like the idea Baaqir's men carry them."

Teddy tried to quell my worries, "We shouldn't have to worry about Baaqir's men anymore. When we get to EV765 he'll hand the gadget over to me, and that should be the end of our dealings with Cyrus Baaqir. After Kleos, I'll just tell Baaqir we didn't find anything."

"Hold on a second, he didn't seem like the kind of man you can just brush off that way. He's going to expect results." I said. "He specifically warned you not to betray him, remember?"

"Let me worry about Baaqir. You've done your part with him brilliantly, Abby." He said dismissively.

"We should finalize our plans; there's little time before we reach EV765, and we must have our plan complete before then. First, and most important, is you Abby. Are you going to come with us?" Kara asked.

If I didn't go with Teddy and Kara, I'd be going to Kleos Prime aboard a CTF frigate under the command of Gordon. Uhg, I wanted to be sick just thinking about it. No, thanks.

"If I help you, will you promise to bring me back to Ampora when we're through. I'll have to think of some excuse, but I don't want to lose my teaching career."

"Certainly." Teddy promised, "We'll take you anywhere you want to go, even if it's to waste your talent teaching snot-nosed brats."

"Alright I'm in, Gods save me. I couldn't bring myself to help the Alliance acquire those artifacts. If I worked on the Academy's dig, I'd be doing just that. So what's next?"

Kara gave me a hug and whispered, "I knew you wouldn't let me down."

"I'll arrange to have the Tito meet us at EV765. Then, it'll take us time to install Baaqir's gadget." Bradley began. "After that, we'll head for Kleos, sneak down to the surface, and beat the Academy to the goods."

"You make it sound so easy. I have no idea what I'm going to tell Dr. Hughes. I don't imagine he'll be too happy when I don't show up." I said.

"Don't worry, you'll think of something, you're a natural. You proved that with Baaqir. You were thinking on your feet bloody well back there." Teddy had more confidence in me than I did.

"It didn't feel like it, I felt like I was going to throw up any minute." I confessed.

"That's how it feels to lie to a dangerous megalomaniac." Teddy teased.

"Lie? I don't think I actually lied to him." I defended myself.

"No, sweetling, you didn't. You don't have a lying bone in your scrumptious body." Kara teased me.

"Now, now, time for that later, my love," Teddy smirked at Kara. "Alright, I'm the one that actually lied to the man. I promised to bring him artifacts I've no intention of bringing him."

"Yes, but," I was starting to have second thoughts, "There's so much that can go wrong. What if they've already found something by the time we get there? What if they're already digging at the coordinates where you and my father were? Or, what if we can't find any artifacts once we get there?"

"Abby, you're having understandable concerns." Kara tried to calm me down. "Don't worry, this is going to work; we know what we're doing. We're smugglers, so we know how to get in and out of places without being caught. We do it all the time. But, if we get into any trouble, we'll get out of there as fast as we can. You have nothing to worry about."

"Baaqir's device should keep us clear of the fleet." Bradley offered, "As long as we arrive at Kleos without being noticed, we'll have the advantage."

There *was* one bit of information I knew that Teddy and Kara didn't. The Academy dig on Kleos Prime was being protected by Commander Gordon and his men; Gordon had told me as much during my interview. Since I didn't feel comfortable sharing the fact I'd been interrogated by the secret police, I had to figure another way of telling them. The information seemed too important to simply ignore.

"Uhm, I think there's something I need to tell you. I was checking my messages earlier today, and I had a message from Dr. Hughes on Kleos Prime. He said it's nothing to worry about, but there's a CTF security team there. I guess, watching over the site and protecting the Academy staff." I informed them.

"That's interesting news," Teddy began, "but, it's not the end of the universe; it's simply a complication. We can deal with it, we'll just have to be more careful, that's all. Right, well, I need to make some calls. Hopefully, everyone we need is available. What do you think Kara, the Tito? Snyder's crew?"

"Yes, the Tito is perfect. Small, but versatile. We'll need a lot of firepower just in case. And tell him to bring my gear too, please."

That seemed to go surprisingly well. I thought they'd be more upset about the presence of green shirts at Kleos, but they took it rather calmly. At least Teddy and Kara weren't frightened by the secret police.

However, my mind was grinding on a few problems. I was wondering how I'd be able to avoid joining Commander Gordon on his frigate at EV765, and how I was going to get my passport back. I was brooding about it when Teddy broke me out of my trance.

"I asked if that was alright with you, Abby?"

"What? Oh, I'm sorry, my mind was wandering. What'd you say?" I asked.

"I was just asking if you'd like a bit of weapons training? Just in case?" Bradley asked.

"Weapons training? Gods' curses, why? I'm just a teacher, I'm not looking for any combat, that's for sure."

Kara said, "Abby, combat usually finds you, most of the time you don't have to go looking for it." Well, *maybe for you*, I thought. She continued, "I'd like to give you some close combat training just in case. It'd make me feel better."

"Just in case of what?" I asked.

"If anything goes wrong, I want you to be able to protect yourself. Plus, isn't it a good thing to be able to defend yourself in *any* situation? Teddy has calls to make to his contacts, arrangements to make with Ernie Snyder, while you and I have some time on our hands. Let's go, Abby Thornwell." Kara wasn't asking.

Kara grabbed my hand and led me out of the suite and in a direction I hadn't gone before. We walked to the end of a corridor and turned down a ramp to a lift.

"Where are we going?"

"You'll see. This is one of my favorite things about this ship. We travel aboard the Archeron a few times a year, and I always make time for the exercise deck. It's nice to have a partner to train with."

We stepped out of the lift and into the corridor. On both sides of us, along the corridor, were rooms with large windows that revealed the interior of the room to us. There were rooms with many passengers using various exercise equipment, rooms with netball courts or bolt ball sets, VR simulation rooms, racket ball courts, hoop courts and many others.

We eventually came to a section where room after room contained people sparring. Martial arts were all the rage, so we saw people sparring using Katabu from Nemea, Luvacca from Pentoff, Karate from Old Earth and countless other disciplines. I'd taken judo classes at home, but I was strictly an amateur.

We arrived at room #65, which Kara had apparently reserved for us. The entire floor was a slightly springy sparring mat. There were two duffle bags against one wall; the demon had already been there and stashed her things. Kara locked the door and when she pressed a button next to it, the large window became opaque so no one could spy on us from the corridor. I began to get seriously nervous. If Kara expected me to spar against her, she was crazy. She had at least 20 cm on me, and I couldn't even guess how many kilos. I was no match for her, I'd seen her in action.

"Let's change." she said, producing outfits from a duffle. They were body suits of the kind she favored. I caught the one she threw at me and was sure it wouldn't fit; it looked 5 sizes too small.

"This looks like it was made for a little girl, Kara. I won't be able to fit one butt cheek in this thing."

"I'm confident I know the size of your butt, little human." She laughed.

Kara proceeded to strip naked and slip into hers, so I figured 'why not' and did the same. I was shocked, as it fit perfectly, miraculously just my size.

Kara laughed, "You forget, little human, I went shopping with you, I know your size exactly. And these things stretch to fit, as you see."

"But where'd you get it? Do they sell these here?" That seemed unlikely to me. "And, don't you ever sleep?"

"Very little. Humans waste far too much time slumbering. I know a woman who makes these for me. She has a shop on board, but these aren't normally for sale, she makes them for me special. You like it?" Kara was proud of herself, clearly.

"I love it, but it fits so tight there's nothing left for the imagination." I said. "You know a woman on board the Archeron who makes these for you?"

"She's an old friend and just recently took up residence here. And, it's supposed to be tight. Don't worry, my imagination is up to the challenge." She teased.

I wished there was a mirror. Mine was pale green and Kara's dark red. They were very elastic and form fitting, hugging every curve. I'm glad the window was opaque or everyone in the corridor would've enjoyed an embarrassing, lewd show. It was basically like being naked.

Kara confessed, "I love these suits. I wear them all the time, it's the next best thing to being naked. Your movements will be completely unencumbered. You'll see. Now, Abby, what kind of self-defense training do you have?"

"Well, I've studied judo at home for years. Something to keep fit, mostly. I'm certainly no match for you, I'm too small. And you're an expert."

"That's exactly what I am. On Nir-Kvek I was Grand Champion three times in a row. The men in those competitions grew quite weary of me," she laughed. "I'll teach you a few lessons I learned when I was young. In truth, when done properly, your size can be used to your advantage. It's all about leverage. Let me show you. After all, isn't a Grand Champion the best possible instructor? Don't worry, I won't hurt you." That wasn't all that reassuring.

However, as it turned out, Kara *was* a fine instructor. Her style of hand-to-hand combat was familiar, similar to judo or jiu-jitsu. I was able to use leverage to topple Kara a few times, although she may have been acting just to be nice. But I believed I could've used her lessons well against a smaller opponent. We worked up a sweat and I was having a good time. Once again Kara and I were like old friends.

It was shocking how comfortable I felt with her. I'd never felt that way with anyone before, even back when I was a child skipping rope with school mates. I'd always felt like I didn't have much in common with people, and making friends had always been a challenge. I guess the same was true for colleagues at the Academy. They were more like acquaintances than actual friends, sad to say. But, with Kara, I'd quickly formed a relaxing bond, even though we seemingly had *nothing* in common. I couldn't understand it, or explain it, but I decided to just go with it and see where it led.

"Kara, what sort of material is this body suit made of? It stretches to fit perfectly but seems truly durable. And it breathes wonderfully, I seem to cool off almost instantly when we take a break."

"It's a natural fiber from my home, called demsai. Nir-Kvek is the only place it's produced. It's perfect for the high humidity at home. Everyone wears it, except the peasants who can't afford it. I bring my friend here bolts of it from time to time. She used to have a shop on her home world in the Jovell system. Teddy and I'd visit there often with luxury cargo; they were good customers. That's where I met her, and we became friends."

"You used to visit her planet, but now she lives on the Archeron? Is business that much better here?"

"Not exactly. It may be, but that's not why she left home. About three of your standard years ago her planet was invaded by the CTF. Thousands of human soldiers landed and seized the major cities. The Tellurians claimed they were preventing a coup against the rightful government. The people were no match for the humans' weapons and were forced to capitulate, and her planet was annexed by the Alliance as a 'client' world." Kara explained.

"That's horrible." was all I could think of to say.

She continued, "Many of the leaders of her planet were imprisoned, their property declared forfeit. Many thousands of other people were gathered up and taken away. The Tellurians claimed the people they took away were part of the plot and no one knows where they were taken. The woman hasn't seen or talked to her brother for more than two years. He was the administrator of a small cooperative farm."

"Kara, I had no idea that sort of thing was happening, I swear. That poor woman."

"I know you didn't. It's not your fault, little human."

As a historian I knew about the many atrocities in human history, of course. But I'd honestly believed that sort of thing was confined to the past. On the Archeron I was learning about more contemporary crimes committed by humans. Before, I would've scoffed at such a tale as propaganda intended to undermine the Alliance. But, I'd come to believe Kara, and my disillusionment was profound.

"Sadly, her world is one of many, and she is one of millions. There are refugees scattered all over the quadrant." Kara told me.

"You know, I'm not sure I'll be of any use when we get to Kleos Prime. I've never been on a real dig before and I'm worried Teddy is expecting too much from me."

"You might be surprised what you can do; the only problem you have is a lack of confidence. Now, what do you know about knives?"

Kara produced a set of sparring knives from her bag. The blades were made of a pliable synthetic material with no edge and blunt points. She handed one to me and the lessons began. Kara was a tireless dynamo as she drilled me in knife combat; stance, balance, defensive moves and killing strikes. It was exhausting, but I kind of enjoyed it. I felt like a badass for an hour or so, something I'd never felt before.

When I was sure we were finished, Kara produced a handgun from one of her duffels. "Have you ever handled a gun, Abby?"

"Of course not. I hate guns."

"Why?" Kara asked, "A gun is nothing more than a tool, like a pencil. You don't hate pencils do you?"

"No, but pencils don't kill people."

"Neither do guns. The person using the gun can kill people, but I could also, quite easily, kill someone with a pencil. Or, a ruler, a desktop and a dozen other things found in one of your classrooms. It's time to demystify a gun for you, Abby."

"Well, I couldn't kill someone with a pencil." I said, but I relented. Trying to talk Kara out of something didn't seem very promising.

So, Kara showed me how to hold, load, unload, and safely carry the handgun. She broke the weapon down and had me put it back together. I'm sure she would've had me fire the thing too, except there wasn't a firing range handy.

Finally, Kara pronounced our grueling session finished. My muscles quivered with exhaustion; I was as tired as I could ever remember being. Kara began to gather her things back into the duffels including our clothes we'd worn into the room.

"Wait, Kara, I need to change before we go back." I didn't want to trek the corridors in nothing but my body suit, it'd be too embarrassing.

"Nonsense, little human, you have a fabulous body. Hold your head high and let people see how amazing you are. You never know, you might cause a riot on the exercise deck." She laughed and sped from the room carrying the duffels with my clothes.

"Hey, you..." I yelled as I followed her. I don't know why she thought it was so funny, she was dressed exactly like me. But, of course, she was proud of her body, and I was a shy little human who was self-conscious.

Eventually, she slowed her pace, and we strolled together up the corridor, into the lift, and back toward 2nd class. I received a few appreciative looks from other passengers along the way. I felt self-conscious, but Kara laughed and teased me.

"You should dress this way more often, little human. We could sell tickets and turn a tidy profit."

I was sure most of the stares were in her direction, but I took her teasing in stride. I'd become quite used to it.

"Tell me more about your home Kara, about Nir-Kvek. What do Tovoleks do for fun?" I asked, as we both turned down the corridor in the direction of my cabin.

"Well, let me see. At harvest time every year there's a big festival called Sart-mek. In the common tongue it would mean something like 'Work's End.' Almost everyone takes part; the peasants from the villages look forward to it all year. For nine days most of the empire celebrates, often even pausing military campaigns. There are live plays, acrobats, carnival games for the children, contests of strength and stamina, races with prizes for the winners, and lots of food and drink of course. It's probably the most joyous time of each year."

"What kind of contests, what kind of prizes?"

Kara laughed. I loved to hear her laugh. "One test of strength is to try to pull a wagon filled with firewood the farthest. One of my cousins, Juxtu, once pulled the wagon all the way to the end of the course. He won a new battle ax for that. For winning a race the children win prizes like a bag of candy or a small animal to raise."

"Did you ever take part?"

"I did, when I was young. I always did well in archery, and won a distance race once. But once I got older, around 12 years I think, my father wouldn't let me compete any more. He said it was *unseemly* for the Lord's daughter to win prizes."

"Didn't you mind?"

"One did not argue with my father."

"What about the plays, did you ever get up on stage?"

"Not me, I'm no player. Sometimes, though, the local lords themselves take part. My father loved to participate. He'd play a Graf-tuk, that's a mythological beast similar to a dragon, or a mean old man, and have the children laughing uncontrollably." Kara smiled, "He was funny when I was young, always quick with a joke. He'd tease me constantly; I was his favorite." Now I knew where Kara got the teasing from.

"You were a daddy's girl." I commented. "Just like me."

"I suppose. We understood each other, and I never saw eye to eye with my mother. My father was a heroic figure to me when I was small. I guess he still is."

"All girls should be the apple of their father's eye. It's the natural way of things." I mused. "And all daughters' hero should be their father. I'm sorry, Kara, I didn't mean to interrupt your tale. Please, continue."

Kara smiled and continued, "In the evenings, when the children go to bed, there's music and dancing, and lots of wine. There's always lots of wine at celebrations. Nir-Kvek is famous for our wine; at least we're famous for *drinking* a lot of wine. And there is always a large number of children born around the same time the next spring." She laughed again. "I even heard some villages hold orgies late into the night, but I never saw it for myself."

"I'd love to visit there someday." I said. "With you."

"Because of the orgies? Abby, you're making me blush." she teased me again.

"Ha, you wish." I laughed, "No, I meant I'd like to see Nir-Kvek with you to show it to me."

"I'd like that too. But it'd be extremely dangerous, for both of us. There are constantly wars raging and I'd be a hunted fugitive; there's a reward for my head offered by my uncle. The usurper would give anything to have my Sur-rok. It traditionally belongs to the lord of Az-Codor, which he believes himself to be. But its mine by birthright, and my first born should've inherited it in turn. Now that will never happen." Kara lamented.

"How old were you when your father was killed? I was 26 when mine died."

"I was 23 of our years, which is roughly 30 Telluric standard years. My father was 51, and in his prime. Many Tovoleks live to be 100 if they don't die in battle or fall victim to a fever. Our medicine isn't as advanced as human medicine. Many people die of fevers, but many more die in battle. My husband was killed in battle."

"I'm sorry, that's terrible. I didn't realize you were married."

"Actually, it's not so terrible. To die in battle is a great honor for a Tovolek warrior. It was an arranged marriage and he was much older than me. That's not uncommon in ruling class families. Dorrict was actually a friend of my father's from a neighboring fiefdom. My father considered him trustworthy, and believed he wouldn't interfere with how I ruled Az-Codor. That was probably true, but we never got to find out. He died during a melee in the battle of Orti river, cleaved through the skull. And I, of course, never had the chance to rule Az-Codor. He was a decent man, I suppose, but rather dull and extremely ugly."

"How long were you married?"

"Three and a half years, and a little more. The best thing to come of it was my daughter, Livva. I loved her very much; she was a sweet, quiet child and loved to be held. And so, of course, I held her constantly. She was *my* 'time borrowed from heaven." Kara's emotion was evident and infectious. I felt tears forming.

"What happened?"

"She died of a fever when she was two, only a few weeks before Dorrict was killed. He was a great warrior, and I've always believed he was killed because when Livva died it broke his heart. He doted on her more than I did, and that's saying a lot. The poor man was crushed when she passed."

"That's so sad, Kara, you lost your husband and daughter only weeks apart. I think I might cry."

"Don't cry, sweetling. I've made my peace with it. In Tovolek culture when children die they immediately ascend to heaven, and I shall be re-united with her when I die. Dorrict died in battle, so he enjoys an exalted place among the fallen there; that means they are together already. I'm sure he dotes on her still. So, you see, there's no reason to be sad." I was only slightly comforted.

"You never re-married?" I was aware my nosiness was my Achilles heel; I just couldn't help it.

"My father and I argued about it. I claimed to be in mourning and refused his suggested mates. In truth I couldn't stand the thought of losing another child. I suppose I would've relented eventually, my duty to my family and Az-Codor would've won in the end. But fate brokered a different destiny for me. I'm content with my place in the universe."

"Kara, do you think you could ever get your fiefdom back from your uncle?" I asked the indelicate question that'd been nagging me since Kara had first told me her story.

"I'd love that, but there are many complications. The usurper has replaced many of the petty nobles of the fiefdom with his cronies. He's also forged many alliances during the time I've been away. I'd need time to gather my own, and then there's the Emperor. I have no idea which of us the Emperor would favor, and on that, much would depend. But, in reality, I've made a commitment to Teddy Bradley I'm not willing to break."

We arrived back at my door in a quiet mood. The conversation had tied my tongue and launched her into silent contemplation. I offered her a glass of water and she accepted gratefully.

"I'm going to take a shower, make yourself at home. I shouldn't be long," I said. "You're welcome to shower here too, if you want."

"Thank you Abby, you're kind." Kara still seemed a bit lost in thought.

I stripped off the body suit and entered the shower. I'd worked up a sweat during our training and my muscles were sore, the hot shower felt wonderful. I was taken by surprise when the shower door opened and a naked, grinning Kara entered. The shower was large but the two of us still squeezed together. Kara said simply "I wanted to conserve water." Rather than stooping lower, Kara lifted me up into her arms to kiss me. We spent a luxurious, long while getting clean.

After we emerged I asked, "Do you want to go find something to eat?"

"Why don't we order room service? How about some cheese and cured meat?" Kara suggested, "And wine, lots of wine."

"Kara, have you ever tried caffarra before?" I asked with a giggle.

She laughed, "Of course. I wish we had some."

I raised my eyebrows and smiled. "I'll be right back."

We shared the rest of my first cheroot. We were giggling like schoolgirls when the food arrived. The Archeron's staff was professional and efficient. They didn't comment on the noticeable odor of caffarra, nor our resultant giggling. We ate, drank, and talked about random nonsense, the minutiae of everyday existence. The wine was particularly good, the caffarra was even better, and I probably ate too much once again.

I, of course, asked many more questions about Nir-Kvek. My curiosity about Kara's home never dampened. I couldn't help it; I'd never seen an alien world and I couldn't suppress my fascination. Eventually, Kara began to ask about Ampora.

"My home isn't as interesting as yours, Kara."

"I'd still like to hear about it. I've never been there; I hear it's quite beautiful. Are all of the women there pretty?" she teased me.

"Quit it." I scolded her. "I think it's beautiful, but I'm biased. There's two large continents on Ampora, but most of the planet is covered in water. The oceans are bright blue, and there are resorts scattered next to the lovely, white sandy beaches. When Ampora was first colonized it was mainly a tourist destination. But that was a long time ago. Millions of people that visited decided to settle there because of the beauty and mild weather. So, the population grew rapidly. Now we have almost 15 billion citizens."

"Quenra be merciful, how do you feed all of those people? Nir-Kvek has a population of less than 2 billion ."

"Well, we don't have seasons the way you do on Nir-Kvek, and the weather is basically the same all the time, sunny and mild. That means our growing season is basically all year long. Most of our food comes from the sea, so I eat mostly fish and vegetables. But don't get me wrong, I like it. The food at home is wonderful, and there is a wide variety. There are gigantic farms on the ocean floor where crops are grown."

"You grow crops in the sea?" Kara asked.

"Sure, on the ocean floor along the coastlines. There are also large nurseries where fish are raised, millions of them, of all different types. I just love fresh seafood. Do you like fish?"

"We have fish at home. Peasant fishermen spend long hours at sea. But I always preferred meat I could hunt." It didn't surprise me Kara was a hunter. "Fish is considered peasant food, but my mother always loved this particular type of fish stew one of our cooks made. She'd ask for it on cold days, but my father wouldn't eat it, and insisted on roasted game instead. My mother would call him a spoiled 'little lord' and laugh at him. She was the only person who ever dared to make fun of him."

"I've never been hunting. There's only small animals in the wild on Ampora, anyway. There are large domestic animals, but they're few and the meat is expensive. It's a luxury I usually can't afford. We don't have any suppett there." We both laughed.

"Where do the people live? Are there farms and villages in the countryside?"

"Not many. Most of the people live in large cities. There are even cities built on the ocean surface. Many of the buildings have transparent bottoms so you can view the sea life below you. It's surprisingly beautiful. The cities are bustling and crowded, though, and some of the buildings reach the clouds, like the mountains on your planet. The city where I live, Pelios, is the Capital city and houses the government buildings and offices. Over 90 million people live there."

"90 million people in one city? That's amazing. Do you live in one of those buildings that reaches the clouds?" I couldn't believe Kara honestly seemed interested in Ampora.

"I live in an apartment not far from the campus where I teach, but the building isn't that tall. There are 30 floors and I live on the 11th. My apartment isn't a great deal larger than this cabin on the Archeron." It sounded boring to me as I described it. My perspective had changed radically since I'd left Ampora.

"What about wars? Are there ever disagreements among the government officials?" Kara asked.

I smiled, "There are constant disagreements, but they don't lead to war. There's never been a war on Ampora since its founding. They argue over things like housing allowances and garbage disposal. Should Pelios have a new hospital or the Academy a new laboratory? The government officials yell at each other or accuse each other of corruption, but that's as violent as it gets."

"I can't imagine that. On Nir-Kvek if the neighboring Lord insults you in any way you're honor bound to declare war. You march your army across the border and burn crops, sack villages and take prisoners. There'd be no yelling."

"We have a sort of festival once per year. It's in celebration of Founder's Day. In Pelios there's a parade, and speeches. Everyone gets a day off work, and there's some drinking I suppose. But no orgies." I giggled.

"What of your job? What are your students like?"

"There are a few curious, serious students, of course. They make my job much more fulfilling. But, in reality, the majority of the Academy's students are spoiled and entitled. They take their easy life for granted, and don't appreciate how good they have it. It's a little sad."

Her comms device gave off a tone. It was a message from Bradley. Apparently, he'd contacted the man called Snyder and the rendezvous was set. He was bringing everything they'd need, including Kara's gear, whatever that was. She seemed pleased.

"What else did Teddy say?" I asked.

"He says not to worry about him. He's going to gamble a little, hit a bar for a nightcap and try getting some sleep. I think he may acquire a woman along the way, since I'm to give him 10 hours or so before I meet him in our suite. He says to have fun."

Cheeky bastard, I thought. I guessed that meant Teddy was fine with Kara and I being together. He even seemed to be encouraging us. Well, I wasn't going to argue with my good fortune; carpe diem, Professor Thornwell. I stood and offered Kara my hand. She took it, and I led her toward the bed. I sat on the edge and patted the spot next to me.

Kara sat and leaned in for a kiss. As our lips parted she said, "You should get some sleep as well, little human."

"We have 10 hours," I sighed, "I'll get some sleep if there's any time left."

Part Eight A Dose of Reality

Interstellar Date: 388-06-21
On Board the Archeron

ONCE AGAIN I WOKE UP alone. Kara was quiet as a ghost when she left my cabin, I had no idea when she'd gone. She claimed she didn't sleep much, and I believed her. Tired as I was I slept like a baby, but I was still sore upon waking. Kara's training had done a real number on me, and the caffarra had worn off. I took two more of those terrific pills room service had brought me and sat down to think.

The countdown timer I'd set on my comms device showed a little less than 77 hours till we reached EV765. That wasn't much time to solve my 'Commander Gordon' problem. I could worry about what to tell Dr. Hughes later, but for now I needed to figure a way to get my passport back and ditch Gordon at EV765. I wasn't completely naïve; I knew trying to ditch the secret police wasn't going to be easy.

My need for coffee reared its head, and remembering many places to get breakfast on the promenade I decided to invite Kara along. But, she didn't answer her comms. I imagined she was helping Teddy put the finishing touches on their preparations for the trip to Kleos, and I probably shouldn't bother them.

Instead, I had room service deliver coffee and began to organize my belongings. Since I'd bought the new clothes I had more things than I could stuff into my bags. I sorted my clothes while I thought about Gordon and my passport.

EV765 was a small planet in the free-trade zone with a busy space port on its largest moon. It was a favorite port of call for cruise ships because there were many attractions for passengers to enjoy. The capital city, Beddan, had shopping, restaurants, and nightlife available. Also, it was the location of 'Edonismo Boulevard,' one of the most notorious red-light districts in the known galaxy, featuring night clubs, strip clubs, massage parlors, and a host of bordellos catering to every taste and fetish.

Since there'd undoubtedly be many passengers disembarking at the space port to visit Beddan, it could be a good place to give Gordon the slip. I might be able to get lost in the crowd. That was a promising idea, but it didn't help with my passport situation. In fact, I might need my passport just to disembark. Being a novice traveler I didn't know how those things worked. I realized I might have to break down and tell Kara my problem and maybe she could help figure a solution.

I gave her another call, but still there was no answer. The lack of communication was becoming stressful, so I called Teddy. Alarmingly, he didn't answer either, and my stress ratcheted up. I could go searching for them, but that was a daunting prospect on a ship like the Archeron, which was the size of a city; searching it wasn't a practical option.

There wasn't anything I could do besides wait to see if they showed up at my door or answered their comms. My coffee was finished and my appetite gone, so I poured myself a tumbler of Cordson's. I'd had more to drink aboard this ship than I'd had the last month on Ampora.

A few sips into my drink there was a knock on my door. I rushed over to open it, and to my overwhelming shock there stood Leanna Callicenna, Baaqir's body servant. Behind her stood Sebastien Fowler, the head of Baaqir's security. But I didn't see anyone else with them. I was at a complete loss for why they might be at my door. If there'd been a two-headed loppa hound with bared teeth at the door I would've been less surprised.

"Hello, Professor, may we please enter?" Leanna asked in her soft voice.

"Hello Leanna. I'm surprised to see you. You can come in, but would it be alright if your friend stayed outside?" I wasn't sure I trusted Fowler all that much, or Baaqir. And Fowler was nothing more than Baaqir's hired muscle.

"That's not what our instructions were, Lea, I'd feel better if I stayed with you." Sebastien said quietly and almost differentially to the young girl.

"I'll be perfectly safe, as long as you guard the door." Leanna smiled sweetly at the burly security guard and placed her hand on his arm. Sebastien smiled back and relented.

Leanna entered my cabin and the door closed behind her. Today, she wasn't in a sheer wrap like before, but was instead costumed like a teenage temptress. Her long hair was in braids. She wore a tight, white, crop top, showing off her small breasts and toned belly to great advantage. She had on a dangerously short, pink mini skirt with a white belt. White fishnet stockings adorned her legs and pink trainers were on her feet. Her face was made up immaculately, and she wore the most eye-catching, fluorescent pink lip gloss I'd ever seen. And, of course, those mesmerizing violet eyes still enchanted me.

"Professor, I'm sorry we surprised you. Did we interrupt anything?" She asked.

"No, I was just having a drink and waiting for my companions from the other day to show up; I thought you might be them. But I'm also glad to see you, Leanna. You look quite pretty in this outfit. Did you pick it out?"

I was almost positive Baaqir had picked it out, she resembled every man's fantasy girl. Her outfit, together with her incredible beauty, would stop traffic at a busy intersection back home.

"Thank you, Professor Thornwell. Yes, I did. I shop for all my own clothes. I just love this outfit; I feel sexy in it. When I stroll the promenade in this outfit, none of the men can keep their eyes off me. I just love having that effect on men, don't you, Professor?" Leanna asked innocently.

"Leanna, I'm afraid I've never had that effect on men." I laughed.

Leanna blushed slightly and began, "Professor, my master, his excellency Cyrus Baaqir... "

I interrupted her, "Please, Leanna, I'd like you to call me Abby. All my friends call me Abby. And all that nonsense about his excellency, you can dispense with that. Just call him Baaqir."

"Oh, alright... Abby. Does that mean I'm your friend?" she asked as she blushed a bit more.

"Of course, Leanna. You're my friend; I think I'd like being your friend." I said casually, but earnestly.

Leanna started to speak but stopped. She appeared to be choked up. I grabbed her some water from the mini bar.

"Leanna, are you alright? Here, have some water." I gave her the container and she took a dainty sip. She carefully wiped a drop of moisture from the corner of her eye and seemed to compose herself.

"I'm fine prof... I mean Abby. It's just that... I've never had a friend before."

"Oh, come now, I'm sure that's not true. Those other girls with Baaqir, I bet they're your friends." I consoled her.

"No, they're *not*. They treat me rudely and I believe they say cruel things when I'm not present."

"Well, what about Sebastien, he seemed to be nice to you. I bet he's your friend."

"Sebastien isn't my friend either, Sebastien's in love with me." she confessed with a small giggle. "At least, that's what he says."

Ahh, that explained the exchange outside my cabin. I began thinking of the burly, serious Sebastien in a new light. He obviously wasn't the cold, businesslike ruffian I'd originally taken him for.

"I see. Well, that's a good thing, isn't it? Being loved?"

"I suppose so. He's a wonderful man, and he's always been kind to me. He says he'd like to take me away from here, so we can be together. He's handsome, and smart, but I'm not sure I'm in love with him. I haven't told him yet, though. I wouldn't want to hurt him." Leanna said with evident concern.

"Aww, Leanna, don't be upset. You can't always love someone just because they love you. And, sadly, someone you love doesn't always reciprocate. That's the way love works, there's no way to control it." I felt like such a hypocrite. I'd never been in love, so how would I know anything about it?

I changed the direction of the chat, "Leanna, wouldn't you want to be taken away though? I mean, Baaqir keeps you as his slave, doesn't he? Wouldn't you want to leave if you could?"

"Oh no, Abby; that's not true. I'm employed by my master... I mean Baaqir. He pays me a generous stipend. I have enough coin to enjoy myself on the Archeron. He's been incredibly good to me." Leanna's defense of Baaqir was unexpected and threw me off.

"How do you mean; he's been good to you? What's he done for you?"

"Oh, Abby, it's a long story."

"Tell me. Leanna, I'd love to hear it."

"Well, as you might've figured out already, but I'm not purely human. My mother was human, but my father was Lirannian. And, they weren't even married. I've been told that half human-half lirannians are incredibly rare. The chances of such a pregnancy reaching full term is almost 50,000 to 1. Even knowing what the chances were, my mother refused to terminate the pregnancy; she wanted me too much. She died giving birth to me."

"Oh, Leanna, that's terrible. I'm so sorry."

"My father had returned to Liranna, and my mother's family didn't know how to contact him. I don't believe they even knew his name. On Dressida, the Followers religion is powerful and influential. They insists on keeping humanity pure. I was an illegitimate half-breed so my mother's family refused me. They gave me away to an orphanage."

"I can't believe they wouldn't take you in, their own flesh and blood. I think that's awful."

"So, when I was young, I lived in an orphanage in the city of Kaart. The other children there were cruel to me, you can probably guess why. The girls hated me, called me horrible things, and never included me in any of their activities. The boys bullied me and sometimes even beat me, or worse. I was lonely and sad most of the time. "

"The people who ran the orphanage allowed that to happen? They let the other children beat you?" I was shocked.

"Abby, the *worst ones* were the priestesses of the Followers who ran the orphanage. They made me work like I was a servant, fed me scraps if anything at all, and usually *punished me* when the others picked on me.

They criticized me constantly and punished me cruelly whenever I acted out. They beat me, locked me away in a small closet or sometimes starved me for days at a time. They said I was an abomination."

"What happened? How'd you end up here, on the Archeron?"

"One day, when I was perhaps 10 or 11 summers, Cyrus Baaqir came to the orphanage. The priestesses treated him like royalty, 'yes Mr. Baaqir,' 'no Mr. Baaqir,' 'whatever you say Mr. Baaqir,'" She giggled.

"What'd he have to do with the orphanage?"

"I don't know for sure. He donates large amounts of coin to charities, so he was probably one of their biggest donors. He took me aside and asked if I liked it there. I told him the truth, that it was horrible and the priestesses treated me cruelly. He became angry and yelled at the head priestess; she was terrified and begged his forgiveness." Leanna giggled again, "So, that's how I became my mas... Mr. Baaqir's servant. He took me with him that day, and I've been with him ever since. I don't think I could ever leave him, even if I loved Sebastien with all my heart." She said finally.

"So, Baaqir saved you from that horrible place. That's an incredible story, Leanna. You're very brave; I don't think I could've been so brave in the same situation. I'm proud you're my friend."

And so, my opinion of Baaqir was under review. How could a man who seemed to be such a lecherous degenerate during our meeting, also be the man Leanna described?

Leanna blushed even more and smiled at me so infectiously I had to smile as well. There was a knock on the door again, Leanna said, "Excuse me" and quickly went to the door to see what Sebastien wanted.

"Leanna, we need to hurry up. Mr. Baaqir has arrived in the bird's nest and is waiting for us." He said.

"Of course, I'll hurry." she responded. Then, rushing back over to me said, "Mr. Baaqir requests another meeting with you, Abby. Can you come with us?"

"You mean *now*? I don't know Leanna, I didn't enjoy the first meeting with him, I'm not sure I'm ready for another. Plus, I think I should wait for my friends to show up here; sorry."

"No, Abby, you don't understand. Your friends won't show up here, they can't. Mr. Baaqir told me to say the meeting was important and concerns your friends." she explained.

"Oh. Can you tell me what's going on with Captain Bradley and his partner?"

"I'm sorry Abby, my friend, but I don't know. Mr. Baaqir surely wants to tell you himself. Please come." Leanna urged.

Grabbing my comms device I followed the odd pair. Leanna, dressed as a sexy schoolgirl, walked next to me while the tall, muscular security guard walked ahead wearing a tailored suit. Sebastien wasn't carrying the imposing Z-gun today but had a handgun of some sort in a holster at his belt. To my surprise we weren't heading toward the 1st class lift.

"Where are we going?" I asked, directing my question toward the man ahead of us.

"To a secure location. Mr. Baaqir is already there waiting for us. We're taking a discrete route, trying not to be seen. We believe the entrance to Mr. Baaqir's suite may be under surveillance. Right this way." Sebastien pointed toward a narrow corridor.

We walked down the corridor and I eventually saw a lift door hidden behind a recess. As we stepped into the lift, no one talked. The atmosphere had become quite tense, a definite sense of foreboding had overcome me. I started having second thoughts about my judgement. It was the second time in a few days I'd mindlessly followed someone to a meeting on their own turf. In reality, I had no damn idea if I could truly trust these people.

The lift door opened onto a set of stairs, like the stairs at the end of the hall in my apartment building. It seemed entirely out of place on a starship. We ascended three flights of stairs as I wondered where in hell we could possibly be going.

Eventually, we reached the top of the stairs, went through a large door, and as we emerged on the other side my jaw dropped in awe. We found ourselves standing beneath a transparent dome enveloped by the cosmos; it was a much smaller version of the dome that encased the arboretum. Billions of stars spilled across the inky black canvas above us, while novas and supernovas flared like angelic fireworks. Nebulas unfurled like glowing testaments to the Gods' artistry, quasars blazed with intensity and galaxies twirled in elegant spirals. In every direction, the universe revealed its treasures. It was wondrous and I was rendered speechless.

"Hello, Professor." Baaqir said from one of several reclining chairs at the center of the space. "Welcome to the Archeron's Observatory Lounge, or as I call it, my bird's nest. How do you like it?"

"I love it, it's amazing. It's like a close-up view of creation."

Baaqir was dressed in a tasteful gray, pinstriped suit, including a vest and tie. He wore freshly polished black shoes, carried a wooden cane with a gold handle, wore a black bowler hat, and generally looked like a completely different person than the day before. Standing a few steps behind him was a tall, swarthy man I hadn't seen before, dressed in tan slacks and a black sweater. He had a sidearm at his belt, and wore a smug look on his unshaven face.

"Thank you, Professor. I come here often, I love it; it's calming and inspiring at the same time. I must be careful; I could waste away hours in this place. Theoretically, passengers can reserve this room for parties, but secretly I keep it almost all to myself. That way I can come here any time I wish, just to relax."

"I don't blame you; this is spectacular. But, you didn't bring me here just to show me this view, did you?"

"No, I didn't. Please have a seat, Professor, we have much to discuss." He motioned to one of the chairs across from him. "Leanna, could you bring our friend some of that fruit juice again, I know she enjoyed it before." then to me, "That juice is a special blend I import from Grovia especially for Leanna. I've grown to love it as well; I have a glass almost every morning."

Leanna scurried away to retrieve my refreshment from an inconspicuous bar recessed into the back wall. I felt guilty being a bother, but remembered she'd said it was a job, she was being paid to serve Baaqir.

"I'm sorry for the urgency. Please don't blame Leanna, she was instructed to tell you nothing. I'm afraid the situation demanded I see you at once. You see, Professor, your comrades have been detained by the Ministry of Security." he confided.

"What! Why? How can you be sure?" Oh, gods, it had to be my fault! Those green shirted creeps must've followed me, and I'd led them straight to Kara and Teddy!

"I'm quite certain, I'm afraid. I wasn't exactly sure what you might *do* when you found out, therefore I sent two of my most trusted people to bring you here. Our immediate concern is what your friends might tell them about *us*."

"Our immediate concern should be to free Captain Bradley and Kara Az-Codor. We can't leave them with the secret police." I argued.

"And just how, exactly, would you go about that, Professor?" He asked in a slightly mocking tone.

"Well, aren't you some sort of wealthy and powerful oligarch or something? Why can't you exert your influence and demand they be freed?" I asked.

"Oligarch? Who uses that term anymore?" He chuckled. "It's true, I have a great deal of influence with Telluric institutions, I won't deny it. But there are certain developments that prevent such a course of action."

"Well, can you at least tell me what happened? Why were they arrested?" I asked as I tried to stem my panic. Leanna handed me my juice; I thanked her and took a big swallow.

"Let me introduce you to the man in charge of the Archeron's security force, Gregor Dementov." Baaqir indicated the man behind him. "Gregor, can you tell our friend what happened?"

"Yes sir, I can. Several hours ago, your two confederates were seen exiting the cargo hold of this ship by my men. Understand, miss, the cargo hold is strictly off limits to passengers while we're in transit. A couple of hours later they returned to the cargo hold, and my men were waiting for them. They were taken into custody." Dementov explained.

"I still don't understand, your security force isn't the same thing as the Ministry of Security." I said.

"That's correct." Baaqir said. "I became aware shortly after they were detained and instructed Gregor to let them go. The Archeron's security basically works for me." Dementov did a slight bow with a crooked little smile. "But, after we released them, the Ministry grabbed them up almost immediately."

"Alright, but why'd the green shirts arrest them?" I was getting impatient.

"We can't say for sure. Knowing Bradley, it could be any number of reasons. It's possible the Ministry has an informant on Gregor's staff." Baaqir suggested.

"If they do, I'll weed 'em out quickly. I can't have my people informing for the secret police." Dementov said.

"You see, just entering the cargo bay would be a minor offense, easily swept away." Baaqir told me, "However, I'm perturbed to say, Bradley had several large pallets of cargo stored in the hold; all of them with convincing, counterfeit lading codes. When Gregor's people inspected the containers, they discovered contraband weapons. Your friend, Captain Bradley, actually had the temerity to *smuggle weapons* aboard this ship."

"That's news to me, of course. And it doesn't make any sense; Bradley has his own ships, why would he risk smuggling weapons on the Archeron?" I asked.

"Who knows? But you have to admit it's a rather daring and clever idea. As for why, well, I understand Bradley's smuggling operation has had several setbacks recently." Baaqir advised, as Tubau approached from near the door. He wasn't there when we came in, I was sure of it; I would've smelled him. He must've snuck in quietly after I sat down.

"I believe you've met Wa' Tubau." Baaqir said. "He keeps me apprised of Bradley's activities."

"We weren't properly introduced, I'm afraid. Wa' L'Kyne Tubau at your service, Professor Thornwell." The little fellow said as he bowed toward me. He took a seat next to Baaqir; his feet didn't touch the floor. It appeared as if an ugly, little child had joined us. A smelly child. I didn't know how Baaqir could stand sitting next to him.

"Nice to see you again." I answered lamely.

Of course, I thought, Tubau worked for the Trade Guild and Baaqir was a powerful member of the organization. Tubau could be the one who followed Teddy and Kara to the cargo hold in the first place. Sneaky little devil, I was beginning to understand why Kara despised him so much.

After our first meeting I was under the impression I was on Baaqir's good side. We'd cut a deal to acquire artifacts for him, and he'd even offered me a job. However, I couldn't shake the impression he wasn't happy with me for some reason.

"These smugglers, like your Captain Bradley, are often quite clever." Baaqir said. "The Archeron wouldn't normally be suspected of carrying contraband. So, if he bribed the inspectors when the cargo was loaded, and once again when unloading, the plan would've come off without a hitch."

"What do you mean about his operations having setbacks?" I asked.

Teddy and Kara had implied their smuggling business was thriving. Not to mention their syndicate.

Tubau answered smugly, "Professor Thornwell, in just the last few months, several vessels suspected of being involved in Bradley's smuggling operation have been captured and impounded by the Trade Guild. His business has suffered greatly. I flatter myself that I've been instrumental in these successes."

"Tubau has been assigned to Captain Bradley for some time. The Trade Guild has been trying to curb his activities but haven't been as successful as I'd hoped." Baaqir told me.

"Mr. Baaqir, we've impounded the majority of Bradley's fleet." Tubau defended himself indignantly.

"Watch your tone L'Kyne, remember who you work for. Regardless of Bradley's other endeavors, this business today puts *us* in an awkward situation, Professor." Baaqir warned.

"Us? What do you mean, *us*?" I asked.

"The Ministry of Security is extremely paranoid; you cannot begin to imagine the extent. Therefore, any mention of our names by your friends, and *you and I* could have a serious problem. Because of those weapons we may be implicated in smuggling charges." Baaqir told me.

"Whoa, I didn't know anything about those weapons. How can I get in trouble for those?" I protested.

"Well, it's actually quite simple; if one of your friends mentions your name in between gasps of pain or in concussed delirium, you will certainly be arrested. Worse, one of your friends could mention *my* name. I'm a controlling partner in Aries, contraband weapons on the Archeron is a bad look. Tell me, just how much do you trust this pirate, Bradley?"

That was an excellent question. What about Teddy? I didn't know anything more about him than what he'd told me. Kara? She wouldn't talk to the green shirts; I was sure of that. I doubted she'd even talk under torture. But Teddy? I didn't know. What could they tell the green shirts about *me* anyway? The most questionable thing I'd done on board was talk to them!

"Honestly Mr. Baaqir, I don't know who to trust. I've only known Bradley for a short time, and I can't answer for him. But I believe Kara Az-Codor is dependable."

"Why is that, Professor, because you've *slept with her*?" Baaqir challenged.

I'm sure I blushed noticeably, with my personal, private business being aired in front of all those people. I chanced a look at Gregor Dementov, he was sneering at me with a creepy grin. I didn't like that guy. Tubau barely suppressed a snicker. I didn't like him any better.

"Uhm, I won't dignify that, Baaqir, it's none of your business. But I do feel like I know her better than I know Bradley, that's all."

"Oh, of *that* I'm fairly certain." He commented sarcastically. Dementov chuckled and tried to hide his sleezy grin with one hand. I *really* didn't like that guy.

"Get to your point, Baaqir." I was getting tired of this conversation.

"Very well, Professor, my point is simple. You don't know either one of them, *at all*. You met them less than 5 days ago. Isn't that true?"

"That's right, but..." I started.

He didn't wait for my response. "I admit at our first meeting I was caught off guard. That rarely happens to me; I foolishly hadn't done my due diligence. After his surprise request for a meeting I fully expected to reject Bradley, whatever his proposal was. I'd describe the man as clever, but entirely untrustworthy."

"The man is nefarious." Tubau said. "I've never met anyone so dishonest."

"At least he doesn't sneak around and listen at other peoples' doors." I said to Tubau; Dementov chuckled. Then I said to Baaqir, "How can you stand to sit next to him, he smells like he fell in a sewer and didn't get rescued for days."

Tubau began, "You filthy... "

"Enough." Baaqir ordered, "I'm able to manipulate my senses. When L'Kyne attends me I turn my olfactory off. If it means anything to you, we smell almost as offensive to him."

I said, "Good."

"Bradley's been an adversary of the Guild's for a long time." Baaqir's tone was condescending. "And these syndicates he had a hand in creating have become a thorn in our sides as well. I never intended to do business with him."

"If you just planned to reject him, why'd you even agree to the meeting?" I challenged.

"Perhaps you're right; perhaps I shouldn't have. But I had the notion Bradley could help us identify Mr. Jelks' killers. When a prominent member of the Trade Guild is murdered, we must bring the culprits to justice, without exception. The meeting with Bradley was successful in this regard, at least."

"So, you didn't even care what Teddy had to propose?"

"No, not at first. I assumed he wanted to discuss syndicate business, or perhaps weapons, something he and I have a common interest in. But I never expected to take his proposal seriously. However, when he said it was about ancient artifacts, and when I realized who *you* were, I knew I'd been too hasty. And of course, when he showed me those astonishing metallic pieces, I naturally became interested in what the three of you were up to. Since our meeting I've had a chance to consult my many sources, research all of you thoroughly, and get some much-needed perspective."

"Mr. Baaqir, I..." but he interrupted me again.

"Leanna, could you bring me a glass of brandy, please? Thank you."

"Yes, sir."

"Simply put, Theodore Bradley is the worst sort of scoundrel, masquerading as a gentleman." He said, "He's a shameless opportunist, only interested in himself and his profit. He's a man completely controlled by his greed, the way an addict is controlled by their impulsive cravings."

"That's funny Baaqir, he told me almost the same thing about you."

"I'm not surprised. I cultivate a certain image, one that's good for my business. It helps when creating partnerships if you have a reputation for making your partners a lot of coin. However, with Bradley it's all about *his* profit; believe me." Baaqir advised.

"I told you I wasn't sure I trust Teddy." Baaqir continued to seem annoyed with me, and I couldn't understand why. He was being inexplicably confrontational.

"Alright then, let's talk about your other friend, the Tovolek. My augmentations don't just improve my memory, they also improve my *perception*. I instantly suspected, the moment you entered my suite, that there was something between the two of you. And when I was rude, she moved to protect you. She placed her hand on your shoulder, and that's when I knew for sure." He said, with an irritating hint of accusation. "She's taken advantage of your inexperience, Abigail. She was aware you'd never been to space, had never met anyone like her before. She exploited the situation to their advantage."

"I don't blame you one bit." Dementov leered. "She's a tasty piece, that's for sure. Once you removed her fangs and claws she'd be a nice bit of sport."

"Shut up, you asshole!" I yelled at Dementov. His leer became a bit more sinister and I practically shuddered looking at him. I turned back to Baaqir, "No one took advantage of anybody."

Baaqir said, "Alright, Abigail, whatever you say. Let's put aside the fact she's a *non-human* from a *primitive* planet. Professor, she's a **dangerous creature**. You have no experience with these sorts of violent, alien races; I do. The Tovoleks are an extremely vicious and war-like race; from all accounts they're quite bloodthirsty. Did you know she's a fugitive from justice? She's a wanted criminal on her home world, with a huge price on her head. She's accused of *Patricide*. She's no one to be trusted or bargained with." Baaqir was starting to piss me off.

"Just wait a second Baaqir, Kara told me all about her fugitive status. She's *not* the one who killed her father, it was her uncle that killed him. Listen, are you going to help me free them, or do I have to try alone?" I didn't want to hear any more of his poison.

"Free them? As I've said, there's nothing I can do at the moment. However, I did have my people jettison Bradley's cargo as soon as I heard the two were arrested. All the Ministry has now is the word of their informant, whoever that may be, that those weapons ever existed."

"So, what *can* we do?" I asked. "Besides destroy evidence."

Baaqir smiled. "We must wait, though patience isn't a natural strength of mine. With no evidence, the Ministry shouldn't hold them for long. Of course, one never knows; lack of evidence doesn't always keep the Ministry from detaining people."

"Well, if you aren't going to do anything to help them, why'd you even send for me?" I was getting frustrated.

"I simply thought you'd like to know your friends were arrested. You're also much safer here with Sebastien and me, in case Bradley talks. In addition to *that*, Leanna insisted we tell you. Leanna asks for so little; I tend to indulge her when she does." Baaqir explained. I didn't know what to say. "But, that's not the only reason I sent for you, Professor. You and I have several topics to discuss."

"We do?"

"I'm afraid so. You see, I researched *you*, as well. I've learned you've never left Ampora before; you've never even been issued a passport prior to a week ago. I must admit you had me fooled. I was convinced you and Bradley had been teamed up for some time, the way he deferred to you. But now it's obvious to me you weren't even with Bradley when he found those fragments on Kleos Prime." My face must've given away my surprise at the planet's mention.

"Oh, yes. I've deduced where those fragments must've come from." He scrutinized me closely, "You see, I've also learned an application for an archeological expedition to the Kleos system was submitted by the Amporan Academy of Sciences only a few short weeks ago. Amazingly, the application was approved by the Cultural Ministry almost instantly; the very next day in fact. Those applications typically take months or even years to process. The Amporan Academy, that's where you teach, is it not?"

"It is, yes."

"A permit issued to dig on Kleos Prime, followed closely by Bradley striking that deal with me? There are no such coincidences, Professor. Bradley's inexplicable fragments of metal *must've* come from there. Yesterday I got the impression the two of you were going to search for our Reges Scientia artifacts together. Imagine my reaction when I discovered you were actually on your way to the Kleos system to participate in the *Academy's* expedition." Baaqir didn't sound friendly anymore.

"That's easy to explain... " I started.

"Save your breath, Professor." he interrupted, "I've deduced your plan, as well as your deception. I don't normally stand for being lied to; that sort of thing gives a bad impression. However, in your case I'm willing to believe you were misled by those two miscreants."

"Lied to? I didn't... " I started, but Baaqir cut me off.

"Please, Professor, don't dig yourself a deeper hole. Correct me if I'm wrong, but I believe your plan was to abandon your Academy colleagues, while you and Bradley attempted to locate artifacts at Kleos behind their backs, which he'd then sell to me." He accused, "Or, perhaps you were going to *steal* artifacts from the Academy, then have Bradley sell them to me. Either proposition seems equally dubious."

"Mr. Baaqir, this is just a misunderstanding."

"That it is." said Baaqir, "I understood I was to have exclusivity when it came to Reges Scientia artifacts. Bradley even promised me so, specifically. And yet, the three of you *knew* the Academy was there digging for artifacts already. How were you planning to fulfill your promises?"

"I guess we were convinced we could find artifacts there the Academy couldn't. Bradley knows where those fragments were found, they don't." I said.

"I see. Apparently, you thought as long as you kept me in the dark about the Academy's dig, *what I didn't know wouldn't hurt me.* Is that it? How do you know the Academy hasn't already found artifacts on Kleos Prime?"

"Truthfully, I guess we can't know that until we get there." I confessed.

"Exactly. Obviously, you were keeping the Academy expedition a secret because you realized I'd never agree with your proposition if I were aware of it. There is no way I'd surrender my QSDM technology if I realized the true nature of your proposal. You lied by omission."

I wasn't sure how to respond. Baaqir was correct in almost all his accusations. In fact, the only thing he was wrong about was Teddy had never even intended to sell him anything at all. But, I couldn't tell Baaqir it was actually *worse* than he thought it was, could I?

"Mr. Baaqir, I don't know what to say. You're right, I suppose Teddy didn't think you'd agree to give us the stealth tech if you knew about the Academy dig. I'm sorry."

Baaqir scrutinized me with his penetrating gaze; his disfigured countenance unnerved me horribly. My palms had begun to sweat several minutes before and were sopping, but I resisted the urge to wipe them on my trousers. I refused to give the man the satisfaction of knowing how the conversation was affecting me. Let him use his cyborg's perception if he wanted to know.

"Abigail, *someone else* knows Bradley found something on Kleos Prime. Not only that, but they've informed the Ministry of Security. You see, I've learned the expedition you were on the way to join was actually proposed and expedited by someone within the Ministry of Security. They recruited your Academy to do the excavation, but they're clearly the sponsor, and will reap whatever treasures are found. That also explains why the dig was approved in only one day. Someone was pulling strings aggressively for that to happen."

"The Ministry of Security proposed the Academy dig? I didn't know that."

"They did, indeed. So, you see, I now have the possibility of *two* Ministry investigations hanging over my head. One about the weapons on board the Archeron, and another having to do with my involvement in your Kleos enterprise. I've been an outspoken critic of the Ministry of Security, calling out their overreach and abuses on many occasions. Therefore, I strive to never give them an excuse to investigate me. You and your friends have certainly put me in an uncomfortable position."

"I don't understand. Why would the Ministry of Security sponsor an archeological dig? That doesn't make any sense." I said.

"I agree. The Ministry aren't collectors, like me. Their interest in culture extends only to the varying ways to destroy it. No, their interest must be far more *practical* in nature; they must expect to find something *useful* at Kleos Prime. Therefore, we must ask ourselves what would be useful to the Ministry of Security? Certainly not clay pots or old bones." He reasoned, "They must hope to discover weapons, or more probably technologies which might lead to weapons. That's what would be useful to the CTF, correct?" Again, Baaqir was methodically logical in his analysis.

"Gods, they have to be looking for Reges Scientia artifacts too." I blurted. "Just like us."

"You've stated it exactly. That's why I said someone *else* knows what Bradley discovered there. It's the only explanation for the Ministry's involvement. Professor, your plan of snatching artifacts at Kleos is even more harebrained considering what we've just discussed. You wouldn't be competing with the Academy but with a far more formidable adversary, wouldn't you agree?"

"Yes, I see that."

I already knew the green shirts would be at Kleos providing security. But I didn't know they were behind the dig in the first place until Baaqir had told me. He was right, of course, somehow Gordon knew Reges Scientia artifacts might be found there, it was the only explanation.

"There is another thing you weren't honest about, Professor." He accused. "Since I know you weren't at Kleos when the fragments were discovered, but your analysis of the fragments was, I believe, accurate, I've come to the logical conclusion it was actually your father who was at Kleos Prime with Bradley when those pieces were discovered. Am I wrong?" Baaqir asked. Clever bastard.

"You aren't wrong. My father and Bradley found those fragments at Kleos Prime over 20 years ago. Truthfully, I only found out about it on board the Archeron." I admitted.

"The strikes against you keep piling up, Professor." he told me ominously. "I'm still inclined to give you the benefit of the doubt and assume those two con artists fooled you into participating in their scheme. However, I still question your judgement in the matter."

"I apologize for my part in the deception. In our defense, the rest of it is the truth. I actually do think those fragments belonged to an ancient, advanced society. And so did my father." I hoped that was enough to placate Baaqir.

"I don't doubt it. And, for what it's worth, I agree with you. But, you're still not being completely honest, Professor. I might've mentioned, that doesn't sit well with me." His voice had taken on an edge. "As I've said, I checked you out. You don't seem to be in any financial distress, so I'm wondering why you'd throw over your Academy in favor of Bradley, a man you just met, by your own admission."

"I don't know what you mean." I said.

"Of course you do. You were already on your way to Kleos to participate in the Academy expedition. You didn't need Bradley, or *me* for that matter. What motivated you to team up with Bradley in preference to your own Academy? The most obvious reason I could think of is coin." he reasoned logically, "Bradley stood to make a small fortune selling artifacts to me, if his scheme succeeded. But, as I've said, you don't seem to need coin that badly. If you did, you probably would've snapped up my job offer." Clever bastard. I'd hate to sit across a thezra board from this guy.

"It's true, I'm not in debt, but I'm not well off either. I make 65 thousand coin a year teaching a bunch of spoiled, entitled brats history that most of them couldn't care less about. I depend on my government housing allowance to pay my rent. A lot of coin sounded good to me. Afterward, I could resign, and find something more interesting to do with my life."

Baaqir sat and studied me. "Like work for me?"

"Possibly. I'm still considering your offer." I lied.

"No, you're not. You have no intention of working for me; don't worry, I'm not offended. Let's return to the topic of the Academy dig. You didn't throw in with Bradley for coin, that much I know. In fact, knowing what I know about him, I'll bet he never even discussed what your cut of the prize would be, did he?"

"Well, I... "

"Did he even promise you a cut, Professor?" He interrupted me again, "Oh, don't get me wrong, you won't turn down the coin if it's offered, but you have *other* reasons for joining Bradley. Personal reasons, most likely. Professor, the perception granted me by my augmentations makes me more or less a human lie detector. Tell me, is it simply a case of sexual infatuation with the Tovolek?"

"Absolutely not!" I protested, "That's insulting."

"No insult was intended. Everyone is susceptible to sexual obsession, Professor; I don't judge. I imagine she's quite a thrilling change from what you're used to; as a lover, I mean."

"As I said, that's none of your business." I fumed. I was getting angry, possibly because he was hitting a little too close to home.

"Or, is it more complicated? There's an aspect to this that illudes me; it sits just out of reach at the edge of my perception. Does it have anything to do with your father? Something to do with finishing what he started? As you've admitted, he went to Kleos with Bradley. Now you've planned to do the same."

That was a perceptive question, I admit. It was actually a question I'd been asking myself. I'd taken enough psychology classes in school to know it was possible I was only going with Teddy and Kara so I could follow in my father's footsteps. Or, maybe it was simply the unexpected excitement I felt when I found out my father was more than the conservative professor I'd always assumed him to be. He'd been adventurous and daring, traveling around the quadrant in search of ancient relics in spite of the danger from the authorities. Surprisingly, those are the footsteps I craved to follow.

"Perhaps. I don't honestly know. Until recently I didn't know my father had ever left Ampora. I suppose I wanted to go where he'd been, I won't deny it. Bradley was friends with my father, and maybe I'm a fool, but he and Kara make me feel closer to him somehow."

"And you miss him. I quite understand."

We sat silently, across from each other for several moments. He studied me, and finally shook his head subtly, as if I was an enigma he couldn't explain.

He looked past me toward the door. I turned to look as well and discovered several more security types had joined us in the observatory. I had no way of telling if they belonged to Baaqir's personal security force, or if they were members of the Archeron's security. They were all dressed similarly.

"Abigail, I have another question, just out of curiosity: Why wait 20 years? If your father was convinced of the antiquity of those metal fragments, why'd he and Bradley not return to Kleos before now? Surely your father understood how important Kleos might be. He was no fool." Baaqir had asked a question I couldn't answer.

"I can't say; I wondered the same thing. Perhaps my father got sick; he was sick often during his last few years. Or perhaps Bradley had other business he couldn't get away from. Maybe my father didn't realize the importance of the discovery until it was too late. He passed away eight and a half years ago."

"That would be exceedingly curious. The Henry Thornwell of my imagination would've recognized the value of Kleos instantly. Maybe I give him too much credit. Either way, I plan to have a discussion with Captain Bradley about it. If we ever see him again." Baaqir said chillingly.

He turned his attention to Sebastien Fowler, and they whispered for a few minutes; low enough so I couldn't eavesdrop. I just sat and sipped my juice. My mind was racing, thinking back over my conversations with Teddy and Kara. The portrait Baaqir painted of my new friends was certainly sobering. And, his opinion of our chances against the Ministry of Security on Kleos Prime was impossible to argue with. Harebrained seemed like a good description.

Baaqir snapped me out of my thoughts, "Professor, I've no way of knowing what that pirate has told you or convinced you to do for him. But ask yourself this: Why now? If he and your father were friends and worked together over 20 years ago, why have you never heard from him before 5 days ago? Bear in mind I ask you these things not to upset you, but to illustrate to you the foolhardiness of trusting Bradley, or his Tovolek."

He stood and walked over to Gregor Dementov, they conversed quietly for a while, and I was losing patience quickly. I couldn't just sit there while Teddy and Kara were in custody.

Our discussion had paused, but I sensed there was more to come. I had nothing to say, so I sat in silence, alone with my thoughts for several minutes. I hated that Baaqir made so much logical sense when he was attacking Teddy and Kara. It made me feel like a fool for befriending them. I hoped that wouldn't be proven true. Finally, I'd had enough of Mr. Baaqir's company.

"I think I'll return to my cabin. I'd rather wait there in case they're released." I announced as I stood to leave.

"I don't think so, Professor, I'm afraid that's not possible. If Bradley is selling us out to save his skin, I have a ship standing by to take us away." Baaqir told me. "Please, have a seat."

"Not possible? Does that mean I'm a prisoner? And take us away to where, exactly? Where can we go the Ministry of Security can't find us?" He wasn't going to let me leave, and I began to realize my situation was more perilous than I'd imagined. Just what did Baaqir plan to do with me?

"I wouldn't call you a prisoner, call it under my protection." He said as he walked back over to join me. "If necessary, the ship will take us to my home planet, Dressida. I hold great sway with the local government, and I also have many powerful friends there. I could take my case directly to the Council of Governors and plead my innocence; and yours, of course. We'd be safe there I believe. In time, I'd clear us of any charges."

"I don't have to be cleared of any charges; I haven't done anything wrong. I had nothing to do with those weapons in the cargo hold. Why would I run away?"

"Well, Professor, let me see." He said condescendingly, again. "How about your plot to sabotage the Ministry's little treasure hunt at Kleos Prime? I'm sure they wouldn't be too happy about that. If they get your two friends to talk, and believe me they *know* how, your friends will probably tell the green shirts all about your little plot. They'd lock you up and throw away the key." Damn him and his logic!

"Worse, Bradley could give them *my* name in connection with your plot to steal artifacts at Kleos, and *I'd* be in jeopardy. Distressing, since I had no knowledge of the Ministry's involvement at Kleos because the three of you *lied to me* about it." Baaqir had raised his voice again.

"I didn't lie, I didn't know the Ministry was behind the Academy's dig." I argued, possibly for my life.

"Semantics; you're aware of my meaning. You kept the existence of the Academy dig to yourself; a deliberate deception. And, don't be so sure Bradley and his Tovolek were as uninformed as you. They might've known all about it. No, Professor, if Bradley or the Tovolek implicate either of us, our best option is to leave this ship and head for Dressida. You must come with me because I can't allow you to fall into their hands either. You could implicate me just as easily as Bradley. In short, the three of you have put me in a terrible position because of your *lies*." Baaqir said with finality, and a bit of venom in his voice.

"I told you I was sorry."

"That might be sufficient, *if you were a child*. I knew better than to trust Bradley, but I was enchanted with those artifacts. For that, I blame myself. However, there's still the question of *your* trustworthiness. I haven't decided yet if I trust you, Professor."

"All I can do is apologize, if you don't accept it, there's nothing I can do about it. But, I honestly don't think Teddy or Kara will tell the green shirts anything; they don't seem like the type. And, I have a question for you, don't your men outnumber the green shirts here on the Archeron?" I indicated the several armed security guards around us, "Why are you so worried about what they'll do?"

He laughed at that, "While there's probably only 10 or 12 green shirts on board, there's also a contingent of allied marines. A full company, more than 200 men plus officers. The ship's security, which works for me, numbers close to 200 also. However, I have no illusions that they'd be a match for a company of Marines. In any case, a firefight on a star liner full of passengers is a terrible idea, don't you agree? I have no wish to leave here, this is my home. But I will if I'm forced to. It just depends on what your friends tell the green shirts."

"How do you know there's only 10 or 12 green shirts on board? Do you keep track or something?" I was just nervously asking questions at that point. I was worried out of my mind about Kara, and yes, even Teddy. I still thought of them as my friends, despite what Baaqir had said.

But Baaqir wasn't done testing me, it seemed. "As a matter of fact, we do keep track. Didn't Commander Gordon tell you how many men he has on board?"

Uh oh, this couldn't be good. Baaqir knew about my interrogation by Gordon. Gods, he knew everything! Fear slithered closer to my consciousness. Teddy had warned me how dangerous Baaqir was, I found myself hoping he'd exaggerated.

"Baaqir, is there anything you don't know about what happens aboard this ship?" I asked, trying to stall and think how I could explain myself this time.

"I certainly hope not. I became concerned when I learned of Gordon's presence on the Archeron. It's unusual for a security officer of such high rank to be on board. Gordon commands his own frigate, you see. So, why would he be on board the Archeron? I'm afraid I can only conclude it has something to do with *you*, Professor."

"*Me?* What could it have to do with me?" I asked. But of course I knew it was because of me. Gordon had practically told me that. And once again Baaqir had deduced another fact from thin air.

"What, indeed? Commander Gordon appearing aboard the Archeron at basically the same time you did is an astounding coincidence, Professor. Shortly after, he grabbed you for what, I can only assume, was an interrogation. There are nearly ten thousand passengers aboard the Archeron, he hasn't arrested or interrogated anyone else. So, clearly, Gordon has a special interest *in you*."

"I wasn't arrested. They just wanted to talk to me." I interrupted.

"With them, there's no difference. I knew about it within a few minutes, of course. I thought little of it at the time, the Ministry questions people aboard the Archeron from time to time and it normally doesn't concern me. I had no idea who you were at the time and never gave it a second thought."

"Mr. Baaqir. It was no big deal. I... " I started, but he once again interrupted me.

"But then you showed up in my suite with Captain Bradley and I began to wonder. So, now we come to my most worrisome question for you, Abigail. One which, I'm afraid, might not leave us friends." He began. "What'd you and Commander Gordon talk about?" the billionaire asked. He made a subtle gesture to Gregor Dementov who, ominously, moved over to stand beside my chair. Tubau, seated next to Baaqir, had a nasty smirk on his ugly face.

"As you probably know, Gordon told me I couldn't divulge what we talked about." I said, hoping Baaqir would take that for an answer.

"I think we're beyond that now, don't you, Abigail? I want to know what was discussed. I know nothing was said about me, after all we hadn't even met yet. *But* you *had* met Captain Bradley and his Tovolek. I must know if you're trustworthy, Professor." he said. "Bradley was traveling under an assumed name, so someone informed the Ministry he was on board the Archeron."

"Well, Tubau was in Bradley's suite at the same time I was. He knew they were here, he probably followed them on board." I offered.

"How dare you, you worthless *bitch*!" Tubau shouted as he stood. "I work for the Guild! I'd never inform for the secret police!"

"Silence." Baaqir ordered. "Tubau is probably telling the truth. Not because he's a shining example of loyalty, but because he knows what I'd do to him if he ever betrayed me. Informing for the Ministry behind my back would be an unforgivable betrayal, L'kyne knows that. Also, he's always been a coward; quite dependably so."

"Hmmf" Tubau breathed out. "Self-preservation is simply an instinct I *do not lack*."

Baaqir chuckled coolly, "Abigail, my apologies. I respected your father greatly, and I'm fond of you; I truly am. But I simply must know if you informed on Captain Bradley. After all, he and his beast are in Ministry custody as we speak."

He seriously thought I might've told Gordon something that got Teddy and Kara arrested. I was in a tight spot; how was I to prove I *didn't* inform on them?

"Come on, Baaqir, you think I'd actually inform on them? You think I'd stoop that low?" I tried.

"Abigail, I *think* you're just a simple academy professor. I imagine, when sitting across from the formidable Commander Gordon, that you were nervous, even a bit scared. Maybe you were *more* than a bit scared. Scared people have been known to say almost anything to stay out of trouble, even to the point of informing on new acquaintances whom they *barely know*." Again, he was frustratingly logical. That's easily how it could've gone, but it didn't.

"Mr. Baaqir, I wouldn't. Please believe me." I pleaded.

I was in a panic; I didn't want to tell Baaqir what Gordon and I'd talked about. The fact the Ministry of Security had found my father's DNA on Kleos Prime didn't seem like something Baaqir would be happy to hear. He was mad because I didn't tell him about the Academy's dig. What would he do when he found out I'd kept the secret police's involvement to myself. Damn.

"Right now, I'm trying to decide if I believe you, Professor." He began, "Now, it's a fact you were questioned by Gordon, it's also a fact you had just met Bradley and his beast, and it's now a fact they've been arrested by Gordon. If I didn't know you to be an innocent professor, clearly in over her head in this business, I'd pronounce you unreliable right now and be rid of you."

"Please Abby, my friend, please tell my master what he asks." Leanna pleaded. I'd forgotten all about her standing behind me.

"Be still Leanna, let her talk. If you can't be silent, you'll have to leave." Baaqir told her.

"Abigail, believe me, I have no wish to harm you. But if I don't hear the *truth* now, I will have Gregor do just that. Bear in mind I'm a human lie detector. Now, *tell me what you and Gordon talked about*." Baaqir was done being Mr. Nice, if that's what you'd call it up until then.

My heart was practically beating out of my chest. "I was told at the beginning of the meeting that since he was in charge of security for the expedition to Kleos, I needed to be screened. He said it was nothing to worry about, simply routine."

"Screened for the expedition you neglected to tell me about. Gordon himself interviewed you, not one of his lackeys?"

"Yes, it was Gordon."

"Senior officers who command warships don't normally conduct simple security screenings. I was correct, Gordon *has* taken an interest in you. Please, go on."

"He asked me if my father had ever told me anything about Kleos Prime. Then..."

"Wait." Baaqir interrupted, "Commander Gordon actually mentioned your father? Why would he do that?"

I bit my lip, but I had to tell the truth. Baaqir was a cyborg lie detector. "Because they'd found my father's DNA on Kleos Prime. Gordon showed me a 20-year-old derma patch they'd found. I think he came to the Archeron just to ask me about it." Silence fell for several moments as he processed this new information.

"So, not only did you neglect to mention the Academy's expedition, but also the Ministry of Security's involvement. Yet another mark against you, Professor. And what about Bradley? What'd you tell Gordon about him?"

"Nothing. He never asked me about Teddy, I swear, They weren't arrested because of me. Gordon was only concerned with what my father told me about Kleos Prime. I said Pop never told me anything, because that's the truth. My father never mentioned Kleos to me in my entire life."

"And Gordon believed that?"

"Honestly, I don't think so. He threatened to lock me up in the brig, but then he said we had plenty of time to talk more before we arrived, and he let me go. That's it, that's everything."

"Do Bradley and his Tovolek know about any of this? That you were questioned by Gordon or that they found your father's DNA on Kleos Prime? Tell me the truth, don't try to protect them."

"I never told them about it. So, as far as I know they have no idea. I told them after our meeting there'd be CTF at Kleos when we got there, but they didn't seem worried about it." My palms were dripping, and I felt faint. If Baaqir had Dementov kill me I don't think I'd even blame him.

"You knew there were green shirts at Kleos Prime, and you agreed to help Bradley take artifacts out from under their noses anyway? Abigail, you have a lot of backbone for an academy professor. Or, perhaps your naiveté hindered your judgement."

"That's it? That's all you're going to say?" Tubau asked him, "She practically served you up on a platter to the Ministry of Security!"

"L'Kyne, if you can't be constructive, I can have Sebastien nail your tongue to the floor." Baaqir said calmly.

Tubau, with those bug eyes, was hard to read, but he clearly believed the threat because he was silenced.

"Mr. Baaqir, Gordon took away my passport and I was preoccupied with that. Honestly, I just didn't think anyone else would care about my father's DNA, I didn't think it mattered. I see now I should've told you about it."

"You should have, but it's spilled milk, as they say. As I've already said, I wouldn't have agreed to Bradley's plan if I'd known of the Academy dig. Gordon is just another complication. And, as I pointed out before, you're just a professor in over your head in all of this. That doesn't absolve Bradley, however. He's no babe in the woods, he knew exactly how I'd react to knowledge the Ministry was involved at Kleos."

"When we met with you, I hadn't told Teddy yet. So, he didn't know the Ministry was involved." I said.

"Don't be so sure, Abigail. Bradley may know far more about the situation than he's shared with us. Just because he's well informed, doesn't mean he shares his information, even with his friends. And he and I *aren't* friends."

Baaqir leaned back in his chair and closed his eyes. I guessed he was thinking. Probably thinking about whether he should have me thrown out an airlock or not.

My heart was thundering, the adrenaline was giving me a headache. Baaqir finally leaned forward again, eyes open, and considered me. He had a look I couldn't read on his misshapen face. I feared what he might do to me if he didn't forgive me. But in spite of my personal peril, I still couldn't get my mind off the vision of Kara being tortured and beaten while she desperately tried to protect me. The thought horrified me worse than anything Baaqir might do to me.

Finally, he spoke. "Alright Professor, you can relax. I don't believe the discovery of the DNA changes anything. Please excuse me for a moment."

He stood and walked over to where Sebastien was standing attentively. Gregor wandered back over to the other side of the room also, helping me to relax a little. I was supposed to be on an *enjoyable* trip into space, my first ever. It was shaping up to be my last, as well. It'd become my considered opinion that space travel is overrated.

Baaqir and Sebastien conversed in hushed tones. They might be deciding my fate, or talking about restaurant reviews or muzzle velocities for all I knew.

Leanna sat beside me, "Abby, I'm also worried about your friends. I hope they're alright." She placed her hand on mine and I took it. We held hands and waited. "Don't worry Abby, my friend. My master is fond of you, I can tell." Hadn't she just heard him threaten to 'harm' me?

Baaqir returned to his seat. Gregor Dementov stood next to him again. Sebastien joined our group as well, standing next to Leanna and me. He'd acquired a Z-gun at some point.

"Abigail, I apologize. These methods are abhorrent, and I'm afraid they may be traumatizing to someone like yourself." Baaqir sounded reasonable again. "But there is another matter that must be dealt with right now. Sebastien?"

The man, Sebastien, raised his Zymtal rifle and took aim. There was a terrifying discharge of light and energy as he fired. I closed my eyes instinctively and leaned away from him toward Leanna. I felt a crackling of static electricity along my arm and side of my neck. When I opened my eyes again, Gregor Dementov lay on the ground convulsing dramatically, a grimace of pain on his face. His spine was bent horribly concave, and his arms and legs seemed frozen in awkward positions.

"Why'd you do that?" I yelled at Sebastien, shaken.

"Dementov is the informant, of course." Baaqir explained, "He's the reason your two friends were arrested. I was questioning you to be absolutely certain, but I already knew, more or less. I was never going to harm you, but I needed to know the *truth*. Threatening you with Gregor was credible, I believed, since you hadn't met him before. It's easier for me to read people when they're under duress. Or, perhaps I should say it's more difficult for people to hide their feelings. I hope you can forgive me; I'd still like us to be friends."

"It doesn't matter. I'm mostly stressed about Kara and Teddy." I said. "So, you're positive Dementov told the green shirts about them?"

"It's simple deductive reasoning. I was sure Tubau said nothing, as I've explained. I was 99 percent sure you'd said nothing, plus I believe you knew nothing about those weapons. Dementov obviously took a bribe from Bradley to allow the weapons to be loaded. It's probably not the first time. When the two were found in the cargo hold, Gregor feared I'd discover his illicit activity, so he informed on Bradley to the green shirts. Isn't that right, Gregor?"

Baaqir poked him with his cane and Dementov convulsed and groaned in obvious agony.

"They say the muscle spasms caused by a Z-gun are excruciating. It can last for several minutes too; the man is suffering badly. But perhaps not as badly as he deserves."

Baaqir called over a couple of the guards standing back by the door. They came and, not too gently, dragged Dementov away.

"What's going to happen to him?" I asked.

"I suggest you forget about Dementov. You won't be seeing him again. I detest the Ministry of Security; my people know that. Betrayal is not tolerated." Baaqir explained. I was left with the assumption he'd be killed, and with the impression Baaqir was just as dangerous as Teddy had claimed.

"I always knew there was something wrong with Dementov, I'm not surprised at all." Tubau claimed.

"And yet you said nothing to me of your misgivings." Baaqir said sarcastically.

He turned to me and said, "Bradley smuggling arms on board the Archeron is disappointing."

"Tell me about it." I said. "I had no idea, but why are you disappointed?"

"You see, when Bradley confines himself to smuggling brandy and cigars, I'm content to allow the Trade Guild to harass him. But when he deals in arms I intervene on his behalf and keep the Guild away. Isn't that true, L'Kyne?" Baaqir asked him.

"Yes sir. Though I've never understood why."

"Well, pay attention and you may be edified. Abigail, can you guess why I allow... no, not allow, but actively *facilitate* the smuggling of arms by Captain Bradley?" Baaqir asked me.

"I don't know for sure, but my guess is it's because your company, DRG, sells to the people fighting against the people Teddy sells to." I answered. "It's good for business, that's all."

Baaqir laughed, and Tubau looked at me slack jawed. I thought it was obvious.

"Exactly, Professor. You have a keen mind, maybe I should give you Tubau's job." He looked now at the little man, "If arms dealers like Bradley stopped selling weapons to the insurgents, the CTF would no longer need to buy billions worth of weapons from me. War creates strange bedfellows; and business is war, war is business. Tubau, she deduced that in a matter of hours, you've missed it for years." He laughed derisively.

"But sir. My job is to catch smugglers, not to anticipate business strategies." Tubau argued.

"This time though, Bradley has gone too far." Baaqir explained, "Smuggling weapons on *my* ship. Can you imagine the audacity of such a thing? I don't know whether to stand him in front of a firing squad or pin a medal on his chest. If it wasn't for Dementov, it would've required only a warning to stop such a thing. But now that the Ministry of Security is involved, we might've finally seen the end of Captain Bradley. I can hardly protect him while he's using *my* ship for his smuggling, now can I? I'd be admitting guilt."

I was getting dirty looks from Tubau. He was jealous of me because he thought Baaqir liked me better. Gods, these people were crazy! Baaqir left to go talk to Sebastien again for a few minutes. I wasn't scared for myself anymore, but I was worried sick about Teddy and Kara.

Leanna leaned close and whispered to me, "Abby, my friend. Sebastien is going to leave soon. When he does, you must insist on going with him. I'll come too."

"Why?" I asked, just as Baaqir returned to his seat.

"I have good news and bad news" he said, "First the good news: it seems they've let your Tovolek friend go. Why, we have no way of knowing. But my people say she was freed several minutes ago."

"Where is she? She's probably searching for me." I blurted. "I need to see her." I was frantic to see Kara and make sure she was unharmed. And to get the hell away from there too; beautiful as it was I'd grown sick of Baaqir's 'bird's nest.'

"Please remain calm, Abigail. Sebastien has ordered his people to find her and take her somewhere safe. He'll let us know when they've got her." Baaqir continued, "Now, the bad news: Bradley is still in custody. I'm not sure what to make of the situation, but we can be sure at this point they don't intend to set him free. It looks like we've seen the last of him."

"I, for one, can't say he'll be missed." Tubau commented. I wanted to punch his ugly little face.

"L'Kyne, please remove yourself." Baaqir said with exasperation.

"Yes, sir. Where should I go?" Tubau asked.

"Away."

The musculux got down from his chair slowly, as if he thought Baaqir might be kidding. He huffed once, then twice, then made his way toward the door. I, for one, wasn't going to miss his stench.

"Now, it only remains to wait for your friend to be located." Baaqir told me. "I'd like to question her about the nature of her interrogation."

There was no need to respond, so I sat silently waiting. It wasn't a long wait.

Sebastien hurried over to our group. "They think they've located her. I have more men on the way here, I'm going to go down and get her myself." This must be the moment Leanna was warning me about.

"I'm going too. I have to see her." I said.

"I'm afraid not Abigail, that would be too dangerous. You'll stay here, with me, until this entire episode is completed to my satisfaction." Baaqir declared. Dammit.

"I'm going Baaqir, and the only way you can stop me is to shoot me. I mean it." I announced. He looked like he thought that might be an excellent idea.

"She'll be safe with me sir. Besides, she might help us capture the woman without force. She's quite a formidable opponent, so perhaps the professor can convince her to come along peacefully." Sebastien proposed. I wished I'd thought of that argument.

Baaqir paused for a few moments, weighing the pros and cons of letting me out of his sight. He clearly wasn't convinced yet he could trust me. I couldn't say I blamed him, as dishonest as I'd been with him. And after he'd threatened me, he knew I wasn't fond of him either.

"Very well, take the professor along. But you're responsible for her, Sebastien, don't let her out of your sight. And bring them both back here when you find the woman. We must speak with her, and then decide our next move." Baaqir ordered.

"I'm coming too, I'll go with my friend Abby." Leanna pronounced. Baaqir didn't argue, he just waved his hand in the direction of the door. Two more security guards had shown up to relieve Sebastien and guard the 'bird's nest.'

Baaqir addressed me again, "Abigail, I'm certain there's still a piece to the puzzle I'm not privy to. When you return with the Tovolek, we'll talk some more. Think about confiding in me, you might be surprised what a good friend I am to have, Professor."

"Alright, let's go." Sebastien Fowler announced. I began to follow him, but Baaqir stopped me once more.

"One last thing, before you go. A simple word of advice: You may believe Bradley's creature cares about you. Who knows? You may be right. But hear this: The Tovolek has been at Bradley's side for many years and they've been through much together. She's his confidant and partner; you shouldn't test her. Don't make her choose between you and that pirate, you may not like how it turns out." Baaqir turned away to speak with another one of his minions.

"Come on Professor, we should hurry." Sebastien told me. So, we left the sanctum of the observatory and proceeded down the stairs to the lift. Me, Leanna and the burly guard who loved her; we made a strange trio. I was thrilled to be away from that observatory, though. The whole vibe had been one of menace while I was there.

"Try to raise her on comms, Professor, she'll answer you if she has her comms with her." Sebastien said.

That made sense to me, and I desperately wanted to talk to her. I tried her code, but got no response. They must've confiscated her comms device. Or broken it.

"We should try their suite; she may be there waiting for me to show up." I advised.

Sebastien said, "I already know; that's where she is. My people followed her to your room. When you weren't there, she went to hers. We must move quickly. Professor, do you trust me?"

"What?" I was caught off guard by his question.

"Yes, Abby, my friend, please trust Sebastien, he has a plan of escape. He's clever, my Sebastien." Leanna said. Escape?

"Alright, Fowler, what's your plan?" I asked.

"First, we collect your friend. The two of you can gather your things, only what's important; we must move quickly. Then we head to Baaqir's ship and get the hell out of here." He said.

"Sorry, Fowler, but I don't want to go to Dressida with you and your boss. I don't trust Baaqir all that much, no offense." And I sure didn't want to be at that guy's mercy again any time soon.

"You misunderstand me, Professor. We aren't going *with* Baaqir; we're going to steal his yacht. I've already packed my things, and Leanna's, on board. There are 16 shuttle bays on the Archeron, Baaqir keeps his yacht in bay 11. I've got the access codes and I can fly the ship myself. The four of us are leaving, but we don't have much time before Baaqir gets suspicious and starts looking for us; we have to hurry."

Well, I'll be damned, Sebastien was running off with Leanna and he offered Kara and me a ride.

"Is this your idea, Leanna?" I asked.

"No, not actually. It's Sebastien's idea. He's wanted to leave with me for a long time, but I always refused. Just a while ago, when you were speaking with Mr. Baaqir, he offered to take me away again, but also offered to save you and your friend Kara as well. He is so valiant and thoughtful, isn't he? Abby, I decided I do love him after all. Isn't it wonderful?" Leanna said excitedly. She was smiling and blushing, and so obviously happy I had to smile back.

"Thank you, Sebastien. I don't know what else to say except let's go get Kara, and as you said, get the hell out of here."

Part Nine There is no Going Back

Interstellar Date: 388-06-22
On Board the Archeron

WE HURRIED FROM THE lift to Kara's suite. I wasn't sure what to expect; what had her green shirted captors done to her? I imagined the meeting wasn't as cordial as mine had been, and mine hadn't been all that cordial. Gordon had unnerved me, he was a cold, calculating bastard. But, Kara was no naïve history teacher, and hopefully she wasn't as intimidated by him as I was.

I knocked on her door as Sebastien and Leanna stayed back. Kara opened the door and I rushed into her arms. I hugged her tighter than I've ever hugged anyone in my life. The raw emotion that engulfed me was unfamiliar and even a bit frightening. I was overcome with all of the uncertainty and stress I'd been storing up all day. Relief, surprise, gratitude, and excitement all combined at once, had me shaking as I crashed from an adrenaline high I didn't even realize I'd been on.

"Thank the Gods; I didn't know if I'd ever see you again." I stammered.

"It's alright, little human, I'm here now." she smiled. "But, what happened to you? Did a Benoan Panther chase you through a swamp?" I must've been sweatier than I'd thought.

"Never mind me, are you alright? What happened with the green shirts?"

"They arrested us, but how'd you know about it? They confiscated our comms."

Kara wasn't sure what was going on, as she eyed Sebastien and Leanna suspiciously. The two had entered the suite after me and paused near the door, politely letting us have a moment.

"These two came to get me and took me to Baaqir a couple of hours ago. He's the one who told me you'd been arrested. I was so worried about you. What about Teddy? Will they set him free too?" I asked, beginning to calm down.

"Don't worry about me, I'm fine. It seemed the green shirts were more interested in Teddy than me. They only asked me a few meaningless questions, cuffed me to a chair for hours, and then let me go with no explanation. But I'm afraid they were much harder on my master. The leader, a man named Gordon, seemed extremely angry with him for some reason." Kara answered.

"Did you and Teddy really have weapons in the cargo bay? Baaqir said you were smuggling weapons on his ship. Why'd you do that?"

"We did it, little human, because that's what we do." she stated, matter-of-factly, "We've done it before and it worked perfectly. Teddy and I are smugglers, remember? We were simply careless and stupid getting seen leaving the cargo hold."

"That Tubau creep was with Baaqir just a while ago, it might've been him that saw you." I guessed.

"That little vermin; I should've known. He better pray we never meet again. We should've been more careful, dammit." Kara responded. "We thought since the Karmarinski brothers were in the casino, it was a good time to check our cargo. We were careless."

"Excuse me, Kara? I'm sorry to interrupt, but we don't have much time. I have a ship waiting to get away from the Archeron, but we must hurry. Please gather your things as quickly as you can and come with me." Sebastien said in a calm and professional voice.

"Fowler, isn't it? I hate to disappoint you, but I'm not going anywhere with you or your boss. And even if I would, I wouldn't leave without my master." Kara declared firmly.

Sebastien remained calm, "I'm sorry, I should've said, we're not going with Baaqir. In fact, I'm stealing his new yacht. But there's nothing we can do about your Captain; the secret police still have him."

"You're stealing Baaqir's yacht? *Your* boss? You have big balls for a security guard." Kara said. "I don't know who's more foolish, you or I."

"Why do you say you're foolish?" I asked her.

"Because I'm going back there and I'm going to kill every green shirt I see; and free Teddy." Kara pronounced. She *was* wearing her 'full battle armor' as Teddy would call it.

Sebastien argued, "I'm afraid that *would* be foolish. You'd have no chance. And anyway, we don't have time."

"Listen, I know exactly where Teddy is, exactly how many men are guarding him and exactly how I'm getting him out of there. Abby and I will gather our things, we'll take them to your ship, then you and I will go kill the men guarding Teddy and free him. After that, we'll go with you." Kara said with authority. I wasn't going to argue, but I wasn't sure about Sebastien.

He said, "That's insane. I came here to collect you and take you away with us. I never volunteered for a suicide mission."

Leanna said, "Sebastien, my love, we must help them. *All of them.* They need our help."

Sebastien sighed and shrugged his shoulders, "Alright. Just how do you plan on rescuing your captain without alerting the entire ship? If we start shooting we'll have marines all over us in minutes." Sebastien asked. He apparently couldn't deny Leanna anything.

Kara simply turned, leaving me to collapse into a chair, and retrieved one of her duffle bags from behind her. She dug into it and produced her answer. "Here" she said, as she threw a long slim blade in its scabbard to the security guard. I recognized it as the second weapon she'd worn the day I'd met her, besides her little tooth. It was a longer weapon, better described as a sword than a knife. She turned to me and tossed a scabbard in my direction too. I barely had the reflexes to catch it.

"What's this?" I asked her.

"That's yours. I bought it for you after our knife lessons. It's your own little tooth." Kara had bought me a dagger. I supposed that passed for romantic on Nir-Kvek.

I pulled it from its scabbard and examined it. It was much smaller than Sur-rok, maybe half as long. The blade was slightly wider, and the point not quite as tapered, but it was definitely reminiscent of Sur-rok. The grip fit my hand perfectly and was ornate as well. It was a beautiful weapon.

"Wow, it's gorgeous Kara. There's inlaid gold here; this is too much. You didn't have to do this. But thank you, thank you. I love it. Only, I don't know if I'll be able to actually use it. I'm no warrior."

"You'll have it with you, just in case. Do you remember your lessons, little human?" She asked.

"I do."

"Fowler, can you use that thing?" Kara asked, indicating the sword she'd tossed at him.

"I've had training, when I was young. But are you telling me you intend to take out CTF security officers with swords? That's crazy, they'll shoot us down before we even get close." Sebastien protested.

"We'll approach casually and ask to speak with their prisoner. Our weapons will be concealed, their weapons undrawn. When we get close, we'll kill them quickly and quietly, raising no alarms. We'll retrieve my master and head to your ship; simple as that." Kara explained. I had to admit she made it sound simple. There was no way it could be *that* simple, though.

"The two of us will be taking on how many?" he asked.

"Only five, perhaps six. I will kill the first one in the corridor quickly. We'll kill another two in an outer room, as quietly as possible. Two more will be inside the room with Teddy, we'll kill them and free him. If the leader, Gordon, is present, leave him to me. I'll kill him as well, with relish. I only regret that death is too good for them, they deserve to suffer. But I'm confident they'll suffer eternally in the afterlife, so that consoles me somewhat." I'd never heard Kara speak like this. She was terrifying, and I was truly glad she was on our side.

Unflappable, Sebastien simply shrugged, chuckled and said, "As you say, then. Let's gather your things. Oh, and just in case." he tossed her the handgun and holster he'd been wearing. "You know what they say about bringing a knife to a gunfight."

"No, what do they say?" She asked.

"Don't." he replied.

Kara quickly packed a few pieces of clothing in small cases for her and Teddy. She grabbed two spare comms from a drawer and her duffels, and off we went to my place. I had even fewer things to gather, just some of my new clothes and personal belongings. I had one piece of luggage as we made our way down twisting corridors and several lifts. I was profoundly lost by the time we arrived at shuttle bay 11.

There were four of Sebastien's men there guarding Baaqir's magnificent yacht. As he talked with them I wondered what he was saying. He obviously wasn't telling them the truth about what our group was up to. At least I didn't think so; I didn't know if those men were more loyal to Baaqir or to Sebastien.

The yacht was bigger than I expected, long and sleek with beautiful lines, and it had *Avernus* painted in gold script near the tail section. It reminded me of the terrifyingly fast racing boats that were so popular on Ampora, blasting their way around the ocean courses at breakneck speeds. They all had names like Banshee or Nightwing painted along their hulls. The Avernus looked capable of lining up in the Grand Championship Rally on Founder's Day.

"Alright, my men have readied the Avernus for departure. Baaqir's plan is to leave quickly if there's any sign of treachery. Kara and Professor Thornwell, you should secure your baggage on board. I've told my men you'll be leaving with us, so they should give you no trouble. Leanna, you'll stay here with the professor, Kara and I will go retrieve Bradley." Sebastien explained. He'd procured another handgun, and it was holstered on his belt.

"No way. I'm coming with you." I didn't want to be separated from my demon protector again, period.

"Professor, I can't protect you if I'm trying to fight a bunch of green shirts at the same time. It won't be safe." he said.

"I don't want to be separated from Kara again. I'll stay out of the way. Please let me come?" I pleaded.

"It'd be wiser for you to stay, Abby. I won't be able to focus on your safety, I'll be killing Tellurians." Kara was in serious demon mode. "A little human might get in the way."

"Kara, I'm coming." I told her with the most serious look I could manage. "I won't get in the way, I promise."

"Do you know how to handle a gun, Professor?" Sebastien asked. "I can grab you one, if you want."

"No, I've never used a gun before, and I thought we were trying to stay quiet? I'd probably shoot my own foot off anyway. No, thanks."

"Let's go." Sebastien said. He'd laid down the law to Leanna and ordered her to stay with the shuttle. She was easier to convince than I was, she was no warrior either. Plus, she had nothing to fear from Baaqir if he surprisingly showed up there.

The three of us left the shuttle bay and headed for a lift. I had my little dagger in its scabbard on my belt but I had no illusions I could help in any fighting. Kara and Sebastien had concealed their weapons as well as they could. But, both of their weapons, especially Sebastien's longer blade, were hard to hide. Each had equipped themselves with a sidearm as well, but of course the plan was to be as silent as possible, so hopefully those wouldn't be needed.

I'd assumed we'd be heading toward the promenade to that dingy little beige office Gordon had questioned me in. But that's not the direction Kara led us. I guessed the green shirts had more than one office on the Archeron, or perhaps they'd borrowed an office from the ship's security.

We traveled through a labyrinthine series of corridors to a section of the ship I hadn't visited. That was no surprise since I hadn't seen a fifth of the Archeron yet. What was surprising was the lack of people. I saw no passengers, stewards, cleaning staff or even security. I had the impression we were in the bowels of the ship.

We came to a lift, but when Kara tried the door it wouldn't open. "Krag Aft!" She exclaimed. "We need to find a steward or something; someone who can access this lift."

"There's no time to look for a steward, I haven't seen any the whole way down here. Sebastien, is there a way to bypass the lock?" I asked.

Sebastien stepped forward, "Let me try something." He placed his thumb to the scanner, and swish, the lift door opened. "I've never been to this lift before, but I have high security clearance aboard the Archeron. I figured it was worth a shot."

"It's a good thing I brought you along." Kara said dryly. "I was worried Abby and I would have to do everything." Now Kara was teasing Sebastien.

Kara explained as we rode the lift down, "When the lift arrives and the door opens, there will be a guard posted in the corridor. We'll casually approach him, and I will kill him quickly. Watch for others."

We exited the lift into a short corridor with doors on either side. Just as Kara had told us, a few meters from the lift was a CTF security officer standing at attention in his green uniform. He immediately approached us with his hand out, palm forward in the universal signal meaning halt.

"Hold it, you people can't be here, this is a restricted area. I'm going to have to ask you to... " and then he noticed we were armed. His eyes went wide, and he reached for his sidearm.

Kara acted instantly, leaping forward and at an angle to the luckless soldier. She was incredibly fast, like a Talvian Leopard pouncing on prey, and that's just what the poor fellow was in fact, *prey*. Sur-rok, the ornate dagger that looked like a treasure from a museum, was out of its scabbard and embedded in the man's throat before his fingers had closed on his gun or he'd been able to utter one more syllable.

The man's eyes bulged even wider, in complete shock, as his arterial blood coated his shirt and jacket. Kara gripped him under his arm and quietly lowered him to the ground against the nearest wall. A crimson pool expanded in the corridor, I quickly stepped aside to avoid it. The entire engagement had taken mere seconds, and the man was dead before Sebastian and I'd closed the distance. I think Sebastien's face was nearly as shocked as the dead man's.

As for me, I was thinking I may be ill. I'd never seen anyone killed before, of course. My father had died quietly in his sleep. The sudden, deadly violence unnerved me to my core, my hands were shaking. I'd never seen so much blood in my life. I didn't think of myself as squeamish, but I was happy I hadn't eaten in hours.

"*Lucifer's balls*, I've never seen anyone move that fast before. What in hell are you?" Sebastien whispered.

"She's a demon." I answered for her.

"So, now what?" asked Sebastien as he shook his head.

Kara, unphased and not even breathing hard, said "Through the second door on the right is a sort of waiting room. There were two guards there earlier. Through another door inside we'll find my master. There were two guards in there with him earlier as well. Gordon wasn't present when I was freed, but he may have returned; he'd be the sixth man." she whispered calmly. "I hope he has returned; his entrails could use some airing out."

"How do we get into the waiting room, knock?" Sebastien asked. He was clearly skeptical whether his clearance gave him access to the green shirts' inner sanctum.

Kara leaned over and grabbed the dead man's right wrist, lifting it up. No, I thought, no she wouldn't! *Yes, she would*! She calmly unsheathed little tooth again and quickly removed the dead man's right thumb.

She said, "Follow me. Abby, you should hang back."

I shifted a little forward, trying to stay out of the dead man's blood, which'd nearly swamped the corridor. I quietly crossed the hall to get a view inside the waiting room once the door was opened. Kara would probably have scolded me, but she was intent on her purpose and had forgotten about me for the moment. She and Sebastien braced themselves as Kara lifted the dead man's thumb to the scanner.

The door opened with a familiar swish. This time both Kara and Sebastien were prepared. They shot through the open door in a flash. I heard a voice from within, though I couldn't see the speaker, "Magnuson, what do you think... " and then only a strangled noise.

I had a bad vantage point and couldn't see what was happening, but I heard a brief struggle and what I guessed was the sickening sound of a sword cutting through a person. Sebastien must've employed his blade to profound effect, as no shouted warnings came, only the faint sound of the bodies being lowered to the floor.

I turned to look back towards the lift. No green shirted reinforcements had shown up yet. But it wouldn't be long, there had to be some sort of digital surveillance in that corridor.

Again, the whole thing couldn't have taken more than a few seconds. Kara and Sebastien were efficient and deadly opponents. I was starting to think this might actually work just like Kara had predicted.

I crept over to the doorway and peeked inside. Two CTF men lay on the floor in rapidly growing puddles of blood. The man at Kara's feet was bleeding profusely from his left ear, a puddle of blood and brain matter collected beside it. Kara had apparently plunged Sur-rok into his skull, ear first.

The man on the floor next to Sebastien had been completely decapitated, a spray of blood painted the near wall, his head was across the room. The gore of the scene was way too much for me, I turned, lurched my way out into the hall, and retched uncontrollably. Dry heaves are the worst!

There was a noise of shuffling chairs from the interior room, the room that supposedly held Teddy. My retching must've alerted them, dammit.

I heard "What's going on out there?" My heart leapt into my throat. What had I done?! I'd jeopardized the whole plan.

As I reentered the room Sebastien gave me a sympathetic look and put a finger to his lips. I realized I wasn't exactly 'hanging back' as I'd been told. Kara, quiet as a cat, slipped over beside the interior door, into an ambush position. Sebastien moved toward me and put his arm out to guide me into the corner behind him. He wiped his bloody sword on his sleeve before putting it back into its scabbard and drew his sidearm. Because of me, we didn't have the element of surprise anymore. Silence was a luxury we could no longer afford.

There was a moment of calm, then "What are you idiots up to? What was that noise?" The door swished open and a secret police officer was standing there, just inside the interior room. His face registered shock and surprise at all the gore, but he reacted remarkably fast, stepping back out of the doorframe, and to the side while drawing his weapon.

I heard him say "Overwatch, this is torch, over." He'd activated his comms device and was calling for help.

I could see Teddy in the interior room. He was zip tied to a metal chair and had blood on his shirt; they'd been beating him.

Then we heard "Torch, this is Overwatch. Go ahead, over."

The conversation didn't have a chance to get more involved. Kara the Demon, wielding Sur-rok, had plunged the dagger into the wall at approximately the height of the green shirt's head. Her blade went through the thin interior wall like it was tissue paper.

We heard a shout and a curse, "*fuck!*," as Kara spun into the interrogation room like a flash. There were sounds of a brief struggle, and a frightening weapon discharge. I think I may've screamed as Sebastien raced forward. Kara's maneuver had surprised him as much as it had me.

"Are you alright? Are you hit?" Sebastien asked her as he rushed into the interior room.

"I'm fine, no problem. We're lucky these walls are so thin. I took his eye out with my blade from the next room." Kara laughed. "I haven't had that much fun in ages."

She'd finished the job on the guard after she'd spun into the room. But he'd had time enough to get off a shot. The noise had been impossibly loud to me, and I was sure there'd be a team of Gordon's goons on us any second.

Kara went to Teddy and removed the zip ties from his wrists. She helped him to his feet; he was wobbly but smiling.

"What took you so long?" he asked shakily.

"We went to have lunch first. You know how I hate to kill on an empty stomach." Kara answered. Then she kissed him on his bloody lips.

"Ouch, easy. My kisser's had a rough day." Teddy said, but it was clear he was elated we were there. Well, at least he was elated to see Kara.

"We need to hurry, that shot must've been heard. Someone is sure to come and investigate any minute." Sebastien advised. "Wait. Kara, you said 5 guards, possibly 6. We've killed 4."

Just then I saw movement in my peripheral vision, coming from my right. I was standing in the center of the 'waiting room' as the 5th guard grabbed me, putting me in a loose choke hold. He held a gun to my head.

There was a recessed storeroom behind the desk, and the bastard must've been taking a nap, or searching for more torture implements there when we entered. None of us had seen or heard him.

"All right you filthy proggs, drop your weapons or this little bitch gets one in the ear." He threatened.

He started to reach for his comms, I knew we couldn't allow him to contact anyone, so I made a split-second, desperate decision; I pulled my dagger from its scabbard and shoved it right into his crotch with all my strength, as I yelled, "Who's a bitch?"

He let out a primal scream that would've curdled the blood of a Pentoffian executioner. I was sure they'd heard it in Baaqir's bird's nest. I guessed I'd hit something pretty vital with my little blade.

As I stabbed him, I tried to wrench away from his grip, but the bastard was strong and held on tight. As he screamed I heard another tremendously loud weapon discharge. For a split second I thought the officer must've fired his weapon, and I couldn't understand how I wasn't dead.

It'd been Sebastien; he'd drawn his gun and shot the man holding me directly through his eye. A pretty nice shot from the next room, and through a doorway. He'd missed *my* face by only a few centimeters. With blood, and I didn't want to imagine what other types of gore, spraying the side of my head and face; I swooned and collapsed on the bloody floor.

Sebastien rushed to me, "Professor, are you alright? You aren't hit, are you?" He lifted me up into his powerful arms and slapped me in the face. He literally slapped me!

"Professor... *Abby*, let's go! We don't have time for this." He said. He was right, of course. I pulled myself together and stood on my own wobbly feet.

We were all thinking the same thing; we'd made far too much noise. We could have company at any minute, so we needed to hurry. Kara had emerged from the office with Teddy hanging on her shoulder. His face was bloody, but his smile was ear to ear. We sprinted and stumbled down the corridor toward the lift. Amazingly, no more green shirts had appeared. The others must've been far away when our clumsy little battle had begun.

"Professor, what are you doing here? This is a bloody battlefield." Teddy asked with a big smile as we got on the first lift.

"Well, *I* came down here to negotiate your release, but these two started killing everyone." I answered. My attempt at humor fell a little flat, but I was sort of proud of myself for trying, given the circumstances.

"I don't understand." Teddy started, "Just what kind of operation is this? There's nowhere to go, we're on a bloody starship. We can't possibly hide from the bastards."

"Master, don't worry. Fowler has a plan." Kara explained. I noticed she was limping as we exited one lift and lurched toward another.

"Oh, *Fowler* has a plan? Don't get me wrong, I appreciate your help back there, but why'd you help me escape?" He asked Sebastien. "Did Baaqir put you up to it?"

"Not exactly." was the response.

We exited the next lift and hurried down another corridor. I was lost, but Sebastien seemed to know where he was going. The blood and guts were catching up with me, I was starting to feel ill again. The last thing we needed was for me to faint.

"Teddy, we're heading to a shuttle bay. There's a ship there waiting for us. We're going to leave the Archeron in it." I tried to explain to Teddy what was going on.

"I'm still wondering why he's here." Teddy pointed toward Sebastien, "Are we leaving with Baaqir or something?" he asked. "I can't believe he'd stick his neck out like that."

"No, not with Baaqir. I wouldn't go around a city block with that son-of-a-bitch." I answered.

"I still don't understand, Professor. Isn't this Fowler chap Baaqir's man?" he asked, motioning toward Sebastien again.

"Not anymore." I answered. "I still don't hear any alarms. Maybe we're good."

"There won't be any." Sebastien told us as we raced down yet another corridor. "They'll try to keep it quiet, if they can. They don't want the passengers panicking. They'll use their comms and spread the word to the marines and ship's security."

"Let's hope the bloody Marines don't get involved." Teddy commented.

Sebastien responded, "We have no way of knowing how long it'll take the green shirts that remain to discover the dead bodies or the surveillance feeds. But you can be sure that once they do, they'll notify ship security and call the marines for backup. Baaqir will realize quickly what's happening, if he hasn't already. But, there may be a few minutes of confusion to help us. Maybe."

We'd found our way through the maze of corridors back to shuttle bay 11. Amazingly, no armed men had appeared to confront us. It seemed incredible that no one had heard those gunshots, but I suppose it was a deserted section of the ship.

"Kara, my love, you're bleeding." Teddy commented. She grunted in response.

I confess I was so worried about the marines following us, and re-living the horrifying slaughter we'd left in our wake, I hadn't noticed Kara was bleeding from a wound in her thigh. A stream of dark blood was seeping down her leg leaving a trail of blood behind us that a simpleton could follow.

"Kara, how bad is it?" I asked as I went to her.

"I've had worse wounds." she said.

She'd stopped, Teddy taking her weight on his shoulder now.

I knelt and examined her leg. There was a frightening amount of blood, partially obscured by her dark body suit. A hole the diameter of my thumb was clearly visible in her upper thigh. My meager medical knowledge was of little help, but I supposed it was a good sign the blood was seeping rather than spurting. Still, it certainly didn't seem insignificant.

"It's nothing. I don't believe it's lethal. We need to get to the ship, there's no time to waste." She said through gritted teeth, clearly in pain. It definitely wasn't 'nothing,' and I felt foolish for not noticing the wound sooner.

"She's right, we don't have time to stop. There's an excellent sickbay on the Avernus. I can look at her when we get there." Sebastien was all business. "Do you need help?"

"I have her." Teddy asserted.

Sebastien typed the code into the wall-mounted terminal and the shuttle bay door opened. Our group practically stumbled inside. The guards Sebastien had left behind ran over to help us; they were clearly shocked to see Kara wounded. I also thought there were pitifully few of them. If the marines showed up we were cooked.

Leanna came running and jumped into Sebastien's arms. She started kissing his cheeks and lips, "My love, what took so long? I've been so worried. Sebastien, our master has called me on comms several times. First he asked what was taking so long, and I told him the woman was being difficult. He called again and wanted us to hurry. I think he was getting impatient. The last call I didn't pick up. My love, if my master thinks something has gone wrong, he will come *here*."

"Everyone get on board; we need to leave. Now." Sebastien announced.

"Who's ship is this anyway?" Teddy asked as we quickly headed for the boarding ramp.

"It's Baaqir's." I answered.

"We're stealing Cyrus Baaqir's spaceship? Do any of you know what that means? We'll be outlaws everywhere in Telluric space. That man doesn't forgive people who cross him." Teddy declared.

He was already an outlaw I supposed, but he obviously didn't want to be on Baaqir's bad side too.

As for me, I had a hard time thinking of myself as an outlaw. However, I'd helped a prisoner escape from the secret police, and in doing so I'd participated in the killing of several CTF officers. Gordon may also have discovered my involvement in a plot to steal artifacts at Kleos Prime. I was clearly an outlaw, whether I wanted to be or not.

"Master, we're already outlaws. We killed 5 men helping you escape. Stealing a ship is a minor offense compared to that." Kara explained groggily.

After we boarded the Avernus, I went to the obviously brand new, high-tech sick bay. I applied a tourniquet to try to stop Kara's bleeding. I only knew basic first aid and wasn't familiar with the sick bay's automation. Kara needed Sebastien, but he was busy preparing the ship for departure.

Everyone was on board, and Sebastien started the pre-flight checklist. Sebastien's men cleared the bay. I'm not sure what he'd told them, but they didn't seem concerned we were leaving without the big man. But just when everything seemed to be going our way, Cyrus Baaqir walked into the bay; he'd finally deduced what we were up to.

"It doesn't matter, he can't stop us now. Just open the bay's outer doors and we can leave." advised Teddy.

"I tried; they won't open." Sebastien said in his calm way.

"The doors won't open. I've overridden them." Baaqir shouted, "Why don't you all just come out of there so we can talk. I saw Captain Bradley is with you. I'd love to know how you accomplished that little feat."

"He's not going to let us go. What now?" I asked.

Kara was reclined and looking pale. She needed medical attention; she'd been shot in the leg and there was no exit wound. Even with no medical training I knew that meant she needed surgery to remove the bullet. We needed to leave; Gordon could show up any moment with a hundred marines. We didn't have time to parlay with Baaqir. But it was clear we didn't have a choice. I opened the Avernus' hatch and walked back down the ramp to talk to the man. Teddy hurried after me, still with blood on his face.

"Baaqir, let us leave." I started. "You don't need us anymore; you called our deal off. We're the ones the Ministry is after now, they have no interest in you."

"I told them nothing about you, Baaqir." Teddy said. "They didn't even *ask* about you."

"I'm to simply take your word, eh Bradley? Meanwhile, you're no longer their prisoner? Just like that?" he asked. "What'd you say to make them let you go?"

"We convinced them to let Teddy go." I answered. "By killing several of the bastards."

"We? Ah, I see. The work of your *creature*, I suppose. I guess they can come in handy from time to time. But why should I just let you fly off in my ship? It's one of a kind and it was *extremely* expensive. In short, you can't have it." Baaqir answered.

I still thought I could reason with him. "Cyrus, we need to leave before the marines show up here. They're after us, not you; you had nothing to do with freeing Bradley. If you let us leave, we'll bring your ship back to you."

"It's *Cyrus* now, Abigail?" he laughed. "I had nothing to do with any of this mess. We dumped those weapons you'd stored below, Captain. That was bold of you, smuggling weapons on the Archeron. I'm actually impressed."

"Master, please let us go." Leanna had come out of the ship as well.

"Why would you want to leave, Leanna? Haven't I always taken care of you? This is your home, darling. No, you can't leave." Baaqir told her.

"You don't need Leanna, she's just a servant to you. You can find another." I argued.

"There you go again, Professor. Have you learned nothing? I didn't say anything about *need*. I *want* Leanna. She's rare, unique even. And beautiful. I'd no more give her up than I'd give up my Mahad." Baaqir was infuriating. "I've grown to care about her; almost like a daughter."

"We'll get the Avernus back to you once we get away from the green shirts. We can take it somewhere and leave it for you." I was still trying to reason with the man. "Leanna is in love with Fowler, they belong together."

He laughed condescending, "Fowler? Oh, yes, I know. They couldn't hide it from me, as much as they tried. I just didn't think they'd go this far. They're more clever than I gave them credit for, and I gave them both a great deal of credit. Where is Sebastien?"

"He's in the sickbay, helping my partner. She was wounded helping me escape." Teddy told him.

"Not too badly, I hope. I know Abigail is quite fond of her." He said with a touch of sarcasm. "Sebastien is eminently competent; the Tovolek is lucky to have him. There are surgeons on Dressida I'd trust less."

"We can still strike a bargain Baaqir. We can still get you artifacts from Kleos if you want them." Teddy offered. "The deal can be the same. We'll bring you whatever we find there. We can meet you at EV765 and transfer the stealth tech. If you let us leave now. What do you say?"

"I don't think so, Bradley. I think I'll keep Leanna and my ship. If all of you disembark, I'll keep you safe till we reach EV765. You have my word. That's only a few days from now. There, we'll go our separate ways, no hard feelings." He offered. "I've slowed Commander Gordon down a bit for you, but they will be along shortly, so we don't have much more time."

He sounded reasonable, but I didn't trust the man. He wanted us to disembark, but after that he could take the Avernus and leave us for the green shirts. Plus, he was being completely unreasonable about Leanna and Sebastien. He clearly thought of her as a piece of property, even if Leanna didn't believe it. She was just another rare, beautiful piece of art in his collection.

"Master, won't you let us go, please? You always said I could leave whenever I wanted to. I want to leave now." Leanna seemed on the verge of tears.

"No, Leanna. I won't let you go. You're mine, one of my most unique treasures. I couldn't think of it." He said with finality.

"Baaqir, please be reasonable. We don't have much time, we need to..." my plea was cut short by the sound of a gunshot. As I turned I noticed, shockingly, Leanna had concealed a small handgun and as I'd spoken she'd fired it at Baaqir.

My ears were ringing as the man staggered, "Leanna, darling, why? You are my special girl, you could have anything, just by asking." A patch of blood appeared on Baaqir's vest, right in the center of his chest. Another trickle of blood escaped the corner of his mouth, reminiscent of a scene in a stage play I'd attended once back home. He took two furtive steps and collapsed in a heap.

Sebastien must've witnessed what happened. He came running out to where Leanna was standing and embraced her, taking the weapon from her hand. Leanna's round had struck Baaqir right in the middle of his chest.

"Lea, sweetheart, what've you done?" Sebastien asked as he went to Baaqir to check his pulse. "We can't open the outer bay doors now, Baaqir locked them with an override of some sort." He said as the sound of multiple boots could be heard outside in the corridor. The marines had apparently arrived in force.

Leanna, in stunned detachment, simply walked over to Baaqir and squatted down next to him. "I've seen him unlock the doors a dozen times. I know how to do it." she pressed something on the embedded interface in his arm and pronounced, "Done. The override is turned off."

We all rushed to the Avernus once again. Bradley and I went directly to the sickbay to check on Kara. All the automated equipment there was unfamiliar to me, but Teddy seemed to know his way around. He called up a holographic display, checked how she was, and pronounced her 'stable.'

Kara was all but unconscious but managed to mumbled something to me in her native tongue. Bradley grabbed an oxygen mask and placed it onto Kara's nose. "She'll be alright" he told me as we left her to find seats of our own. I hoped he knew what he was talking about. Kara was secured on the sickbay's bed, and as we belted ourselves into our seats I thought 'Go Sebastien, go!'

This time the outer doors opened when Sebastien beckoned them to. Leanna was a clever girl. Opening the outer doors automatically sealed the interior door against the marines on the other side. Bizarrely, it felt almost anti-climactic as we left. Even with 5 green shirts along with the oligarch Cyrus Baaqir dead, Kara shot, and us leaving in a stolen vessel.

Shock from all of the violence I'd witnessed that day left my thoughts in a tangled web of contradictions. Delighted to be alive and escaping that chaos, but horror stricken by my part in the events of the day. Kara was shot and lying in sickbay, 6 men were dead, and I'd been actively involved. My culpability hung over my head like the Sword of Damocles.

As the Avernus' engines roared to life, everyone secured in their seats, a brief moment of weightlessness caught me by surprise; I felt my stomach rising to my throat. A sensation of acceleration hit me and we were suddenly free of the Archeron. The realization struck me: I wasn't only leaving the giant cruise liner behind, but also shedding my past life. My very identity was altered in that moment of acceleration, I was being reborn as an outlaw, a fugitive from my former hum-drum existence. As we escaped into the dark void of space there was no doubt in my mind: I could never go home again; there'd be no going back.

Part Ten More Secrets Revealed

Interstellar Date: 388-06-23
On Board the Luxury Yacht Avernus

AS SOON AS WE CLEARED the Archeron, Sebastien raced to the sickbay to help Kara as I followed close on his heels. The automated system would handle the physical tasks of surgery to remove the projectile and seal the wound, but her problems weren't so simple.

"She's lost a lot of blood, and the automated system can't create whole blood for her, it doesn't recognize her blood type." Sebastien said. "What species is she again?"

"Tovolek, from the planet Nir-Kvek. That's what she told me." I said.

"That's right. The sickbay aboard the Tito has been programmed for her; I'll try to contact them. They're on the way to EV765, so they may not be far." Teddy said before he headed for the bridge.

The scene reminded me uncomfortably of my long vigil at my father's side as he died. His health had been declining for years, gradually reducing him to an invalid. I'd applied to the Health Service for a live-in nurse, but delays in the bureaucracy meant I took on much of his care myself. However, near the end he'd required hospitalization. I stayed with him, read to him, spoon fed him and patiently waited for the inevitable.

My devotion to him was absolute and I was devastated when he died. I couldn't have asked for a better father, but knowing what I know now, it would've been nice to have known the man Teddy described; who wouldn't enjoy hearing tales about their father artifact hunting all over the galaxy? I felt a bit cheated, though I realized that was unfair.

Sebastien brought me back to the present. "A 7.7mm slug, at point blank range like that, should've passed thru and thru. It certainly would have if she were human. Since there's no exit wound I guessed the slug must've hit her femur, but it missed the bone completely. Amazingly, her muscle fiber is so dense it stopped the slug part way through her thigh."

I held Leanna's hand with my sweaty one. We watched as the sickbay's automated system performed surgery on my friend. Two robotic arms descended from the recess above Kara, each with a myriad of instruments, tools and attachments. There was a monitor on the side wall that showed an x-ray view of Kara's leg as the surgery progressed. Fascinating as it all was, my emotional state made it impossible for me to watch objectively.

In all honesty, Kara was the reason I found myself there, with those people. Had she not made such an overpowering impression on me from the start, I'm positive I'd never have agreed to Bradley's proposition. If she were to die, Gods forbid, I wasn't sure what I'd do; literally. Could I continue with Teddy to Kleos Prime? I didn't want to think about it.

The micro-surgery on the damaged blood vessels would've demanded the skills of a gifted human surgeon, but the automated system performed the same task with speed and relative ease. When the surgery was complete, Sebastien came to speak to us.

"She's more or less stable now. There's nothing for us to do now except hope her blood loss is manageable. The equipment in this sick bay is the best available. She wouldn't be any better off if she were in the finest hospital on Dressida. It's too bad none of us can donate blood for her, though."

I shouldn't have to tell Sebastien the finest hospital on Dressida wouldn't even admit her.

"Come Abby, my friend, let's go. Sebastien knows what he's doing." Leanna suggested as she led me back to the salon.

The interior of the Avernus was reminiscent of Baaqir's luxury suite aboard the Archeron. Lustrous wood floor, gold fixtures, and accents of the same wood were visible on the furnishings. Everything was beautiful, if a little over-the-top. There were even a few lovely paintings on the walls. I knew it was unreasonable, but it annoyed me Baaqir had such exquisite taste.

The salon was located just behind the bridge, and consisted of several leather-bound couches and chairs, with a few small tables. At least there were no great beasts' mounted heads. The salon would accommodate at least a dozen people comfortably. On the ceiling above the salon was a duplicate mural to the one in Baaqir's suite on the Archeron.

"Leanna, what's the meaning of the mural on the ceiling?"

"That's a painting of Dressida and its moons. Isn't it lovely?"

I nodded, thinking Baaqir sure did love his home planet, especially for someone who'd chosen not to live there, but on the Archeron.

The bridge was visible through a large, arched doorway, and I could see Teddy at the comms console, but couldn't hear what he was saying.

"Abby, you should go to a cabin and get out of those bloody clothes. I'll go to the galley and prepare some food; I'm sure everyone is hungry. It'll give us a chance to think about our situation while we eat." Leanna suggested.

So, I went to find my suitcase, claimed the first cabin down the hall, and stripped my bloody things off. The mirror revealed a bedraggled soul, hair caked in blood and gore, and an expression of mild bewilderment.

There was an ensuite attached, so I jumped in and took a quick shower. The water probably wasn't as inexhaustible on the Avernus as it had been on the giant Archeron, so I kept it brief. Somewhat refreshed, I went looking for the galley, which turned out to be just aft of sickbay.

Entering the galley was a foray into a sea of stainless steel and strange contraptions. It was easily twice the size of my kitchen back home, sparkling clean and brightly lit; I thought maybe even an average cook like me could create amazing fare in a kitchen like this. If someone could tell me what half the equipment was used for.

Leanna seemed right at home, gliding around the space like a spatula-wielding ballerina. While I showered she'd prepared a lovely, green leafy salad with a tangy dressing. The greens were unfamiliar, but a stolen bite while she wasn't looking proved crisp and delicious. In addition to the salad Leanna prepared a stir-fry of vegetables in a spicy sauce. Once again, most of the veggies were new to me, gorgeous and tasty. But my favorite was a dish of grain, similar to long-grain rice but the flavor was nutty and rich, seasoned with herbs and spices from Dressida. My contribution was nothing more than a bit of chopping and good-natured encouragement. The lack of meat gave me the idea she was a vegetarian.

"Leanna, you don't eat meat, do you?" I asked.

"No, never. But I could find some if you'd like. The Avernus is well stocked." she answered, "My mast... I mean Baaqir likes meat from time to time. But he eats mostly vegetables, like me."

"Leanna, I'm truly sorry you had to shoot him. I know you were trying to help us, and I appreciate it. I understand he was good to you."

"Oh, don't worry, Abby, Mr. Baaqir is fine. But he's probably furious right now."

"Leanna, I saw you shoot him in the chest. You must've hit him in the heart, I'm pretty sure he's dead."

"That was only *one* of his hearts; he has two. The other, artificial one, would've taken over almost instantly."

"Wait, he's *got two hearts*? Leanna, what are you talking about?" But then I remembered the augmentation on the left side of his chest.

"One of Mr. Baaqir's augmentations is an artificial heart. Once his real heart stops, the artificial one takes over. His body automatically goes into a coma-like state while his real heart is repaired."

"Did you say, 'while his real heart is repaired?' What's that mean?"

"Mr. Baaqir owns a biotech engineering firm; he has millions of nanobots in his bloodstream. They automatically repair any kind of damage to his biological systems. The nanobots will repair his original heart in a few hours, but he'll only be in a coma for a brief time. Possibly as little as one hour. His augmentations are truly amazing." Leanna sounded proud of him.

We were wanted by the Secret Police for murder, and if that wasn't bad enough, Cyrus Baaqir (one of the most powerful men in the galaxy) was still alive and probably raging mad at us for stealing his prized yacht. Not to mention Leanna shooting him. We were in about as much trouble as people could be in.

"Well, nanobots aside, that was a pretty good shot; you hit him right in the heart. I'd like to know how you managed it."

"Oh, Sebastien taught me to shoot. He says I'm a natural. The security guards practice quite often at the shooting range on the Archeron, but Sebastien is the best; he is amazing. Sometimes, when no one was using it, Sebastien would take me there and teach me. I even used the same gun. It's actually Mr. Baaqir's gun he keeps here on the Avernus; I know where he hides it."

Leanna went out and announced to the others that *we'd* made food for everyone. I had mostly just watched, but I appreciated her giving me a little credit.

"What's this called?" I asked, indicating the rice-like dish.

"Gorna. It's popular with vegetarians because it's high in protein. I make it for Mr. Baaqir all the time."

"You used to make it for him sweetheart, not anymore." Sebastien corrected her. "Now you cook for whoever you like."

"Oh yes, I forgot."

"Well, I love it. I've never had it before. Thanks for the meal, Leanna, it was delicious." I said.

Teddy and Sebastien agreed, thanking Leanna profusely. I believe she was thrilled; she was grinning from ear to ear.

"Thank you, Abby. I enjoy cooking. Mr. Baaqir had me take lessons from the executive chef at his palace on Dressida." She smiled. "The chef, Arno Tessimi, is quite famous. He was kind and patient with me during my lessons. His daughter, Rissa, participated too, she's a prodigy; she was only 10 summers at the time, but she could cook almost as well as her father. You should've seen her, rushing around the kitchen, correcting him every few minutes. He'd simply smile and shrug, he obviously adored her."

When we finished eating, I stored away the leftovers and placed the dishes in the cleaning chamber while the others chatted. After a while Sebastien went back to the sickbay, Leanna said she was tired and headed back toward the cabins, so it was just Teddy and me.

"Teddy, how bad is Kara? Will she be ok?"

"Don't worry, Kara's an amazing physical specimen. That's not hyperbole, trust me. I've seen her do things I would've sworn were impossible." Teddy reassured me. "In my experience, her body heals much more quickly and thoroughly than ours do. If it were my decrepit old carcass in there, you'd be right to be worried. But, since it's Kara, there's nothing to worry about."

"I hope you're right. I've only known her for a few days, but I honestly don't know what I'd do if I lost her." I confessed.

"She'll be fine, trust me. I know she's grown pretty fond of you, too. I can see how protective she is of you. Maybe more than she is of me, I'm the one who's her Gal-Vek. That means... "

"I know what it means." I interrupted.

My irritation seemed to surprise Teddy. In my limited experience, handsome, charming men can never fathom why any woman would be irritated with them. Teddy seemed to suffer from this same annoying affliction.

He continued, "Well, ahh, I've contacted the Tito. I'd hoped they were closer, but they're running far behind schedule. We won't meet them for almost 22 hours. Come with me, Abby, I'll show you how the comms work."

Teddy led me to the bridge and guided me to one of the six cushioned, contoured chairs. My attention was drawn to the viewscreen, a massive, curved window which dominated the front of the bridge. It displayed a star chart, an intricate web of crisscrossing cosmic highways and celestial bodies, the significance of which was lost on me, a novice.

Six separate consoles full of sleek surfaces and touch pads could be seen. The high-tech gadgetry of the bridge was impressive, but I had more important things to discuss with Mr. Bradley. He and I had to get a few things straight. Sebastien and Leanna had retired to one of the seven cabins in back, so we were alone, for now.

He sat next to me and spoke in a hushed tone, "Abby, we need to talk, you and I. Especially with Kara... out of action. You and I must trust one another."

"You're right about one thing, we need to talk. Either you're not telling me something or you *don't know* something, and I don't know which is worse. Whether I can trust you remains to be seen."

Baaqir had made his opinion of Teddy painfully clear, and it was hard for me to dismiss entirely. I was determined, now that I had Teddy to myself, to get to the bottom of this whole thing. I wanted to know what he knew.

"We're in this business together now, Abby, like it or not. Trust is vital. And as I said before, I need you. You have an important role in all of this."

"So you've made clear, but you haven't told me *what* that role is yet. I want to know what the hell you expect of me, Teddy. But first, I have some information for you."

"Ok, shoot."

"When you and Kara were with the green shirts, Baaqir had me up to his observation deck to talk."

"What about?"

"It wasn't a friendly chat; I'll tell you that. He was pissed at us for not telling him about the Academy's dig. Plus, he told me the Academy's dig was sponsored by the Ministry of Security."

"Sponsored? Are you sure that's what Baaqir said?"

"I can't remember the exact words, but yes, I'm sure. He practically slapped me in the face with it. He said the whole thing was the Ministry's idea, and they'd simply recruited the Academy to do the dig. Why is the Ministry of Security interested in Kleos Prime, Teddy?"

"I must apologize, Abby. You're in all this trouble because of me, and that was never part of the plan." Teddy's apology didn't cut it; and he avoided my question, to my immense irritation.

"Shove your damn apologies, Teddy! Do you *realize* what's happened to me since I met you? My life has been turned upside down *because of you.* I've lost my position at the Academy, I've lost my home; I can never go back to Ampora now. I like my home, Teddy! I liked my job! Now I'm a damn *criminal.*" I ranted, "On top of that, your big plan to beat the Academy to artifacts at Kleos is ruined now. We needed that stealth tech from Baaqir, didn't we?"

"All is not lost, my dear. I'm a smuggler, remember? A damn successful one. I've slipped past the CTF many times before, I can do it again."

"You know, when you say I'm in all this trouble because of you, I don't think you realize just how true that is. Care to guess why they sent for me after the dig had already begun?"

"I have no idea. My man at your Academy didn't know and couldn't find out."

"They sent for me because they found *my father's DNA* on Kleos Prime. I was told about it the day after we met. They found an old derma patch and it still had his DNA on it."

"Damn. We must've done a shoddy job of collecting our garbage. We were so careful; I can't believe it."

"Believe it. So, you *truly are* the reason I'm in all this trouble. You and Pop were sloppy." I accused him.

I didn't tell Teddy that I'd heard about the DNA from Gordon; I didn't think it was relevant where I'd heard it. Plus, I was reluctant to bring up my dealings with Gordon, it would steer our discussion in a direction that was beside my point.

"That doesn't change anything. So, they know your old man was there, but they have no idea whether he found anything. The situation hasn't changed, we still have an excellent chance of success."

"Maybe. Baaqir said a lot of other things too. He researched us all since our meeting. He found out about the Academy dig, so he deduced those fragments must've come from Kleos Prime. He knows I've never left Ampora before in my life, so, he knows I wasn't there when you found them. Therefore, he guessed it was my father that went to Kleos with you. I admitted as much to him when he asked me. The man seems to know everything; he even knows about Kara being a fugitive with a price on her head. And he warned me not to trust you, or Kara. He said you were the 'worst sort of scoundrel, pretending to be a gentleman,' or something like that."

"So, now you don't? You trust that greedy degenerate more than me?"

"I'm not sure yet. That's another thing he told me: he said you were controlled by your greed, and only worried about your profits."

"Well, that's the high priest calling the novice a zealot, isn't it?"

"Maybe, but I'd go crazy trying to figure out which one of you is more greedy. But, that's not even what's important. The real question is which one of you I can trust; if either."

"Baaqir's a clever bastard, he knows exactly what to say to drive a wedge between us. He's simply trying to manipulate you, Abby. Don't let him."

"It seems like everybody's trying to manipulate me. But Baaqir said more than that. He believes there's only one reason the Ministry would send an expedition to Kleos Prime; they must be looking for Reges Scientia artifacts. Logically, that's the only explanation."

"You agree with that bastard?"

"As a matter of fact, I do. His logic is sound. They wouldn't be searching for artifacts to put in a museum and they aren't collectors. The only reason for them to send archeologists to Kleos is to search for artifacts that might be of value to *them*, right?"

"And Baaqir believes the only thing of value to them would be artifacts that could lead to technological advancements and new weaponry." Teddy finished my explanation.

"Exactly. Something or someone gave the Ministry of Security the idea Kleos Prime is a good place to look. You avoided the question before, so I'll ask again: Why is the Ministry interested in Kleos Prime?" I demanded, frustrated.

"I honestly don't know. Look, all we know is the Ministry set up an archeological expedition to the Kleos system, and we only heard that from Baaqir."

"I believe him, Teddy. What's his reason to lie?"

"People don't always need a reason to lie, some do it out of habit. A man like that might lie just to entertain himself. I suspect he's just trying to sow mistrust. Seems like it's working."

"Baaqir may be a lot of things, but I don't think he's a liar." I declared. "I believe him."

Teddy looked exasperated with me. "Alright, let's assume the Ministry is behind the dig. But that doesn't prove they know anything was ever found there, that's just supposition. And it certainly doesn't mean they have any idea where to look for artifacts once they get there. It's a big planet, they're just wandering around hoping they stumble on something. I know where your amulet was found, they don't."

"I hope you're right. But they stumbled on that derma patch. There's something else, Teddy. It's been nagging me since you first told me the story about you and my father. Baaqir brought it into focus; he said, the Henry Thornwell of his imagination would've quickly recognized the importance of Kleos Prime. I don't need to imagine; I *knew* my father; he *would've* quickly seen the importance."

"What's your point, my dear?"

"Dammit Teddy, if my father believed Kleos was important, a herd of wild katapans couldn't have dragged him away from there. He would've at least demanded to return. Why'd you wait 20 years, Teddy? You're still not telling me something, and I'm telling you right now, if you want my help you better come clean."

He lowered his voice even further, and peeked past me into the center of the ship to make sure no one else could hear.

"Alright, Abby. I have to tell you sooner or later anyway; it might as well be sooner. But you must swear to me this goes no further. You can't tell anyone, especially your new friends back there. I don't trust that Fowler chap, he's too clever by half. And his little girlfriend doesn't have the subtlety required to keep secrets. But first, you haven't shown your amulet to anyone else, have you?"

"No, only you and Kara know about it. Some friends back home, but they don't know what it is."

"Good. Make sure to keep it that way. You mustn't tell anyone what it really is, that's crucial."

"Alright, alright, I won't. But *why*, dammit?"

"What I'm about to tell you, no one in the universe knows but me, not even Kara. I've kept this secret for over twenty years, only because Henry made me swear. He made me swear on my *life*, Abby. There *is* more to the story, just as you say."

"I want to hear all of it, no more secrets."

Teddy rubbed his eyes and leaned closer, "We didn't have to go *back* to Kleos Prime. Once was enough; we found what we went there for. Ancient artifacts from a civilization never recorded before; Henry and I both believed so. A technologically advanced civilization."

"So, you found something more than my amulet and those other metal fragments?"

"We did." Teddy stood, "We should have a drink. Or, I should say I *need* a drink. Will you have one with me?"

"Why not; I get the feeling I might need one after you tell me this secret of yours."

"Not *my* secret, my dear. Your father's."

He left me for a few moments and returned with two glasses and a bottle of brandy. An expensive brand, the only kind someone like Cyrus Baaqir would stock on his personal yacht. He poured us each a snifter and sat next to me again.

"To be fair, I suppose it's accurate to say it was *our* secret, Henry and I. But it was his idea to keep it secret. Abby, you told me before that you're familiar with your father's codex, the Codex of Kafo. How familiar?"

"I studied that damn thing, off and on, for half my life growing up. I confess I haven't looked at it in ages now. I never had the knack for understanding it like Pop did."

"But, you know Henry thought that thing was full of galactic history. Even predictions of future events?"

"I'm aware."

"I always thought it was crazy, I mean why would a petty despot from an otherwise unimportant planet like Galbrod know anything about galactic history? Let alone the future. The Galbrodi weren't even capable of interstellar travel. But your father was convinced Huru Bastar was some kind of clairvoyant or something. Turns out your father was on to something."

"What does that codex have to do with Kleos Prime?"

"*Everything*, as it turns out. You see, Henry pinpointed several references in the codex to an ancient civilization which Bastar referred to as the Hoji Mubrani."

"What's Hoji Mubrani mean?" I asked. My father had been the only person alive who could actually read ancient Galbrodi. Now, there was no one.

"Henry said it meant 'Holy Scientists' or 'Priests of Science' in ancient Galbrodi. That was his translation. Those passages refer to the demise of the Hoji Mubrani civilization. Their 'Armageddon,' so to speak. In addition, there's passages that contain distances from the galactic center, proximities to other astronomical bodies, and descriptions of nearby historical events. Henry believed the codex gave the location of the Mubrani Armageddon."

This was getting good. For an archaeologist, a location meant one thing: A dig, and physical artifacts.

"I can see where this is going. My father thought these Hoji Mubrani were the Reges Scientia civilization of legend, because he translated their name as 'Priests of Science.' That sort of sounds like wishful thinking."

Wishful thinking, but not entirely illogical either. Gods, could it really be possible? My irritation with Teddy was forgotten as he continued his story.

"I know it sounds crazy, and that's what I thought too. But Henry and I'd been partners for years by then and I knew better than to doubt him."

"You two traveled all over searching for the site of this Armageddon, is that it?"

"Simply stated, yes. We spent years chasing dead ends. I told you Henry was obsessed, and that's the truth. Eventually, all he seemed to care about was finding the place." He downed his drink, and poured another.

"What was he hoping to find?" I asked, unable to hide my excitement. I knew my father wouldn't have obsessed lightly. There had to be something to it for him to go to such lengths.

"He claimed a passage in the codex told of something left behind, hidden under a mountain. A legacy."

"A legacy? What kind of legacy?"

"The codex isn't specific. You know how that thing reads, all metaphors and allusions, riddles and allegories. I humored him, and the whole time my business suffered. We searched more than a dozen worlds before we finally went to Kleos Prime. When we got there I didn't think it could be the same place. The codex describes a lush and beautiful planet, but Kleos Prime is ugly, and desolate. The planet has several small mountain ranges, but one that's clearly the most prominent, so that's where we searched."

"What'd you find, for Gods' sake?" I asked, "Stop torturing me."

"Deep below a mountain on Kleos Prime there's a chamber, inside of which was what I can only describe as a large vault, half buried in volcanic rock."

"What do you mean, a vault?"

"Exactly that. Listen, the vault is made of the same material as your amulet. There was a door on the exposed side with a set of large dials in the middle. Those dials had hundreds of the same style of markings as your amulet. It was reminiscent of a bank vault, so we started calling it 'the vault.'"

"That's incredible, and perfectly logical. Many societies bury things; remains, treasure, religious or cultural items. My father must've been thrilled out of his mind; it's the sort of thing archaeologists fantasize about. But, something buried by an ancient, *technologically advanced* civilization has never been discovered. How big was this vault?"

"Big." Teddy chuckled, "Our scans showed it was a little more than 10 meters wide, about 14 meters deep, and around 3 ½ meters high."

"Gods, Teddy, that's bigger than my apartment. There could've been anything in that thing."

"That was our reaction, exactly. As you can imagine Henry wouldn't rest until we found out what was in it. I had no tools that could cut into it, and besides, Henry didn't want to damage the vault. So, we spent several weeks there with Henry attempting to open it using those dials. The problem is there's 17 dials on that door, creating billions and billions of possible combinations."

"I'll bet that didn't deter him at all, did it?" I smiled.

"Not a damn bit." Teddy chuckled. "We spent weeks there, Henry never gave up, and he eventually figured it out."

"How?"

"After weeks of failure, Henry finally realized the symbols weren't letters from an alphabet, they were numbers. The Mubrani used base twelve mathematics."

"Like the ancient Egyptians on Old Earth. So, what was the combination? What was in that vault?" I asked.

Teddy shook his head, "I don't know about any Egyptians, but Henry unlocked the vault by using your amulet; don't ask me how, but it's the key. Your amulet apparently contains a mathematical equation or something. Something about fibba somebody."

"Fibonacci?" I excitedly reached inside my shirt and pulled out my amulet.

"I think that was it. I was never any good at math, I just figured what's the point? You always have a comms or computer at your fingertips. But that sounds right."

"Come on Teddy, I'm dying of suspense. What was inside? Gold? Jewels? Engineering specs? The secrets of the universe?" I pressed him. "All of the above?"

"Books. Hundreds and hundreds of books, all the same size and shape, about 30 x 20 cm, with two rings for a binder. Some were just a few pages; some were dozens of pages. The vault was a library, or as Henry called it, a treasure house of the culture's history."

"Books? Just books and nothing else? Why'd Pop think the civilization's history was in the books?"

"It's a logical guess, I suppose. But, he believed strongly the vault was an attempt by the Mubrani to preserve their accumulated knowledge for posterity, in tangible form. According to the codex, they knew they were about to be destroyed. Given that context, I suppose burying a library isn't so crazy."

"But the civilization could be hundreds of thousands of years old. No book could last that long."

"Abby, the books were made of paper-thin sheets of that same alloy. They were as good as new, no corrosion, no rust, no patina of any kind.

There was etching on both sides of the pages resembling the symbols on the vault's door. The Hoji Mubrani language is incredibly complex. There were hundreds and hundreds of unique symbols we identified while we were there. Who knows how many there actually are; maybe thousands. Henry told me there were languages on Old Earth, like Mandarin, that had thousands of unique symbols."

"That's true. Theoretically, it could take a lifetime to decipher a language like that."

After I said it I realized the man most able to accomplish such a feat had been dead for 8 ½ years.

Teddy said, "Not surprisingly, that's almost exactly what Henry said."

"This amulet didn't come from any core sample, did it Teddy? Where'd you really find it? The truth."

"We didn't drill any core samples, and there was no ruined city. The amulet was attached to the vault itself. It had a release switch or something, Henry's the one who discovered it. I made up the story about an ancient city because I wasn't sure yet if I could trust you with knowledge of the vault. I'm sorry, but I thought it necessary to be cautious. After all, you and I'd just met."

I was looking at the amulet in a new light. If the symbols were numbers representing the Fibonacci sequence there was a chance I could figure out how to open the thing. I couldn't be sure until I laid eyes on the door, but I thought I might at least have a chance.

"He didn't tell you the combination?"

"Unfortunately, no. I wasn't present when he opened it. The only thing I know is that fibba, equation thing. Perhaps, between the two of us we'll figure it out. And, Kara; she's uncommonly clever. We'll put our heads together."

"Gods, Teddy, it was a jackpot. Not one codex, but hundreds of them. The entire recorded history of an ancient civilization. It literally *could* be the secrets of the universe. What'd the two of you do with all those books?" I asked, visions of the alien library permeating my thoughts.

"Nothing."

"Nothing? What do you mean, nothing?" I was raising my voice, Teddy signaled me to lower it. "Surely my father tried to decipher the language, right?"

"The rest of the story I told you was true, my dear. After his Dectus Artiga friends had all been killed or imprisoned, Henry wouldn't risk the Alliance getting their hands on that library. We'd been there half a year already, there was no time for deciphering. Like you said, that could take a lifetime. He took his notes with him when we left, though."

"He did? Our little house was packed to the rafters with boxes of papers when he died. Gods, I donated it all to the archives. Those notes are still there, probably unpacked."

"Very likely, I'd say. That's an excellent place for safe keeping. We debated how best to hide the library from the Alliance. Henry didn't want to risk taking it back to Ampora, the Academy is crawling with secret police informants just like all the universities. He had no place to store so many books in his little house, and I had no place *safe* to keep them either. I have a villa on Kyntava, but it's no place to hide the secrets of the universe from the Ministry of Security. Kyntava is an Alliance planet, it's also crawling with informants."

"So, you left them there, on Kleos Prime. In the vault."

"Exactly. What place could be safer than an impenetrable vault, hidden deep underground, on a remote planet with no life. It was the perfect hiding place for thousands of years; until now, that is."

"And, now, we've come full circle, Teddy. We're right back to the question of why the Ministry is interested in Kleos Prime."

"I have no idea, and it doesn't matter. I'll be damned if I'll let the bloody bastards lay their hands on that library. I owe Henry that, at least."

"You didn't board the Archeron just to meet me. All you really wanted was my amulet, isn't that true?"

"Nonsense, my dear. You were always an integral part of ours plans. The fact is, I don't think I'd have much luck opening the vault without you, even with your amulet. And, in the back of my mind I wondered if maybe Henry had relented and told you about the thing. And how to open it."

"Well, he didn't. He kept the secret, just like you did."

"More's the pity. I would've told you about the vault sooner, but I had to be sure I could trust you. Now, I am. And *that* brings us full circle to my point: You and I need to trust each other. Do you trust me, Abby?"

"As long as there's no more secrets, my friend. I want to open that vault, and I want to keep it out of the hands of the Alliance as bad as you do. The enemy of my enemy is my friend."

"Friends, then." Teddy shook my hand. "The secret of the vault would've died with me, except for this expedition by your Academy. Ironically, I'm beginning to think, in a way, the expedition was a stroke of luck."

"Bad luck, I'd say."

"Possibly, but think about it like this: If not for the expedition, I might've died thinking the secret would be safe forever. *You* might've died never knowing what your amulet actually is. That vault might not have been discovered again for hundreds of years, maybe thousands of years. I'm pretty sure Henry intended just that." Teddy took a deep breath, "Abby, what if I told you I think Henry and I made a huge mistake all those years ago?"

"What mistake? Besides leaving the patch behind?"

"We have a second chance, you and I. If we can get to that vault before they do, and take that library away, we can share it with the rest of the galaxy. I think that's what Henry and I should've done 23 years ago. When Dectus Artiga was wiped out, it twisted our thinking into knots. We were so worried about what would happen if the Alliance got ahold of the library, we didn't stop to consider what might happen if they *didn't*."

"What do you mean?"

"Abby, what if the library holds secrets that could end war forever? Or feed everyone who's hungry? Or, make unlimited energy for everyone? That library could actually be the key to *defeating* the Telluric Alliance once and for all. We successfully kept it out of their hands, but here we are 23 years later and nothing has changed. The Alliance is still rolling over everyone in their way. Their racist laws keep billions in submission; millions more have lost their lives to the CTF. Maybe the secrets hidden in the library can put an end to all of that."

"We have no way of knowing what's in that library, remember that Reges Scientia stuff is just a theory. But, having said that, I think I agree with you. Whatever's in there shouldn't be hidden away for thousands of years a second time. We need to grab it before they do."

My mind was racing, running away with visions of all the amazing discoveries to be had from the alien library. I was more excited than I could ever remember being. I couldn't wait to see that vault, touch it, open it and reveal its secrets. But, I had one more question for Teddy.

"Teddy, I understand why you kept the vault a secret from everyone else. But, honestly, I would've liked to have known about what you did with my father; why'd he never tell me about it? And why didn't I meet you before a few days ago?"

"Abby, I'm sorry, but that was Henry's idea."

"What? Why?"

"He thought, in order to keep the secret, we shouldn't tell you about our partnership. He believed you wouldn't be satisfied just hearing about our activities, you'd want to follow in our footsteps. That would've put you in great danger. In fact, it has. Just look what's happened."

"He couldn't have known that." I argued.

Teddy laughed, "Really? Be honest, you could've left our suite that first night we met and never spoken to me again. Did that even cross your mind? Or were you champing at the bit to hear more about Henry's exploits?"

"Well... I guess you have a point."

"We need to share the library with everyone in the galaxy, not just humans. If only we'd had the courage to try that 23 years ago, things might be very different now."

"Alright, I'm sorry for tearing into you like I did earlier. I shouldn't have blamed you for everything that's happened, I'm an adult and I made my own choices. I'm glad you introduced yourself to me, Teddy. I'm happy you told me about my father's *exploits*, as you call them. Without you and Kara I wouldn't know about any of that, or what the Alliance has been up to. So, thanks."

"Actually, it was Kara's idea to come find you. It was a good idea; Kara's ideas often are. Now you know the whole story, and why I needed you *and* your amulet. I really am sorry about getting you in trouble with the green shirts; that was never part of the plan."

"What're friends for, right?" I smiled. "Teddy, that little Tubau guy was with Baaqir in the observatory. He said they've impounded several of your ships and your business is suffering. Is that true, or was he just trying to make himself look good in Baaqir's eyes?"

"You're worried I'm broke, Abby?" He chuckled. "Don't worry, I've lost a few ships to the bastards but we've recently branched out into more lucrative pursuits than smuggling brandy; we're currently more profitable than ever."

"More lucrative pursuits? Like smuggling weapons to rebels? Does that pay well?"

"As a matter of fact, it does. But, it's also for a good cause. You might be surprised, but there are plenty of people in the quadrant besides Kara and me who don't like the Telluric Alliance; including many humans. There are a few brave, resilient people fighting against the CTF. I try to provide them with the means when I can. That shipment aboard the Archeron was on the way to some of them."

"Do those Karmarinski brothers have anything to do with your arms dealing?"

"How do you know about them?"

"I was in Tasha's and saw you arguing with them."

"You were in Tasha's? Well, well, you do get around. Those two are erstwhile suppliers of mine, Benny and Orlo Karmarinski. Two extremely unpleasant brothers from the seedier alleys and festering slag heaps of New Britain. They're nothing more than bloody gangsters, but as it happens quite useful to me, until now. I'm afraid any trust I had in them, and there was never much, has disappeared."

"They looked like they were ready to kill you. How were they useful?"

"They're certainly capable of such a thing, but I had Kara with me so I wasn't worried. They were there to collect payment for some weapons they procured for me. They're very bold and skillful hijackers, you see.

We had a difference of opinion about my payment. I paid the price agreed upon in advance, but they wanted me to pay a bonus because of the difficulty they'd had. The reason we went to the cargo hold to check our goods was to make sure the Karmarinskis hadn't discovered them. There was no reason to believe they knew the merchandise was aboard the Archeron, but Benny and Orlo are clever, resourceful, and dangerous. It always pays to be careful."

"So, you're not going to do business with them anymore? How will you get your weapons?"

"We have other sources. Weapons can be bought on several different free planets, but they aren't as good as the Telluric weapons the brothers steal. Abby, I appreciate your concern but you shouldn't worry yourself about that part of my business. Kara and I have it under control."

"I know, I'm obnoxiously nosey, but I need to know what kind of people I'm involved with. You know, Baaqir admitted to me he's been 'facilitating' your arms dealing. Did you know that?"

"No, I didn't know for sure, but I suspected something. The devious bastard, he's the high priest of greed, you see? He's so greedy he assists me selling weapons to the insurgents, so he can sell more to the oppressors. Kara and I turn a decent profit, but Dressida Research Group makes billions; war is big business. This was good, this talk. It's good to get things out in the open, and I'm unbelievably relieved I finally told *somebody* about that bloody vault; it's like I've been set free after all these years. And, I'm certainly glad to have you with us."

"I'm with you, Teddy. There *is* one big problem with your whole scheme, though: I'm not Henry Thornwell. My father was a legendarily brilliant puzzle solver, and I'm not. It seems to me your plan depends on opening that vault."

"We can work on it together. Besides, I have confidence in you."

"That makes one of us. And, the Academy expedition is already at Kleos Prime, we might be too late."

"We have one huge advantage going for us. They don't know about the vault nor do they have the slightest idea *where* to look. It'd be a minor miracle if they found it."

"Let's pray you're right."

He smiled and said, "I'm not the praying type, my dear, but you go ahead if it'll make you feel better. I'll take all the help I can get."

"Alright, I'm going to sit with Kara for a while. Let me know if you remember anything else my father told you about the vault combination, besides the Fibonacci sequence." I said as I left him alone on the bridge.

"Will do, Abby."

My mind was in a whirl after the conversation with Teddy. One thing of concern dampened my enthusiasm: It was clear to me my father didn't completely trust Teddy. Bradley didn't know how to open the vault. Obviously, Pop had purposely never allowed Bradley to watch him open it, and just as obviously it was because he didn't want Teddy to know how. With this realization, only a fool would trust Teddy Bradley completely.

Pulling a chair from the galley next to Kara's bed in sick bay, I sat with her for a long time, just watching her breath and thinking about what Teddy had told me. I wanted to be mad at him for not telling me about the vault sooner, but I honestly understood completely. He deserved a great deal of credit for keeping the existence of the vault a secret for so long. In his place I don't think I could have.

He and Kara had shamelessly manipulated me into coming with them, but I couldn't be angry about that either. Their stories about the CTF, and the stressful interview I endured with Commander Gordon helped to make up my mind. But again, honestly, I chose to go with them for personal reasons, like Baaqir had guessed. My burgeoning relationship with Kara, along with the fact I was following in my father's footsteps were the true reasons I found myself there. And after the revelation about the vault, I was determined to see my adventure through.

Once I succumbed to exhaustion, I was tormented by feverish nightmares in which I was being chased by green shirts, or perhaps a squad of allied marines. I also dreamed about our rescue of Teddy, reliving the moment I'd stabbed the nameless green shirt officer; the sickening 'shlock' sound of my dagger sinking home finally waking me. The memory of the gore in that waiting room brought me to the brink of being sick all over again.

Still exhausted, I slept once more, this time dreaming of sitting cuddled up next to Cyrus Baaqir on his wide sofa. I was dressed in a sheer, see-through wrap like his little slave girls had been, and stroking his hairless head as he said, "I told you I'd add you to my collection, Abigail. It amuses me."

Part Eleven Sebastien Fowler

Interstellar Date: 388-06-23
On Board the Avernus

WHEN I FINALLY WOKE up for good, Kara still hadn't regained consciousness. Restless and tired because of the poor sleep, I went looking for Teddy and found him with Sebastien on the bridge, in the midst of a heated debate about something.

"Look, I appreciate your situation, but there's no way I'll abandon my goods back there. I have to go back and retrieve them." Teddy said.

"Bradley, I don't give a rat's ass about your 'goods.' Leanna and I want to go to MK141. That's all there is to it." Sebastien replied. It was about as animated as I'd seen him.

"What are you boys talking about?" I asked cheerily, trying to ease some of the tension. "Have either of you checked on Kara recently?"

Sebastien sighed, "Actually, Professor, I just came from there. She seems to be doing much better. Her vital signs are good, at least based on what Captain Bradley told me is normal for her. Her pulse has improved, and her breathing has eased. She was resting much easier than you were, if you don't mind me saying. However, for some reason I can't figure out, she hasn't woken up yet." His usual calm demeanor had returned. "I suppose, if she were human, I'd say she's slipped into a coma. With a Tovolek, I'm not sure."

"Thank you, Sebastien, for helping her. I owe you." I said.

"No one owes me anything, Professor. I've been trained and I consider it an honor to help." Sebastien said. "I only hope I didn't do something wrong; I've never encountered a Tovolek before and neither has that sickbay."

Teddy said, "You did a fine job, Fowler. She simply lost a lot of blood, and her natural regenerative processes have taken over. Based on past experience, once she wakes she'll be good as new."

"I hope you're right." Sebastien offered.

"Never fear. Tovoleks are notoriously difficult to kill." Teddy smiled, seemingly unworried. "And Kara's more difficult than most."

"So, we shouldn't be worried that she hasn't woken up yet?" I asked him.

"Why hasn't who woken up?" Kara asked as she entered the bridge.

Teddy's face lit up like he'd won a lottery, "There's your answer, Professor. I told you she was a quick healer."

Incredibly, Kara had simply walked to the bridge on her injured leg, without crutches and without assistance. A clear, medical sleeve was wrapped around her thigh, and at first glance it appeared the incision was practically healed already. The sickbay had done a marvelous job on her leg. Or, perhaps, Teddy was correct about her incredible healing abilities.

I rushed over and gave her a hug, saying to Teddy as I went, "Don't call me Professor, Teddy. I'm not one anymore." Then to Kara, "Hey you, I forbid you to get shot ever again, you scared me half to death." But I couldn't keep the smile off my face as I said it.

"Don't worry, little human, it would take many more projectiles than that to do me any real harm." she replied, but she sounded tired for the first time since I'd known her.

"Alright, Kara, let's get you to my cabin so you can take a shower and get some rest. Then I'm going to come back and speak to these two about what we do next." I grabbed Kara's hand and started toward my cabin.

"I'm fine Abby, I need to talk to Teddy." she said.

"You will, but you need to get out of these bloody clothes, get cleaned up and changed and then you can join our discussion, no arguments." I told her. "I'll ask Leanna to make you something to eat while you shower, you must be starving. Leanna's our executive chef, it's like eating at a 5-star restaurant."

"Yes, Dr. Thornwell." she said sarcastically, but she went with me anyway.

I left Kara in my cabin and went to find Leanna. I knocked on her door and I asked if she'd prepare some food for Kara. "With meat."

Returning to the bridge, I said "Alright, fill me in on what I've missed while I slept."

Teddy went first, "We're on course to rendezvous with my ship, the Tito, near where Baaqir jettisoned my cargo. We should meet them approximately 12 hours from now. Fowler and I were just discussing what to do afterward. He and I have different plans for the Avernus, it seems."

Sebastien, clearly irritated, said, "This ship doesn't belong to you, Bradley. I'll be damned if you're going to tell me what to do with it. Professor, I was unaware until just a few minutes ago that Bradley had set a course *back* to where he thinks his cargo is."

"Strictly speaking my friend, this vessel doesn't belong to you either. It doesn't belong to Baaqir anymore either, poor devil. Your lady friend has made sure of that." Teddy said.

"Well, about that. It still belongs to Baaqir; I'm 99% sure he's still alive." Sebastien said.

Surprised, Teddy said, "What are you talking about? I saw the man go down in a heap, shot through the chest."

I interrupted before Sebastien could answer, "The bastard has two hearts, Teddy. Leanna told me he's got an artificial heart attached to his chest that takes over when the real one stops, it's one of his augmentations."

"I wondered what that contraption on his chest was. That'd make him hard to kill, that's for sure. Maybe I should get one of those. Too bad, I was hoping we'd seen the last of him." Teddy said.

"Baaqir, alive or dead, isn't here." I said, "So, in my opinion this ship belongs to the five of us, like a pirate crew. Don't pirate crews share equally in all the spoils, Teddy?"

"They do, at that."

"I'm not sure I agree." Sebastien argued, "I'm the one who had the idea to take it. I'm the one who had the access codes to the shuttle bay and ship. Leanna 'persuaded' Baaqir to let us go and opened the bay's outer doors for us. I'd say the Avernus belongs to Leanna and me if it belongs to anyone." I didn't know if I could argue with any of that.

Leanna called, "Everyone, please come to the galley. I've made a meal, you three can talk in there."

We all filed into the galley and sat around the largest table. Kara soon joined us, and it was the five conspirators, all together. We sat and ate the excellent food Leanna had prepared, which included some chops just a little past bloody, the way Kara liked them.

Sebastien began, "We can assume Baaqir will be looking for us. I've disabled the Avernus' transponder, and we're proceeding on autopilot and in dark mode. It's possible he's placed tracking devices on board. I've done a cursory sweep and discovered none, but that's a guarantee of nothing. The CTF is also looking for this vessel. I shouldn't need to say we *do not* want to be found by either of them."

Kara asked, "Speaking of the CTF, what sort of armaments does this ship have? What are our chances if we encounter one of their ships?"

"This ship is surprisingly well armed. We have anti-matter torpedo launchers and particle guns fore and aft. But the main weapon is a mid-ship MIP Plasma Cannon which, when coupled with our reactor output, is guaranteed to ruin someone's day." Sebastien told us. "I've seen the thing test fired once and it was rather spectacular."

"What's MIP mean?" I asked.

Sebastien answered, "Magnetic-Induced Phased Plasma. It fires a bolt of superheated hydrogen plasma. The usual drawback is the power it takes to fire it, but the Avernus doesn't have that problem. Our reactor is a prototype, experimental model that produces 3.3 times the normal output for one its size."

"That's fantastic," Kara said, "I've never heard of a ship this size equipped with that type of weapon."

"The armor and shielding are also state of the art. Dressida Research Group is the most prolific weapon manufacturer in Telluric space, and Baaqir controls DRG corp. The Avernus is basically a gunship disguised as a luxury yacht." Sebastien sounded proud. "But, I'm not sure about our chances with a CTF warship, let's hope we don't have to find out."

"What about cargo space?" Kara asked.

"There's a fairly large cargo bay below us. Not as big as a ship designed specifically for it, but everywhere Baaqir goes he looks for things to buy to add to his collection." Sebastien answered.

"Excellent." Kara said. "I'll take a look in a while to make sure our goods will fit."

Sebastien said, "It'll probably fit, but is your cargo safe?"

"Not for our enemies, it's not." Kara answered sarcastically.

Sebastien remained calm, but I was starting to see when he was annoyed. He clinched his jaw slightly and shrugged his muscular shoulders noticeably. He was a man used to command and didn't like it when he wasn't in control. Our little group might have too many leaders to function properly, I realized.

Teddy said, "We'll be rendezvousing with the Tito in a few hours, near where Baaqir jettisoned my cargo. I'll not just leave it out there floating in space, it's too valuable. Besides, we may need it. But getting the Tito to Kleos will be problematic without the stealth gadget we were supposed to get from Baaqir."

"Why not just take the Avernus to Kleos?" I asked.

Several voices started, but Kara spoke over them, "I agree. I love the Tito, but after what Fowler told us, this ship is better armed. I like our chances better aboard this yacht."

Teddy said, "If Baaqir is still alive we need to contact him. The entire point of meeting with him was to gain access to that stealth tech. Nothing has changed, whatever ship we take to Kleos Prime; it'll be far easier if we're stealthy. So, we should try again to negotiate for the tech. I'm sure you all agree."

There were murmurs of agreement from around the table. However, I wasn't so sure Baaqir would even talk to us. He'd probably like to see us all with ropes around our necks.

"Sebastien, when I walked in on you and Teddy earlier you said something about taking Leanna to MK141. Where is that and why would you go there?" I asked him to change the topic.

"Well, Professor, MK141 is a free planet outside of Telluric space. And, I have a good friend there who can help us start a new life, away from Mr. Baaqir and his cronies."

The two lovers were simply running off to be together, they had no stake in our Kleos adventure. My problem was I liked Leanna and I'd even grown fond of Sebastien. He'd saved my life in the fighting against the green shirts aboard the Archeron. And he'd proven himself capable under pressure.

"Sebastien, how can I persuade you to put your escape plans on hold for a while and help us at Kleos Prime? You're very capable. I've seen you shoot." I laughed, "And we could certainly use your help. Afterward, I'm sure no one would object to you taking the Avernus. What do you say?"

"Another suicide mission? You people don't have much of a plan, just rush there and beat them to it? I'd be a fool to sign up for that."

"It won't be a suicide mission. Those green shirts are easy to kill. You and I killed 5 of them in as many minutes." Kara said with a big smile. I wanted to say she also got shot and damn near bled to death, but held my tongue.

"We'll have a plan by the time we meet the Tito, I guarantee." Teddy asserted.

In this discussion our problem was revealed. If we wanted Sebastien's help at Kleos(and I did), we probably had to tell him about the vault. Otherwise, he'd just think we didn't have much hope. But Teddy would never agree to that. In twenty years he hadn't even told Kara about it; he'd never agree to tell Sebastien.

"Sebastien, you could help them devise a plan. You're very clever." Leanna said helpfully.

Kara interrupted, "Fowler, I've been thinking about something you said just a while ago. You said we were proceeding on autopilot and in dark mode."

"Yes?"

"Well, what exactly does 'dark mode' mean? I don't think I've ever heard that term before." She asked.

"It's a capability the Avernus has. It dampens the signature of the ship and lowers our profile to other ships' sensor arrays. The controls are on the console next to the autopilot. It's simple to use, I can show you." He explained.

"Holy hell! This ship has the bloody stealth device installed!" Teddy exclaimed. "This whole time it's been right under our noses. Can you believe that?"

"Is that what it is?" Sebastien asked. "I never heard it referred to as stealth tech, just dark mode."

"I'm absolutely positive! Baaqir called it a QSDM, Quantum State something, something." Teddy said, "Kara, you're a damn genius as well as beautiful."

"Thank you, master." Kara said, "You're not bad either, but it's called a Quantum State *Disruption Manipulator*."

"Well, that's a mouthful; what exactly does it do?" Leanna asked.

"From what I understand, the device creates a pocket of space inside of which the quantum state of matter has been altered." Teddy explained. "Rendering the ship undetectable."

"You told Baaqir you didn't know how it worked." Sebastien said.

"And I don't; not really. I'm no engineer, I couldn't tell you how a bloody toaster works." Teddy claimed.

"I'm beginning to think you know way more than you like to admit, Bradley." Sebastien accused.

Teddy smiled and replied, "A universe without guile would be a boring place to live."

"And this device is on right now? Our quantum state has been altered? I don't feel any different." Kara said.

"It's on." Sebastien said. "I've been aboard the Avernus many times when the thing was on, I've never noticed feeling any different. It must not be noticeable to people on the ship."

"Creepy." said Leanna. "I suppose I've also been aboard when it was on. I never noticed anything."

"So, if we take the Avernus to Kleos Prime, the CTF warships won't be able to detect us, right?" I asked.

"Theoretically." Teddy said. "Though Baaqir said it hasn't been tested thoroughly. I guess we'll get the chance."

"Wait, don't I have a say in this?" Sebastien wasn't giving in that easily.

"Come on Fowler, surely you can see the Avernus will make it easier to get to Kleos, right? This ship already has the stealth tech installed." Teddy reasoned. "I can have the Tito give you a lift anywhere you want to go. Even to MK141; though why you'd go to that backwater hell, I can't imagine."

"I told you; my friend lives there. He has a government position and can help us."

"Fowler, obviously we can use the stealth capability. Dodging frigates is for desperate fools or idiots." Kara told him. "Plus, we could use *you* too, you're an excellent warrior." That was a meaningful compliment coming from Kara the Demon.

"I'll second that, Sebastien. We want you with us, you've saved my life once already." I told him. "I'd hate to lose you now."

"I'll think about it." he said. "But, I was planning on selling the Avernus to raise coin for a new start. Leanna and I have deposit accounts on the Archeron, but Baaqir will've frozen those by now. We aren't exactly well set for coin as it stands."

"I sympathize, Fowler. But, we're trying to save the bloody galaxy; you don't want to miss out on that, do you?" Teddy asked. "I can offer you some compensation if that's what you're worried about. I have ample coin."

Sebastien did his shrug again but said nothing. We let the discussion drop at that point. We were still a while away from our rendezvous. Sebastien went to the bridge to stand watch on the sensors. So far, we'd been lucky, we'd seen no other ships.

"Is it unusual to go so long without seeing any other ships on the sensors?" I asked.

"Not really. That's one of the wonderful things about space, there's so bloody much of it." Teddy said.

Kara, Teddy, and I took seats in the salon. I found the climate on the Avernus a bit claustrophobic after the huge cruise ship. The artificial gravity on the Avernus was less consistent, the air was less sweet and more humid, acoustics were less subtle, etc. I preferred the larger ship, which Kara assured me was common.

"Those huge cruise ships like the Archeron are designed to seem as close to being 'planet bound' as possible. The wealthy passengers don't want to be inconvenienced by feeling like they're in space while they're in space." She said, sarcastically. "Don't worry, little human, soon you'll be an old hand at this. You'll be able to join a pirate crew."

"I thought I already had."

Leanna brought a pot of coffee and joined our group. "Can I sit with you? I'm letting Sebastien have some time to consider your proposal." she asked as she poured us each a cup.

"Of course, make yourself comfy, Leanna." I told her. "I never turn down a cup of coffee." But I noticed a look pass between Teddy and Kara. Teddy had admitted to me he didn't trust Sebastien; I guess that went for Leanna too.

"Do you think he'll come along with us?" Teddy asked her.

"He's a careful person and will take his time to consider his options. I don't think he makes hasty decisions; but, I believe he'll consider your proposition with an open mind." Leanna answered.

I took a sip of coffee and asked, "Teddy, do you think it's possible to remove the stealth device from this ship and put it in the Tito?"

"It's possible, but now it seems like an unnecessary hassle. Snyder is a talented engineer, but there's no sense in ripping the thing out of this ship if we don't have to. We just need to convince Fowler to come with us, and none of that is necessary." Teddy said, then he turned to Leanna again, "If it's a matter of coin, I'm positive we can work something out."

"Mr. Bradley, not everything is about coin. I don't think that's what concerns Sebastien. I'm afraid he's awfully protective of me, and he might consider joining you an unnecessary risk." Leanna explained. "Frankly, I'm not sure he's wrong. I'm sorry."

"If we want to convince him to join us, he needs to believe there's a reasonable chance of succeeding." I said. "One of us needs to talk with him and explain what we're after. But, I don't think there's any point in telling him it won't be dangerous, he wouldn't believe it anyway."

"We have to stop the Tellurians from acquiring any new technologies there." Kara said. "Plus, the difficult part will be convincing them there's no reason to try again."

"What do you mean?" I asked.

"Well, this is hypothetical, but imagine we simply attack the expedition and wipe it out, scientists and green shirts included. That would gain us nothing but a bit of time, because the Alliance would simply mount another expedition, one that's more heavily defended. We need a way to stop them now, *and* make sure they can't succeed in the future." Kara summed up.

Wiping out the whole expedition, even as a hypothetical, wasn't something that would've crossed my mind. I was still thinking like an academy professor, not like an anti-Telluric Alliance subversive/terrorist, if that's what I'd become. It might take a while before I could think like Kara.

"We should find a way to do what we need to do, but without killing any more than we already have. I've seen enough bloodshed this week to last me for the rest of my life." I said.

"I have no problem killing those CTF scum. Sorry, Abby, I know you're new to all of this." Kara told me. "But you have a point. We can accomplish what we've set out to do without killing. Ideally, we land, find whatever artifacts are there, and lift off without them even knowing we were there. We just have to make sure we find *all* the artifacts, leaving nothing for them."

We all went quiet for a while. Teddy was unnaturally silent, deep in thought about our situation, I assumed. Leanna had been noticeably quiet, as well. I knew her bubbly personality hid a clever mind. She must've had thoughts about our situation, but she was keeping them to herself.

I turned to her and asked, "Leanna, do you want to come with us?"

"Abby, my friend, I'll do as Sebastien pleases. I'll go where he goes. I chose Sebastien over my master, and therefore I've committed myself to him. My opinion doesn't matter."

"Leanna, that's just not true! Your opinion absolutely matters. You didn't just swap one master for another, you're free now. I know Sebastien values your opinion, if he loves you, he *must*." I argued. I hoped what I was saying was true. Perhaps I'm just too idealistic, or naïve.

"Abby, I think maybe you're right about Sebastien. But, even still, I'll do as he says. He's incredibly clever, and I trust he'll decide what's best. But, if I may, I think there's a significant problem with your plan."

"What's that?" Kara and I said at practically the same time.

"Your plan is to gather all the artifacts on Kleos Prime, leaving nothing for your enemies. But how will you be sure you've collected them *all*? It's a whole planet, you could spend years looking and still not be *positive* you've found everything. I'm sorry, but that's what I think."

The three of us sat silent, struck by the realization Leanna was certainly correct. There'd be no way of knowing if we'd collected *all* artifacts on Kleos Prime. Even Teddy and I, possessed of the knowledge of the vault, couldn't be *positive* the library within it was the only valuable artifact to be found on the planet.

Teddy announced as he stood, "If you'll excuse me, I think I'll turn in. I have some thinking to do. Kara, would you join me, I believe I could use your input."

I wanted to argue, but as Kara stood to follow Teddy, I couldn't come up with anything to say. I assumed he'd decided to confide in Kara, and didn't want to speak in front of Leanna. How could I convince him to include Leanna and Sebastien in the secret?

"I think your point was made, Leanna." I told her. "You've given us a lot to think about."

I wasn't sleepy, so I decided to go to the bridge to talk with the former head of security; Leanna joined me. We found him scrolling through star charts, apparently in the midst of some calculations.

"Hey, Sebastien." I called as I entered. "Do you have a little time to talk? What are you doing?" I asked, indicating the charts.

"Hello, Professor. I'm trying to determine how far we are from Kleos, how far to MK141 and so forth. I guess you could say I've been thinking how to stay clear of Baaqir."

"Mr. Baaqir is probably furious at me." Leanna said.

"Why do you say that?" I teasingly asked.

"Abby, it's no joke. Baaqir doesn't get angry often, but he'll stop at nothing to punish those who've wronged him." She said.

"Oh, I'm sorry. I was only teasing. Actually, I think what you did was heroic. You probably saved all our lives. At the very least you saved us from being arrested by the secret police. I should be thanking you instead of teasing you." I said as I put my arm around her.

"Yes, Lea. What you did was certainly brave. I'm proud of you." Sebastien told her. Leanna smiled.

"Speaking of brave, I should also thank you for saving us, Sebastien. We'd never have gotten Teddy out of there if it weren't for you. And you got us away from the Archeron safely, as well. I guess I owe both of you." I told them. "I'm sure Leanna is better off now, with you, than she was with Baaqir."

"I appreciate that, Professor, but I'm not as sure as you are. Leanna's given up safety and security for.... well, I'm not sure yet."

"For love." Leanna said as the big man smiled at her. I thought to myself what an odd couple they made, with Sebastien towering over the diminutive Leanna. But I realized Kara and I must give the same impression. Although she and I weren't what I'd call an official 'couple.'

"Sebastien, you don't have to keep calling me Professor, you know. That's all through now."

"When I look at you, I think 'Professor.' It's about respect, I suppose. I've always respected academic types like you. How about Doctor? You have a PHD, right? You're still a doctor even if you quit teaching."

"I didn't quit teaching, that decision was made for me. But, yes, I suppose I'm still a doctor."

"Excuse me, *Doctor*, but your teaching career isn't over unless *you* want it to be." Sebastien scolded, "There are at least a dozen worlds I can name off the top of my head, free planets, where you could still teach. Those places would love to have you, they're always interested in teachers who speak the common tongue. And, they won't give a damn if you're wanted by the Ministry of Security. That'd probably be a plus on your resume."

I guess I hadn't thought of that. I *could* go someplace away from Telluric space, and teach. The Ministry of Security could still find me I'm sure, but would they even bother? I honestly didn't know.

"Why don't you just call me Abby? I like my friends to call me Abby, and I'd like us to be friends."

"I'll try to remember." he smiled.

"Yes, my love, Abby is my friend, so she should be your friend as well." Leanna told him. "Maybe we can all live in the same place together."

"That'd be nice." I said, "Wherever you and Leanna go, you're better off than you were with Baaqir."

"Abby, no offense, but you don't know what the hell you're talking about. Baaqir was good to me. He was good to Leanna too. Did you know she was in an orphanage run by a bunch of racist, religious fanatics before Baaqir found her?" He asked. I was a little startled at his exacerbated tone.

"I did, Leanna told me." I said. "She said it was pretty bad there."

"I guess you could say that. She was worked, starved and tortured. The priestesses abused her horribly; it was a terrible place. Baaqir saved her and gave her a good life. She was living in luxury on the Archeron; she had everything she could ever want or need. To tell you the truth I'm feeling pretty guilty about the whole thing. Not that I wouldn't do it all over again if I had the chance." He admitted as he grinned at her. She blushed and smiled back at him, slapping his arm.

"But he treated her like a possession; like a slave even." I argued. "You heard him in the shuttle bay saying he wouldn't let her go."

"You may discover, Abby, out here in space among us barbarians, that the universe isn't made up of only black and white, good and evil, heroes and villains, with everything all cut and dried and easy to label. All of us exist in a constant state of flux between not all good and not entirely evil. You want to label Baaqir evil, but I'm telling you it isn't that simple. I think he even loves me and Leanna, in his own way. We're like the children he could never have." Sebastien explained.

"He can't have children?" I asked.

"He told me once the doctors said there was a 75% chance he'd pass on his disorder to his children. He couldn't stand the thought of condemning his offspring to what he endured as a child. So, he decided not to have children of his own. Leanna and I, along with several other fortunate people he's helped over the years, are like his adopted children."

He was speaking calmly as always, but I could feel the emotion behind his words. It seemed Sebastien Fowler was a philosopher, and a romantic.

"I see. Does that mean you think of him as a father?" I asked.

"It's complicated. I grew up on Dressida also; it was my mother, my older brother and me; I never knew my father. We mostly lived in run-down apartments and barely scraped by. My mother would float between jobs; maid, waitress, store clerk, even hard manual labor from time to time. But in truth she was primarily a prostitute."

Leanna said, "She was nice, though. She was a good mother, that's what Sebastien told me."

"She did her best, I believe. Abby, Dressida's religious majority, the hypocritical bastards, deemed bordellos sinful and outlawed them long ago. So, she had to try to hustle on her own without the protection of unions or the law, like most planets."

"Sebastien, you don't have to tell me any of this." I told him.

"I know, Abby, but I'm making a point." He said as Leanna took his hand. "From time to time, she'd have boyfriends, sometimes they'd even live with us, but they never lasted long. They'd eventually get drunk and beat her or beat my brother and me, so she'd kick them out. Or they'd get fed up with the situation and leave. Then we'd have visits from 'uncles' that'd stay a night or two."

"Sebastien, I don't mean to interrupt, but there's something I don't understand. Dressida is an Alliance member. Your mother should've been eligible for housing allowance, food allowance and guaranteed income; all kinds of government assistance."

"Ah, there's where you're wrong, Professor. My grandfather was from Marmo. My mother's father; he was half human and half marmoan. The council of governors, in their *infinite wisdom*, judged marmoans to be humanoid, but not *human*. So, that made my mother one quarter non-human and therefore ineligible for government benefits. I'm officially one eighth 'mongrel' and therefore only eligible for half benefits. My mother whored herself to put food on the table because of the bigotry of the Telluric system."

"I'm sorry, Sebastien, I didn't understand." I apologized sincerely.

"As soon as my brother turned 16, he left. He joined the marines and he's still a marine to this day. It suited him well, I guess. One night, not long after, when I'd just turned 15, my mother brought a John home with her. It was nothing out of the ordinary, except at some point this man began to beat her. I decided I'd had enough, so I took a knife from the kitchen, broke down the bedroom door, and killed the man."

"That was brave of you, protecting your mother like that at just 15." I said.

"I'd like to agree with you, but it wasn't entirely noble. I mostly did it out of anger and hatred. I was an angry and hateful little shit when I was young. I ran with street gangs and did all sorts of horrible things. But I'd never killed anyone before."

"Tell her what happened then, my love." Leanna urged.

"The courts might've been lenient, since he was beating my mother viciously. She spent a lot of time in the hospital, running up medical bills she couldn't afford to pay. But, as it turned out, the man I killed was a politically connected High Priest of the Followers. Like I said, *hypocrites*. They sentenced me to 21 years in prison. Since I was only 15, they sent me to a juvenile work camp to begin my sentence. The place was a hell hole, my best friend there was a rat that shared my bunk with me."

"21 years for defending his mother. Can you believe that?" Leanna asked me. I couldn't answer, I had no words.

"They typically worked us 10 or 12 hours a day. A day on Dressida is approximately 22 hours. We cut the weeds along roadways with scythes or carried buckets of gravel back and forth. Sometimes we dug long trenches, then went back the next day and filled them in. It was hard labor for a skinny punk like me." he smiled. "But I grew muscles fast in that place. It was called Coula, an indigenous word meaning redemption. Redemption Farm. What a joke."

"My Sebastien was a child in that horrible place. We have that in common, I guess." Leanna said.

"The larger and older boys terrorized the smaller and younger ones. The guards either laughed or participated. Beatings and rapes were a near daily occurrence. Hardly a week went by when I wasn't in a serious fight. I ended up in the infirmary more than once. I spent over a year in that place."

I was horrified by his story. I'd never talked to anyone who'd been in prison before. It was tough to imagine such a place.

"That seems so unfair, you were only 15. That judge should be stripped of his gown and gavel." I told him.

"I agree." said Leanna.

"One day, much like Lea's story, Mr. Baaqir came to Coula Farm. After inspecting the wooden barracks we slept in, which were freezing in winter and broiling in summer, he had them bring me to a room where we could talk. I told him my story, and he told me he could get me out of there that very day." Sebastien said.

I was beginning to believe Cyrus Baaqir ran Dressida.

"He offered me a job as a member of his private security force. I'd finish my education, and train in every form of combat. I'd be paid handsomely, enough to support my mother even. I only had to promise one thing. Just one. Can you guess what that was, Abby?" He asked me.

"No, what?"

"Absolute loyalty. I had to swear absolute loyalty to him, no matter what. Now I've betrayed that oath. And for strictly selfish reasons, too. I love Leanna, and I knew we could never be together while we were with Baaqir. He's too jealous, he'd never stand for it. I chose Leanna, but I'm not proud I betrayed Mr. Baaqir." He told me. "You see Abby, I'm no different than everyone else, not good, not evil; not right, not wrong, but somewhere in between. Just like you."

"What do you mean, like *me*?" I asked, shocked.

"I was there, Abby, in the observation lounge when you were talking to Baaqir. I heard the whole conversation. Did you ever tell your friends Captain Bradley and his girl, Kara, you'd been interrogated by the secret police? Why is that?"

"Well, I... "

"You also lied to Baaqir during your first meeting. You didn't tell him about the expedition you were supposed to be part of. You didn't tell *him* about your interrogation either. You weren't honest with Baaqir about several things. You were upset about the way he treated you during that meeting in the observatory, but think about it? Can you blame him? We all live in a constant state of flux between right and wrong, battling our inner demons; all of us."

"Alright, I see your point. But I still think Leanna is better off with you." I tried to placate him. "Baaqir keeps slaves, which is unforgivable to me."

"Time will tell, Abby, whether I did the right thing or not. Wait, did you say slaves? Do you mean those two girls you saw with him? Those two are spoiled mistresses. He pays them outrageous amounts of coin to dote on him. They waste most of their days spending coin and goofing off on the Archeron. And when they visit ports of call, they go shopping and night clubbing with armed guards protecting them; always wearing expensive clothes and too much jewelry. They could leave anytime they want, but why would they?"

"Well, what about the twins, the blue skinned twins? Aren't they slaves?" I asked, still not convinced. "He even told us how much he paid for them."

"Professor Thornwell, you certainly are single minded, aren't you? Do you want to know where those two came from? They were incarcerated in a forced labor camp on one of the moons of Goz 5. They were political prisoners because they took part in an anti-Telluric demonstration on their home world. They were sentenced to life at hard labor." he told me. "*Life*, for holding signs and singing. Baaqir got several people out of that place by saying he needed workers and bribing the commandant of the camp. The aurics he referred to was the bribe he paid for their release."

"I don't understand, why would he do that?"

"Baaqir despises the Ministry of Security. Those camps are run by the Ministry." He said.

"Gods, I didn't even know there *were* forced labor camps for political prisoners. How long has that been a thing?" I asked.

"Abby, when it comes to humans, cruelty never surprises me. Most of the time I think humans are instinctively selfish and cruel, like it's hardwired into our DNA. We have to fight against our instincts to be decent; I know I do. That's why Leanna is so good for me, she makes me want to be decent, and that makes it easier."

"Nonsense, my love. You're the best person I know." Leanna said, "You've conquered your inner demons."

Sebastien smiled, "No, not conquered. Suppressed, maybe; never conquered. Millions of years of evolution can't be conquered, but we can fight it. As for the Telluric Alliance, it rules its conquered planets with an iron fist, as the saying goes. The CTF is brutal, ruthless and doesn't tolerate dissent. Believe me, I know all about it from my brother. He's bragged to me about pillaging planets. Sometimes it's hard to listen to. One time a few years ago, right after our mother died, he told me his squad had shot 135 'agitators' in one day on Erestis 3."

"Agitators?" I asked.

"Yep, you know, *school teachers*, politicians, business leaders, government administrators, people who didn't toe the line right away, or who actively spoke against the Telluric occupation. Agitators."

"Orah's spite, that's awful. I can't believe it." I said.

"Oh, give it time, Abby. Soon, you'll be able to believe almost anything. Ian's staff sergeant would regularly take a few marines and go gather up some young girls, or boys, depending on what they could find. 'Morale' specialists he called them. These weren't prostitutes or anything like that, just ordinary citizens unlucky enough to be caught out in the open when the marines came around. The marines would keep them in the barracks for a few days or weeks, then turn them loose, naked, raped, and bloodied. Ian, that's my brother, once bragged he probably has a couple dozen bastards spread around on different planets."

"Oh." was all I could say.

"Abby, Baaqir saved those twins; they literally beg to serve him. They'd do anything for him. Everything isn't always how it seems. When Baaqir called you and Kara slaves, he was trying to get a rise out of you. I guess it worked." He explained with a grin.

"Yes, I guess it did. You've made your point." I told him. "Is your brother still on Erestis 3?"

"No, he's moved on, I believe. I'm not exactly sure where he is right now, we haven't spoken for a while. I'd like to tell you Ian's nothing like me, but that wouldn't be true. He and I grew up in the same home, had the same experiences. We both ran with street gangs in our teens and grew up in an atmosphere full of violence. If it wasn't for Mr. Baaqir, I might've ended up in the marines too. They sometimes parole prisoners if they sign up. I imagine I would've volunteered if I'd been asked."

"I'm sorry, Sebastien. I guess I have a bad habit of talking about things I don't understand. Can we still be friends?" I asked, trying to lighten the mood.

"Of course. I'm certainly not in a position to turn away any friends. Leanna and I are pretty much out of friends right now, except for you. I should tell you, I'm not sure I trust those other two." he said ominously. "Bradley isn't telling me everything. And the woman is strangely devoted to him."

I couldn't believe how right Sebastien was about Teddy.

"Honestly, Sebastien, I feel ignorant about everything. This last week I've discovered so much I didn't know, it's scary. I had no idea forced labor camps even existed. Or, that Allied marines were doing the sort of things you describe. How is it possible?"

"It's simple: Telluric citizens only care about their free government handouts and whatever mindless entertainment has been devised to distract them and keep them tame. They don't care or even *think* about their *own* freedom anymore, let alone the freedom of people they've never met on some alien world they've never even heard of. Humans are the most self-centered bastards in the galaxy; as long as they have it good the rest of the galaxy can burn for all they care." Sebastien explained. "Sorry, Abby. I didn't mean you, I meant in general."

Sebastien sought to exempt me from the failings of my fellow citizens, but I couldn't honestly exempt myself. There was undeniable truth to what Sebastien said, and I feared I was just as guilty as anyone else. However, the revelations of the previous week had been profound for me. The lack of information I'd suffered on Ampora was shocking and unforgiveable. I silently vowed to never be ignorant again if I could help it.

"Don't feel so bad, Abby. I'm just as clueless as you are about these things. Sebastien and Mr. Baaqir have rarely talked of Telluric Alliance politics around me. And the people I meet on the Archeron never talk about it. I'm learning things too." Leanna consoled me by calling me clueless. Somehow that didn't help.

"Sebastien, won't you please help us? I think we need you." I asked. "I've come to believe that *someone* must do *something* to stop the CTF. We might make a difference at Kleos, with your help."

"Alright, Abby," he said with a sigh, "why don't you start by telling me just what you think the Ministry of Security is trying to find on Kleos Prime?"

So, I proceeded to tell Sebastien and Leanna everything I knew about my father and Bradley and Kleos Prime. For not being historians or scientists, they easily grasped the concept of a Reges Scientia civilization. And they understood right away the interest the CTF might have in artifacts that could lead to better weapons, and more advanced technology. Sebastien is extremely intelligent and asked excellent questions. I decided not to mention my amulet though, or the vault, of course. I guess I just couldn't bring myself to divulge all my secrets. Constant flux, indeed.

Just when I was thinking of knocking on Teddy's door, an alarm sounded on the bridge.

Part Twelve The Arsenal of Dissent

Interstellar Date: 388-06-24
On Board the Avernus

"WHAT'S THAT, WHAT'S it mean?" I gasped in Sebastien's direction. I'd been lost in my own little world, thinking about what I was going to ask Teddy, and the sound of the alarm had startled me.

"It's just a proximity alert, probably nothing. It means the sensors have picked something up. Come over here, Abby, and we'll check it out together."

As we crossed the bridge an insistent orange, flashing light drew us to the sensor console. Sebastien's fingers moved with practiced ease as he silenced the alarm and ceased the flashing. It wasn't until Sebastien had silenced the alarm I realized it hadn't been that loud, it probably couldn't be heard outside the bridge.

"That alarm probably wasn't loud enough for the others to hear, should I go get them?" I asked.

"They couldn't hear it, but there are warning lights throughout the ship that would've drawn their attention. I imagine Captain Bradley is already on his way here. Come here and take a look at the display." He told me as he brought up a 3-dimensional holographic image above the console.

The display had a white dot in the middle I assumed must represent the Avernus. Above and toward the left (my left) of the display was a small orange dot; the source of the alarm. Several sets of numbers and a couple of sets of letters were displayed next to the orange dot.

"This is us", he pointed to the white dot, "and this is the target the sensors detected. This shows the range, approximately 1.7 billion kilometers. UNK, of course, stands for unknown target. That means the Avernus' computer has never encountered this target before. The system has determined the target is a small vessel, but doesn't have enough data to give more information."

"1.7 billion kilometers? That's a long way away, isn't it? The sensors can detect things that far away? How's it know it's a ship and not just an asteroid or something?" The display was fascinating, unlike anything I normally dealt with.

On Ampora, low-orbit shuttles ferry passengers gracefully from city to city around the globe. I dared to travel that way only once, becoming quite sick in the process. Therefore, I'd never become an enthusiast for all things that fly the way many Amporans did. There were clubs that met regularly, flew homemade craft of various design, studied the physics and engineering of flight, and generally wasted away their free time on the hobby. I'd never understood the attraction, but sitting there on the bridge of the Avernus among all of the high-tech gadgets and holographic displays I began to feel a small amount of empathy for their obsession. A *small* amount.

"It sees a heat signature from the ship's reactor, plus the velocity is a giveaway. There aren't many asteroids bending space/time out there." he chuckled at me, "The sensors on the Avernus are state of the art, just like everything else on board. But there are limits to sensor effectiveness while using the REL drive. If we were to disengage REL and stop bending space/time, our sensors would give us a far more accurate reading. But then, of course, the target would be long gone."

"This is so interesting. I have no idea how any of this stuff works." I confessed. I felt like a small child in a confectionary shop, mesmerized by all of the enticing goodies.

"To answer your first question, is that a long way away? Yes and no. It's a long way away for sensors, but in the relative vastness of space 1.7 billion kilometers is practically right on top of us. I don't think we have to worry about them detecting us though. We're using dark mode; we should be all but invisible to them." Sebastien made a few adjustments and the display changed.

"You see, Professor, the target is 0.0002 light years away. Approximately, of course." He made another adjustment, "And now you see it says it's approximately 94 light minutes away. That makes it sound even closer to me." he chuckled. "I can change the display to show distances in many different units. Kilometers, astronomical units, parsecs, light minutes, and light years; you get the idea. But, with dark mode on, they couldn't detect us even if we were much closer. At least, I don't think they could."

"What if it's a Combined Fleet vessel? Can CTF ships' sensors see us in dark mode?" I asked.

"I don't know for sure, yet. The device hasn't been fully tested, and combat vessels are equipped with the best tech available. We might not be visible to an older CTF gunship, for instance, the Avernus would have newer, better sensors than they do. If it was a battlecruiser I imagine their sensors might have more range and better capabilities than ours." Sebastien said.

"You bet they would." Teddy said as he entered the bridge. "But there aren't any capital ships within 500 trillion kilometers. They're off doing horrible things to innocent people, I'd wager."

"Anyway, the dark mode makes it unlikely the ship can detect us, even if it was a CTF battlecruiser." Sebastien said to me, ignoring Teddy.

Kara stepped onto the bridge. She was strangely standoffish, not approaching me and staying clear of Teddy also. She just stood at the back of the bridge and listened.

"The CTF vessels we're likely to encounter in this area would be small gunships, simply patrolling for pirates." Teddy said. "And there's few of them anyway. The CTF doesn't patrol Telluric space aggressively."

"I imagine, by now, Baaqir will have half the Trade Guild's fleet looking for us. He's probably offered a reward for our capture. And the CTF will be looking for the people who killed several of their officers. We must be wary of any targets we pick up on our sensors." Sebastien warned, reasonably.

"I've had a great deal of experience dealing with the Trade Guild as well as the CTF. As long as Baaqir's gadget works, we should be fine." Teddy said confidently.

"I hope you're right." Sebastien said. "We're getting close to the area where your cargo was jettisoned. Just how do you plan to find it? It's a large area to search."

"Never fear, Fowler. My goods have transponders attached for just such a situation." Teddy told him. "All we have to do is follow their signal."

Teddy approached the sensor console and began entering something on the display. I walked over toward Kara and stood beside her. She didn't say anything to me, which was odd. She'd never failed to make me feel welcome. In fact, she'd gone out of her way to act like my friend from the first time we met.

"Kara, is there something wrong? How are you feeling, is your wound healing?" I asked lamely. I was a bit wary of her mood. She seemed agitated.

"I'm feeling much better. There's nothing wrong, exactly. We can talk about it later."

"We can talk about it now. Come with me, Kara Az-Codor." I grabbed her hand and pulled her toward my cabin. She resisted at first, so it was like trying to pull a full-grown tree from the ground, roots and all. But after a few seconds she reluctantly followed me.

Far from home, surrounded by people I barely knew, my need to preserve the profound bond I felt with Kara was paramount. She was my tether keeping me sane in this crazy, unfamiliar situation.

We entered my cabin, and I closed the door behind us. "Kara, whatever's wrong, you can tell me about it. I consider you my closest friend now, possibly my only friend. I've always had a hard time trusting people, so I'm not sure whether to trust Teddy or Sebastien; Leanna is nice but not someone I feel comfortable relying on yet. But, I do feel comfortable relying on you! I need you Kara, I need our friendship."

"I'm sorry, Abby. I'm not upset at you; how could I be? And your friendship is important to me too. Now, maybe more than before." She said. "You might be right to doubt Teddy."

"What do you mean? What's happened?"

"He just confessed he's been keeping a secret from me; about Kleos Prime. The whole time I've known him. We're not supposed to keep secrets from one another."

"I understand." I said, trying to help. It didn't.

"No Abby, you don't. Do you remember the story I told you about being ritualistically committed to Bradley? As part of the ritual we performed in that shrine on Nir-Kvek, we swore not to keep secrets from each other. That was a sacred ceremony, and I took it seriously. I've committed my life to it. Now it seems like he didn't think it was as binding as I thought it was. I feel like he's betrayed me." She confessed.

"So, he told you about the vault?" I asked.

"You knew? How long have you known? Have you known this whole time?"

"No, of course not. My father never told me about it. Teddy just told me a few hours ago. Kara, did he tell you why he kept it a secret?" She didn't answer, so I continued, "He swore to my father never to tell anyone about it. You see? He had a prior promise before he performed the ritual with you. Which one do you think he should've honored?"

"I see your point, little human. Teddy had promised your father first, years before we met."

"And he tried to honor both as best he could. I think it's admirable he kept his promise to my father as long as he did. I'm not sure I could have." I said, amazing myself by defending Teddy.

"So, if I understand correctly, there's an ancient library of some kind on Kleos Prime. Hundreds of books in an alien language. But it's sealed in an indestructible vault, deep under a mountain."

"That's what he told me."

"He should've told me about it. He should've trusted me. I thought he did. I'm known as protector of the weak and keeper of secrets. My father gave me those appellations, and he didn't do it lightly. Teddy should've trusted me; I know I've earned it."

"You're probably right. But, Kara, the fact Teddy kept it secret in order to keep his promise to my father makes me trust him more." I confessed. She nodded thoughtfully.

"Abby, what do you plan on doing with those books?"

"I don't know. Honestly, I've just been worried about opening the vault. Teddy seems to think I can if my father could. He told me he wants to share the library with everyone in the galaxy."

"He told me as much, but I don't think that's a practical plan. My master has a tendency not to think things through logically sometimes. I'm often required to do it for him. How would this 'sharing' be done, practically speaking?" she asked me.

"I have no idea, what do you think?"

"Abby, I don't think we should even open the vault. I think we should destroy it. That's the only way to make sure it stays out of the hands of the Tellurians."

"*Destroy it*? Kara, it's the archeological find of.... well, the most significant in history. We owe it to all the peoples of the galaxy to see what those books have in them. Besides, that material it's made of is indestructible."

"We *can't* let the Tellurians discover more weapon technology; they have plenty as it is. *That's* what we owe to the people of the galaxy."

"We don't have the right to destroy that library."

"Quenra's ass. Not only do we have the right, we have the *responsibility*. Why are the Tellurians at Kleos? They don't care about new ways to grow crops or cure the sick. All they care about is the probability a super advanced civilization would also have super advanced weapons. We should destroy it." Kara reasoned.

I saw her point. But it'd be a catastrophe to destroy all that knowledge. As a historian and an archeologist it'd be a betrayal of my ethos if I allowed that to happen. There had to be another way.

"No Kara, we can't do that. The library belongs to everyone, every race, not just humans. We must find a way to share it with the whole galaxy. If we did, it could change everything. If everyone had access to the contents of the vault, then everyone would have access to any advanced technologies discovered. The Tellurians would gain no advantage."

Kara disagreed, "No, Abby, you're wrong. Think about what happens when everyone has more advanced technologies; wars simply become more destructive. As soon as everyone becomes aware of these theoretical new weapons, it'll inevitably lead to an arms race to see who could build them fastest. Right now, that'd be the Telluric Alliance because they have the facilities in place. No one else in the quadrant can match the Tellurians' industrial might. Not to mention their research and development capabilities."

Again, Kara made an excellent point. "But, what if there's something in the vault that can change all of that? What if there's a way to end wars forever?" I borrowed Teddy's argument.

"The whole point of this was to keep the Tellurians from finding *anything* at Kleos. That hasn't changed now we know what's there. We have to stick to the original plan." Kara argued.

"But think of the secrets we could learn. Maybe there aren't even any weapons technologies in the library. There's no reason to assume that ancient alien culture was warlike." I argued right back.

Kara laughed derisively, "Of course there is. Those fragments Teddy showed to Baaqir didn't start out as fragments. They were a part of *something* to begin with, and that something was destroyed. Those fragments are evidence these genius aliens of yours *were* warlike. Someone or something of tremendous power destroyed your aliens. It's only logical to think it was a weapon of some kind. That kind of rules out the idea there's something in the vault that'd end war forever, don't you think?"

It was tough to argue with that logic. I guess I hadn't thought enough about what to do with the books once we had them. On that, Kara was already ahead of me. She certainly thought the vault could be destroyed, and she knew a lot more about weapons than I did. She was right, Teddy probably hadn't thought this through. Or, perhaps he had and he wasn't being truthful with me. Maybe he had plans for the library he wasn't sharing.

The Avernus' intercom buzzed and over it came Teddy's voice "Kara, my love, I need you."

I told her, "I can't believe I'm saying this, but you should forgive Teddy for not telling you about the vault. He would've been breaking a vow to my father if he had. I have the feeling he'd fall to pieces without you, Kara."

"You're certainly right about that, little human. And you're right, I'll forgive him. But if he keeps secrets from me again, I'll split *him* from lips to giblets. What are giblets, by the way?" Her mood had improved vastly, and her smile had returned.

"I've no idea." I laughed. Kara leaned down and kissed me. Not a kiss born of passion and desire, but one more akin to genuine affection; simple and therefore more meaningful.

Kara and I made our way back to the bridge where we found the rest of the crew. That's how I'd started to think of the five of us, like a pirate crew.

Teddy said to Kara, "Fowler says there's no grappling equipment on this ship, so you and I'll have to suit up and manually load our cargo. We can only get it so close with the tractor beam, the rest we have to do ourselves."

"How many suits in the airlock?" Kara asked.

"Four, but we're the only ones qualified. Fowler's never spacewalked before. He'll stay on board and operate the tractor beam." Teddy replied.

"Wait, you're going outside the ship?" I asked.

"Don't worry, it's perfectly safe. We have to get the goods from out there into the cargo hold somehow. Don't worry, it won't take long; we've done this sort of thing many times."

Teddy didn't understand. I wasn't worried about their safety; I sort of wanted to go with them. Spacewalking sounded fun. I couldn't believe how much I'd changed in a week; I'd never have tried something so adventurous before. Oh, well; maybe next time.

"Hey Leanna, how's it going?" I asked as I went over to sit beside her on the bridge. Teddy and Kara had left for the airlock and I found myself with nothing to do.

"Hello, Abby. I'm fine, but Sebastien is worried."

"Lea, sweetheart, I'm not worried. I just don't see the importance of this. Bradley's weapons could be dangerous. I have no idea what he's bringing on board, and he wouldn't tell me. The Avernus isn't a damn warship."

"See? Worried." Leanna giggled.

Today was the first time I'd seen her wearing boring clothes. Don't get me wrong she still looked beautiful, just not as flamboyant as usual. Her hair was in a ponytail, her face was made up less elaborately. She wore black slacks and a green pullover sweater with military style, thick soled, black boots. The boots were like a miniature version of the boots Sebastien was wearing. She looked like a parody of a soldier.

Sebastien did something at his console and the giant viewscreen at the front of the bridge changed displays. Replacing the usual star chart was a view of the space outside the Avernus. The pallets of cargo Baaqir had told me about, resembling travel chests but much grander in scale, could be seen in the near distance.

With painstaking precision Teddy and Kara maneuvered one of the surprisingly big pallets toward the Avernus. The pallet must've been five meters square and three meters high, and it was only one of several in Teddy's illicit weapons cache.

As they neared, the markings on the crates became discernable, clearly legible was 'Property of the Combined Telluric Fleet' above the iconic insignia of the Alliance: A dark blue, circular field with 32 planets around the circumference, representing the members of the Alliance. In the center of the field, a gold shield with a stylized depiction of a spiral galaxy. Under the galaxy, even though it was too small to read, I knew was written, in Latin, the motto of the Alliance: Simul Invictus. *Together Unconquerable.*

"Those suits aren't meant for manual labor. The hydrogen thrusters have small capacities, and I'm not sure they'll last long enough to retrieve all of that cargo." Sebastien said. I think he was talking aloud to himself more than he was talking to us.

"Sebastien, is there space for all of those pallets in the cargo hold?" I was simply curious, I didn't mean to aggravate the man, but that's apparently what I did.

"Yes, but there won't be room for much else. I wish I knew what was in those containers. Those cases have military markings on them, and from the size of them there could be some serious ordnance. The military markings mean they're stolen from the CTF. Probably equipment meant for the marines." He said, clearly annoyed.

He bent over the comms console, "Captain Bradley, check the gauge on your hydrogen pack. Those suits don't have a large capacity, so you'll probably have to recharge them before you're done."

"Roger that." came the response.

We sat in relative silence, watching the show on the viewscreen. The operation seemed to take forever, as it was slow going. Teddy and Kara had to slowly travel approximately 200 meters to where the pallets were drifting, use their thrusters to tow a pallet back into the cargo hold, secure it, and start again. They did need to recharge their hydrogen before they were done, but eventually the job was accomplished.

After they returned to the bridge, Sebastien commented, "I hope that was worth it."

"I can assure you it was, my good man." Teddy said, "We just brought a few million coin worth of goods on board. Things that'd be beastly difficult to replace. And one or two items that might come in handy on the Avernus. There's one container of the CTF's new series of ship-to-ship missiles down there. My sources tell me they can defeat any known shielding."

"How is that possible?" Sebastien asked.

"Technology is a viscous advisory. You never want to be on the wrong side of the equation. Come, Fowler, let me show you what we have." Teddy beckoned Sebastien to follow him down to the cargo hold and the whole crew followed.

"This first pallet," Teddy began as he opened one of the cases, "contains 2500 brand new EM85 Electromagnetic Gauss rifles, 300 round capacity with recharge at .04 seconds. These are the latest series of the standard issue small arms the CTF marines use, straight from the factory. They still have the inspector's seal on them, see?"

"Over here we have 1000 DRG Multi-Phase Plasma rifles. The latest series; the marines haven't even been issued these yet. These are the small arms the elite troops will be issued in the future."

Sebastien asked, "DRG? As in Dressida Research Group? How the hell did you get your hands on those, Bradley?"

Teddy was clearly in his element and was enjoying himself. "Some disreputable brothers I know hijacked a shipment recently. Abby knows them." He chuckled. "This next pallet has several dozen 40mm, high impact photonic mortars. There's different types of ammo for different purposes. These things can provide a small group of guerilla fighters the means to fight back when confronted by allied marines in armored vehicles. A seriously important piece of equipment for our friends who normally don't have armor support."

"Gods, this is enough to start a war." I blurted. "Where were you taking this stuff?"

"Abby, my dear, you're missing the point; the war started long ago. We're simply trying to even the playing field a bit....ah, this is the best of the lot. This pallet has four K2-7a fighter drones, deadly and completely automated once they've been programed properly. These drones can provide ground support or fight air-to-air combat. They're compact but powerful." Teddy was exuberant. "I've seen a couple of these decimate a regiment of resistance fighters. It's about time the resistance had a way to fight back."

"Lucifer's balls, my brother described those drones to me; they're murderous bastards. Each one is equipped with two 25mm cannons that fire armor piercing rounds." Sebastien said.

"Indeed. Ah, ha, this one over here contains no less than ten low yield tactical nuclear weapons. About 8 kilotons each. They can be dropped as a gravity bomb, or missile fired from a shoulder launcher." Teddy explained. "Or, with these special attachments here, they can be rigged for timed detonation."

"Woah, did you say nuclear weapons? Teddy, those were outlawed years ago. Where in the hell did you get those, they must be a hundred years old. Are those even safe?" I asked, stunned. I couldn't believe any of those things still existed.

"That's an excellent question, Bradley. If those things are that old, they can't be safe to have on board." said Sebastien. "And, I'm not sure it's a great idea to give those to insurgents. Think what they might use them for."

Kara stepped forward and spoke, "Where'd they come from? Abby, where do you think they came from? Where is all this other stuff from? This is *all* CTF ordnance, all of it. And it's not a hundred years old either." she pointed to the markings on one of the cases, "This was produced less than 6 months ago, at a facility on the planet New Gotah. The Telluric Alliance is still producing these *and* still using them."

"Orah's tits, that's insane! How can that be? It makes you wonder who they're fighting that they need those things at all." I said.

Leanna whispered in my ear, "What's a nuclear weapon?"

"Who says they need them?" Kara answered me, "They use them because they're effective and cheap. If you want to level a village that's giving you trouble, just launch one of those at it and it's gone. You don't need any marines to go house to house and endanger themselves. Afterward, they just send in a radiation mitigation crew and that's all there is to it."

I whispered back to Leanna, "It's a weapon invented long, long ago on Old Earth. It's ridiculously destructive for its comparative size. They literally split atoms apart to release energy, the result is a huge explosion, and a release of deadly radiation. They've been outlawed, like nerve agents and biological weapons."

Kara heard me, "Outlawed for everyone else, but the Telluric Alliance doesn't follow its own laws." She had excellent hearing; Leanna was sitting right next to me and could barely make out what I was whispering. Kara was 5 meters away.

Teddy told us, "These are small yield compared to some they use. Seven years ago, on Capira 4, insurgents took control of a whole city. They fortified it with around 20,000 freedom fighters and held it for three months against two brigades of marines. The CTF got fed up, pulled the marines back, and nuked the city from orbit. 850,000 were killed, including women and children."

"My Lord." Muttered Leanna. I was just as shocked as she was.

"I heard about that at the time; Baaqir had a few meetings with the defense minister after it happened, lobbying to get the CTF to stop using nukes. DRG doesn't produce them, so they ignored him."

I decided to take this opportunity to press my case with Sebastien. "You see, Sebastien. That's what the Alliance is capable of. If they discover new weapon technology at Kleos Prime, they won't hesitate to use it; that proves it."

Sebastien said, "Bradley, where were you taking these weapons, and to whom? This is all quite impressive, but there's not enough weapons here to defend a planet. 2500 EM rifles would be a drop in the bucket against 50,000 Allied marines equally well armed. My brother's a marine, he's told me the CTF's tactics. He says battlecruisers sometimes bombard a planet for days, and by the time the marines land the locals are begging to capitulate."

"Point taken, my friend. No, I wasn't taking these to some planet that's under siege. They are bound for some insurgent friends of mine. Their tactics are small groups, striking quickly and pulling out: guerilla tactics. So far, they've been successful attacking isolated CTF installations, ammunition depots, deep space comms relays, and a few small ships. They're just getting started, so they pick small targets, but they have big plans in time." Teddy told him. "The average citizen has no idea, but there are insurgencies on-going right now on nearly twenty planets."

"That hardware is expensive; how can insurgents afford to pay for that stuff?" Sebastien asked.

"Their finances are a mystery to me; all I know is they pay promptly and in Telluric coin. They'll purchase anything I can get my hands on." Teddy replied.

"Isn't that suspicious?" Leanna asked.

"Of course. However, I don't ask questions. For the time being the situation suits me perfectly, why disrupt my good fortune?" Teddy reasoned.

Kara added, "Those insurgents are at least fighting the Tellurians, we feel we should support them as much as we can. 'Never scorn simple beginnings. No fortress is built in a day; the first stone's importance does not diminish as towers soar and moats fill."

"Who said that, some famous Tovolek philosopher?" I asked.

"A poet, of some renown." Kara answered, smiling at me. "His name was Zu'rra Corda Az-van Az-Codor, 59th lord of Az-Codor. He was my father."

A red light on the wall began flashing, cutting Teddy's weapons tour short. Sebastien left quickly, heading for the bridge. The rest of our little crew followed closely behind.

As I entered the bridge, Sebastien was already at the sensor console. We'd been stationary here for quite a while. Teddy and Kara's work collecting their weapons had taken hours, so I think everyone was concerned about this newest target on the sensors.

Part Thirteen A Little Trust is a Dangerous Thing

Interstellar Date: 388-06-24

On Board the Avernus

"IT'S A LIGHT SHIP, with no transponder signal. Could it be CTF or Trade Guild?" Sebastien asked Teddy.

"Probably not. They would normally operate with transponders on. Part of their mission is to be seen by other spacecraft. It's meant to be a deterrent, 'showing the badge' as the saying goes. Also, if they decide to board a ship, they want the other crew to know it's them and not pirates. Trying to board another ship unannounced would encourage a fight, and they don't want that if they can help it." Teddy answered.

I chimed in, "So who is it?"

Teddy again answered, "Well, there's several possibilities. A ship without a transponder could be a pirate, or it could be a smuggler. It could also be a private yacht like this one trying to stay incognito. It could even be some chap who simply forgot to turn his transponder on. I don't think it's the Tito, I wasn't expecting them for a few more hours. Oddly, it seems to be heading right for us. With our gadget engaged it's highly unlikely they would've picked us up on their sensors."

"Bradley, this is your area of expertise. I'm no smuggler, so I'm not much help here." Sebastien said.

Kara said, "These are the coordinates you gave to the Tito, so it's at least possible it's them. Maybe they're early, shouldn't you try to raise them on comms?"

Teddy didn't question Kara for a second. He simply turned to the communication console and waved a few fingers back and forth to initiate a call.

"Crescent, this is Castle, over." he said into the console. "Crescent, this is Castle. Do you copy, over."

After a brief silence, a voice replied, "Copy Castle, this is Crescent. Over."

"It's them. They're ahead of schedule. Probably the first time ever." Teddy laughed. "I'll turn our transponder on so they can pinpoint us. Fowler, can you disengage the gadget?"

"If you're sure it's them." Sebastien went to the pilot's console and turned off the QSDM device. I couldn't tell any difference with it off, I felt the same. The thing was fascinating technology.

"It looks like it's decision time Fowler. We need this ship, and we all want you with us as well. What do you say?" Teddy asked him. "If your answer is still no, I'll buy this ship from you and have the Tito deliver you anywhere you want to go."

Sebastien said, "It's doubtful you could afford this ship, the reactor alone cost over 30 million. I've already endangered Leanna more than I ever intended to; going to Kleos would be irresponsible of me. I'm supposed to be the one to protect her."

"Sebastien, I'd like to go. Abby is my friend, and I think she could use our help. Isn't that what you do for friends, help them when they need you?" Leanna said.

"Leanna, I think I'm starting to like you." said Kara, smiling. "Anyone who's loyal to their friends is alright with me."

"Lea, it's going to be dangerous. Do you understand? We could even be killed." Sebastien said.

"I understand. I still want to go." she said.

"Alright then, we're in. I must be as crazy as you people are. We'll take the Avernus to Kleos." He said. "But if we get killed I'll never forgive any of you."

I grabbed Leanna in a hug and kissed her on the cheek. "You've got more friends now, Leanna." I said. I went to Sebastien and stood on my toes to reach his cheek and give it a kiss. "Thank you, Sebastien Fowler. Thank you."

Teddy spoke into the comms again, "Crescent, this is castle, over."

"This is Crescent, go ahead."

"We have new plans, Crescent. We'll be using this ship to get to our destination. We'll need to transfer some things over from the Tito, and maybe three or four people too. We could use an engineer, Ernie. Are you up for it?" Teddy asked.

We waited, but strangely, there was no immediate reply. The Tito had responded quickly to every transmission before, and Teddy seemed irritated.

"Ernie, are you there? What's up? Did you copy my last?" Still, no reply.

Sebastien changed the display on the large view screen. We now saw a view of the Tito as it approached. My initial impression was the Tito was squat and ugly compared to the sleek Avernus.

"Do you think their comms failed? It was working fine a few minutes ago." Kara said.

"Tito, this is Bradley. If the ship's comms have failed switch over to personal comms, we're easily in range." Teddy said into the console. "Kara, try to raise Ernie on his personal comms. Maybe they don't realize the ship's comms have failed."

Kara took out her comms device and began calling Ernie Snyder, the engineer and temporary captain of the Tito. Again there was no reply.

"This is getting weird, maybe we should raise shields." Sebastien advised.

"Shields? Isn't that Captain Bradley's ship? Aren't they his men?" Leanna asked.

"Master, it's unlikely the Tito's comms and Snyder's comms have both failed simultaneously. Perhaps Fowler is right." Kara warned.

"Kara, try someone else's comms over there. Someone has to be paying attention." Teddy told her.

They were in the midst of their discussion while only Leanna and I were watching the view screen. We saw a plume, like a small explosion, at the top of the Tito's silhouette, followed by several fast-moving objects moving our direction.

"My love." Leanna tried to get Sebastien's attention.

I was less subtle, "Guys! I think they just fired at us!" I said, pointing at the screen frantically.

Teddy, Kara, and Sebastien turned to look and they all jumped into action in surprise. Sebastien rushed to the pilot's console, Kara raced to the tactical console next to him and Teddy lunged toward the sensor display.

"Bloody hell, she's right! Those bastards fired missiles at us. Fowler, take evasive action." Teddy assumed command.

"Fowler, tell me what's what here." Kara shouted. But Sebastien was engaged with his own console, trying to move us away from the oncoming missiles.

Teddy addressed Leanna and me, "You two, take a seat and strap in. Now!" Then to Kara, "Kara, engage the EM shielding. Quickly, there may still be time." Then to Sebastien, "Fowler, engage the QSDM. I've turned off our transponder, but it might be too late. At this close range, those missiles have locked on already. As soon as everyone's strapped in, turn off the artificial gravity and divert power to weapons and shields."

Leanna and I found seats as fast as we could and harnessed ourselves in. Sebastien had started the Avernus moving, but I had no idea if he was in time or not. Teddy joined Kara at the tactical console and was helping her arm the Avernus' weapons. It all was happening so fast I hadn't had time to fully realize we were in terrible danger. Unexpectedly, we were smack-dab in the middle of a battle!

The Tito, Teddy's own ship, had ambushed us. The attack had caught us completely by surprise and unprepared.

Leanna whispered, "Abby, why are they attacking us? I thought they were our friends."

"I don't know. I guess they're not friends anymore."

"Kara, can our shields handle their attack?" Teddy asked.

"4 R-type, armor piercing anti-ship missiles and 2 EM-1700 Varga missiles. The former shouldn't be a problem, the 2 Vargas could penetrate our EM veil, but our armor should hold." Kara told him.

She yelled, "Brace for impact."

Amongst all the shouted orders, descriptions of missiles and general confusion, the main thing I heard was our armor *should* hold.

A moment after Kara's warning, tension palpable in the air, it happened: the first missile struck. The Avernus shuddered violently; my body was thrown forcefully against my harness. A deafening roar was accompanied by the illumination of emergency lighting, casting a blood-red hue across everything on the bridge.

To my horror, the relentless assault continued, each hammering impact sending shockwaves through the ship's frame. We were tossed about like rag dolls in our seats as the Avernus absorbed a half dozen missile strikes. Leanna, her complexion drained of color, couldn't conceal her fear; her eyes betrayed the terror gripping us both. This harrowing ordeal was entirely new to us, and it was nothing short of astonishing that we were still alive. How could the ship endure such an onslaught?

"We have additional company." Teddy announced. "There's two more targets approaching quickly."

"Two more targets? I wish we'd have had time to load some of those missiles we brought on board. What's the range of these anti-matter torpedoes Fowler?" Kara asked.

"They're in range already, but make sure you have target lock, we don't want those things coming back our way." Sebastien said.

"They had their shot, now it's our turn. We have the gadget engaged now; their weapons won't be able to lock onto us anymore." Teddy stated confidently.

"Theoretically." said Sebastien, with less confidence.

"Kara, target the Tito and try to disable them. We don't want to destroy them if we don't have to." Teddy ordered.

He said into the comms console, "Unidentified ships approaching, this is the Avernus. Identify yourselves. Over." There was no response.

"Crescent, this is Castle. Who're your friends? Over" Teddy asked. Still no response.

Why wouldn't the Tito answer us? They'd already attacked us, the surprise was complete, the ambush was sprung, but we were still there, still breathing. Perhaps they were stunned into silence.

"Unidentified ships, this vessel is registered to Dressida Transport Corporation, back off now or you'll have to answer." Teddy said into the comms.

"Nice try, Teddy." a woman's voice came from the console. "We know who the ship belongs to, and it's not you. Standby to be boarded."

"God dammit, that's Ghaz Parzok's voice. Snyder must've sold us out."

"Who the hell is Ghaz Parzok?" Sebastien asked.

"She's a pirate from Runivia, and part of a rival syndicate. She and her crew stalk the trade routes between New Britain and the Reaches of Kator. They're a long way from their usual territory. Snyder must've decided to betray us and teamed up with Ghaz." Teddy guessed. "I can't understand it though, Snyder's been my friend for twenty years. I'd never have guessed he'd do this."

"He even called your ex-girlfriend to help. That's low." Kara said. "I'm powering up the main gun."

"Girlfriend?" I asked.

Teddy said, "Kara's joking. Ghaz was just a casual fling."

"He broke her heart, now she wants to kill him." Kara laughed.

"Can we focus, please." Sebastien said.

I asked. "Can we out-run them?"

"No, my dear, we can't out-run them, but with Baaqir's device we could maybe lose them. However, that's my bloody ship out there, I don't feel like running." Teddy told me.

"There's three of them Bradley, we might do well to escape while we can." Sebastien suggested.

"There's rewards posted for us by now. These bastards are just after an easy payday, so they think. We'll discourage them a little," Teddy said. "Ghaz won't want a fight, pirates try not to if they can help it. But if Snyder's set us up, he can't back down now. Our problem is the Tito is *my ship*. I don't want to destroy it."

"We don't know how much damage we've suffered. Maybe we should just get the hell out of here." Sebastien advised.

"They all have their weapons powered up, but they aren't firing. I think they've lost us. The QSDM must be working." Kara pronounced. "If so, we aren't in any more danger. And they deserve some payback."

"Crescent, this is Castle, come in Snyder." Teddy said into the comms. "What do you think you're doing? That's my bloody ship you're in, you idiot. You think I don't know what it's capable of? You can't beat this ship Snyder, give it up."

"Snyder's not available, Captain. He's currently enjoying a holiday. You're outnumbered 3 to 1 Teddy. Lower your shields, prepare to be boarded and I promise not to hurt anyone." came the reply. "That's the best deal I'm gonna offer."

"That's Jorra's voice, he must be in charge over there. Snyder's dead." Kara whispered.

Teddy said, "That cold blooded bastard. Snyder must've resisted him. Jorra killed him for being loyal to me, the son-of-a-bitch."

"How do you know he's dead?" Sebastien asked.

"Going on holiday is slang for being released into space. It's a coward's way of killing someone. I didn't think Jorra was that much of a scum." Kara explained.

Our eyes were drawn to the screen as Kara's missiles found their mark on the Tito. As Teddy had asked, the little ship wasn't destroyed; but it's movement was slowed significantly. The damaged vessel was leaving a stream of iridescent residue in its wake.

"Teddy, we've no wish to mess up that pretty vessel or your pretty face. Lower your shields and stop where you are, or we'll be forced to fire." Ghaz Parzok's voice came from the comms. Parzok spoke the common tongue with a pronounced runivian accent.

"You're making a big mistake, Ghaz. We've known each other a long time, so if you turn around and go back to the Reaches, I'll forget this ever happened." Teddy offered. "You don't know what you're up against, this ship isn't what it seems."

"Teddy, my friend, you make me laugh. You're outnumbered, and aboard a luxury yacht. What're you going to do, throw champagne bottles at us? Be realistic; no one needs to die here today. The rewards offered for you are posted dead-or-alive. I prefer alive, but my crew is not so picky. Halt where you are; I'm not telling you again." Parzok threatened.

"She still sounds confident." I said, "I thought they couldn't see us anymore because of the QSDM?"

Sebastien said, "They probably think their sensors are malfunctioning. She wouldn't admit that in the middle of a battle; she must be bluffing."

"Then she's a fool." Kara commented.

"Ghaz, you said you know whose ship this is. You know Baaqir is the biggest arms manufacturer in the galaxy, right? Go home or we'll destroy you." Teddy warned.

"Too thin, Teddy. I've played cards with you, remember? I know how you like to bluff." She said.

"Have it your way, then." Teddy said. He turned to Kara, "My dear, do we have weapons lock on Ghaz's flagship, the Plavic? If so, let 'em fly."

Kara didn't answer, she simply made some entries on her tactical console, and we felt the salvo of torpedoes leaving as the Avernus shuddered again.

"Fowler, is the REL ready?" Kara asked. "If not, come about so we can use the main gun."

"Captain, what are your orders? Should I engage the REL and get us out of here, or come about to target the plasma cannon?" Sebastien asked Teddy.

"Incoming. We have 8....no 12 more incoming missiles. All 3 enemy ships launched." Kara announced calmly.

"I'm not so squeamish, Teddy." came Jorra's voice from the comms, "I prefer dead. Is that flea-bitten slut with you over there?"

"I'm here, Norassa." Kara spoke up, "Is this all because I laughed at your little nubbin when you showed it to me? I thought that was the whole point, I figured you got off on humiliation."

"Laugh now, Kara. You'll be dead in a few moments." Jorra Norassa replied.

"Damn. 12 missiles? They must think this is a CTF battlecruiser." Sebastien commented. "Kara, are their missiles on target?"

"Not one. All 12 failed to lock on. I can't believe that stealth device works so well. We're lucky."

"I never doubted it for a second." Teddy said, "Come about, Fowler. Kara, target the Plavic with the plasma cannon, fire as soon as you get target lock."

His customary rakish charm had been replaced by an intensity I'd not seen before. Teddy was in 'Captain Bradley' mode now, and the change was drastic.

"Coming about." Sebastien answered.

We all watched the view screen as our salvo of torpedoes hurtled toward the notorious pirate ship. A series of blinding flashes obscured our view as our attack struck home. The ship emerged from a cloud of debris, damaged but defiant. The forward section bore unmistakable scars, the hull now marred with fractures and scorched plating.

"I have target lock on the Plavic with the MIP cannon." Advised Kara.

"FIRE!" ordered Teddy.

We felt a shudder and heard a muffled roar as the plasma cannon discharged. The red-tinged emergency lights blinked out momentarily, and Leanna squeezed my hand so hard I thought she'd break a finger. I hadn't even realized she was holding my hand. I looked up to see the plasma bolt, glowing with the blinding intensity of a miniature star, traveling toward the pirate's ship. It's progress was far more rapid than the missiles from earlier, closing quickly, burning a spot in my vision as it went.

"Main gun plasma charge impact in 5 seconds. It's right on target and the Plavic is stationary, without shields." Kara told us.

On the large view screen was the pirate flagship. With their shields gone, the impact of our plasma bolt was nothing short of cataclysmic. A blinding eruption of light obscured our view, and as the flash dissipated, a mangled wreck was revealed where the Plavic had been. The pirate vessel had been ripped apart by our terrible weapon; two large sections of the ship now floated separately and cascades of debris scattered in every direction.

A chilling wave of horror swept over me as a grim reality sunk in; mere moments ago, living souls had inhabited that vessel. Now, the stark truth hung heavy in my mind: no one could've lived through that impact. My conscience now had more deaths to rationalize away.

"Direct hit, the target has been destroyed." Kara told us unnecessarily. "Quenra be merciful, that cannon is awesome. And those anti-matter torpedoes played hell with their shielding. They didn't stand a chance."

"What's the status of the other two targets?" Teddy asked her, with no apparent remorse in his voice.

"The second pirate vessel is retreating; I bet they've seen enough." Kara reported. "The Tito is stationary, but under power. They might've lost their shields too. If so, we should finish them."

"That's still my ship, don't forget." he said. "Take us closer, let's have a look."

"What about the other pirate? Do you want to pursue?" Sebastien asked.

"Let 'em go. Hopefully, they'll warn others to leave us alone. This ship just might become notorious." Teddy smiled.

"Let's board the Tito. Jorra Norassa is a traitor and a murderer. I want to kill him slowly and painfully." Kara said. "We have to deal with those traitors, master."

"We will, my love, we will. But we don't have the numbers to board. Jorra probably has 7 or 8 men with him over there, we can't hope to overpower them. And, if we get close enough to take a launch over, we'll be exposing ourselves to attack. We don't know exactly how badly damaged they are." Teddy told her.

"The other pirate vessel has gone out of sensor range." Sebastien said. "I don't think they'll be back. Should I re-engage the artificial gravity and bring us back to normal power?"

Teddy thought about it for a moment, "I suppose so. I don't want to use the plasma cannon on the Tito anyway, I want my ship in one piece. Kara, what are they doing now? Any sign of activity?"

"No, master, they're just sitting there. They're still capable of launching more missiles, but they haven't recovered shields yet, if I'm reading this correctly." she answered.

Teddy tried them on comms again, "Alright Jorra, our sensors show your shields are down. You saw what our plasma cannon did to the Plavic; I want you to power down all your weapons. In fact, turn all your systems off except life support. Over."

"Or what, Teddy? You won't destroy your own ship." Jorra responded, his voice noticeably less arrogant.

"It's nice to hear you say it's still my ship. Power down now or we'll fire. I can't let you leave."

"Kiss my pucker, Teddy. You don't command me anymore."

"Master, they haven't powered down yet, I'm actually detecting a power surge in their reactor. They're probably powering up their REL to try to escape."

"Alright, launch 2 more of those torpedoes." Teddy ordered. After we heard and felt the launch Teddy said quietly, "Dammit."

We sat quietly for a few moments while the torpedoes closed in. The Tito began to move after we launched, but not fast enough. Our torpedoes impacted with a flash on the viewscreen, but the Tito was still there. It was still moving, but much more slowly.

"Two hits, port side, midships. I see gas venting to space; they have a hull breach. But they're still under power. Damn, incoming missiles, I count 4." Kara said.

"The fools know their last launch amounted to nothing. Why bother?" Sebastien asked.

Leanna leaned over to me and whispered, "Abby, why don't they just surrender? I don't understand."

I didn't know anything about this Jorra Norassa person, but I assumed the mutineers aboard the Tito thought surrendering wouldn't save them. So, they decided to go down fighting, forcing Teddy to destroy his own ship at the same time.

"I'm not sure, Leanna. It seems hopeless for them to continue fighting. But I don't know anything about combat in space."

Kara launched another salvo of anti-matter torpedoes. I was pretty sure about one thing, surrendering wouldn't save them from Kara the Demon and they knew it.

Our torpedoes struck the Tito once again. This time there appeared to be a secondary explosion, and a part of the tail section was separated from the rest of the little ship. The Tito ceased to move, dead in space.

Our view screen suddenly went blank. "The forward optics must've been damaged in the first attack. Looks like it's out." Sebastien, calm and controlled as usual, made a few entries on his display and the viewscreen changed to a star chart again.

"Their missiles failed to lock onto us and scattered." Kara announced. "We've learned one thing for sure, we know that QSDM device is effective against missile attacks."

"As long as you remember to turn it on." Sebastien said, wryly.

Kara remarked, "I guess our shields weren't completely effective in the first attack, a couple of those missiles must've hit the hull full force. We're lucky, so far I don't detect any loss of cabin pressure, so there's no hull breach. But we'll have to go outside to check the damage and see if there are any repairs we can make."

"What about the Tito? What can you tell me about them?" Teddy asked her.

"The sensors detect no movement. There's still a heat signature from their reactor, so presumably they have power. But we know they had at least two holes in their hull we could see before our optics failed." Kara reported.

"If they have power, they're still dangerous." Sebastien stated. "We should finish them off. We can't afford to take a chance on more missile strikes."

"I want to see if there's a chance to salvage my ship." Teddy said.

"Dammit, Bradley! If we screw around anymore, we're the ones who'll need to be salvaged. We have no idea how badly the Avernus is damaged or if they're still capable of attacking us. The smart thing to do is... "

"Alright, alright." Teddy cut Sebastien off, "We'll do it your way. Kara, prepare to fire another salvo."

"Avernus... Avernus... this is the Tito. Come in, Avernus." came from the comms.

"Go ahead Tito." Teddy replied.

"We lost propulsion and have minimal life support. We surrender, Cap'n Bradley, get us out'a here."

"Who is that? That isn't Jorra's voice." Kara said. "You think it could be Yoshi?"

"Is that you, Yoshi? What happened to Jorra?" Teddy asked.

"Aye, Cap'n, this is Yoshi. It's just Del, Haney and me left. The four guys that were on the bridge are dead. We were workin' on the damage amidships when your last attack hit. Can you evac us Cap'n?"

"Stand by Yoshi." Teddy told him. "Well, what do you think?" He asked the rest of us.

"It could be a trick. They could be trying to draw us in and hit us at close range." Sebastien said, "Plus, didn't those clowns just try to kill us? We don't owe them a goddamn thing. The prudent thing would be to leave the area as quickly as possible. All this fire being traded might've drawn attention. Long range sensors can pick up all this energy being released pretty easily."

"However, if we rescue them, we can take the opportunity to salvage as much from the Tito as we can, and then scuttle her. I don't like the idea of someone towing her in and making repairs. I'd rather no one have her if we lose her." Kara argued. "It's up to you master, whatever you say. But Fowler's right, we should be as quick as we can, whatever we do."

Teddy turned back to the comms, "Alright, Yoshi, we'll come get you. Shut down your reactor and go to batteries. Make your way to the starboard airlock and wait. You all better be unarmed when we get there or we'll kill every one of you, clear?"

"Aye, clear, Cap'n." came the reply.

"Why tell them to shut down their reactor? Don't you need that to scuttle it?" Sebastien asked.

"True, we could scuttle by overloading the reactor, but there's always a chance a damaged reactor could vent radiation, or even explode before we want it to. Plus, they can't fire any weapons on battery power." Teddy smiled and turned toward Kara, "Love, grab us a couple of those rifles from down below and meet me at the runabout. Fowler, you have the bridge. Take us in to about 1000 meters and lock on with the tractor beam. Can you power up the runabout from here?"

"Already done. Listen, don't approach that ship until they've disabled their reactor, the runabout launch has no shields or weapons. You'll be sitting ducks if they try anything, understand?" Sebastien asked.

"Don't worry, I was born in the morning, but not *this* morning." Teddy said with a grin. "You know, I'm beginning to like you, Fowler. You handled yourself damn well under fire. I'd say you're a born bootlegger."

"Great, thanks."

"And, you were right. We should've raised shields when you suggested. I almost got us killed from sheer stupidity. Next time I promise to pay better attention."

The runabout launch they were speaking of was a small, 6 or 8 passenger vessel that was neatly concealed along the starboard side of the Avernus. It could be used to transfer people between ships in orbit, or in open space like our current situation. It could also be used as an escape pod in case of emergency, but it was little more than a life raft as it had no reactor of its own and no REL drive.

"Alright Bradley, they've shut down their reactor. Everything seems quiet over there." Sebastien reported.

"Thanks, we'll make this as quick as we can, and see you in a few minutes. Keep an eye on the sensor display and alert us if you see anything." Teddy said.

We'd lost our forward optics, so Sebastien cleverly turned the Avernus about so we could watch the launch travel towards the crippled Tito. Seeing it on the viewscreen I couldn't believe there was anyone still alive over there. There were ragged holes all over the port side of the ship, and black burn scars all over the front. There appeared to be a hull breach up front as well, and debris floating near it. Leanna was the first to notice a body floating a few meters away from the forward breach.

"Abby, look. There's a body there. Oh, how awful, it's missing an arm." she said.

It was, indeed. The sight was gruesome and only a few days before I would've been horrified, but now it had a negligible effect on me. I was becoming used to slaughter, and I wasn't sure how I felt about it.

The situation reminded of a quote from the violent despot from Vanu Kina, Quarto Pei, 'My vineyards are watered with the blood of thousands of enemies, and I don't regret a single flagon of wine.' I guess ole Quarto was just saying 'better them than me,' a sentiment I wholeheartedly agreed with.

The runabout had reached the Tito and docked with it. "We're opening the airlock, standby." came Teddy's voice. There followed several minutes of silence, and I could tell Sebastien was trying hard not to ask what was going on. I have to admit, I was getting anxious by the time Teddy returned to the comms.

"Everything's good. The prisoners are bound and secured in the launch, so we're gonna try to retrieve some things. We shouldn't be long. Any targets on the sensors?" he asked.

"None. But hurry, I'd like to get the hell out of here." Sebastien responded.

We waited several more agonizing minutes for Teddy and Kara to finish whatever they were doing over there. I wasn't happy about them bringing their three former comrades back with them. Those assholes had just tried to kill us, and apparently, they *had* killed the fellow named Snyder.

I found myself pacing around the bridge and I couldn't even remember getting up from my seat. I went quickly back to my cabin and retrieved my dagger. Kara had shown me how to clean and oil it earlier, and as I attached the scabbard to my belt, I felt a certain comfort having it with me.

As the launch slowly made its way back, I asked Sebastien, "What's the plan with these prisoners? Can we trust having them on board with us?"

"That's a damn good question, Professor. My answer would be no, but they're comrades of your friends. I'm not sure what to think. Listen, whatever happens I'll have your back. You can count on Leanna and me to be your friends, do you understand?"

"Thank you, Sebastien. And if it means anything, you can count on me. I'll have your back too, yours and Leanna's." I assured him.

Teddy made a slow circuit around the Avernus in the launch, I supposed to inspect the damage. They stopped at the bow and spent a long time there. Eventually they made their way back to the docking cradle.

We headed to the starboard airlock to greet our guests. Sebastien wore his sidearm and carried a rifle as well. Leanna had her little pistol in a holster at her hip too. We probably looked like a bunch of desperados from an old film.

The airlock opened and out stepped Teddy with a concerned look on his handsome face. Kara barked "Let's go" at the three men she led behind her. Their elbows were tied together behind their backs and it looked quite uncomfortable. One was an older fellow with a pot belly and unshaven face. Another was a skinny young man, barely more than a boy. He even had pimples on his beardless face, and a look of abject fear etched upon it. The third man was in between the other two in age, handsome and fit. He had bushy brown hair and a disconcerting look of smug calm on his face. I instantly didn't like him.

"It seems we have a few problems." Teddy began, "The bow looks like we passed through an asteroid field. There's dents the size of an assemblyman's ass out there. It also looks like there may be a place or two where the armor has been compromised. One of the forward sensor pods is completely missing and the other is heavily damaged. The optics are damaged too, as we already know. Those missiles nearly did us in, that's for sure. We should find some place to make repairs."

"Any suggestions where we can go to make repairs?" Sebastien asked. "Or how long it'll take?"

"Well, there's many places we could go, but finding a place out of the Alliance's reach might be a trick. Don't forget about Baaqir, but you'll know his reach better than me." Teddy answered him. "But, if we can find a place to dock, the repairs shouldn't take that long. One thing's for sure though, we'd be fools to try for Kleos without our forward sensors and optics."

"What should I do with these three?" Kara asked.

"The furthest cabin toward the back is the 'brig.' It can be locked from the outside." Sebastien suggested.

"That'll do for now. Kara, my dear, lock them up and come back. We have some decisions to make." Teddy said.

Kara marched the men back to the last cabin and shoved them in. As she returned to the salon she said, "Abby and Leanna, can I get your help?"

We followed Kara and Teddy as Sebastien went back to the bridge. Kara led us back to the launch, where we found the thing stuffed with boxes and crates of equipment and supplies.

"I'd appreciate it if you can help us move this stuff to the salon where we can sort through it. This is everything we could salvage from the Tito. Just carry the smaller boxes and leave the heavier ones for me, thanks." Kara said as she grabbed a huge crate and headed back to the salon with it.

"Well, I guess we better get to work" Leanna laughed.

Professors don't do much manual labor and I was sweating in no time. There were boxes of food, mostly dehydrated single portion meals known as PPRs or pre portioned rations. Boxes of electronic equipment and spare parts. There were quite a few weapons, mostly small arms but also a few tubes with grips that I learned were handheld, shoulder-mounted missile launchers. There were several duffels Kara grabbed and took to she and Teddy's cabin. She didn't share with us what they held.

When we were done, we headed back to the bridge just in time to witness Sebastien launching another set of anti-matter torpedoes at the Tito. Teddy didn't want anyone to be able to salvage his ship, so he'd decided to blow it up instead. We all watched the ship come apart on the screen as Teddy looked away.

"Where to, Captain? Seems to me, as wanted criminals, we should leave Alliance space to make repairs. I was just thinking that MK141 is outside Telluric space, and I have my friend there who could help us. It's also relatively close to us, just a few days with the REL. Unless you have a better idea, that's what I suggest." Sebastien said.

"No, I don't have a better idea. Do you think there'll be a space dock available? And skilled workers? This is damage I can't fix myself, and we'll need parts and specialized equipment." Teddy asked him. "Snyder was my top engineer."

"Certainly, if you can pay. Telluric coin might not answer though, we may need something more universally accepted." Sebastien answered.

"They'll trade, won't they? It's been my experience that guns are pretty universal. And if that doesn't answer, I have gold, precious stones and bluster." Teddy laughed. "Don't worry, if they have the expertise, I have the payment."

Sebastien set a course for the planet MK141. The REL drive worked perfectly, even after all the damage we'd suffered. But he was worried about our sensors, they were severely compromised without one of the forward arrays. He told me we weren't exactly flying blind, but with one eye closed.

We sat down to another meal together; nothing fancy this time, just some dried meat, cheese, nuts and dried fruit. Teddy brought out a case of Nir-Kvekian wine he'd salvaged off the Tito.

"Is this the wine you told me about, Kara?" I asked.

"Ah, yes. This case is a vintage from before I was born and is particularly well regarded. This wine is prized among connoisseurs, isn't that so, master?"

"That, it is. For a time, I was the exclusive interstellar dealer of Nir-Kvekian wine. I'd tell you what my mark-up was but I'm afraid Kara might skin me." Teddy smiled.

"My master was a famous vintner before I corrupted him." She smiled, "I think you'll enjoy it but be careful. It's mild and sweet to the palate but is actually quite strong. One can get very drunk, very quickly."

"My kind of wine." Sebastien said. "Pour me a double."

"Take a small sip and let the wine rest at the tip of your tongue for a few seconds. Then chew the wine softly a few times before swallowing. The flavor explodes, and you'll be delighted." Kara advised.

Following her suggestion, I lifted the glass to my lips, allowing the velvety liquid to caress my palate. A faint, involuntary giggle bubbled up from within me. It wasn't just the wine's delightful flavor that tickled my senses; it was the unexpected bliss of the moment. As I pondered my emotions I discovered, to my amazement, I was quite content. Despite the hair-raising dangers we'd shared and the looming uncertainty of my future, I was happy. Perhaps as happy as I'd ever been in my entire life.

We ate, drank, and joked as if we'd been comrades for a decade. Teddy even told an embarrassing story about escaping a customs official on the planet Temorin 4. He claimed to have hidden in an empty barrel in the loft of a barn for a day and a half. He'd lost 140 cases of wine and barely avoided jail by bribing the farmer to smuggle him into the city.

The adrenaline from the battle had worn off, much wine had disappeared, and the party was winding down. But before we could call it a night, Kara threw a bit of cold water in our collective faces.

"We came through that pretty well, considering. I'd say we were lucky, but I don't believe in luck. However, before we all break our arms patting ourselves on the back, we need to get some things clear. We have a mission on Kleos Prime, and we can't be fighting it out with every motherless scum that gets in our way. We have to avoid more battle, because Kleos Prime is more important than any phallic measuring contests." She pronounced. "*And now*, I need to know what you plan to do with those three scum back there before we go any further." This she said directly to Teddy.

The room fell quiet. I hadn't before heard Kara speak that way to Teddy, and I was surprised. Since I'd known them he'd repeatedly relied on her advice, but she'd mostly acted differential towards him. This seemed like a direct challenge to his authority, or his judgement.

Sebastien broke the silence, "I concur. I don't know those men personally as you both do, but I do know they just tried to kill us. Or, at the very least they meant to turn us in for a reward. I'm not sure what benefit we gain from having them with us."

"I see." Teddy began, "Perhaps I was wrong to save them, I admit. But Del is a man I've known and trusted for many years. Yoshi is just a kid, I don't think he could've had anything to do with killing Ernie Snyder, he was like a father to him. As for how they can help us, Del Malcolm is a fine engineer and Yoshi is his apprentice. We lack an engineer among our little crew presently, so perhaps they could be of use."

"What about Haney? He's a pilot and navigator, what need do we have for him?" Kara challenged.

"Would you prefer I send him on holiday?" Teddy challenged right back.

Kara's neck turned pink. She clearly wasn't in the mood for Teddy's flippant attitude. Leanna and I exchanged a look of worry. Just a few moments ago we were all in a good mood, laughing and having a good time drinking Nir-Kvekian wine. The tension in the galley had quickly become unbearable.

"No." she said, close-lipped, ferocity in her eyes, "I'd *prefer* to slice his living heart from his chest right here on this table and feed it to him."

Leanna gasped quietly at the lurid statement. I wasn't as shocked by Kara's hatred of traitors, of course; I knew the story of her father's murder. Still, Kara's demeaner was frightening and I once again felt the hair at the back of my neck stand up. Baaqir's words came to mind, 'Tovoleks are a blood-thirsty race.'

"So, you'd answer murder with murder? A man you've known and worked with on many occasions?" Teddy asked her.

"Not murder, *justice*. It's what mutineers and traitors deserve. It's what they *all* deserve." Kara answered vehemently.

Teddy stood up and proceeded back toward the cabins. Kara followed him and Sebastien stood but stayed with Leanna and me. The three of us felt like outsiders in this, at least I did. Those men were comrades of Teddy and Kara, none of us had ever met them. It didn't seem like our place to have an opinion.

Soon, Teddy returned leading the older man, still bound, back with him. Kara followed them back into the galley and stood to the side. Teddy grabbed a chair and placed the man on it. The poor fellow looked terrified.

"This is Del Malcolm, an old friend of mine. I'm going to ask him a few questions about what happened aboard the Tito. When I'm done, any of you that want to, can ask him questions too. When we're all through we'll vote, the five of us, on what to do with the three of them. I chose Malcolm to question because I've always known him to be honest, and I don't think he'd lie to save himself." Teddy said.

I was to be a part of a makeshift jury it seemed. I didn't want to take part but I didn't see a way to argue my way out of it. I was part of the crew now, and with that came responsibility to the rest of the crew. So be it.

"Del, what happened on the Tito? Why was Ernie released into space?" Teddy asked.

The fellow, Malcolm, swallowed; then asked for some water. I quickly grabbed a cup and gave him a drink. I had to hold the cup because his hands were still tied behind him. He gulped the water and cleared his throat.

"Well, about a day after we set out, Jorra found on the web that there were bounties offered for the capture and return of you lot. Big time coin, enough to make us all good financially." He told us. "He made a speech about how it was in our best interest to go for it, to turn you in. Ernie argued against it, of course, and a few others. Me, Sam, the kid."

"You? You argued against it? That's convenient. You didn't do a very good job if it." Kara said. "So, why is Snyder dead? Tell us that."

"Yes, me!" Malcolm asserted, "Jorra dropped it, and I thought it'd all blown over, until the next day Jorra brought it up again, this time with several others supporting him. He had 4 with him, and when Snyder ordered them back to their posts, Jorra drew a handgun and put it to Ernie's head. He said he was taking charge and anyone who didn't like it would get shot. I swear, I tried to argue, but Jorra marched Ernie down to the airlock and put him in. Sam and I tried to force our way to the door to open it and let Ernie back in, but Jorra shot Sam in the head, right there. Murray and Griche grabbed me and dragged me to the brig."

"That's when they opened the airlock and killed Snyder?" Teddy asked.

"I didn't see it, I only heard about it later."

"What about the kid, Yoshi? What'd he do while this was going on?" Kara asked.

"I don't remember, he was probably scared to death. Yoshi fears everyone anyway, and Jorra had a gun threatening to kill anyone who opposed him. I didn't see Yoshi till he came and freed me from the brig when the battle started. There was a hull breach and Yoshi needed my help to plug it." Malcolm answered.

"And Haney? What about him?" Teddy asked.

"Trick was with Jorra from the start." Malcolm said.

"Haney was bridge crew. How is he still alive when the rest were killed?" Kara asked.

"I have no idea. After the second round of explosions, he just showed up where Yoshi and I were. I swear Captain, all I've told you is the truth." Malcolm said.

"Alright, Del. Alright." Teddy said.

"Wait." Kara interrupted, "There's something I don't understand. You say Norassa killed Snyder because he opposed him. Snyder argued with him and tried to stop him from taking over, right?"

"Right." Malcolm agreed.

"You also said you argued with Jorra and tried to stop him. You said you tried to open the airlock to let Snyder back in. Actually, you said you and Sam Hawksbrook tried to save Snyder, and Jorra shot and killed Sam, isn't that what you said?" Kara asked.

"That's what happened." Malcolm said.

"Why, Del, did Jorra kill those two and not you? You claim to have done the same thing they did, but for some reason Jorra didn't kill you. Why not?" Kara asked.

The man, Malcolm, looked around the room at all of us. His eyes were big, and his lower lip trembled noticeably. He was clearly terrified.

"I don't know. I don't know why. They wrestled me to the ground and tied my hands and dragged me to the brig. That's what happened, I don't know why they didn't kill me. Maybe they didn't want to kill the last engineer on board, I don't know."

"Does anyone else have any questions?" Teddy asked the rest of us.

"Del, you don't know me. My name is Abby Thornwell. You said that other man, what was his name? The pilot?" Kara spoke up and told me his name. "Yes, the pilot, Haney. You said he was with Jorra from the start. How do you know that?"

"The first day, when Jorra brought the idea up, Trick was right there at his side. He made a comment about how none of us owed Teddy anything, and you all deserved whatever happened to you because of how stupid you were killing green shirts. I think Trick was in on it with Jorra to begin with."

"Fowler, you have any questions for Del?" Teddy asked.

"Nothing that matters."

"Kara, my dear, would you please take Del back to the lockup?" Teddy asked.

Kara went to Del Malcolm and helped him from his chair, then walked him out of the room. We all sat quietly until she returned. She seemed to have lost a bit of her anger when she came back, and I was happy to see it. Kara was my friend, of course, but she was frightening when she was angry.

"Well, what do you think?" Teddy asked the room.

"It all depends on whether you believe him of not. If he's telling the truth, he's innocent." Sebastien said. "He seemed to be truthful."

"I've never known Del to be dishonest. But, then again, he's never been accused of mutiny before. Some people will say anything to save their life." Teddy said. "But I agree with Fowler, I think he's telling the truth."

"If he's telling the truth, it means Haney was one of the ringleaders. I don't see how you could think Malcolm told the truth about one thing and not the other." I said.

"He never liked Haney, but no one does. He's a good pilot, but I never liked him. I didn't think Jorra liked him either. I suppose Del could be innocent, it's possible they kept him alive because he's a good engineer. But the fact is we'll never know. All three of those men have every reason to lie to save their skin. I don't know how we can believe anything they say." Kara reasoned.

"I'd like to suggest something." Leanna spoke up, "I, myself, wouldn't like to be involved in any more killing. What if we kept them locked up until we get to MK141, then set them loose there? I don't trust them enough to have them with us, but I can't see the harm in just turning them free."

"That's a good idea, Lea." Sebastien chimed in. "We wash our hands of them. Like Kara said, we'll never be able to believe anything they say.

So, we can't ever trust them. I don't want them with us either, and this way we don't have to kill them."

"That's two votes, and I'll make it three. I'd hate to kill Malcolm or Yoshi; I like both of them too much. As for Haney, I have an easy time believing he's a rat bastard, but if we bring him in here and question him, I have no doubt he'd have a story all about how he tried to stop the mutiny but just couldn't. We can't prove anything either way." Teddy agreed.

"So be it. I'll go along with the majority. But I think you all know, if it were up to me, we'd kill them all now and get it over with. I hate the idea of letting a mutineer and murderer go free." Kara told us. "Plus, they're responsible for the loss of the Tito, don't forget about that."

I sat there and stayed silent. I understood Leanna and Sebastien's position. They didn't know those men and sentencing them to death would be a harsh thing to do to a stranger. I agreed with that sentiment. The man, Malcolm, seemed sincere to me. And Yoshi was just a boy. But I kept quiet, because in my heart I agreed with Kara about Trick Haney. Since I believed Malcolm, I had no doubt in my mind Haney was a mutineer and a murderer. Gods forgive me, but I would've voted to turn him over to Kara the Demon.

We decided to take turns getting some sleep. Kara, with her preternatural ability to go without sleep, took the first watch on the bridge. The wine had helped make me tired, so I crept to my cabin and dove into the luxurious bed with silk sheets and eiderdown comforter. Baaqir sure knew how to live, the bastard.

A few hours later I woke to the smooth, silky feel of a naked Az-Codorian crawling into bed with me, spooning me from behind. Kara wrapped her arms around me and nestled her face into my hair and neck. Her soft kisses gave me goosebumps and lit a fire in my belly.

"Kara, won't Teddy wonder where you are?"

"He knows, little human. He relieved me on the bridge. Don't be jealous, my pretty professor, you are mine and I am yours until you tire of me."

"That'll never happen." I whispered.

"You say that now, but what about when I get old and ugly? When I have wrinkles, age spots, and walk with a cane. Will you not tire of me?" she teased.

"We'll be old and ugly together. I'll put cream on your spots and whittle a cane for you from driftwood. That would make me supremely happy."

"Me, too. Not the old and ugly part, but certainly the part about being together." she kissed my neck some more. "I like driftwood."

Rotating, so I was facing her, I whispered "Kara, are you sure Teddy won't mind? I don't want my desire for you to cause trouble between you and your Gal-vek. I'm starting to like Teddy; I don't want him to hate me."

"Mmm, your desire for me. I like that, Abby Thornwell." She kissed me sweetly on the lips, "Teddy knows I've decided to be your lover, and he understands. My question is for you, little human. Do you want me?"

"You know I do; from the moment I met you."

"Good. Now, I think I'll give you a thousand kisses all over your body. One thousand, and I won't stop until you beg me to."

"That'll never happen." I whispered once more.

Part Fourteen Excursion to Fort Eversun

Interstellar Dates: 388-06-25 thru 07-01
The Avernus arrives at the free planet MK141.

THE TRIP TO MK141 WAS relatively uneventful. We kept the three mutineers locked up in the last cabin and periodically brought them food and drink. The trips to the 'head' were handled by Teddy or Sebastien. I didn't venture back there, having no wish to involve myself in their pleadings and apologies, of which I was told there were many. Apparently, Teddy hadn't confided in the men what our plans for them were, and they were still afraid Teddy would turn Kara loose on them. None of them had any illusions about what that'd mean.

Once, I happened to overhear the boy, Yoshi, while they were bringing him food. He was begging Teddy for mercy and he sounded like he'd been crying. He asked Teddy to tell his mother what'd happened to him so she wouldn't be worried.

"Just tell my Ma where my body is. I know she'd wanna know, Cap'n. If she never hears from me, it'll kill her. You can do that for me, can't you?"

"Yoshi, there is every possibility your mother will see your body again with breath still in it. But, if you ask me about it again, I'll toss your body into a crevice on one of the moons of Pentoff."

"Does that mean you ain't gonna kill us, Teddy?" This was the voice of the murderer Haney. I took a couple of steps closer to the door so I could hear his response.

"I wouldn't say that, Trick. You see, right now we're trying to discover if there's any bounties available on *your* sorry carcass. I seem to recall you were hiding from the law when you joined Snyder's crew.

291

Hopefully, the bounty is available dead or alive. That way I can slit your throat, so I won't have to listen to your idiot voice anymore." Teddy told him. Haney shut up after that.

After about four days in REL drive, we arrived in the MK141 planetary system. The planet itself had defensive shielding surrounding it, as was common, and we had to get permission to land. Unlike at home, where the space ports and docking facilities were in orbit around Ampora, the space port at MK141 was on the planet's surface near the capital city.

Sebastien sat at the comms console and spoke to the orbital controller about landing. "Miccon One, this is the Avernus. We're requesting permission to approach. We need repairs and supplies."

"Stand by Avernus." came the reply.

"If they don't know you already, these places usually require a hefty bribe or two to the local officials to get anywhere." Teddy said. "If that comes up, let me do the negotiating."

"Don't worry, Bradley. I don't think that'll be necessary. If they think we're buying supplies they're more likely to welcome us with open arms. Commerce is always a high priority. These folks need the business just like everyone else does; more even. Plus, I told you, I have friends here." Sebastien said.

"Excellent. We may need a few things now that you mention it." Teddy agreed. "Let's hope your friends are still friendly."

"Your vessel has been flagged Avernus. We may not be able to accept you. It's possible a repair dock may be available in a few weeks. However, I'd have to get special permission from the government to allow you to land." The planetary controller advised.

"A few weeks, my bloody uncle. Bloody extortionists." Teddy exclaimed, "They know we're not holding in orbit for weeks."

"Take it easy, Bradley, I think you're right, they're just fishing for a bribe. I've no doubt the Avernus is flagged as stolen, but I don't think they'll care about a stolen ship as long as we can pay our way while we're here." Sebastien said. He turned back to the console.

"Miccon One, we're here on a diplomatic mission as well. Can you please inform Commerce Director Damon Offerton that Sebastien

Fowler has arrived with an envoy from Kyntava and his entourage? We'd be happy to pay a fee for your assistance. A reasonable fee, that is."

"Rodger, Avernus. Stand by." came the response.

"Who's Damon Offerton?" I asked.

"Yes, and who's the envoy and who're the entourage?" Kara asked with a laugh.

"He's a very old, very dear friend of mine. We grew up together, for a while anyway. He was one of my best mates in the 'sliders,' our street gang back home. Damon was never a great fighter, but he's as clever as they come." Sebastien told me. "Last I heard, he was a big wheel here."

We waited for several minutes while the orbital controller was silent. Our aft optics were still functional, so I took the opportunity to examine MK141 through the viewscreen. From orbit, the planet presented a desolate picture. Muddy browns, muted beiges, and faint hints of weary yellow stretched across the landscape. The absence of vibrant greenery was painfully obvious, and only sporadic pockets of civilization were visible. The scarcity of cities left me with an overwhelming impression of loneliness and isolation.

The dominating feature was an inland sea in the same hemisphere as the capital city. However, it's modest size was shocking, as it was the *only* water visible; a solitary oasis in this arid expanse. MK141 from orbit appeared to be about the opposite of Ampora, which was brilliant blue from horizon to horizon and had hundreds of large cities.

"Sabes, is that you, you old dog? What in hell are you doing way out here? Why aren't you back in that fatted pig you call a ship, with all those trollops and rich widows?" came a voice from the comms console.

"Easy, Damon, there's mixed company up here." Sebastien laughed. "I just thought we'd give you a little business, we had a bit of trouble and need to repair our ship. Nothing major, but we're in a hurry. Can you fix us up?"

"You came all the way here for a repair job?"

"It's a long story."

"Don't get me wrong, I'm glad you're here. I'm sending the access code now, and you can use dock 1744, out on terminal K. I'm on my way down to meet you right now. I can't wait to see if you're still as ugly as I remember." Damon joked.

"He seems a jovial chap. Well done, Sabes." Teddy teased.

"Ah, come on. You know how it is with old pals. We keep in touch, but we haven't seen each other in years. I hear he's pretty well set up here, some kind of bigshot in the government. I can't say it surprises me; Damon was always two steps ahead of everybody." Sebastien said. "Let's get down there and see about the parts we need."

We all strapped in again as we began our approach. I asked Kara if the 'prisoners' would be all right while we descended, she shrugged and said she didn't care. The ride got bumpy as we hit the atmosphere, but it didn't last long. As we broke through the clouds, I got a closer look of my first alien planet. It didn't get any greener as we descended.

"There's a city there, see it?" Leanna said excitedly. "And mountains. Look, beyond the mountains is a sea. It's so beautiful."

I wouldn't say it was beautiful, exactly. Fascinating perhaps. And the city Leanna spied was small and dingy, with few buildings being more than a handful of stories. It was nothing like my home. My *former* home.

"Yes, Leanna." I smiled, "And it has the added advantage of being a highly unlikely place to have missiles launched at you."

Sebastien slowed our descent, and a planet-based tractor beam guided us into our docking area. The dock was little more than a concrete platform next to a worn looking warehouse, or quonset hut. The building didn't look large enough to house the Avernus, so I guessed the repairs would have to be completed outdoors. After we landed, the five of us gathered in the salon.

"Well, Fowler, I suppose your friend will be along. Should we wait for him to arrange our repairs?" Teddy asked.

"I think that'd be best. He can certainly help finding a trustworthy contractor, and we need to keep as low a profile as possible. Remember, we're wanted criminals now." Sebastien said.

"We aren't wanted here though, right?" I asked, "I mean, we're not in Telluric space anymore."

"That's true enough. I don't suppose the local militia will bother us, but a place like MK141 could be teeming with bounty hunters. I'm not talking about the unshaven, pot-bellied local slobs. I'm talking about the professionals. Ex-military, sometimes mercenary, well-armed and knowledgeable kind of bounty hunters. They sometimes work in teams and are well organized. If they're around, they'll know all about us by now and be on the lookout." Sebastien told us.

"Fowler's right. We see those types quite often in places like this. The bounties on us are probably substantial and would be tempting to anyone, let alone professional bounty hunters." Teddy agreed.

"But I was hoping to go shopping in the city." Leanna practically whined, "I need some things. Plus, we've been cooped up on the Avernus long enough, I want to see the sky overhead and breath some fresh air." Leanna apparently agreed with me about the Avernus' claustrophobic effect. She missed the massive Archeron, which had been her home for so long.

Sebastien simply shrugged and smiled. Again, it seemed he couldn't say no to the girl about anything. I had to agree with Leanna about having the sky overhead and fresh air. My first sojourn into space had been less than relaxing. I turned to my girl (oh how delicious it felt to think of Kara that way) and gave her a sort of pleading look.

"It's alright, Fowler, I'll take Leanna and Abby into town and have a look around." Kara volunteered, "We'll keep a low profile and try not to get into any barroom brawls. I'll go armed and ready; I'm used to being a fugitive."

Remembering my lost passport I said, "I'm afraid I left my passport back on the Archeron. Do you think they'll let me disembark here without one?"

"Places like MK141 usually aren't worried about that sort of thing. I don't think it'll be a problem." Teddy told me. "They'll be more concerned with your ability to spend coin while you're here."

"What about the prisoners?" Sebastien asked.

"We have to keep them here for now." Teddy answered, "We can't turn them loose until we're ready to leave. If we let them go now they could give us away to those bounty hunters you were talking about. We can't trust them, especially Haney."

We three women started getting ready to go into the city. I donned some of the new clothes Teddy had bought me, attached my dagger to my belt and I was ready in no time. Leanna appeared from out of her cabin wearing a halter top, miniskirt, knee socks and heels. Her long hair flowed down her back in crimps and curls, and as usual her face was made up perfectly. She looked like a teenage celebrity about to hit the town. She and I, with my beige safari clothes and boots, made an odd couple.

"Lea, we said low profile." Sebastien began, "You look amazing, but that's certainly not low profile. At least change the heels, those aren't practical if you have to run from danger. Go put on your boots I bought you, please."

"Oh, you're no fun." Leanna teased. But she did go back and change her shoes like he'd asked.

Sebastien's friend, Damon, had shown up while we were getting ready. I hadn't seen Kara yet. Teddy, Sebastien, and Damon were sitting in the salon negotiating. Offerton himself was a tall, thin man with sandy blond hair and a clean-shaven face. He was dressed in an azure, silk suit; or a material much like silk. He had a new haircut, gold rings on his fingers and a gold tie clip in the shape of a palm tree completed his outfit. He was the most prosperous looking thing I'd seen on MK141 so far.

They paused their discussion and rose from their seats when Leanna and I entered. Teddy came to my side and said, "Offerton, let me introduce my friend, Abigail Thornwell. She's a professor of history from Ampora, and one of the partners in our current endeavor. The brains of Aristotle and the beauty of Aphrodite in one package."

"Such praise; and yet I find myself unable to disagree. I'm humbled to make your acquaintance Ms. Thornwell." Offerton bowed, "I'm Damon Offerton, administrator of this port, and I'm at your service, madam."

"That's Doctor Thornwell to you, Damon." Sebastien smiled. "Damon is the friend I was telling you about, Abby. He's the Director of Trade and Commerce for the planetary government."

"And who is this ravishing creature, Sabes?" Offerton asked as he gazed at Leanna.

"That, you silver tongued rascal, is my fiancée, Leanna Callicenna. Lea, this is Damon, the one I was telling you about." Sebastien said.

"Don't believe a word he's told you, miss Callicenna. Sabes was never a reliable story teller. My, my, I'm certain I've never met a more charming pair of ladies." Offerton flattered us. "Wait, did you say fiancée? Surely, an oaf like yourself couldn't possibly have ensnared such a beauty. I refuse to believe such nonsense."

"Sebastien, this the famous leader of your gang from when you were young? Why, he looks almost respectable now." Leanna teased.

"Don't let him fool you, he claims he went straight, but I'd still check your pockets before he leaves." Sebastien laughed.

"Ha, if I remember right, you were the gifted pickpocket. I never participated in anything so risky. I apologize, ladies. Sabes and I are old friends from the slums of Broyden City, on Dressida. Unfortunately, our hardboiled youth seems to have left us unworthy of gentle company."

"Gentlemen, there's no need to apologize on my account. It's entertaining seeing old chums reunited. It's lovely to meet you, Mr. Offerton." I said.

"Call me Damon, please. That goes for you too, Leanna. And congratulations on your betrothal. I like to tease, but in all seriousness, Sebastien is the most reliable chap I've ever known. A lady could hardly find a better fellow to attach herself to." He turned back to Teddy, "Now, where were we, my friends?"

"You were telling us about this contractor." Teddy told him.

"Ah, yes. Petyr is the best man we have, Sabes, trust me. He and his crew will fix you right up in no time. The parts may be a little trickier; the original optics on your ship are like nothing I've seen before. And, when I checked on those forward sensor arrays the company that made them says they won't be available for at least nine more Tellurian months. Where'd you get this ship, the future?"

"That's not far off." Sebastien chuckled. "And, I suppose Petyr the contractor will kick a significant portion of the bill back in your direction?"

"Sabes, I do have a family to feed." Offerton said good-naturedly.

"Well, what parts do you have on hand? Can you replace our equipment with something approximate?" Teddy asked.

"Approximate? I believe so. The stuff we have in stock is the absolute best available here, it comes from a free planet called Winthra. The place is known for its excellent engineering firms. Many of which are involved with construction projects here, and I can vouch for the quality of their technologies."

"That's fine, Offerton, just set us up with the best you have available. Speed is the overriding concern. We are in an unholy hurry. We're far behind schedule as it is." Teddy said. "How much for the repairs and parts, all in?"

"Well, now, these are friend prices you understand. I guess we can make an exception and do the whole thing for 30 thousand Telluric coin." Offerton offered. "That includes around the clock work. Petyr could have it done in two or three days."

Teddy let out a long whistle, "For those prices we might not be friends for long. If you could replace those original parts, we might have a deal, but since you can't and we're forced to accept lower quality components, I think 20 thousand is more in line."

"I just told you, these components are top quality, the best available." Offerton argued.

"Come now, let's not haggle. How about we split the difference and say 25 thousand? I want to remain friends and get the work started before Kator goes supernova." Sebastien laughed.

"How about this, 20 thousand, all in gold?" Teddy, shockingly, produced ten shiny new aurics from his jacket pocket.

I must've looked stupid, my mouth agape, as I stared. I'd never seen that much gold before. Ten aurics amounted to 500g of pure gold, a resource average citizens like me didn't see often. Most of the 'gold' jewelry sold was different alloys manipulated to appear gold. Real gold was almost exclusively used in high-tech devices and manufacturing, usually for the military. Aurics were minted, in limited amounts, on the planet Theta Barriso, the banking and financial center of the Telluric Alliance.

"Excellent. Sabes, you didn't tell me you had all that shine. I guess we have a deal." Offerton couldn't hide being impressed.

"I didn't know." Sebastien told him.

Offerton said, "I'll have Petyr start right away. I want all of you to come to my home this evening for dinner." Damon Offerton proposed. "Now, I won't take no for an answer. I'll have the militia send some men here to guard your ship as we sup, and I'll have my chef prepare something special for us. Here's the address." he tapped Sebastien's comms device with his.

Kara appeared from her cabin decked out in full combat gear. She wore one of her body suits, and her familiar armor, but this time all of it was in tactical black. Both of her blades were in scabbards at her waist, and she also wore a handgun in a holster. Her hair was pulled back into a tight ponytail making her facial features more stark than usual. She was fearsome looking, to put it mildly.

Offerton stopped in his tracks and stared for several seconds. He'd obviously never seen anyone or anything quite like Kara before. "Say, now. What have we here?" he finally asked.

"Damon Offerton, allow me to introduce my partner and confidant, Ka'rra Corda Az-Mur Az-Codor, Pont-jar of Az-Codor. Also known as Kara the Demon or if you prefer, simply Kara. Kara, this is the director of trade and commerce for the planetary government here, Damon Offerton. He also, conveniently, manages this port facility." I think Teddy got a kick out of introducing Kara to people for the first time.

"Well, I'm not usually at such a loss for words. I'm extremely proud to meet you Ms. Az-Codor. I have to admit I've never met a Tovolek before, but I've always wanted to. You make a formidable impression, madam. You are exceptionally beautiful, and yet terrifying as well." He smiled as he indicated Kara's armor and armaments. We all laughed, even Kara smiled crookedly at him.

"Thank you, Mr. Offerton." Kara responded. "I'm glad to meet you too. And, since we've just met, you have no reason to be terrified. *Yet.*"

He seemed to take Kara's teasing in stride. I have to admit Offerton was a charming fellow. It wasn't hard to understand how he'd climbed so high in the government here. After he left, we had another brief meeting in the salon.

"I suppose you three are going out? Are you sure I can't dissuade you? It's a bit foolish in my opinion." Sebastien asked.

"We'll be fine, Kara's with us." Leanna reasoned. "I need some clothes and makeup, and I want to see the city. Maybe we can even find somewhere to eat lunch while we're out."

"What'll you use for coin, Lea? You can't use your deposit account here and we don't have any local coin. What we have is a bit of Dressidian coin. That's only good on Dressida, I'm afraid." Sebastien told her.

"It's not even certain Telluric coin will be accepted by the local merchants. But, we are not without means, Fowler." Kara told him, as she showed him a small velveteen pouch.

Kara undid the leather cinch and spilled a small pile of precious stones into her hand. There were red gems, pink gems, blue gems, green gems, and several multi-colored stones I couldn't possibly name. The collection was quite beautiful.

"Kara, where's all these gems and gold coming from?" I asked, awed.

"We were able to salvage this from the safe on board the Tito. Ironically, the idiots who tried to capture us to claim the bounties on our heads were unknowingly sitting on top of this treasure the whole time, the morons. This was a big reason I wanted to board the Tito before we left."

"And you don't mind financing Leanna's shopping trip? That's generous Kara, thank you. I'll pay you back, I promise." Sebastien offered.

Teddy told him, "Don't worry about it, my friend. You're both part of the crew now, and this is the crew's hoard. Besides, I owe you more than this for helping me escape from the green shirts back on the Archeron."

"I appreciate that, Bradley. It's still generous of you, thanks." Sebastien said.

Teddy explained, "Kara will take these gems to a jewelers or pawn broker's shop here and see what they'll give her in local coin. It'll be far less conspicuous shopping with local coin than with gold or gems. But,

Kara my dear, don't make too large an exchange in one spot. It might bring too much attention. Spread it around as much as possible."

We disembarked the Avernus and walked together through the bustling workshop next door. The place was filled with machinery, and we saw several mechanics sorting through crates full of parts. As Offerton had promised, our components were already appearing.

Exiting the workshop we found ourselves in the surprisingly busy port terminal. Hundreds of people scurried about, many carrying luggage. Up ahead we spied an office with a sign that read 'Customs and Immigration.' Behind the desk sat a disinterested clerk, who, with a practiced nonchalance, accepted the modest Telluric coin bribe Kara discreetly offered. He wished us a pleasant visit and waved us on; none of us showed him a passport.

We walked out onto a crowded thoroughfare, merchants' shops displaying every sort of ware lined the street. Indiscernible conversations could be heard from the many open-doored cafes and pubs. The sun wasn't yet high in the sky but the heat was already oppressive. The city's name was appropriate: Fort Eversun. If I had to guess, I'd say it was 40 or even 45 degrees Celsius. Honestly, it sort of took my breath away. Even though, mercifully, there was no humidity. The temperature on Ampora rarely topped 30 degrees. I found myself searching for a place to get a drink before we'd gotten far down the street.

Kara, however, was intent on finding a shop to exchange the stones. We garnered many looks, the three of us. Because of our mismatched appearances we were obviously drawing too much attention, but there was nothing to be done about it. I marveled at the diversity of the population there. It was more like what I'd expected on the Archeron. Many different races were evident, humans as well as Runivians, Jijians, Betrads, Windrites, Lirannians and more than a few I couldn't name.

A Lirannian man crossed the street ahead of us at one point. He was short in stature, as all Lirannians are, but had delicate features to go with his pale complexion. He also had those same stunning, violet eyes that Leanna had; I found him quite handsome and secretly wondered if Leanna's unknown Lirannian father had been as handsome as this stranger. He must've been, for her to be as beautiful as she was.

We turned a corner and were confronted, unnervingly, by a group of red-skinned, yellow eyed Pentoffians armed to the teeth. There were four men and two women, dressed in military style uniforms, carrying rifles, and armed with several different styles of weapons on their belts. They coolly regarded us as we passed by, but didn't speak. Kara, walking calmly beside me, hardly seem to notice them. I must confess to being frightened, those Pentoffians were a scary looking bunch. It wasn't that long ago humans had been at war with the Pentoffian Empire.

"Kara, did you see those Pentoffians back there?" I asked her, "That was a sight I could've done without. They were armed and looked like they were angry at us for breathing the same air."

"I thought the one on the end was sort of cute." Leanna said of what appeared to be the youngest man of the bunch. He did have a bit of a baby-face, but 'cute' wouldn't be my choice to describe him. That leathery, red skin and those disconcerting yellow eyes creeped me out.

"Shh, Leanna, you're terrible." I said. "Be careful, Pentoffians supposedly have a thing for human females."

"That's just propaganda, Abby. Don't believe everything you hear." Leanna said.

"Oh, you can believe it." Kara told us. "Supposedly, during the war, Pentoffian soldiers went out of their way to capture human females if they could. Brigades of their soldiers would keep them as concubines and even bring them along on campaign. Many of the soldiers even married their human captives and had families together. I think it's safe to say the Pentoffians aren't as prejudiced as most humans are."

"But who were they, Kara?" I asked. "They weren't the bounty hunters Teddy and Sebastien were warning us about, were they?"

"They were probably local militia." she answered, "You see them on many worlds doing similar jobs. Pentoff was decimated during the war, and the Tellurians have placed many economic restraints on the Pentoffians. There's not many opportunities left on Pentoff for young people, so they emigrate all over. They mostly seem to gravitate toward police or militia careers, but they're excellent soldiers and there's several well-known regiments of mercenaries made up of Pentoffians available for hire. The ones I've met are usually decent fellows."

"Militia? Aren't they like policemen?" Leanna asked.

"Very similar, yes." Kara answered, "They're sort of para-military police. They keep the peace, investigate crimes, and make arrests. But they're also, theoretically, responsible for defense in case of invasion or insurrection. They may or may not be interested in our bounties, so it'd be wise for us not to run afoul of them."

We eventually found a small jeweler's shop on a narrow side street. The proprietor was a Jijian man of advanced years. Jijians are well known to be extremely devout religiously and Kara thought the man would give us an honest price for some stones because of that. She produced a few stones without revealing the pouch.

"Ahh, yes. Quite nice, quite nice. Loose stones are in demand now miss, and these are fine." he said as he examined the gems slowly with his jeweler's glass.

The man placed the gems on a tray and held a small scanning device above them for several seconds. "The stones appear to be natural. Have you had them appraised recently?"

"Yes, several Telluric months ago on Marmo. My auntie left them to me when she passed, and I never wanted to part with them because of the sentimental value, you understand. But my friends and I find ourselves in want of local coin here. Can you tell me what the exchange rate is for Telluric coin? Your local coin is the kel, isn't that correct?" Kara asked the man. It was obvious Kara had done this sort of thing before. I had to stifle a giggle when she talked about her 'auntie.'

"Yes, the kel is the local government's unit of coinage. I think it's roughly 25 kel per Telluric coin. Can you tell me how much you were offered for these on Marmo?" he asked.

"I can't remember, and I didn't write it down. Is there an offer you'd like to make, sir?" she asked sweetly.

"Well, for the ruby I could give you 25 thousand kel, I'm not sure of the emeralds, they aren't in high demand just now." the jeweler offered. "I could offer you the bulk, wholesale value. But I'm afraid that wouldn't amount to much. Grevin!" he shouted.

I was trying to figure out what 'grevin' meant when a tall, skinny young man came out from the back of the shop. He wasn't Jijian or human; I couldn't tell exactly what race he was for sure. Part Betrad probably, because of his height.

"Grevin, do you remember what the bulk price for emeralds is?" the old man asked.

The young man, Grevin, said, "I think it was fourteen hundred per carat, boss."

Kara drew little tooth from its scabbard and placed it on the counter. I thought maybe she meant to show the man the gems embedded in the handle; he seemed nice.

"Sir, what about me leads you to think me a fool?" Kara inquired, with just a bit of venom in her voice. "The ruby you refer to isn't a ruby but a Katorian Painite, as you well know. One of the rarest gems in the quadrant. The two emeralds aren't emeralds either, but Stamolites, also known as Alexandrites in some places."

"Oh, I see. Miss, I would never mistake you for a fool. Let me take a second look." the man said.

"If you examine the three stones closely, you'll see they are of exquisite quality and clarity, and obviously not synthetic. My auntie had erudite tastes and only collected the absolute best. In addition, the exchange rate is nearer to 30 kel per Telluric coin. I don't begrudge you your profit sir, but let us be reasonable. I'll give you an opportunity to... *adjust* your offer."

"Of course, please forgive me, I must've made a mistake. The exchange rate fluctuates daily. Let me take another look at these gems of yours." He said, his eyes taking in Kara's dagger. "Grevin, can you please give us a more accurate exchange rate, kel for Telluric coin?"

The old man retrieved a tray covered in black felt, pulled a lamp from under the counter which lit the felt tray up brightly and placed the stones on it. He began to examine them more closely with his jeweler's glass. Grevin disappeared again to the back room.

He returned quickly and announced, "29.08 kel per Telluric coin, via the Central Bank, as of this morning."

"Thank you, Grevin. Now that you say it, miss, I can see this is clearly a Painite. It's nice, if somewhat small. I can offer you, say, 75 thousand kel?" It was suffocatingly hot in the shop, but I could swear the man was sweating more profusely than he was when we'd walked in.

"I will accept 150 thousand kel for the painite which is worth nearly twice that." The man huffed at her, but she continued, "I'll accept 60 thousand kel for the Stamolites which is a fraction of their worth as well; as long as you promise not to disclose where, when and most importantly *from whom* you purchased them. You must not attempt to re-sell them for at least one tenth of your local year. If I hear you haven't lived up to your end of the bargain, you'll have a more intimate introduction to my friend here." Kara tapped her dagger.

"Miss, I will... " He started to make a counteroffer but looking at Kara and her dagger he surrendered to common sense. "You bargain well. Let me go to my safe and I'll return shortly." He knew when he was defeated. If you could call purchasing three beautiful gems for nearly half price being defeated. He and Grevin disappeared again.

After he left I said, "Kara, was it necessary to threaten the man? We could've gotten him to make a better offer eventually."

"The threat wasn't about the price. I was trying to make sure he doesn't talk about us. The last thing we need is talk getting around about the three crazy, off world women selling gems for half-price. That'd get too much attention. The advantage of dealing in loose stones rather than jewelry is there's no arguing over provenance. Whoever possesses them, owns them. I used a threat to keep him quiet and sold cheap to make sure he bought. His greed overcame his fear, just as I expected. He's jijian, but he *acts* about as jijian as Teddy, if you know what I mean."

"So, how much coin are we getting?" Leanna asked.

"210 thousand kel, which is a little more than 7 thousand Telluric coin. The sad thing is I could've probably gotten close to 15 thousand coin for those stones on the Archeron, but we aren't on the Archeron. And, we couldn't have gotten kel aboard the Archeron either. However, it's probable that 7 thousand coin will buy more here than it would've on the Archeron where everything is overpriced, so we probably came out about even, all things considered." Kara explained.

The man returned with a briefcase. Grevin went and locked the front door and came to stand beside his employer. The jeweler placed the case on the counter and opened it, revealing stacks of old-fashioned bank notes inside. He slowly counted out 210 thousand kel and handed the stack over to Kara. He also produced some sort of paperwork or contract for her to sign.

"I prefer to simply transfer Kel electronically to you if you have a local account. These bank notes are hard to come by. I would increase my offer by 5 thousand Kel if you were amenable." He said.

"Sorry, we don't have a local account, and we aren't staying long. We'll take the notes. Also, you must know that whatever name I were to scribble on your paper won't be my own." Kara said.

"It matters little to me, miss, but I need the paperwork for the commerce commission's inspectors." he told her.

Grabbing the pen, I signed the thing. My throat was parched, I must've lost a kilo sweating in that oven of a shop. After I signed, we bid farewell to the Jijian and left. Stepping out into the 45-degree heat was refreshing by comparison. As we walked down the narrow street Kara started handing Leanna and I wads of bank notes. It was an odd feeling holding currency this way, I'd only ever held bank notes a handful of times in my life, and never this many. Everyone at home used Telluric coin for everything.

"Abby, who's Bianca Steenburg?" Kara asked.

I laughed, "She's an assistant history professor at the Academy. I figured Bianca wouldn't care if I signed her name, we're thousands of light years from Ampora. Let's find a drink, what do you say?"

We quickly spied what appeared to be a public house and made our way there. There was a hand-painted sign above the door that said Hedrick's.

As we entered, our nostrils were assaulted by an offensive deluge of smells better left uncontemplated. With herculean willpower, bolstered by a thirst of epic proportions, I resisted the instinct to leave the foul place. Hedrick's was a bit cooler than outside in the street, so it obviously had rudimentary conditioned air which the little jewelry shop had lacked, but it was still too warm for comfort.

The pub's decorations were an eclectic collection of every manner of home-spun curiosities. Shelves held jars of rocks, rusted tin cups, varmint skulls bleached white by the relentless desert sun, nearly spent candles and even a pair of boots hanging by the laces from a nail. Grimy mirrors, faded photographs and even a frilly pair of women's knickers also decorated the walls.

Kara went to the bar as Leanna and I found a table nearby. She asked the fellow behind the bar, "Are you Hedrick?"

"Nah, Hedrick's dead. I took the place over after he was killed, but I never got round to paint'n a new sign." There was a smattering of laughter from the twenty or so patrons in the place.

"How was Hedrick killed?" Kara asked.

"Got'na fight wit a Runivian pirate and sprung a leak in his head." This caused more mirth among the patrons.

"That'd do it. So what's your name?" Kara asked.

"Yarmoulachuck."

"That's why he ain't painted a new sign yet." Came from one of the patrons sitting at the bar. "Can't afford the paint."

Several other patrons laughed good naturedly, and the barman didn't seem to take offense. I had the impression the crowd was mostly regulars, and the source of at least some of the smell.

"Let me have three ales please, in clean glasses, if you have them." Kara asked sarcastically, and received a few laughs too. Mr. Yarmoulachuck just shook his head and poured the ale.

The three of us had drawn a great deal of attention. The locals seemed quite curious about the 'outworlders' among them. They seemed to be hanging on Kara's every word.

One of the patrons, a corpulent fellow in an old, threadbare, stained suit, asked Kara as she carried the glasses to our table, "Where'ya from? What'r ya, some kine'a commando or som'n? I ain't ne'er seen a giddup like that before."

"Really?" Kara answered, "This is the latest style in the Nenevar system."

"Nin'var? I ain't ne'er heard'a that place." The man retorted.

"That, sir," said Kara, "Is why you're so obviously out of step with fashion."

The man, and the other regulars, were momentarily thrown off, not sure if Kara was serious or teasing. Some of the locals chuckled, and eventually the man began to scowl as he slowly realized he'd been insulted.

The ales Kara brought us were smallish glasses of weak, flat, cloudy, room temperature beer. On the plus side, it was only 2 kel per glass. Still, I believe you would've had a difficult time finding worse ale anywhere in the galaxy.

"Sir?" I addressed the barkeep, "Do you have anything stronger? Any whisky?"

"We ain't got no whisky, lady. Ain't nobody here can afford the stuff. We got some sandrob if you'd like to try it."

"Sandrob? What's that?" I asked.

"Local hooch, distilled from beets. Beets is about the only veg'able that grows here." He told us. "My missus makes beet soup 3 times a week. I'd divorce her, but there ain't no better cooks around that ain't married already." Several of the patrons guffawed.

"Give us three glasses of sandrob, please." Leanna said. The patrons guffawed again.

When it arrived, we sipped the stuff and grimaced. It tasted nothing like beets and was as harsh on the palate as pure grain alcohol. The patrons guffawed at us again and shook their heads. I was glad we amused them so much.

"That ain't the way you drink it." the barkeep told us. "You just toss it back, quick like, and try'n miss your taste buds." He poured himself a shot and tossed it back by way of demonstration.

So, we did the same. I gasped, my esophagus on fire, and coughed a few times. More guffaws followed, but good naturedly. A few patrons offered to buy us another round which we politely declined. As we stood to leave, the barkeep gave us some advice, along with a much-appreciated glass of plain, ole water for each of us.

"If you're looking for real whisky, like the stuff that's imported, head downtown to the Billet Hotel bar. That's where the fancy folks drink. They got lots of stuff there, but bring yer wallet wit ya."

Leanna wanted to shop first, so we asked a few people in the street where the best shopping was. It was beginning to be evident the spaceport was in the working-class part of the city, and the more gentrified area was further 'downtown.' We grabbed a cab, a rusty old jalopy with holes in the floorboards, and proceeded toward the Billet Hotel as the barkeep had suggested.

Sure enough, as we neared the hotel the neighborhoods progressively got nicer and there was a shopping district near the hotel with more up-scale shops and even a few restaurants. We exited our cab and went on foot toward a ladies' boutique.

"Oh, this place is lovely." Leanna told us, "This will do fine."

Leanna was in her element, buzzing around the place and running the salesgirl ragged. Her purchases began to pile up as I wandered around the place. I have to admit, I'd rarely ever shopped in these types of places at home. I didn't own much I'd describe as 'frilly,' but I found a section of the shop dedicated to lingerie. Leanna had already bought some things there I believed, and I picked up a set I thought was quite sexy. I carried it over to where Kara had been standing and observing events with amusement. I showed her what I'd found and smiled.

"Should I, Kara? Do you think this would look good on me?" I asked shyly, blushing furiously, I'm sure. Kara smiled back at me.

"I've no doubt you'd look ravishing in that, little human. You look completely delicious in everything you wear. But, to be perfectly honest, I prefer you naked." I put the lingerie back.

When Leanna had exhausted the salesgirl and burned through most of her portion of our kel, we went searching for a more practical shop. Kara was determined to convince Leanna to buy some more sensible clothes. Trousers and knit shirts and maybe even another pair of boots. Leanna found a place that sold makeup and exited with another large bag, but we did eventually get her to buy some trousers and shirts in another shop. I gave Leanna a bunch of my kel to cover these last items. So far Kara and I had been spectators.

As we left the last shop, I noticed two men across the street wearing gun belts and camouflaged clothing. They were humanoid, large and dark skinned; I couldn't guess where they came from. The two were staring at us quite obviously and I managed to nudge Kara and nod in the men's direction.

"I know, Abby. I saw them earlier today, but when they didn't follow us I thought they weren't interested. Now they're back, so we have to assume differently. I think it's time to end our shopping trip."

We hailed a cab again, this one only slightly less decrepit. And proceeded back toward the space port. I didn't see the men follow us, but I was new to all of this. Kara wore a concerned expression but said nothing.

Kara had the driver stop a few streets from our destination and we jumped from the vehicle and practically dove into a small cafe. We grabbed some seats facing the door with a view of the street and waited silently for a few minutes.

"Do you think they followed us here?" Leanna asked worriedly.

"I don't think so." Kara answered, "But they escaped my attention once already today. They aren't unskilled. I think they're probably bounty hunters, but I've no idea yet if they know who we are. I didn't want to lead them straight back to the ship, but clearly, we can't stay here. I think we should hurry back and hope we've lost them." she pronounced.

Kara asked the woman behind the counter if there was a back exit from the shop and handed her a 1000 kel note. She quickly hustled us out the back and into an ally. We proceeded as quickly and quietly as we could toward the port facility. There was no sign of the two men until we reached the end of another alleyway and Kara stopped abruptly and held her hand out for us to stop.

"They've gone ahead of us to the port entrance and are waiting there." She said. "They're rather clever. They surmised we were from off world and would eventually return to our ship. I only see the two of them, but they may have confederates. If I kill them, that might not be the end of it."

"They're armed, Kara. What makes you think you can kill them?" I asked. Kara simply smiled at me and shook her head like I was being ridiculous.

"Do we have to kill them?" Leanna asked, "Maybe we can sneak past them."

"How about a distraction?" I asked, and told them my idea.

We retraced our steps back up the ally and down another street. We came up from another direction and crossed over. As expected, there didn't appear to be a side entrance to the terminal; the only way in was through the main terminal entrance, which was staked out by the bounty hunters.

Leanna and I left the side street and walked out into the main thoroughfare in front of the spaceport. As we'd hoped, the street was busy with pedestrians, and Leanna spied a couple of men walking alone: our target demographic.

"Sir? Sir? Can you please help me with my packages?" Leanna said to one of the fellows walking down the street and minding his business. She had a stack of packages, fumbling and pathetically trying to balance them all. I was a few steps behind her, Kara was still hidden. The street was busy and noisy, so Leanna tried speaking louder, "Sir? Come here and help me, please."

The man finally stopped and glanced over. Seeing Leanna, his eyes grew large and he quickly began walking toward her. Leanna cultivates that effect on men. I moved up beside her and noticed the two bounty hunters finally begin approaching us. Other men began to approach the damsel in distress as well, and soon there were three men bickering over who'd help her with the packages. A modest crowd was beginning to gather near the scene. We were still only a few steps from the street corner as the bounty hunters neared us.

Kara had waited, concealed behind the corner of the building. The two bounty hunters, carelessly overconfident, had rushed over to where Leanna and I were, without drawing their weapons. It was a crucial mistake. Their attention was focused on the scene Leanna was causing, and they no longer had the building's corner in their field of vision. Kara the Demon bolted blindingly fast from cover and attacked the two careless manhunters.

Like the green shirts on the Archeron, they were unprepared for her speed and agility. She struck the first with a vicious chop to his throat before he could draw his weapon; I actually heard a sickening crunch as his larynx was crushed. He fell to the ground gasping for breath as the second man went for his sidearm.

Kara seized his wrist, twisted his arm up horizontal and brought her other elbow down viciously, shattering his humerus with an ear-splitting crack. The man screamed as Kara bent his broken arm behind his back and shoved him to the ground. She disarmed him and handed his weapon to me. Surprisingly, she produced a zip-tie and tethered his good arm to his bad behind his back. He yelled and cursed in an unknown language until Kara kicked him and threatened to slit his throat if he couldn't be quiet.

She'd disabled the two men in no more than fifteen seconds. The whole crowd was stunned into silence by the feat, including me.

The first man, sprawled at her feet, was violently gasping for air, his eyes literally bulging. Kara knelt over him, handed his sidearm to me and drew little tooth from its scabbard. She placed the dagger at the man's throat and sliced a small hole there. She reached up and grabbed a straw from an innocent bystander's drink, placed the straw in the hole she'd created, blew into it to clear his airway, stood up and pronounced, "They'll probably live."

The innocent bystander, a middle-aged woman, began loudly berating Kara for taking her straw without asking. Kara simply took the drink from the woman's hand and tossed it into the gutter. "Now you no longer need a straw, so be silent."

The crowd had grown considerably around the men sprawled in the walk. The three of us gathered Leanna's packages as quickly as we could and raced toward the port entrance. As we ran through the terminal building I heard a loud whistle behind us, and yelling from the street. Someone must've alerted the militia of the skirmish.

We raced through the workshop next to our dock platform amid a dozen or more workmen busy with the Avernus' repairs. Teddy happened to be standing outside the ship and turned to greet us, but instantly realized what was happening and followed us up the ramp and into the ship. The ramp retracted and sealed with a vacuum-like thwump.

Sebastien came from the bridge. "What happened? Is everyone alright? Lea, are you alright?"

"I'm fine, my love. You should've seen; you should've seen Kara. It was amazing! She bested two of them in like 10 seconds! She's incredible!" Leanna was out of breath from running but managed to tout Kara's violent, virtuoso performance.

"I've seen it, sweetheart. I've seen it. But who'd you best?" Sebastien asked Kara.

Kara, again not the least bit out of breath, said, "There were two well-armed men following us today. I thought we'd lost them, or they'd lost interest, but they appeared again staked out at the entrance to the port. By their looks and actions, I guessed they were bounty hunters. There was no way to sneak past them, so I was forced to disable them."

"And there were witnesses, correct?" Teddy asked. Kara just shrugged.

"Well, the most important thing is, did you at least get your shopping done?" Sebastien asked sarcastically.

I couldn't help but laugh. I was getting used to the danger and I found myself, shockingly, wishing I'd been able to help Kara more against those men. I was disappointed my dagger hadn't gotten bloody. My lover was rubbing off on me, so to speak.

"Well, I *did* get my shopping done." Leanna said, and we all laughed; the tension was broken.

Sebastien went back to the bridge and got on the comms. I assumed he was talking to Offerton, trying to gauge how much trouble we were in. I had no idea what would happen if those pentoffian militiamen came pounding on our door. How did things work on a free, alien planet? What would they do if we resisted?

"Well, how much did you get for the stones?" Teddy asked Kara. "Did you spread them around like I asked?"

"I only went to one shop and sold three stones. You know the little painite? That one and a couple of stamolites. I got about 200 thousand kel, the local currency. That's about 7 thousand coin or so. Though I think Leanna spent about 2-thousand-coin worth today." she smiled.

"Three thousand." I said with a laugh.

"That's fine. It's nowhere near what they're actually worth, but that's to be expected. We can use the local currency to purchase whatever supplies we need. We should try to stock up on fresh produce if we can find it. Coffee, sugar and take on as much water as we can. Well done, my dear." Teddy pronounced.

"And whisky. This ship has no whisky on it. There are 20 different varieties of wine including champaign, brandy, dressidian grog, whatever that is, but no whisky. I thought Baaqir had good taste till I tried to find a drink on his ship." I said.

"I must admit I like a glass of good whisky sometimes." Teddy agreed. "We must ask Offerton about it tonight at dinner."

"I should've bought you a bottle of sandrob today, Abby. We could've had a toast." Leanna teased me.

"What the bloody hell is sandrob?" Teddy asked.

"The local hooch. It's hideous." Kara chuckled.

We sat around the salon and chatted, everyone in a good mood. The incident on the street outside virtually forgotten. Leanna showed us her purchases, some of which were even a bit practical, though not many. Eventually Sebastien came back to join us.

"Damon says not to worry about the two men. He's already spoken with the militia commander, and they say the men weren't local. The local authorities don't appreciate off-world bounty hunters here. However, he says the incident will probably create a good deal of talk on the streets. That means other bounty hunters will be aware of us now if there's any around."

"Speaking of bounty hunters, I looked us up on the web today." Teddy told us. "There are rewards offered by the Ministry of Security for me, Fowler, and Kara. However, interestingly, there's no rewards offered for Leanna or Abby."

"Why would that be?" I asked. "I had to be on the surveillance feeds from the escape."

"The Ministry's post doesn't offer a reward for your capture; it just says you're wanted for questioning. It doesn't mention Leanna at all." Teddy said.

"That's because Leanna didn't do anything to the green shirts. But she did shoot Baaqir, I bet he offered a juicy reward for her." Kara opined.

"That's the most curious thing of all." Teddy said. "I couldn't find anything about a bounty offered by Baaqir on *any* of us. Do you think he forgave us? Fowler, you know the man, why wouldn't he offer rewards for us?"

"I can't say. He might have something else in mind for us. Maybe he's hired his own people to come after us; mercenaries, or private contractors. He definitely wants the Avernus back unscathed. Those idiots back there would have bounties on their heads if Baaqir knew they fired missiles at his ship." He chuckled.

"I suppose that's possible. If that's true, we must be cautious. Baaqir may think we still plan to go to Kleos. His private contractors could be waiting to ambush us." Teddy said.

Sebastien agreed, "Mr. Baaqir will've examined all our options more thoroughly than we have. If he's deduced we're heading for Kleos, we must be cautious indeed."

"What about dinner, are we still going?" Leanna asked.

"You still want to go?" Sebastien asked.

"Don't ask such silly questions, my love."

We, that is Sebastien, fed and watered the prisoners once more as we all prepared for our dinner party. I hadn't brought any evening wear with me from the Archeron, so I was at a loss for anything to wear. But Leanna thought she could help me. I was seriously doubtful; Leanna was slimmer than I was, and we didn't exactly have the same taste in clothes. I couldn't imagine any of her clothes would fit me.

Later, when I went to Leanna's cabin, she had several dresses spread out on the bed for comparison. They were various colors, but all were skimpy and looked exorbitantly expensive. To my surprise, I found an emerald hued dress that fit and it was even one of the more modest ones. She said the dress was a little loose on her, but it fit me super snug. I'd never worn anything so revealing before, and was nervous about it.

She asked if she could do my makeup and hair. "I always wanted a sister so I could do her makeup and hair. This is sooo much fun, Abby." Leanna giggled. After that I couldn't protest.

I needed a drink before I wore that dress in public, so I went out in search of some of Teddy's brandy. As I entered the galley Sebastien let out a wolf whistle from behind me.

"Wow, sweetheart, you look amazing. We might have to let the others go to dinner and stay here alone instead." he said from behind me. I turned slowly around.

"Why, thank you, Sebastien. But I think we should go along with the others."

"I, ahhh, sorry, Professor. I thought you were Leanna. But you do look amazing. Leanna's work, I assume?" he recovered nicely. I took his mistake as a nice compliment.

"Leanna's clothes, Leanna's hair and makeup, even Leanna's shoes. I can't believe she found something that fits me, but she's a magician." I smiled. I couldn't wait for Kara to see me.

"What's this? My dear, you look stunning." Teddy said as he entered. "Pour me one of those too, will you beautiful?" He asked as I was pouring myself a brandy. Sebastien asked for one as well. I downed my brandy and poured another, an uncontrollable smile on my face.

Leanna entered the galley a few moments later and the whole room lit up. The girl sure knew how to dress. She wore a full length, platinum colored gown falling in gossamer layers down her petite body. Her face was a masterpiece too, showing off her incredible violet hewed eyes and beautiful smile. Her makeup skills were peerless.

"Where's Kara?" I asked.

"She's outside, speaking with one of the guards." Sebastien said.

"It never fails, Kara has a way with soldiers everywhere we go. She instinctively knows how to ingratiate herself; she speaks their language, as the saying goes. Kara's the reason our arms dealing has been so successful, we always have eager customers." Teddy confided.

"What guards?" I asked. Just as I asked the outer door opened and Kara called us.

"Our ride's here. Come on, let's get a move on." she said.

Part Fifteen Dinner with the Offertons

Interstellar Dates: 388-07-01, 02
On MK141

AS WE EXITED THE SHIP and walked down the ramp, I saw Kara in conversation with a rough looking, rifle toting Pentoffian militiaman. There were several of them standing around outside the Avernus.

Leanna and I were dressed to impress, Teddy and Sebastien had put on suits and were looking quite dapper, but Kara wore her customary armor and weapons. She was apparently accompanying us tonight as our bodyguard.

"Abby, come, let me introduce you to Kutta Kuttoriff, the man in charge of security for the Avernus. These are his men. He wanted to meet me after he heard about me saving you from those gunmen who attacked you this afternoon." she said. "Kutta, this is my beautiful lover, Professor Abigail Thornwell. Abby, you look so gorgeous, you take my breath away."

"I have Leanna to thank for it. Hello, Mr. Kuttoriff." I said to him. I got an unexpected thrill out of Kara introducing me as her beautiful lover.

The Pentoffian, Kutta Kuttoriff, was as tall as Kara and wore a military style uniform. His rugged appearance was enhanced by several scars clearly visible on his face and neck. His nose was crooked, giving the impression it'd been broken more than once, and one of his ears was missing a lobe. The man was ugly, even by Pentoffian standards.

"Mr. Kutta. Kutta is his family name, Kuttoriff is his given name. Isn't she stunning, Kutta?" Kara asked him.

"Easily the most beautiful creature I've met since you introduced yourself, Kara." He took my hand and kissed it with a flourish. "Call me Kutta; everyone does. The two of you make a charming couple, I must say. I'm equally jealous of you both." He laughed. "But is she as deadly in combat as you are, Nir-Kvekian?"

The Pentoffian's demeaner belied his appearance. He was well spoken and genial, and his laugh was quite infectious.

"Not quite, but I'm getting there. Soon I'll be her bodyguard when we go out." I told him. He laughed again. I liked him instantly.

"You were right, Kara, she is something. You'd better keep a close eye on this one, I may just steal her away." he said with a big smile. "Although, my wife might intervene."

"Oh, you're married?" I asked, "Do you have children?"

"I have four; three boys and a girl. I know what you're thinking, 'he doesn't look old enough to have children.' But I'm much older than I look." He laughed again.

"You must be ancient." Kara said.

Kutta produced his comms and showed us pictures of his kids. "Durra is 11, he's the eldest. Very studious. And little Cietta is the baby, she's 4."

"You have beautiful children, Kutta." I said.

"Yes. What happened?" asked Kara.

"Ah, come now, it's not sporting to make fun of a fellow's looks when you are, yourself, such a beauty. It's like shooting an unarmed adversary." He smiled.

"Sorry, Kutta, I had no idea Pentokreegs were so sensitive." Kara said. Kutta said nothing, simply performed a small, formal bow at Kara.

We left him to guard our ship as I took Kara's arm. Damon Offerton had sent an airship for us. The driver/pilot came around and opened the door for us. Leanna and I took our seats first, followed by the men. Kara climbed in last, eying the driver who was having a difficult time keeping his eyes to himself. Leanna and I were both in revealing dresses.

As we took off I asked Kara, "What's a Pentokreeg?"

"That's a slang term for a Hero of Pentoff. That's the highest military decoration that's given there, reserved for only the most heroic deeds.

Doing something spectacular on the battlefield, or sacrificing yourself to save your comrades. It's a rare award, incredibly prestigious."

"That guy back there, Kutta, won that decoration? Hero of Pentoff?" I asked.

"He didn't deny it. He has a small pattern tattooed on his neck I believe represents it. Why a Hero of Pentoff is way out here, working as a militiaman has got to be an interesting story." Kara said, almost whispering to herself.

The trip to Offerton's villa was a short one by air. We passed over the city center on the way and in the waning light the city seemed less dingy and run down. The central plaza was lit up brightly and hundreds of people could be seen milling about. But outside the center of Fort Eversun there were streets and streets of slums. Obviously, a sizable portion of the population on MK141 were desperately poor.

After we set down on Offerton's private landing pad behind his residence, the man came out to greet us with his family. His wife was tall and willowy, with long blond hair. She also wore a long, beautiful gown, which made me feel better knowing I wasn't overdressed. She had two small children with her, each holding one of her hands. The kids each had long blond hair like their mother.

"Friends, let me introduce you to my lovely wife, Mariella, and my children Stavros and Jenni. As you can see, they take after their mother, thank Ova. And this is my humble home, the Oasis." Offerton told us.

Offerton's home was anything but humble. It was, in fact, a sprawling mansion built on the crest of a hill. The front overlooked the city, the rear had a view of the desert and distant mountains. There was a large swimming pool in the back which included a waterfall, and I'm talking about a two-story waterfall cascading down a rocky slope. I'm guessing that's what inspired them to name the villa 'The Oasis.' There was a tiled courtyard between the pool and the villa with two fireplaces, a huge bar, and enough furniture to seat 30 or 40 people.

The rear wall of the villa consisted of six massive, sliding glass panel doors from floor to ceiling which had been opened to give a magnificent view of the villa's interior. Above the glass doors, on the second floor, was a wide veranda with more furniture. Presumably, the sleeping quarters were behind the tinted glass doors up there.

Behind us, beyond the landing pad, was a beautiful vista of the desert valley and the mountain range beyond. There were a few homesteads in view, but sparse vegetation. However, it was undeniably gorgeous with the setting sun as a backdrop.

"I love what you've done with the place, Damon. It's a little cozy, but I'm sure you make do." Sebastien teased him. "I fully intend to make use of all 20 WCs before we leave."

"Ah, you scoundrel. I wouldn't put it past you. But, for your information there's only 7. Mari, did I ever tell you about the time Sabes and I cut the beard off a high priest as he slept?" Damon asked as he laughed.

"Yes, dear. That and a hundred other stories." Mari turned to Sebastien, "My husband never shuts up about his friend Sabes. It's so lovely to finally meet you. And, who, may I ask, are these ravishing young ladies?" she asked as she motioned to Leanna and me. It was then I noticed the absence of Kara. I had no idea where she'd gone.

Mariella was slightly built and, while she was quite beautiful, her facial features were distinctly not human. I wondered where she came from. The children favored her more than their father.

"I'm sorry. This is my friend Theodore Bradley; he and I are partnering on a venture currently. This beautiful girl here is my Leanna. We're engaged but haven't made our wedding plans yet. And this beauty who looks like her sister is Abigail Thornwell, eminent historian and adventurer. They aren't sisters, but I do consider Abby one of my closest friends." Sebastien told them. I felt quite touched by what he'd said, and I'm sure I blushed.

Leanna and I talked over each other trying to say hello, and finally got it out. Mari had the children each introduce themselves to us and I couldn't help being impressed by Offerton's little family. Beautiful and charming wife, adorable children, a high-ranking position in the local government and a gorgeous villa. He seemed to have it made.

"Beautiful home Offerton, quite splendid." Teddy said as we entered the villa and moved toward the spacious, centrally located family room. "What is it you do for the government again?"

"My title is Director of Commerce and Trade, but I do a little of everything. After the planetary premier, a man named Jaxx, was elected 3 years ago, he elevated me and tasked me with improving the economy. I've been quite successful, increasing the GDP here by nearly 200 percent, mostly through trade. I've been on the Mick for about 8 years now." Damon said. "I'm even in nominal charge of our terraforming efforts."

"The Mick?" I asked as we all began to find seats.

From this interior room we still had a marvelous view of the mountains. The room included a massive fireplace and stylish yet comfortable furnishings.

"Oh, sorry. Yes, that's what we call our little planet, the Mick. MK141 is such a mouthful. We've applied to the interstellar planning council to have our designation changed, officially, to Miccon." he explained. "That's what the original settlers called it before it was ever registered."

"What does it mean, Miccon?" Leanna asked.

"It's a Benott word meaning 'refuge.' The very first settlers here were Benott refugees, and much of the population here is of Benott heritage. My department has many, and they are capable, trustworthy employees. Fort Eversun is the original settlement, as well as the surrounding valley."

"Well, it's lovely." I commented as servants began circulating and taking drink orders.

Damon laughed. "No, it's not. I appreciate the kind thought, but the Mick is far from lovely. But I'm working on that. In twenty years, this rock is going to look quite different. It'll never be Grovia, but just wait, it's going to be more garden than desert, I guarantee."

A servant asked what I'd like to drink. "Whisky, preferably Cordson's. If you don't have that, then the best whisky you have, on the rocks."

Offerton continued, "Anyway, I began in the commerce department when I got here, my superiors wasted my abilities at first; they were shortsighted. Once I showed what I could do I rose rapidly up the ranks of the bureaucracy. But it was Venson Jaxx who recognized my potential. He and I agree completely about the future here. We see great things where others, in the past, have sold the Mick short."

"Damon was always the smartest of us all. When we were teenage delinquents together, our crew always listened to what Damon said. He was *almost* always right." Sebastien said. "Although, there was one time he talked us into hijacking a lorry full of wheat."

"Ah, come on man, not that story." Offerton pleaded.

The waiter came back with my drink, which wasn't Cordson's, but was quite good.

"The sacks inside were 50 kilos each. We were 13 or 14, so the bags were as heavy as we were." Sebastien laughed. "We unloaded half the truck before we realized it wasn't wheat, but fish food. We'd stolen the wrong shipment. We abandoned the lot and skipped; though not before hours of back breaking work."

"I still think I could've gotten some coin for that stuff. You ingrates never gave me the chance." Offerton complained.

Mari called a nanny into the room and told the children good night. They told us all good evening politely, and left with the nanny, presumably for bed.

Several more servants began to circulate with platters of bite-sized hors d'oeuvres. I couldn't believe how many servants they had. I knew a few people who worked in government jobs on Ampora, and they mostly lived in apartments similar to mine. I was beginning to think it had something to do with being director of 'commerce and trade.' That could be lucrative I supposed, if you were just a *little* unscrupulous.

The conversation meandered about the room, Leanna and I visiting with Mari. Damon and Sebastien regaled Teddy with stories of their youth. Leanna joined Sebastien and told the story of their relationship, with Damon and Mari listening attentively. As awkward as I've always been in social situations, I was never one to seek out parties of any kind. But I had to admit I was enjoying myself greatly. I missed Kara though.

Finally, Kara showed up. She waltzed in and stood behind me casually, not saying anything.

"Well?" Teddy asked her.

"I checked the perimeter. It's walled for the most part, but there are access gates at three points. They seemed secure, but I believe they could easily be scaled. I spoke to the security detail employed by Mr. Offerton, and they seem competent. Though I did find one fellow lounging, smoking and not paying close attention. I had a talk with him." Kara told us. She'd been checking the security. Of course, she had.

Offerton, mouth agape, took in Kara's report. He looked to Sebastien, who just shrugged, then let out a genial laugh and asked a servant to take Kara's drink order.

"These hors d'oeuvres are terrific Damon. I'd love to know what's in this, but I've learned not to ask such things. Haven't I, Kara?" I said.

"There are some things better left unknown, Professor Thornwell." Kara teased.

"Offerton, did I hear you correctly, did you say you're in charge of the terraforming here?" Teddy asked. "Terraforming has always fascinated me. It's the literal act of conquering nature."

"Well, yes, I did. This might sound crazy, but I don't know much about it to tell the truth. When you break it down it's all about common sense. I don't actually need to know how it works; just how much it costs. I figure out what the Mick needs, hire experts to give me cost estimates, and hire terraforming engineers and contractors to make it happen."

"So, how do you decide what needs to be done?" Teddy asked as we made our way into the dining room.

We all took seats around the long table. The servants were bringing around larger platters now, offering to fill our plates. Fruits, bread, vegetables, and roasted meats, it was a feast. But I saw no fish.

"The Mick is basically a baren rock, *almost*. When I got here the population was around 90 million. A ragtag bunch of rejects and refugees trying to scrape out an existence here. The soil is very poor, verging on poisonous. There's little water, as I'm sure you've noticed. You must've seen our inland sea as you arrived. The sea is briny, and supports almost no aquatic life, but it's the only water we have. So, we have desalination plants operating at maximum capacity trying to provide enough water for the population to cook with and drink, let alone bath." He grinned.

"There's no subterranean water? No aquifers?" Kara asked.

"None. Believe me we've searched." Offerton said. "What's complicated the problem is all the turmoil and upheaval in the quadrant. Our population has boomed all the way to nearly 210 million now. Millions of emigrants but also a lot of refugees. As a result, the level of the inland sea has dropped 35cm in the last 3 years. Obviously, we can't sustain that sort of attrition to our water supply. Are you sure you want to hear all of this?"

"Absolutely, I'm fascinated by it." Teddy said. We all agreed as we began the meal.

"So, our surveyors located water, in the form of ice, in our asteroid belt which lies just beyond the 5th planet in the system, MK145. There are huge rocks consisting mostly of ice out there, and we've begun harvesting them. Barges tow them back here. I've had 4 massive underground reservoirs constructed at great expense near Fort Eversun, and we've begun filling them up. Some of the ice is now going into the inland sea, so hopefully the level will stop falling. I'm pretty proud of the work we've done."

"And you should be. It's impressive work man, you're fixing an entire planet." Teddy congratulated him.

"You might've noticed an unpleasant consequence of our hydration campaign. The average planetary temperature has risen substantially because of the imported water. As you know, water vapor is a highly efficient green-house gas. But, the terraforming engineers tell me there are solutions for that as well. As you solve one problem, another sticks it's ugly head out."

"I imagine there may be a shift in the weather, eventually. More rain as the atmosphere incorporates the added water from the asteroid belt." Teddy said, "That'd make food production much easier."

"Exactly. At least, that's the hope. In the meantime, the largest portion of our food is imported. Nearly everything we're eating tonight came in on transports. It's extremely expensive to feed 200 million people this way. So, the other terraforming project we have going on is rehabbing the land. Huge hovercraft infuse millions of tons of organic material into the topsoil. Fertilizer and nutrients and so forth. It takes years to accomplish, but hopefully we'll eventually be able to feed ourselves. Our population crunch is forcing us to rush the whole thing, and they tell me it's dangerous to go too fast. But we have no choice." Damon told us. "The catch is, once the soil is rehabbed, we'll need even more water for irrigation. Meanwhile, we're borrowing like mad, and creating a massive amount of debt."

"I think it's noble what you're doing here, Damon." I said. "Making the whole planet a better place for people to live. It's incredible."

"Thank you, Abby. I have to admit I find it quite satisfying. Though it takes up much of my time. There's never enough hours in the day." He said.

Mari added, "And now there's a new complication."

"Mari, please. Not tonight." Offerton said.

"What is it, Mari?" I asked.

"It's not about the Mick, necessarily." Damon began, he looked at his wife, then "Alright. Mariella is from the planet Furanix Prios originally. She emigrated here with her father when she was young. For years, the Furanills have dreaded a confrontation with the Tellurians. Their planet has abundant resources, it lies in a strategic location and so forth. So, the high council has been preparing to defend themselves for some time. Beefing up planetary defenses, expanding enlistments, and purchasing large amounts of weapons. The Furanills have never been expansionists, so the Telluric Alliance has always left them alone. Until now."

"What happened?" Kara asked.

Mari said, "When I emigrated here with my father, he started an import business and did well, but we left behind a large extended family. Not long ago a cousin of mine sent me a message that the Tellurians had arrived with a huge fleet."

"Oh, gods." I said, "That's horrible, Mari."

"Her father, may Ova give him peace, did exceptionally well on the Mick. Most of what you see here was inherited from him." Damon told us, sweeping his arms around the villa. "Anyway, we've lost contact with Mari's family there, and now she fears the worst. No one had heard anything from there, I assume because the Tellurians blocked communications somehow, until a trader I know told me a few days ago the fighting was still going on weeks after it started. That's unusual, isn't it Sabes?"

"Yes, I think so." Sebastien answered, "From what I've been told, these invasions are normally over quickly. It's unusual for the inhabitants to even fight back for long. Mostly they just surrender, limiting the damage to their planet."

Kara said, "It's a good thing, though. They aren't giving in to the Tellurians. It's great they're fighting them."

"I'm not so sure." Damon disagreed. "It means thousands, maybe millions of Furanills might die. The trader told me something else interesting. He said the Furanills had dealt the Tellurians a solid defeat initially. He said the CTF retreated out of the system and were gathering more ships and troops for another attack."

"That's even better news. I don't know what could be better." Kara said.

But I could see the look on Mari's face, and she didn't think it was good news at all.

"Kara, don't you understand?" Sebastien said, "The Furanills can't win, they're just making it worse for themselves. The CTF will attack again and this time with overwhelming force. Millions will be killed. And, because of the resistance there may be horrible reprisals against civilians. Abby, you remember what I told you about the marines on Erestis 3? The CTF will punish the Furanills for resisting."

"So, everyone is supposed to just surrender to them, is that it? That's cowardice. Everyone should be standing up to them." Kara said with her customary certainty.

"That's been tried before." Damon said dryly. "It didn't end well for the Pentoffians."

"Mr. Bradley, tell me, what do you know about the Laprows?" Mari asked.

"They're a race of avians, from what I understand. Isolationist, apparently. I've never met one." Teddy told her. "Mari, do you think they're somehow involved in this attack on your home world? If so, it would be surprising. As far as I know, they don't venture out of their own star system."

"The high council of Furanix Prios has been in negotiations with the Laprows for years, trying to acquire weapons and technology from them." Mari told him. "I have an aunt who's in the diplomatic service. What if it worked?"

"Mari, that's conjecture. We've no reason to suppose that's true." Offerton said.

"But your trader friend said we'd handed the Tellurians a defeat. Doesn't that make it possible? With technology from the Laprows, isn't it possible we could beat them?" Mari argued.

Teddy offered, "I've heard Laprow technology is highly advanced and completely different from Telluric technology. But, even if it that's true, it doesn't necessarily mean Laprow tech is better than Telluric tech, or could win a war against them. The Tellurians easily outnumber the Furanills a thousand to one. I doubt a slight technological advantage could make that much difference."

"The Laprow rumor is a bunch of wishful thinking in my opinion." Damon said.

"My point is it's possible, that's all. Don't you want us to defeat them?" Mari challenged Damon.

"Of course, darling, you know I do. But right now there's nothing we can do to help them. It's the Mick I'm worried about. We recently discovered palladium in the asteroid belt. Our mineral deposits here on the Mick have always been of the ordinary variety, nothing special. Palladium changes that. We've been a backwater, joke of a place, with 200 million poor folks who have no place better to go. But now, with our terraforming efforts and the discovery of actual, valuable mineral deposits in our system, we could become a target of the Tellurians too. We'd be easy pickings for the CTF."

"And soon we'll be flooded with refugees from Furanix Prios, isn't that right Damon?" Mari asked. "And we can't afford them. We can't afford to feed them and house them because our government's budget is stretched to the limit already. The government here has great ambition, mostly from my husband and his friend Jaxx. But we have little means to see it through. Damon and I have gambled on this place also. My father's fortune is all but gone, invested in government bonds. If a hundred of my relatives show up here, we'll have to take them in. Just like the Mick will take in all the other refugees from Furanix Prios. If the government here goes bankrupt, Damon and I will be ruined along with it."

"It's true, this war on Furanix Prios has come at the worst possible time. We're one of the nearest planets to them, and the only one that has a history of accepting refugees in large numbers. Our resources are strained as it is. Our salvation should be our deposits of palladium, but I'm afraid if we start a large-scale effort to harvest and sell it, the Tellurians will simply come and seize it. Palladium is used for most things the military needs. That's why it's so valuable. It's a real conundrum, I tell you." Offerton admitted.

Sebastien said, "Damon, if there's anyone who can figure out a way to make it all work, it's you. You're the cleverest guy I've ever known; without cerebral implants, that is."

"Yes, Offerton, a clever chap like you can manage it. As for your palladium, there are ways. Perhaps I can lay out a plan for you which will enable you to harvest the stuff and smuggle it out of the system to be sold elsewhere. With luck, you may be able to avoid the notice of the Tellurians. I know a few smugglers who could help." Teddy smiled.

"That'd be greatly appreciated, Captain Bradley, thank you." said Offerton. "I'm sorry friends, I never intended to lay all of this at your feet. It doesn't even concern you. Ah, the unrewarding, weary life of a bureaucrat."

Damon laughed as he lifted his brandy snifter, dipped his cigar in it, and took a puff.

"Anyway, how was the meal? Not too shabby, eh? My chef does wonders with what we have. I have warehouses stuffed with things; I speculate in all sorts of commodities. You let me know if there's anything I can get you before you leave, alright?"

"Cordson's whisky. From Nemea 2, I think. I'll buy a case if you have it. Hell, two cases, I have 50 thousand kel burning a hole in my pocket." I told him.

"Now that you mention it Offerton, I might have a little shopping list for you. Can I get in touch with your office tomorrow?" Teddy asked.

"Of course, Captain, you make sure you do. Anything I can do to help." Offerton offered helpfully.

The evening was slowly winding down. I'd eaten my fill, there'd even been an assortment of delicious desserts. We left the table and wandered toward the large courtyard outside. The air had cooled considerably, as I've always been told happens in desert environments. The stars were out, the evening was mild, and the Oasis was almost what I'd call magical. We'd continued to converse in small groups, but finally we reached the edge of the pool.

"Goodbye to you ladies, it was a treat to host you all. Next time you're in the vicinity, look us up, will you?" Offerton told us. "Gentleman, I'll see you tomorrow. I'll do what I can about your list, Bradley."

Sebastien said his goodbyes with Leanna on his arm, proudly showing her off to his old friend. We leisurely walked around the pool and toward Offerton's airship for our ride back to the port. Kara drew Teddy and I close to her and whispered.

"Master, did you tell Offerton anything about yourself?"

"Like what? I don't think I talked about myself at all." Teddy said.

"Stick close to me, there may be trouble." She told us.

"What do you mean? What trouble?" I asked.

"Offerton called Teddy 'Captain' just now. The only way he'd know he was a captain is if he'd been researching him. That means he's researched us all, which means he knows precisely what the prices on our heads are. I wouldn't be surprised if those two bounty hunters from this afternoon were sent by our friend Offerton." Kara explained.

"Kara, my dear, I believe you're being too suspicious. Why would the man invite us to dinner to meet his family if he was intending to betray us? He undoubtedly researched us; I'd do the same in his place. In fact, I *did* do the same thing; I researched him before coming here." Teddy admitted.

"What'd you find out?" I asked.

"He apparently spent time in prison on Dressida, but only served 4 months of a 3-year sentence for larceny. He then became a marketing agent for an arms manufacturing firm on Astraea after prison. Before emigrating here, he was the CFO of a small firm producing agricultural equipment on Grovia. The man got around and was obviously successful. He knows his way around in the business world and now, here, inside of government bureaucracy. But the main reason I don't believe he's planning to betray us is that he just offered me a job, not 20 minutes ago." Teddy chuckled.

"Offered you a job? What job?" Kara asked.

"Some silly government moniker, import licensing agent or something like that. But in reality, he wants me to use my contacts to organize a campaign to import as many luxury items as I can here. He wants to systematically improve the standard of living of everyday citizens on this rock and make himself a pile of coin in the process, of course." Teddy chuckled again. "He liked my idea about the palladium too. I wouldn't be a bit surprised if he's offering Fowler a job as we speak. They've been chatting for quite a while. Offerton is an opportunist and a hustler; my kind of fellow."

"You may be correct, master, but something here doesn't feel right. I've had a bad feeling all evening and I can't wait to get back to the ship." Kara said. "How close are the repairs to being finished?"

"Offerton has those men working around the clock. I think they should be done, perhaps, by midday tomorrow. Or, in a worst-case situation, they should be done by the following morning." Teddy said. "I have to say, Offerton has himself quite a fiefdom here. The Premier lets him have a free hand to do as he wishes, and opportunities abound."

Baaqir had told me Bradley was controlled by his greed, and I could see Teddy was tempted to take advantage of this 'rock' as he'd called it. Sebastien and Leanna walked over to us and asked if we were ready to leave.

"Your friend is quite an operator, Fowler. I like the man." Teddy began, "He offered me a government job with benefits just a few minutes ago."

"You too, eh?" Sebastien said, "He offered me my pick. I could be the head of the Premier's security detail, or the commandant of the entire militia force. I told Damon I had no military experience and he just laughed. He asked me how much terraforming experience I thought he had."

"I wonder if he has a job picked out for me?" I joked. "I agree with Kara though, I think we should get back to the ship."

We boarded Offerton's airship and once again flew over the center of the city. The flight was enjoyable, and the city was sort of beautiful at night, all lit up. After we landed, Kutta Kuttoriff quickly approached us.

"Kara, may I have a word?" he asked her, but we all gathered around to listen. "I just received a call from the Oasis, armed men are on their way here to detain all of you. I was ordered not to interfere."

"Offerton! I knew there was something up, I'll strangle him with his own entrails!" Kara exclaimed.

Kutta laughed and said, "As much as I'd like to see that, it wasn't Offerton who called, it was his woman. I don't take orders from that Furanill bitch. Apparently, she's hired some mercenaries to capture you."

"Thank you, my friend, it's bloody decent of you to warn us." Teddy said. "So, am I to understand you don't intend to stand aside?"

"I was assigned to protect this ship, so that's what we'll do. My people love a good fight, there's no better way to put starch in your stinger." He laughed.

"Any idea how many mercs we can expect? Or how they'll come at us?" Teddy asked.

"I've no idea how many they'll be, but it's a good bet they'll come by air. The port is walled on all sides, and the main entrance is guarded. They'll want to be quick to ensure surprise, that means dropping from above. That's what I'd do if I were them." Kutta explained.

"How many men do you have here?" Kara asked.

"I've sent the workers away, but I have 12 militia here with me; and I could call for reinforcements."

"I don't think that'll be necessary." Teddy said. "I doubt those mercenaries have a clue what's waiting for them. Come with me, my friend, I have some gifts for you and your men."

We scrambled inside the Avernus. Teddy and Kara disappeared into the cargo hold as I went to my cabin to change. I didn't want to get blood all over Leanna's beautiful dress.

When I came out, Sebastien was helping unpack a crate of EM85 rifles. Kara began carrying rifles out and handing them to Kutta's militia. The militia guards included a few women and several Pentoffians. One of the women in camouflage was a Pentoffian; she was smaller than the males but just as fierce looking. By their reactions, I guessed the EM85s were a serious upgrade over what they'd been armed with. They all looked pleased and excited.

Sebastien handed me a handgun in a holster, "Do you know how to use this, Professor?"

"Kara taught me how to handle a gun, load it and unload it. I even took one apart and put it back together. But I've never fired one."

"Lea, give Abby a crash course in how to shoot a gun, will you?" he asked her, then left to help arm the militia.

Leanna came to me "Abby, it's very simple. Hold it like this," as she demonstrated with her personal weapon, "release the safety, here, and just point and *squeeze* the trigger. Take your time and aim carefully. Don't point it unless you intend to use it. And don't point it at any of your friends, especially me."

Kutta's militia had set up barricades and taken defensive positions around the platform. I asked where Kara was, and Teddy told me she was on top of the Avernus. I noticed a ladder to a hatch above the cabin doors and went to climb it. When I got to the top, I saw Kara setting up a vicious looking gun of some sort on a tripod.

"What kind of gun is that?" I asked.

Startled, she turned, and the look on her face froze my blood. Note to self: try not to startle Kara.

"Get below, Abby, this is no place for you. There will be fighting soon." she ordered. I quickly retreated down the ladder, sobered by the intensity Kara demonstrated. My palms began to sweat.

Leanna and I grabbed a spot in the solon, with an unobstructed view of the ship's exit ramp. Sebastien and Teddy were each armed with a rifle and had joined Kutta's militia on the platform outside, out of our sight.

Our vantage point was a poor one, depending on how you looked at it. We couldn't possibly see the mercenaries approaching from where we were inside the ship, but they couldn't see us (or shoot us) either.

Several agonizing minutes passed silently. I couldn't even hear any chatter from outside, the militia had become as quiet as prayerful worshipers. I was just beginning to wonder if the whole thing was for nothing when weapons began to sing loudly. I heard automatic rifles discharging in their rhythmic staccato, but also a much deeper, booming staccato from above, on the roof of the Avernus. The entire ship vibrated as Kara fired the weapon she'd set up.

Amidst the general clamor I began to hear a different, distinct sound. It sounded as if a hail storm had begun, with a rhythmic clickety-clack sound that could only mean one thing: the Avernus was under fire. Panic seized me as I realized what it meant. Kara was on the roof!

My instinct was to rush to the ladder and scream for her to join us inside, but before I could act there was a distant explosion. The Avernus shook as I heard what sounded like a cheer from Kutta's people outside. The noise of rifle fire and the hateful pinging against the ship's hull stopped shortly afterward. Ominously, the rocking of the ship caused by Kara's gun had stopped as well. I did run to the hatch then, climbing the ladder with dread in my heart.

I yelled, "Kara, are you alright?"

"Yes, little human, more than alright." she poked her head into the hatch, "Whoa, what a night! That was more fun than a Targa hunt. Oh, I hope I get to see that woman again. She and I will have a long talk, and I doubt she'll enjoy it as much as I."

Teddy re-entered the ship, his rifle slung over his broad shoulder. "They won't be eager to return, I can tell you that!"

"Teddy, what happened? Is everyone alright? Did the mercenaries leave?" I asked.

"The lucky ones did. They came in two hover copters, up over the rooftops of the neighborhood next door, just as Kutta predicted. We opened fire on them and one of their ships exploded spectacularly. The other banked hard and sped off in the distance; I can't imagine they'll be back." He laughed.

Sebastien came up the ramp and Leanna leaped into his arms and started kissing him. Kutta followed him aboard, grinning exuberantly.

"How is everyone? Anyone injured?" he asked. Teddy assured him we were fine. "That was fine sport; I'll wager those mercenaries filled their breeches when we opened fire." He laughed.

"Kutta, my friend, I'm hiring you and your men to be my personal security force for the next day or so. At least until our ship is ready to depart. You do fine work." I heard Teddy say as I returned to the salon.

I went over to Kutta and gave the man a hug, "Thank you. That was quite decent of you, defending us like that. We owe you."

"Think nothing of it. It beats rounding up vagrants and drunks. I can't believe the nerve of that Furanill harpy, giving me orders like that; who's she think she is? I'd love to see her face when she hears what happened to her hired goons. Besides, Abby, it's a pleasure to serve such a lovely lady." he said with a bow. "Now, where is your woman?"

"Right here, you big flirt. I told you to stay away from her." Kara said as she descended the ladder carrying the tripod and a bandolier of ammo. "If I hadn't shot that copter from the sky, you might've had to do something except look mean."

"Oh, *you* shot the thing down, is that right?" Kutta said with a wide smile. "I believe it was *I* that shot the pilot right between his beady little Caladrian eyes. I've been known to shoot the eye from a bird at 100 paces."

"Braggart. We'll test ourselves at a firing range one day and see who's the better shot." Kara teased back, "but first, give me a hand with this, will you?"

Kutta disappeared with Kara toward the cargo hold. A younger looking pentoffian scampered up the ramp and into the salon. Sebastien went over and shook the man's hand.

"Thank you, Bunta, that was excellent work. We certainly owe you all a debt that'll be hard to repay." Sebastien told him. "If we hadn't had advanced warning of their approach, it might've been a disaster."

The man (boy?) just stammered "That's alright, don't worry about it, we had fun. I hadn't fired a weapon in anger for ages. I was looking for my uncle, is he in here?"

"What is it boy? Can't you see I'm busy here trying to look important to this bevy of beauties?" Kutta laughed. "How can I get anywhere with you hanging around, eh?"

"Sorry uncle, but the men want to know what your orders are." Bunta said.

"Just like always, secure the area, police up your spent rounds, and try not to step on your peckers!" He laughed again. "Children!"

"Come in, sit down, have a drink my friend." Teddy told him.

"I never turn down a drink after a fight. Come to think of it, I never turn down a drink!" He said. "Say, Bradley, that's some serious ordinance you have in your cargo hold. What're you going to do, start a war?"

"Perhaps; we shall see." Teddy smiled. The pentoffian's affable personality was infectious.

"I tell you, if we'd had *that* sort of cookery during the war, all you humans would be speaking pentoffian now, instead of this ugly, clumsy common tongue you belch at each other." He laughed again. "*Av necta do fluvessa, to fu doa fluvessa fa.* Pentoffian is the most beautiful language in the galaxy."

"What'd you say, Kutta?" I asked him.

"I had never seen beauty, till you showed beauty to me." He recited. "It's a traditional part of our marriage rite. Though, in my case, a slight exaggeration on the part of my lovely bride. We Pentoffians are the greatest lovers in the galaxy!" He declared. "Everyone knows that!"

"You're married, Kutta?" Sebastien asked him.

"Of course! My Tressa is still a vision, even after 13 years of marriage and 4 children. She's far too pretty for me and was very young when we married. She was betrothed to a friend of mine named Ugett when we met. I asked her to marry me less than a month after I met her. I still can't believe she accepted. Ugett still can't believe it either!" He roared with laughter again at his own joke. None of us could resist laughing with him.

Kutta Kuttoriff, the pentoffian, came and sat beside me in the salon. Teddy poured him a dram of the Kyntavan brandy, and we had a little discussion. Sebastien wanted to make sure it was Mari Offerton, herself, that'd called Kutta.

"You're sure it was her, not someone else?"

"It was she, alright. I've had dealings with her before. She considers herself an *aristocrat*." He stated with scorn. "She was born with an electrum prod up her honey pot. Excuse my soldier's language."

Teddy asked, "Do you have any idea who those mercenaries were?"

"I can't say for sure, not having laid eyes on them. The pilot was a Caladrian, I believe. The dead one, I didn't get a good look at the other. In this place, men like those come and go all the time, I'm afraid. But I'll try to find out if you want me to. Shouldn't be too difficult, if there's grieving widows they were local. If not, they were outworlders and we'll never know for sure who they were."

Teddy poured him another drink, "Kutta, I really would feel better if you stuck around here until we're ready to depart. I'll make it worth your while."

"Ha! Here I am on a civil service stipend, with four brats to feed, and you're asking if I'd like some extra pay? All I can get!" he said, and left the ship in a flourish.

After Kutta left, Teddy asked, "The question, in my mind, is did Offerton know his wife was setting us up?"

"Of course he didn't. She must've done it behind his back. She made a big deal at dinner about how they were in debt and so forth. She must've decided our bounties were too juicy to pass up." Sebastien reasoned. "Plus, Damon wouldn't do anything like that. He owes me too much."

"What do you mean, he owes you?" I asked.

"You remember I told you about Coula? After I'd been there almost a year, Damon showed up. I'd grown several centimeters and put on 25 kilos by then. But he was still the same: skinny and weak. He was never a good fighter. So, I ended up protecting him all the time in there. Then, when Baaqir got me out, I had one condition. I told Baaqir I'd take the job if he'd get my friend an early release too. So, you see, Damon would never betray me. Never."

"Alright, so it was the wife, but what do we do about it? They have two kids; we can't do anything to hurt her." I said.

I was trying to keep Kara from suggesting what I thought she'd suggest. Kara didn't have a forgiving bone in her body.

"We'll continue on as if we know nothing. We were attacked by some bounty hunters, *again*, and we bloodied them in the process of defending ourselves. That's all Offerton needs to know. Let him worry about his two-faced, backstabbing hartha of a wife." Kara said. "We have more important business."

So, we went back to business as usual. Kutta called the workers back to finish repairing the ship. We took turns getting some rest, and when morning came, we started getting deliveries of supplies. Offerton had filled Teddy's shopping list, and more. There were containers of foodstuffs including some fresh produce. More of the ubiquitous PPRs, coffee, milk, eggs, cheese, fresh bread, all of which must be expensive here. There were cases of wine and brandy, ale from Furanix Prios, believe it or not, and even a case of Cordson's Whisky. Oh, and several thousand liters of fresh water too, enough to completely top off the Avernus' storage tanks.

As midday approached, the man himself, Offerton, showed up. Either he's a tremendous actor or he was completely oblivious to his wife's skullduggery.

"Hey Sabes, the ship's looking much better than when you got here." he said. "She's very pretty, are you sure your boss won't miss her?"

"Not as much as he'll miss my charm and wit. But, he's not my boss anymore."

Offerton chuckled. "Just be careful, men like that don't forget or forgive trespasses. He's going to want his fancy ship back. Did you get all the goods I sent?"

"You bet, Damon, thank you. What do we owe you for all this stuff? Some of this must've been hard to get, and I imagine it was all expensive." Sebastien asked.

"Don't worry about it buddy, I owe you this and more. This is all my pleasure. I understand you folks had some more trouble last night. I can't tell you how embarrassed I am. You've been attacked twice in as many days; I need to get the militia to clear all of these bounty hunters out of here."

"They were no trouble at all. I just hope the wreckage didn't cause any damage to the neighborhood next door." Kara told him.

"None, I'm told. A couple of abandoned warehouses burned for a while, but they were put out by the fire brigade. There were no survivors from the bounty hunters ship though." Offerton said.

"Good." Kara said.

"Damon, I want to thank you sincerely for the Cordson's. I can't believe you found it." I said.

"We found that case in one of my warehouses. It was the last one on the Mick, and you're welcome to it. Someone Sabes refers to as one of his closest friends is also one of *my* closest friends. And, I have one more present for you." He said as he produced a passport from his jacket pocket.

"What's this?" I asked as he handed it to me.

"Sabes said you'd lost yours, so I had this one made up for you this morning. I hope you like the photo. I had one of my people taking pictures at last evening's dinner, and we used one she took."

I opened the passport and saw a photo of myself from the night before; hair, makeup and green cocktail dress included. It looked like a photo from the spring social. I was shocked as I noticed the title next to my name: Assistant Director of Trade, MK141 Planetary Government, with a stamped seal in the shape of a palm tree. Offerton had given me an official diplomatic passport labeling me as a member of the Mick's government.

"Damon, I can't accept this. I'm not assistant director of anything. Thanks, but this is too much." I said.

"Nonsense; take it. It might get you in the short line at customs when you travel, who knows? If they call to check you out, they'll be calling my office, so you have no worries. Just don't declare war on anyone without asking me first." He winked.

I gave him a hug and thanked him again. He said, "You'll *have* to come back and visit again now, since you'll have to renew your passport here. You can visit Sabes while you're here, he's going to stay on as head of security for Premier Jaxx, aren't you?" he asked as he glanced in Sebastien's direction.

"Ha, nice try. I never said that." Sebastien told him, "I'll tell you Damon, the offer is tempting, but I'm sort of in the middle of something right now, and I can't walk away. Maybe after we're done, I'll return. There's a few things I'd still like to talk over with your wife."

Kara and I laughed, Leanna giggled, and I'm sure Offerton wondered what was so funny. Teddy changed the subject.

"Listen, Offerton, is there any more news from Furanix Prios? I like to keep my ear to the ground when it comes to Alliance difficulties. I'm rather invested in such things, if you know what I mean."

"So I've heard." Offerton admitted. "Nothing new today I'm afraid. Communications are still down. The Furanills were giving them all they wanted last we knew, hopefully they can keep it up. It's possible if they can bloody the Tellurians' noses enough, they might decide the whole debacle isn't worth it and bugger off."

"That's probably too much to hope for." Teddy said, then handed something to Damon.

"What's this?" Damon asked.

"A dedicated, secure comms device. It's encrypted, and paired with another device in my possession. With it, we can safely send messages which are impossible for anyone else to decrypt. I'd appreciate it if you'd keep me apprised of events on Furanix Prios." Teddy explained.

"You're recruiting me?" Damon asked with a grin.

Teddy shrugged, "Information is *the* most valuable commodity, my friend. More valuable than gold, or even your palladium, for that matter. Once our current project is complete, there may be something you and I can do to help the Furanills."

"I'll see what I can find out." Damon agreed.

"Excellent. And now, we need to prepare the ship for departure. Thanks again, Offerton, you're a fine chap. And, I'll be in touch." Teddy said.

"Bon voyage, my friends. You are always welcome on the Mick." Offerton declared as he exited down the ramp. "And don't forget my offer, Sabes, we could do great things together!"

"Just as long as you stay clear of his better half." Kara whispered to me.

Kara headed back to the last cabin. When she returned she was leading the three bedraggled looking men behind her, still bound. Teddy cut their tethers and handed each of them a bottle of water.

"This is the end boys. You've proven you can't be trusted, so we can't have you with us. But we don't want to follow your sorry example and murder you like you murdered poor Ernie and Sam. So, this is where you get out." Teddy told them. The boy, Yoshi, looked ready to cry.

"Captain, where are we? What are we supposed to do?" he asked. "I didn't kill anybody! Why can't I come along with you?"

Kara grabbed him by his hair and violently turned his head towards her. "Because you stood by and watched it happen you little bastard. My father used to say no man who sits and eats with a traitor is guiltless. Be glad I'm letting you live." Kara shoved the boy down the ramp, and he tumbled all the way to the concrete pad outside.

Teddy handed the engineer, Del Malcolm, a small stack of the kel bank notes. "Here, Del, take this. It's not much, but a man such as yourself should be able to find work here. This planet is called MK141, it's removed from Telluric space. We're actually in the port facility right now, so you shouldn't have to go far to find work. It makes me sad to do this Del, but I have no choice. Help the kid out, will you?"

Malcolm simply nodded. "I'm sorry Captain. I know I should've done more. And thanks for this." He indicated the kel notes in his hand. He slowly walked down the ramp, and I found myself feeling sorry for him and the boy. I'd hate to be abandoned somewhere I didn't know anybody. The thought was frightening.

"What about me? Do I get some of that too?" Haney asked Teddy, pointing at the kel notes.

"I have something better in mind for *you*, Trick." Kara announced as she grabbed him by the arm.

She marched him down the ramp and out onto the landing pad. You could see the man flinch when he was hit by the sun, it was hot on the Mick. I stood at the top of the ramp, watching to see what would happen. Leanna joined me.

"What's happening, Abby?" she asked.

"I don't know, Kara didn't tell me."

"Kutta, this man is a mutineer and a murderer." Kara announced. "He helped kill two of his shipmates in cold blood. He also betrayed the five of us, attempting to sell us for a bounty. What do you think the punishment should be for that?" She asked the Pentoffian.

Kutta marched over to where they stood and glared at Haney. Haney tried to pull away from Kara's grip but there was no chance of that. Haney trembled and started to speak, but Kutta back handed him viciously, snapping his head violently to the side.

"On Pentoff, a man found guilty of betraying his comrades is sentenced to be beaten to death, by *them*. They use long, thin poles made of Chitra wood which are flexible. There's no Chitra trees here on the Mick, but we adapt to our environment when needs be." Kutta said as several of his men approached carrying metal poles close to two meters in length. "These aren't Chitra wood, but a local substitute. I imagine the effect will be similar."

"What're you gonna do? Wait, stop." Haney pleaded.

I saw the boy, Yoshi standing to the side, watching. Malcolm stood beside him, a horrified look on his face.

The pentoffians surrounded Haney, and as Kara turned him loose, they began to beat him viciously. Haney again tried to plead for mercy, but soon his jaw was shattered by a skillful stroke, and he wasn't able to speak after that. Leanna and I turned away, sickened by the display. The sound of the beating continued for an unholy amount of time. Whip-thud, whip-crack, eventually becoming nothing but wet sounds as Haney was methodically reduced to a puddle of bloody pulp.

It was clear Kara had set the whole thing up in advance. As she returned to the Avernus with Kutta, Teddy addressed her.

"Was that absolutely necessary? We all agreed to let them go. We took a vote."

"I didn't vote to let them go, I only agreed to abide by the vote. And I did, I *turned him loose*, right before the pentoffians beat him to death. What Kutta's men did was justice; Pentoffian justice, but justice all the same. I couldn't be more pleased how it turned out." Kara declared. "He got what he deserved."

Teddy shook his head slowly, "Well, Kutta. I can't say I approve, but I also can't say the man didn't deserve what he got. Regardless, we all owe you a tremendous debt. Without your warning those mercs would've caught us by surprise. We'd have had no chance, and I'm a man that likes to pay my debts. The rifles we handed out are our gifts to you and your men. I've unloaded two crates of ammo for them as well. This, my friend, is for you." Teddy handed the pentoffian three shiny aurics, close to 6000 Telluric coin worth of pure gold, almost 180 thousand kel. Kutta smiled widely.

"And this" Teddy handed Kutta the remainder of our kel bank notes, "Is for the rest of your militia to share. It's the least we can do for you. And, you'll always be considered our friend, Kutta Kuttoriff." He said as he shook his hand.

Kutta smiled, "And you, Teddy Bradley, are a credit to your race. *Any* fellow who pulls gold coins from thin air is my kind of fellow!" he laughed again. "I've known you for two days and haven't once thought of killing you; a new record for a human."

"Take care, you villain. Next time we meet, we should go to a shooting range." Kara told him. "I could show you a few tricks."

"Oh, never mind Nir-Kvekian, the last thing you want is to see me shoot again!" Kutta turned toward me now, "And, you, Abigail. You watch yourself, and take care of this braggart Nir-Kvekian. Her boasting will be her undoing!"

"I will. Thank you, Kutta." I said. "Buy something nice for Tressa with that gold. I wish I'd gotten to meet her."

"Next time, Abigail. You and your boastful friend will come to supper, and Tressa will make a pentoffian norek pie for you. You've never eaten so well." He called as he left down the ramp.

Sebastien went through his pre-flight check list methodically. I checked to make sure my gear was secure, and by gear, I mean my whisky. Teddy found a seat at the comms console and Leanna found a seat on the bridge next to Sebastien.

As I buckled myself in, Kara entered the bridge. She took her accustomed seat at the tactical position and buckled her harness. I gazed at her trying to reconcile the amazing woman I now realized I loved, with the 'dangerous creature' Baaqir had warned me about, and of which I'd recently seen disturbing evidence. I wasn't sure I could.

"Miccon One, the is the Avernus, requesting clearance to depart." Teddy broadcast.

"Avernus, this is Miccon One. You are cleared to depart. Avoid passing above the city, please. Have a good trip, Avernus." came the response.

We felt a brief instability as the Avernus left the pad, and a tilt to our left as Sebastien avoided the city. Then the sudden acceleration as we rapidly rose above the clouds. Sebastien brought up the forward view on the screen to test that our optics had been repaired properly.

The Mick was more appealing from low orbit, the multi-colored mountains and inland sea were actually quite impressive. I realized I was going to miss it. As the first planet I'd ever visited besides Ampora it'd forever hold a place in my heart. I wanted to return some day, to see how Damon's terraforming progressed.

Kara pronounced the sensors functional. Apparently, all the repairs had gone off smashingly. The nav computer made a few calculations and the course to Kleos was set. We'd be passing through a wide area of Telluric space enroute, so Sebastien engaged the 'dark mode' and activated the REL drive.

Following in my father's footsteps had finally become a reality.

Part Sixteen Kleos Prime

Interstellar Dates: 388-07-03 thru 08

Enroute to, and arrival at Kleos Prime

WE WENT THROUGH THE fresh food we'd gotten from Damon Offerton first. I've always enjoyed eggs, when I could get them. Ampora doesn't have a large domestic bird industry, but there were imported eggs available. Of course, they were relatively expensive, so I ate them sparingly. The eggs we got on the Mick were a delightful treat for me, so I had them almost every meal. Scrambled, poached, boiled, and pan fried, I couldn't get enough.

Leanna was a magician with omelets, as you'd expect, but I hated to impose on her constantly so I did a lot of the cooking myself.

It was only after I'd polished off at least a couple dozen that Sebastien told me they didn't come from birds. There was a reptilian creature, similar to a large tortoise, which was raised for their eggs on MK141. That's why the eggs were so fresh and delicious he said. He liked them too, so he and I gobbled most of them.

Speaking of Sebastien, he and I started to spend a lot of time together on board. He was a remarkable fellow, and I enjoyed his company, but mostly it was the fact he and I were both enthusiastic Thezra players. The Avernus had a beautiful Thezra set carved from stone. We'd set it up in the salon and have epic matches. Leanna and Kara began to watch the matches and cheer us on. I also discovered, before long, the two of them would gamble on the outcomes. Neither Sebastien nor I could stand to lose, so the matches were both enjoyable and contentious.

Thezra is a strategy game for two competitors. Each player starts with 24 pieces of various values and usefulness. It's an ancient game

347

that originated on the planet Runivia and is widely considered the preeminent two-player strategy game in the quadrant. Games between masters sometimes last for days, and often end in draws. I was taught to play by my father, and I've always enjoyed the challenge of it. I fancy myself something of an expert and have won several tournaments on Ampora. I even managed to defeat Cortland Brentford, a professional player rated as a master, in a best of 5 set once. The trophy I earned sits on my mantle at home.

I'd get a glass of ice from the galley, open a bottle of whisky, set up the board, and call out 'game on' so everyone could hear. Time passed quickly during a game, and that was sort of the point. We had time to kill on the way to Kleos, and it gave us a chance to strategize as well.

On the second day out from MK141, Sebastien stunned Teddy. "So, Bradley, just how do you propose to grab that library out from under the Ministry of Security's noses?" Teddy looked from Sebastien to me, and I threw up my hands.

"Don't look at me, Teddy. I never said anything."

"I told him." Kara confessed. "There should be no secrets among crew mates, it's counterproductive. Sebastien and Leanna are taking the same risk we are by going to Kleos, and they deserve to know everything we do. I told him everything I know, so now there's no secrets. Right?"

This last question was for Teddy. Kara was basically demanding to know if there was anything else Teddy hadn't told us.

"Quite right, absolutely. There should be no secrets. I was planning on telling you Fowler, just picking a good moment." Teddy said.

There was something else I noticed in this exchange; a subtle little thing that was meaningful to me. Kara had referred to Sebastien as 'Sebastien' instead of 'Fowler.' As far as I can remember she'd always, before, called him Fowler. To me, it meant my love had finally accepted him as a close comrade, instead of just a fellow tagging along with us. 'Fowler' was an acquaintance, 'Fowler' was a hired gun; 'Sebastien' was a friend.

Kara and I cohabitated in the first cabin. Teddy never said a thing to me, but I wasn't sure about his interactions with Kara. In the sheltered existence I'd lead 'before,' what'd happened between the three of us,

I would've considered a problem. In my mind I'd basically stolen his woman. Kara continuously told me not to be jealous of him, and he certainly wasn't jealous of me. But I still didn't understand how that could be. Kara was so incredible; how could he *not* be jealous?

Leanna and I also become closer friends as we traveled to the Kleos system. Sebastien took to calling us sisters, I guess because of our red hair, but I also think he got a kick out of our friendship. We were so different, but when we were together, we became like peas in a pod. Even I didn't understand it. She confided some of her horrible experiences from her childhood, and I confided embarrassing episodes from my adolescence. Like the time I got caught making out with one of my friends. We were supposed to be studying, and her mom walked right in on us kissing. I never got invited back to their house.

Leanna routinely did my hair. I'd sit patiently as she performed miracles, braiding my locks in dozens of different configurations, trying to find 'my' perfect style. She'd gossip about people she knew aboard the Archeron, and I'd tell her about Ampora as she worked. It was actually quite relaxing, to be honest. All my life, as an only child, I'd never realized what I'd missed growing up without siblings. My relationship with Leanna was a breath of fresh air.

One day, after a particularly frustrating Thezra loss to Sebastien, we gathered in the salon to plot. Annoyingly, I'd finally come to the realization Sebastien was just a *little* bit better than me. The first time we played I'd taken it easy on him, thinking he was a novice. I was shocked when he used a series of complicated advances to neutralize my defense. After that, I didn't underestimate him anymore, but he still gave worse than he was given. Dammit.

"So, here's our tactical situation as I see it." Teddy began. "After we drop out of REL drive, short of the Kleos system, we'll approach Kleos Prime slowly, using dark mode. The CTF will most likely have a ship in orbit there. But if we're careful, we might be able to enter orbit on the opposite side of the globe from it. Then we can descend to the surface when we're geosynchronous above the mountain which holds the vault."

"That sounds like an excellent plan, as long as there's only *one* CTF ship. If there's more, that won't work." Sebastien said. "Most importantly, we need to avoid a fight. They'd call in reinforcements and our whole plan would be ruined."

"Agreed." Kara spoke up. "The last engagement showed us the danger of fighting in space, anything can happen. Without an engineer on board, even relatively minor damage could prove catastrophic for us."

"Yes, we slip in without being noticed, that's the plan." Teddy said. "Then, Abby opens the vault, we pack all those books on the Avernus, and we slip out quietly. Easy."

Our sensors picked up several targets as we went. Traveling in REL drive we couldn't glean much info on each target, but it was a fair bet some were CTF. The dark mode never failed us, the technology worked like a charm, as if we were all but invisible. Sebastien and Teddy collaborated on our navigation, avoiding star systems Teddy knew to be active with insurgencies (there were a few), because of the inevitable CTF presence; while also steering clear of systems Sebastien knew to have Baaqir's businesses and interests, just to be safe.

Eventually we came within sensor range of the Kleos system. Teddy's information was that CTF frigates were patrolling the sector, so everything rested on the effectiveness of the QSDM device. Apparently, a frigate was a significantly more dangerous ship than a simple 'gunship.' Sebastien gave me the lowdown.

"A CTF gunship is a formidable platform, it usually has a crew of 7 or 8, carries missiles and uses particle cannons. The sensors and defensive systems are comparable to the Avernus." he told me.

"However, one of their frigates has a crew of 30 or 40, often including marines. Their armor and shielding is more formidable, and their weapons would include some sort of plasma energy weapon along with the missiles and particle guns. A gunship might have 16 or so missiles equipped at a time, a Frigate more like 40 or 50. And, frigates usually have a couple of small, two-man 'fighters' they can deploy during combat. We're no match." he finished.

"So, we stay in dark mode and hope Baaqir's fancy tech works as well as my sources claim." Teddy added. "We are about to give the tech a major test."

We dropped out of REL at the outskirts of the system. Right away we got proximity alerts on two targets. One target was in orbit around Kleos Prime, just as Teddy had predicted. It was probably the frigate Gordon himself commanded, and that meant the bastard was most likely on Kleos Prime already.

But, of more immediate concern was the second target that was on our side of the solar system, and too close for comfort. We were well within range of both ships' sensors.

"Damn, there's two of the fuckers." Sebastien told us. "Just what I was afraid of."

"Never fear," Teddy said. "The gadget hasn't failed us yet, but let's give them a wide berth, just in case."

"Wide berth, aye, aye." Sebastien set a course to avoid them.

Even with the course correction we passed relatively close to the nearest ship. The computer told us it was most likely military, and medium sized. When we ran the transponder code through the computer it confirmed the ship was a CTF frigate named the Trident; a new class capable of carrying much more cargo than earlier models.

"It's damn odd." Sebastien said. "Two CTF warships in one lifeless solar system? Isn't that unusual, Bradley?"

"Quite so. Damn unusual." Teddy agreed. "I hate to admit it, but there has to be a connection to the Academy's presence on Kleos Prime. This isn't a simple patrol."

"Where's the Academy's ship?" Kara asked. "It has to be here somewhere. What's it called again, Abby?"

"The Bishop Ambrose."

"Presumably it's on the surface of the planet. They'd be using it as a base of operations." Teddy said.

"If so, that complicates our plan. Without knowing where it is, we risk detection if we try to land." Kara observed.

"It's a risk we can't avoid, we don't have a choice." Teddy said. "We'll drop into orbit on the other side of the globe from the CTF ship, then do a few turns in orbit trying to locate the Academy ship on the surface. Hopefully, they'll be thousands of kilometers from our mountain."

"That's the plan? *Hopefully,* they don't see us? *Hopefully,* they're thousands of kilometers away?" I asked, worriedly.

"Abby, my dear, we have a skilled pilot, a stealthy ship and the greatest smuggler in the galaxy on our side." Teddy smiled.

"Thanks, but I wouldn't call me the greatest. Maybe top 3." said Kara.

"Smartass." said Teddy.

"If there's any sign they've detected us, Abby, we'll leave immediately." Sebastien reassured me, "We'll engage the REL and get the hell out of here, I promise. We obviously can't fight two warships."

Leanna and I stood at the back of the bridge watching Teddy and Sebastien fly the ship for several minutes.

"There's no indication they can see us." Teddy said, "If they had, they'd be moving to intercept. This might just work, boyo."

"It looks that way, for now." Sebastien said.

Kara said, "I've got everything ready, master."

"Good. Now, everyone gather around for a moment." Teddy said. "The atmosphere on Kleos Prime is breathable, but just barely, at about 17% oxygen. It's alright for short periods with no exertion, but after a while the higher-than-normal concentrations of gases like xenon and argon start to have a narcotic effect."

Kara said, "Therefore, I've rigged up some small respirators for us to wear while on the surface. Here, Leanna, let me show you."

She took one of the devices and placed it around Leanna's neck, then strung the little respirator up over her ear and down to her nose. A little bubble went over her nostrils and fitted snugly.

"Just breath normally through your nose and you'll have no problems. If you start to get dizzy or short of breath, the nose piece isn't sealed properly and needs to be adjusted. Or, perhaps you've been breathing through your mouth too much. Simple." Kara told us.

There were several tense minutes as we made our way to Kleos Prime. No one spoke. Kara sat at the tactical station monitoring the sensors. Leanna had sat down next to Sebastien at the pilot's console. Teddy sat at the comms position, and also watched the sensors closely. I stood at the back of the bridge feeling like a third thumb.

"We're approaching the planet, everyone strap in." Sebastien announced.

"Fowler, this Quantum disruption device will *probably* work as we descend to the surface; however, it won't be able to hide the heat shockwave we create as we enter the atmosphere. Hopefully, if they detect us, we'll just appear to be a meteor." Teddy warned.

"Damn big meteor." Sebastien said. "Don't worry, Bradley. We'll enter orbit on the opposite side of them, no problem. I have it under control." Sebastien told him calmly.

"Alright then, place us in orbit." Teddy instructed.

Sebastien carefully brought the Avernus towards Kleos Prime. The orbital window was narrow as Sebastien attempted to keep the planet between us and the CTF ship. Eventually, we entered orbit almost exactly opposite the enemy vessel; apparently, an impressive bit of piloting.

"Well done, Fowler." Teddy complimented him. "Where'd you learn to fly? That was quite well done."

"I went to pilot training for nearly a year on Dressida. Baaqir insisted I be well rounded and as useful as possible. I've also had survival training, zero-G combat training, medical training, studied computer engineering and I can bake a mean apple pie." He smiled. "I'm multi-talented."

"And so modest." Leanna added, soliciting a round of laughs.

"I can't see any signs of an Academy vessel on the surface." Teddy stated. "In fact, I've seen no signs of any activity down there. That's damn odd too. How do you conduct an archeological dig without digging?"

"What do you think it means?" I asked.

"I'm not sure, we should've seen some evidence of a dig by now." Teddy answered. "But, it appears the Bishop Ambrose has gone; if it was ever here."

"Well, we can't stay in orbit, so let's get down there already." Kara said.

"We've made one pass over the mountain range that holds our vault." Sebastien told us. "Everyone get strapped in; I'm going to try a descent the next time we're in position." Sebastien announced.

We took our seats and fastened our harnesses. The viewscreen showed an unobstructed view of the desolate waste that was the surface of Kleos Prime. There were no clouds and no water in sight on the surface. Compared to Kleos Prime, the Mick had been a garden of eden.

"Alright, everyone hold on." Sebastien told us as he began our descent. The ride was much smoother than at MK141, with virtually no turbulence. We descended rapidly toward the mountains, the dry, rocky terrain on the viewscreen was rushing at us alarmingly fast. Sebastien, after slowing our descent, skillfully set the Avernus down in a small canyon between high peaks. We'd officially arrived at our destination. I couldn't wait to put my eyes on that vault.

"Brilliant job again, Sebastien. When this is all over I'll hire you as my pilot, you have a natural knack for it." Teddy gushed.

He turned to the rest of us, "Alright, this is the closest spot we could find to land. The cavern that leads to the vault is still a couple of kilometers from here, but this location hides the ship from view in three directions. I'm afraid my sources tell me the QSDM device doesn't work perfectly if the ship is on the ground."

"Does that mean the frigate in orbit will be able to detect us now?" I asked.

"We'll know soon enough; if they see us they'll quickly come and investigate." Teddy said. "But, I don't think we need to worry. Between Fowler's skillful piloting and the gadget, I think we've avoided detection. This canyon should keep the ship out of view, but it might be a good idea to shut down all non-essential systems just to be careful."

"I'll do that right now." Sebastien said.

"I'd like to head for the vault as soon as possible; I can't wait to see it." I said.

"We have rough terrain between here and there, and we'll have to hike it. We don't dare use the runabout; it might be spotted from a distance by sensors, we need to keep a low profile. I think perhaps this first trip will be myself, Kara, and the Professor. Fowler, I'd appreciate it if you'd stay here with the ship, and Leanna can stay here with you, for now."

"I can do that. How long do you think you'll be gone?"

"We'll travel light. Canteens, weapons, and torches. It's been a while since I've been here, so I might take a few minutes to find the cavern entrance. Say, 45 minutes there, 30 minutes to locate the entrance, 45 minutes back."

"Wait, we're not going to the vault?" I asked.

"From the mouth of the cavern it's several hours descent to the vault chamber, my dear. Are you sure you want to take that on the first day? It may take us a while to get accustomed to the climate here. Atmospheric pressure, gravity and air quality all take a toll; especially gravity. If I remember correctly, the gravity here is a bloody pain."

"The mass of Kleos Prime is 20% greater than Ampora, Abby." Sebastien said, "It'll take some getting used to."

"To hell with that, I'm here for the vault. I'm not here to do a survey. I thought we were in a hurry to grab those books before the Ministry can find them. I need to snap some pictures of the vault door so I can work on opening it. The sooner I get started, the better."

"I agree," Kara said, "Time waits on no one."

"As you say, then. Let's gear up." Teddy took charge, "Make sure your canteens are full and weapons loaded. Kara, you better go below and grab us rifles and the climbing equipment we brought over from the Tito, we'll need it. Abby, go to the larder and grab some PPRs, just in case. Wear your jacket, the daytime temp is around 5 or 10 degrees, but at night it drops considerably; well below zero. We only have a couple hours of daylight left."

He turned to Sebastien again, "It looks like we'll be several hours. We'll try to stay off comms, obviously, but I'll set up a small relay transmitter on the surface. That way we should be able to raise you if we get in trouble. Emergencies only. Alright?"

"Aye, aye, Captain." Sebastien smiled. "What do I do if the green shirts appear?"

"We have to pray that doesn't happen. But, in the unlikely case, forget about us, save yourselves. Blast off and avoid the bastards. Wait a few days and try to come back using the dark mode. We'll try to stay hidden. If that doesn't work, it's been an honor working with you, Fowler. Take care of your girl, and good luck." Teddy told him.

"I'm not going anywhere, you pirate. If they show up here, I'm taking off and coming to get you at the cavern mouth." The two shook hands and that was that.

I dressed in a few layers, clipped my little dagger to my belt and wore a backpack with PPRs, some flares, extra socks, first aid kit, electric torch, gloves, hat, and other paraphernalia I imagined I might need. I hiked frequently at home, but never anything like this rocky, mountainous terrain on Kleos Prime.

Kara returned from the hold with three rifles, not two. She handed one to me and started a quick tutorial on its functions and abilities. It was one of the EM85 rifles like the ones Teddy had given to Kutta's militia.

"Kara, do I really have to carry this thing? It's too damn heavy." I asked. "I'm no soldier. What if I just carry a handgun? I probably couldn't hit anything with that rifle anyway."

"It's up to you, little human. I'll make a deal with you, if you don't want to carry the rifle you can carry some of these for me in your pack." She showed me what looked like a little rocket. It was several centimeters long, cylindrical with a pointed nose and three fins on the bottom.

"What the hell is that?"

"A mortar round. I use them like a grenade, I flick the arming switch here," she showed me the small lever between the fins, "and then throw it. I set it to ten seconds so it's similar to a grenade, but much more powerful. You just have to make sure you throw it far enough." She laughed.

"You want me to carry bombs in my pack? That can't be safe; what if I fall?"

"It's perfectly safe. They won't detonate unless the arming switch is activated. They come in a case of four, sheathed in foam. They'll be perfectly safe in your pack. You carry a case of these and a handgun, and we'll leave your rifle here."

"Alright, if you say it's safe. Do you really think we'll need any of this stuff? We're just hiking to the vault." I asked her.

"This is my area of expertise, Abby. I won't tell you how to give a lecture, if you don't tell me how to arm myself in hostile territory. Deal?"

"Are you two ready? We're wasting daylight." Teddy asked.

"Almost." Kara replied. "Abby, you must promise me, if we encounter CTF soldiers you'll do as I say, understand?"

"Aye, aye, commander."

"I'm serious. I'll protect you as much as possible, but you have to do as I say. Keep your head down, no sneaking closer to get a better view, and no heroics."

"Ok, I promise."

We left the relative safety of the Avernus and hiked out onto the surface of Kleos Prime. Teddy wore heavy boots, hiking gear, a large pack on his back and carried one of the EM85s. I was wearing my new hiking gear, my good boots, and my heavy pack on my back. Kara's mortar rounds weren't light. I didn't carry a rifle, but I'd strapped a handgun to my belt as well as my dagger. But instead of the gun making me feel fierce, I felt foolish.

Kara, however, looked like a one-person army. She'd made mention of her 'gear' before on a few occasions. Now, I knew what she was talking about. From her metallic cladded boots to her helmeted head, she was armored. She called it a personal, exo-armor combat chassis. A Tellurian design, the thing had its own power source and assisted her movements, giving her immense strength (as if she needed it) and speed. She claimed the suit would allow her to leap several meters high and run as fast as a gazelle.

The suit was heavily armored as well, apparently it could withstand direct hits from energy weapons as well as projectiles. She carried one of the multi-phase plasma rifles, had a shoulder rocket launcher strapped to her back and also carried a large duffle full of ammo. She had to be carrying close to 100 kilos of equipment on our hike. Conspicuously absent were her edged weapons. I suppose she'd decided she didn't need Sur-rok when she was carrying all that fire power.

"Are you sure you have enough weapons, Kara?" Sebastien teased as we left. "I could strap one of the antimatter torpedoes to your back if you'd like."

"Only a fool gets killed for lack of firepower or ammo. Preparedness is the soul of professionalism. I would've thought you knew that, Sebastien." She teased back.

THE HIKE WHICH FOLLOWED was an absolute back breaker, surpassing my initial worries. Teddy's cautionary words about the increased gravity proved all too true. The landscape itself was unforgiving, featuring unstable gravel paths, steep inclines, obstructive boulders, and rare moments of relief. I found myself tripping repeatedly, my breath labored throughout. My respirator, fastened to my nose, proved irksome, necessitating frequent adjustments in a futile attempt to find a more comfortable fit.

"Remember to breath in through your *nose*, Abby. When we get winded, we instinctively tend to breath more through our mouths. But here, that's a mistake. That air has less oxygen in it." Teddy said helpfully.

Teddy, though older than me, trod steadily ahead, his confident stride betraying no hint of fatigue. Kara bore the weight of her equipment with ease, aided by her powered combat suit, which ensured she never wavered or slowed. It was painfully evident I was the weakest link, causing the others to pause and wait for me repeatedly.

Eventually, we reached the spot where Teddy believed the cavern to be, only to discover it wasn't there, much to our chagrin. We stumbled around for a few minutes, but couldn't locate it. Teddy questioned whether we were at the correct elevation, as the mountain's peak soared at least a thousand meters above us.

"It's near here, I know it. At one time I had the coordinates memorized, but that was years ago. I never thought I'd return." Teddy explained. "We should split up; Kara, take Abby with you and work your way that direction three or four hundred meters, then come back here. I'll head this other direction and do the same. The aperture is six or eight meters across, you won't be able to miss it."

Kara and I began our scouting mission in the direction Teddy had indicated. The terrain, although not terribly steep, was a constant challenge. Walking sideways along the hill was murder on my hips and I was starting to think I'd bitten off more than I could chew in this whole excursion when we crested a small rise and there, about 30 meters to our right was a cave entrance. It looked exactly like Teddy had described, so we decided it had to be what we were looking for.

When we returned to the place we'd left Teddy, he was nowhere in sight. So, Kara and I took a break, setting down what we were carrying, taking a sip or two of water, and relaxing.

"This place isn't just ugly." Kara said. "There's an echo of death here, I can almost feel it. MK141 was dry and dusty, but it was a paradise compared to this place. It's hard to imagine these ancient geniuses of yours even stopped here, let alone settled here."

"We don't know if they stopped or settled, but they were supposedly wiped out here. Kleos Prime probably looked completely different thousands of years ago." I said. "Teddy said the codex referred to this place as lush and green."

"If that's true, what do you think happened to it? There must've been a catastrophic disaster, or a *devastating war*." Kara guessed.

"War? You think some kind of super weapon could have done this?"

"Those genius aliens of yours, the Reges Scientia, it stands to reason their enemies would've been just as advanced, don't you think?" she asked. "They could've launched some kind of weapon from space that devastated the whole planet. Or used some unknown technology to disrupt the planet's orbit or rotation. Looking around, it's not hard to believe."

"Maybe. It's possible they were the Reges Scientia civilization people have speculated about; my father seemed to think so. But his Codex referred to them as the Hoji Mubrani, and gave this place as the location of their armageddon; the end of their civilization."

"Theoretically, they were so advanced they had cures for every disease, genetic engineering to make them live longer, technologies to grow plenty of food or overcome any problems they could possibly have, right?" Kara asked.

"That's the theory. We still don't have any proof of all that."

"But, if it's *true*, what could possibly have destroyed them? Abby, it must've been a war, and this was the final battlefield. They were wiped out by some sort of super weapon and all of their advanced technologies couldn't save them."

"You believe the theory, about the ancient, advanced civilization?" I asked, surprised.

"Maybe, I'm not sure. But, if that library is what you and Teddy think it is, and this place was the site of a devastating war, it stands to reason that vault is probably filled with military secrets; don't you think?"

"What are you ladies talking about?" Teddy asked as he walked up. "Can I join you? I'm bushed."

"Grab a seat. We think we found your cavern." I said.

"Excellent; I'm already tired of searching. How are you two holding up?" Teddy asked. "I have to admit that hike took a lot out of me. It was a great reminder I'm twenty-three years older than the last time I was here. The gravity is a killer, just like I remembered."

"I have another of these exo-suits stored in the hold. I could run back and bring it here for you.' Kara offered. "Sorry, Abby, I don't think it'd fit you."

"Don't worry about me, fresh as a new-cut flower, I am." I said. "Just how hard is the hike from here down to the vault, Teddy?"

"Well, it's several stretches of steady slope to walk, interspersed with a few steep descents. We have rope and I brought some repelling harnesses. If my memory serves, it should take us two and a half or three hours, maybe a little more. If we keep a steady pace."

"That sounds fun." I said sarcastically. "I'm sorry, but I'm not sure I'm up to the descent and the climb back up too. Not to mention the hike back to the Avernus. But, I need some photos of the vault door."

"Henry had a difficult time with the climb, eventually he started camping out down by the vault. There's a fairly large cavern just above the vault chamber where we set up a small camp. We can do that again if you want, Abby. Come, let's at least get you inside and out of the worst of the cold."

Teddy took me by the hand and helped me up and we started for the cavern entrance. The going was awkward, as I've said, but before long we arrived at the cave. Teddy fished in his backpack and came out with a transceiver booster and placed it near the cave mouth.

"Our comms won't penetrate all of the rock once we start down, the vault is deep inside the mountain." he said.

The three of us ventured inward, and as we stepped further into the cavern, it gradually grew wider. Inside, we found a cave that measured roughly 30 meters in width and stretched 60 to 70 meters in depth. The ceiling overhead was about 10 to 12 meters high. What caught our attention most was the unexpectedly level and smooth floor, suggesting a deliberate touch in its creation.

"Henry and I scanned these hills from orbit, looking for irregularities or anything that looked like it might be ruins. This cave showed up prominently. Once we laid eyes on the inside of this cave, Henry was convinced it wasn't a natural feature."

"That's the first thing I thought when we walked in. This floor's too flat and smooth to be natural." I said.

"Then, we saw this." Teddy grabbed my hand and led me back toward the far end of the cave. He indicated a path that was clearly carved into the rock leading to another opening the size of a large, arched doorway. Just inside the doorway a set of stairs had been carved into the rock leading downward into the mountain.

"When we saw this, we knew we were on to something."

"Wow, this is incredible." I declared. "Who do you suppose carved these stairs?"

"That's an excellent question. Who, indeed?" Teddy asked. "Was it the same chaps who put the vault down there, or someone that came along later? Who knows?"

"Well, let's not waste any time." Kara said. "Abby, make yourself comfortable here, and I'll be back with photos of the vault as quickly as possible. Master, are you up for the hike?"

"Absolutely. Being here again is giving me new energy."

"I'm coming too. I can't just sit here waiting for you to get back, I'll go crazy." I said. "My father used a cane. If he could do it, so can I."

The stairs led us deeper into the tunnel, their rough-hewn edges gradually giving way to a smoother path. The passage remained consistently more than a meter wide, occasionally expanding to accommodate two or even three people side by side. The ceiling overhead was generously high as well, allowing us to move without having to stoop. It was as though someone had meticulously crafted this tunnel with our needs in mind. Whoever the engineers had been, they must've been humanoid, or at least the same size as us.

As we advanced, we reached an abrupt break in the path; a chasm roughly a meter and a half wide. On our side, a primitive ladder had been carved into the rock's face, descending into the depths of the tunnel. Kara, resourceful as ever, withdrew a length of rope and fastened it securely to my harness, then lowered me down the approximately four meters to the path below. She repeated the process with Teddy, effortlessly attaching the rope to a metal anchor she hammered into the rock face above.

After Teddy and I had safely reached the bottom, Kara simply leaped down, landing like a cat, disdaining the rope completely.

We continued this way for hours, stopping to take breaks every few minutes. I was glad I'd decided to join them, the climb down wasn't nearly as trying as I'd feared. Going up might be a different story though. Finally, we came to what Teddy called the 'campsite.' It was a large cavern, as he'd said. Most likely natural in origin, about 15 meters across and 4 or 5 high. The engineered pathway continued downward at the far end.

"This is where we set up a campsite 23 years ago. Henry stayed here for weeks, literally. I carried supplies down here to him. He was obsessed with finding the combination to the vault and refused to leave this place. The vault is only a couple dozen meters down that way."

We left the campsite and proceeded down the path, which veered sharply to our right. There was another set of carved stairs, at least the 20th we'd encountered during the descent, and finally it appeared. Jutting several centimeters from the side wall of the path was the so-called vault. It was the same dull, matt bronze color of my amulet with a textured appearance but the characteristic smooth feel. There was no doubt in my mind it was constructed of the same material; what I'd decided to call Mubranium, after the inventors.

"The path ends just up ahead there." Kara advised. "That leaves no doubt; this entire pathway and tunnel was constructed to arrive here at the vault. But, how was the vault placed here? How was it buried in the heart of the mountain, in rock that's probably millions of years old. What sorcery was used to do this?"

"Clearly, it was done with technology we don't understand. Maybe one of those books inside it will tell us how it was done."

Teddy asked, "Well, what do you say, Abby, do you think you can you open it?"

"I don't know yet, we just got here." I laughed. "Give a person a chance to think."

Kara dropped her duffle and began rifling through it. Meanwhile, I took my canteen and started to clean the dust and dirt from the symbols embossed on the vault door. The door was tall enough I couldn't reach the top, so Teddy helped me in the cleaning.

Seventeen circular dials of varying widths adorned the door, radiating out from the smallest dial in the center. Each dial was covered in alien symbols, and I needed them all clean so my photos would show every detail, every nuance in the symbology. My plan was to take a catalog of photos and feed the data into the Avernus' computer in order to work on a solution.

After recording the vault's symbology on my comms device, I tried moving the dials. Unbelievably, they moved freely, the dust and age seeming to have no detrimental effect on them. Mubranium, whatever the hell it was, didn't seem to corrode. The dials on the door were most likely incredibly ancient, yet showed virtually no signs of age. Exhausted and needing rest, I eventually went and sat on the floor against the far wall to organize my thoughts. The grueling ascent back to the surface was a daunting prospect.

Kara set down a small, battery powered heater between the three of us. The temperature had started to drop a while ago, and it was becoming uncomfortable. As we warmed ourselves, resting for the hike back to the Avernus, I noticed something.

I rose and walked back over to the vault and ran my fingers along a subtle indentation below the dials, near the floor. It was a rectangular shaped void about 3mm deep, 4cm wide and 7cm tall. It was as if a piece of a jigsaw puzzle had been removed.

"Try your necklace, Abby." Teddy suggested.

Goosebumps had sprung up as I lifted the amulet from around my neck. I knelt and placed the thing against the rectangular shaped space on the vault. It was the exact size and shape. I removed the leather string from the small aperture in the amulet which it was threaded through, placed the amulet against the little void and it clicked into place, a perfect fit.

"We followed the directions in the codex, and came to Kleos Prime looking for this place." Teddy said. "Henry found your amulet right where it is now."

"What about those other pieces, the ones you showed to Baaqir?" Kara asked. "Where'd you find those?"

"Believe it or not, those and 40 or so others were in a neat little pile near the cavern entrance. Like someone had gathered them and placed them there. I still have all of them, buried under a half meter of tile and concrete below my patio on Kyntava. All torn, twisted and discolored as if by some type of conflagration."

"Probably caused by a weapon of some kind." Kara said as she looked at me.

"Possibly, who knows?" Teddy said.

"Well, I have what I need, let's get going, I want to get back to the ship and start my analysis of this door." I said.

Coming face to face with that vault door forced me to acknowledge a sobering fact: There were trillions of possible combinations using those 17 dials. *Trillions.*

We gathered up our gear and started to climb back to the surface. The going was difficult and slow but aided by Kara and her powered suit of armor we made steady progress. She'd have Teddy and I attach our harnesses to a rope, and she'd haul us up any vertical obstacles hand over hand, like some sort of mythical hero.

After three torturous hours, my leg muscles cramping and my lungs burning, we finally started up the last set of stairs to the cavern at the service. As Kara, who was leading the way, reached the top of the stairs and entered the cavern I was contemplating how lovely a glass of Cordson's and a steaming hot shower on the Avernus would be. Teddy and I reached the top and began walking toward the exit; what I heard next chilled my very soul.

"Good evening, Professor Thornwell. It's so nice to see you again."

I'd know that voice anywhere, including in a nightmare. It was the voice of Commander Percival Gordon of the CTF security forces.

Part Seventeen Commander Percy Gordon

Interstellar Date: 388-07-09
On Kleos Prime

THERE MUST'VE BEEN at least 20 heavily armed soldiers in the cavern with us, a mix of green shirts and marines. Two marines stepped out from cover behind Teddy and me. We raised our hands without being told, but Kara raised her weapon and pointed it at Gordon. For a moment I expected her to fire, and despite the near certain deadly reprisal from the marines if she did, part of me hoped she'd go ahead and kill the bastard.

"Kara, stop!" Teddy shouted. "They have us surrounded, Abby and I are trapped."

"You'd better listen to your boss." Gordon told her, "Lay down your weapons and your friends may live. If you open fire, you all die."

Kara quickly evaluated the hopeless situation and reluctantly did as she was told. She laid her rifle and rocket launcher on the ground at her feet. Several soldiers raced over to grab the weapons, keeping their rifles trained on her the whole time. They were obviously aware of how dangerous she was, as 6 marines surrounded her.

"Gentleman, please remove that tactical suit, I believe it's CTF property." Gordon ordered. One of the marines told Kara "Don't move" and he began to unbuckle her armored suit.

"Twenty against three." Kara said. "If you people ever showed up and the odds weren't stacked in your favor, you'd all shit yourselves and run away."

It took a few minutes to get the armored suit off Kara. All she was wearing underneath was one of her formfitting body suits and the temperature was below zero. But Kara gave no indication of being uncomfortable. The soldiers made her lie down face first on the cold, dirty cavern floor and proceeded to bind her arms and legs in a set of manacles behind her back. She was completely immobilized; they weren't taking any chances.

While this was happening, the men behind us relieved us of our weapons and shoved Teddy and me over in front of Gordon. The marine behind me kicked the back of my legs forcing me to my knees. They quickly delt with Teddy the same way.

Kara said to Gordon, "Careful. I swear, every injury they endure will be visited a hundred-fold on you, Gordon, you Var-luk."

Gordon crossed the short distance to where Kara lay prone on the ground, securely manacled. "That's *Commander* Gordon to you, trash breed. You don't look all that dangerous now, you murderous bitch. Tell me, what does 'varlook' mean in your primitive language? I mean, *Jesus*, is every Tovolek word only two syllables? When you're all sitting around a campfire telling stories you must sound like a bunch of cavemen grunting at each other. Oo-oo, ah-ah." The marines all laughed as Gordon delivered a vicious kick to the side of Kara's head.

"Don't!" I screamed.

"Gordon, you son of a bitch, she's defenseless. I wouldn't expect that, even from you." Teddy yelled at him.

"Gag it." Gordon told the marines.

He placed a boot between Kara's shoulders and pressed down. "This *thing* killed five good men on the Archeron, it deserves whatever it gets."

Three marines jumped on Kara as Gordon came back toward us. Two of them held her down as the other forced a painful looking, studded metal gag into her mouth and buckled it tightly behind her head.

"What *are* you doing here, *Theodore*?" Gordon asked.

"I was going to ask you the same thing, *Percy*." Teddy answered. "How in hell did you find this cavern? And where'd you find that blasted derma patch, I was careful to make sure we left nothing behind when we left."

Gordon laughed, "The professor told you about the patch? Let's see, hmm, where did I get that thing? I think it was on aisle 2, third shelf on the left in the pharmacy on board the Archeron. I think it's for hay fever." Several of the soldiers standing around laughed with him.

I said, "You ass! You made that all up? Why?"

With a big grin, Gordon responded, "It's an old interrogation trick, you hit the subject with something shocking to throw off their guard. I thought maybe if I could shock you enough, you'd give up what your father told you about Kleos Prime. It didn't work, but I have many, more effective techniques I can try, don't worry."

"Then, how'd you know my father was ever here?" I asked.

"Confused?" Gordon chuckled, "It's pretty simple: Teddy told me."

"That's bullshit." Teddy said.

"Teddy, what's going on? What's he talking about?" I asked. He ignored me for a moment and spoke to Gordon instead.

"You're a bloody liar, you know I never told you a thing about this place, or Henry." Teddy argued, "All I told you was I knew of a planet where Regis Scientia artifacts might have been found."

"Teddy, you told him that?" I asked, bewildered at the turn of events.

"I did, but that's all I told him. They'd arrested Kara, and I was trying to convince them to set her free. I simply hinted about a possible discovery, that's all. I said I'd tell him where if they'd release her."

"At first, Teddy." Gordon taunted. "But, think about it, the only way I'd know about this cavern is from you. Don't be too mad, Professor, he doesn't remember a thing about it. Poor old Teddy here was under the influence at the time." He laughed wickedly.

"You drugged me? You bastard!" Teddy exclaimed and tried to rise. The marine behind him kicked the back of his legs again sending him sprawling. Gordon simply smiled.

"Of course. I like you better when you're drugged, Teddy, you don't lie as much. To be honest, when the motion detectors in here were tripped earlier today, I was genuinely surprised. I was in the middle of drafting my report, and contemplating my ruined career. I was sure I'd lose command of the George Upton and probably get assigned to some desk job shuffling papers on some God-forsaken client world." Gordon explained.

"You'd probably fuck that up too." Teddy said as the marines were binding his wrists behind his back with a zip-tie.

Gordon gave a subtle hand signal, and the marine beside me drove the butt of his rifle into the side of Teddy's head. Sprawling to the ground and landing with a thud, at first Teddy appeared to be unconscious. But he groggily rolled himself onto his side and spat out a gob of bloody spittle. A thin trickle of blood flowed down past his temple, falling in droplets to the ground between us.

In that moment, Teddy Bradley's face transformed into a mask of pure hatred, his eyes smoldering with intense fury. I wished with all my being that he was free and the marines weren't there; Teddy was bigger than Gordon, and a highly skilled combatant. It would've brought me great satisfaction to watch Teddy mop the cave with him.

"But then, of course, I realized: *it had to be you*. After all, you and I were the only two people who knew about this cavern. Still, I couldn't imagine why you'd be here, on Kleos Prime. After you kidnapped the professor, the last place I thought you'd turn up is here. I assumed the kidnapping was an effort to steal the professor away from me."

"I didn't kidnap anyone; Abby came along with us by choice." Teddy argued.

"And you delivered her right to me, saving my mission and possibly my career. I thank you, Teddy, that was considerate of you. But, enough of the joyous reunion, where's your ship?" Gordon asked. "You three didn't walk to Kleos Prime."

"Gone. I told our crew to leave and return in 3 days to retrieve us." Teddy said. "There's a platoon of mercenaries with them."

"I seriously doubt that. You haven't got enough supplies to last 3 days. It doesn't matter, there's nowhere for them to hide, I have two frigates at my disposal. We'll capture or kill them sooner than later." Gordon opined.

"Teddy, will you please tell me what's happening?" I asked him, exasperated.

"He drugged me before, the bastard; weeks ago when they arrested me on Kyntava. I'm sorry I never told you, Abby. I thought we could pull this off, really. I have no recollection of being drugged." Teddy pleaded. "I never would've told him about this cavern, I swear. I only wanted them to free Kara, and they did."

"Truthfully, that could be all he remembers, Professor. But after we applied the needle he spilled his guts about this place; all about Henry Thornwell, even about the vault down below us. That's why I'm here. The only thing remaining is to open that thing, and I'll be a hero."

Gordon spoke to one of the green shirts, "Bradshaw, take Mr. Bradley to the Upton and place him in the brig. I'm arresting you, Teddy, for illegal arms dealing, smuggling, trespassing into a restricted zone and generally being a pain in the ass. I may charge you with treason too, it just depends on the professor's cooperation. Take the Tovolek bitch to Krieg, he'll know what to do with her. I'll keep the professor here with me."

Teddy said to me as the marine, Bradshaw, led him away, "I'm sorry, Abby. This wasn't the plan, but I can make this right; as soon as I sort out this ugly bastard." He indicated Gordon.

Gordon taunted, "Good luck with that; in a few days you'll be locked up in the highest security prison in the galaxy, Teddy."

Four of the marines picked Kara up and carried her away as well. The way she was gagged and bound tore at my heart; I knew she longed to be fighting.

Cyrus Baaqir had been right when he told me someone else knew about Kleos Prime. It was Gordon, and incredibly, Teddy *himself* had told him.

"Alright, Gordon." I said. "What do you want from me?"

"Professor, never fear, you and I are going to have a *long* talk, but not here. This place is cold and dirty, and I have a comfortable office back on my ship to talk in. Come with me."

We left the cavern accompanied by several armed green shirts and marines. Outside, there were several armored vehicles waiting. Down the slope of the mountain, jolting and careening on the rough terrain we went, to the wide plain below us, where the CTS George Upton, Gordon's frigate, awaited. They must've landed while we were climbing down to the vault. I guessed it was the ship in orbit as we arrived at Kleos Prime.

We rode in silence, and I took the time to assess my options; there weren't many. Teddy had sold us out, if unintentionally. Sure, I was shocked, but not as much as you might imagine. It'd seemed from the beginning Teddy had secrets he wasn't sharing. That'd been proven true, of course. I just hadn't known the extent of his secrets. Maybe I still didn't.

Gordon's ship dwarfed the Avernus in sheer size, and obviously in firepower as well. It literally bristled with cannons, missiles and numerous other appendages that were a mystery to me. We boarded via an elevator platform that dropped down underneath the ship. The platform was large enough to accommodate numerous men or a substantial piece of machinery. Evidently, the armored vehicles must've been lowered to the ground using this ingenious mechanism.

As promised, Gordon showed me to an office in the interior of the vessel marked simply with the word 'Captain' stenciled on the door. The office was spacious and comfortable looking, furnished with a grand, polished wood desk, plush leather chairs, and adorned with an array of wall decorations. Among these hung a sizable, carved wooden crucifix, apparently a testament to Gordon's Christian faith. Framed diplomas and certificates shared wall space with photographs capturing various moments from his life and career.

One prominent photograph depicted Gordon in a dress uniform, holding a plaque and shaking hands with an older officer whose uniform included numerous stars on his epaulettes and a forest of ribbons on his chest.

Another photograph caught my eye, showing a younger Gordon, clad in weathered camouflage fatigues, standing alongside fellow officers behind a mound of dead bodies. Despite the grim backdrop, their faces bore smiles as they proudly displayed gruesome trophies for the camera. Beneath the image, the caption read 'Victorious! Members of Special Unit 19 pose with the fallen after the battle of Yarnua City, Erestis 3. 382-02-14.' In the photo, Gordon held aloft a grisly necklace crafted from a string of severed ears.

"Please, take a seat Professor Thornwell, you must be exhausted." he began. "I've made that hike to the vault a few times myself. Would you like something to drink besides water?" He indicated a large bottle of water sitting on his desk, apparently meant for me.

"No, thank you." I said cautiously. I didn't feel comfortable drinking anything he gave me, but I had to be realistic. I was thirsty and they'd confiscated my gear, including my canteen. I wouldn't be any good to anyone if I died of dehydration, so I grabbed the water and took a big drink.

"The dry climate here makes one incessantly thirsty. I've been to more inhospitable places, but none where I wasn't being shot at. You can take the respirator off aboard the Upton, Abby, our life support is working perfectly." I did as he suggested.

"Since when does the Ministry of Security have their own warships?" I asked. "I didn't realize you people were given command of fleet vessels."

"It's a fairly recent development. The Ministry took delivery of eight new frigates about three years ago. Now, we no longer need the regular fleet to carry us around like a bunch of glorified taxis; we can transport ourselves wherever we need to go."

"And, I imagine it's easier to keep your atrocities a secret this way. That must be very convenient."

He ignored my jab, "Before, fleet command was always sticking their noses into Ministry business. You're right, it's much more convenient this way. How do you like my office, Professor?"

"It's pretty much what I expected, except for the crucifix. I'm surprised you're a christian, you don't seem like the type."

"The accoutrements of being a preacher's son. It's beautiful isn't it? That crucifix is hand carved and over two hundred years old; my mother's family has passed it down. She gave it to me when I was given this command and I consider it good luck. You're not christian, Abby?"

"No. I cannot believe in a God that wants to be praised all the time."

"Ahh, Friedrich Nietzsche, I believe. How *professor* of you, Professor. If I remember my entry level philosophy, he wasn't a fan of religion in general. Most people on Ampora belong to that polytheistic Gremism religion, don't they? How many gods do you have, again?" He asked sarcastically, with obvious amusement. So, Gordon was educated; he was still an asshole.

"Why am I here and not in the brig with my friends?"

It was my fault for bringing up the crucifix, but I wasn't going to get into a religious debate with Percy-Fucking-Gordon.

"Not in the mood for theistic comparisons?" He chuckled, "I thought it'd be obvious why you aren't in the brig: I need you. I sent for you for a reason, Abby. I went all the way to Ampora and boarded the Archeron for a good reason."

"Alright, you've stumped me, what reason is that?"

"It's very simple: You're going to open the vault for me. Afterward, I can fetch the contents back to Titus. There, I'll receive accolades and congratulations from my shocked and impressed colleagues and superiors. I'll be promoted to Captain, forthwith, and eventually of course, to Admiral. I plan to become the youngest Admiral in the history of the service. That vault is my ticket to stardom, and you're the key, quite literally." He'd poured himself a glass of amber liquid as he spoke, and took a sip as he finished his little speech.

"It's nice to have goals."

"Abby, you're a historian, surely you know what 'Kleos' means?"

"It's Old Earth, ancient Greek for 'renown,' I believe."

"Very good, that's correct. Fame and glory; it's what the heroes in Homeric poetry were after. They wanted their names to outlive them. I have the chance to emulate them here on this dustbin of a planet."

"You're certifiable, Gordon. You do realize Achilles had to die to achieve Kleos, right? He was killed by the Trojan hero Paris with an arrow. And then Paris himself was killed by an arrow."

"You miss my point, Professor. The name of this planet is prophetic. I'm going to be famous, and you're going to help me."

"What makes you think I'll open that vault for *you*? Are you unhinged, or simply an idiot?" I asked, attempting to hide my fear with bluster.

He didn't get upset at my remark, he just smiled thinly and continued, "Because I'm going to make you the same offer I made to your friend, Teddy. He didn't want to cooperate either, *at first*. But he eventually saw things my way. I always get what I want... one way or another."

"I guess I'm supposed to ask you what you offered Teddy, is that it? I don't care, because I'll never help you. Besides, I don't know if I'll be able to open that vault anyway. The locking mechanism looks complicated to me. Even if I wanted to, I'm not sure I could open it."

"You're correct about one thing, it's complicated; much more so than I anticipated. I've had several experts examine it already. Including some of your friends from the Academy. What a waste of time that was. But, I'm positive you'll be eager to help me when we're through here."

"What makes you so sure?"

"After our talk aboard the Archeron I had you followed, Professor. The Tovolek and you, shall we say you're... 'romantically involved.' That's the polite way to put it."

"What makes you think that? We're friends, that's all."

Gordon chuckled, "Abby, you're a terrible liar. Like when you told me your father never mentioned Kleos Prime. You were supposed to come here with *me*, Abby, on the George Upton. If I'd thought for a *second* Bradley might show up there, I'd have taken you into custody the instant you boarded. Strictly speaking, I screwed up. I should've thrown you in the brig like my instincts told me. But, that's what I get for being a nice guy."

"Nice guy? Right. What'd you mean about my friends from the Academy?"

"Dr Hughes and his outfit. They were as good as useless when they encountered that vault. They had no idea how to open it. Just like my encryption experts that looked at it; all useless."

"Where are the Academy people? Are they still here? Can I see them?"

"They're being held at a safe location, far from Kleos Prime. I can't very well turn them loose until I collect the contents of that vault. What do you say, Abby, we should be friends you and I, don't you think? An upstanding Telluric citizen like yourself should be eager to help out the CTF, wouldn't you agree?"

"I'm not going to help you. You just carried my friends away in chains, that didn't exactly get you on my good side."

"You might want to worry a little more about getting on *my* good side. I'm afraid it's just as I feared. Your time with those two has poisoned your perspective, Abby. They aren't who you think they are."

"They're my friends, I know that much." I declared.

"No, they *aren't*. Listen, Bradley only sells weapons to rebels to line his pockets. He's about as idealistic as a sewer rat. And that sub-human monster he travels with is a murderous savage, driven by her hatred of us humans. She murdered her own father in a failed coup attempt, for Christ's sake. I'm sorry to be the one to tell you this, but she only seduced you in order to get you to help them. Let me guess, they asked you to open the vault for *them*, am I right?"

"It's easy to tell when you lie, Gordon, your lips move. Kara didn't kill her father, his brother did."

"Is *that* what she told you?" he smiled wryly, "On the Archeron, you attended a meeting between Bradley and a man named Cyrus Baaqir, did you not?"

"If you were following me, you know I did."

"Baaqir's a notorious collector of black-market artifacts. My guess is Bradley promised to sell Baaqir artifacts from Kleos Prime. Did Bradley confide his knowledge of the vault to Baaqir?"

When I didn't answer, Gordon continued, "You may as well tell me, Professor, I'll find out soon enough. My guess is Bradley filled your head with a bunch of idealistic mumbo-jumbo to get you to help him. But, believe me, he's only in this for the huge payday when he sells those books, or whatever they are, to Baaqir. They're conning you."

"I don't believe that."

"Alright, let's forget about the Tovolek for now; and Bradley. Because, simply put, they just don't matter anymore; they're out of the picture. Now, it's just you and me. Tell me, what do you think the CTF is doing out here, Abby?"

"Well, judging from that photo," I pointed to the one with him holding the necklace made of ears, "I'd say mostly killing people. A couple of those dead bodies look like children, Gordon. I wasn't aware you Ministry of Security types participated in actual combat."

"Many of us do. The Minister himself encourages us to get our 'hands bloody,' as he puts it. It's the fastest way to advancement, that's for sure. As for that photo, when an enemy combatant is shooting at you, trying to kill you and your comrades, you don't stop to consider how old they are."

"I look at that picture and wonder what you did to those people that made them want to shoot at you."

"I'll tell you: A few weeks before that photo was taken, a group of those insurgents had gathered up 200 or so human civilians; mostly bureaucrats and administrators. They abducted them from their homes and offices, along with their families, gathered them in the city square and executed them. A few were tortured and beheaded, but most just got a bullet to the back of the head; women and children included. Do you think we should've just turned the other cheek?"

"Whoever fights monsters should see to it that in the process he does not become a monster."

"More Nietzsche. Boilerplate philosophy doesn't impress me, Professor. To be honest, I expected more from you."

"I can't believe anything you say, Gordon. You'd say anything to get what you want. I'm sure there's horrible deeds done by all sides in war. Maybe we should try to have fewer wars, what do you think?"

"I agree, but this is about survival of our species. The CTF has the responsibility for protecting humanity. Right now, we're trying to secure our borders, which are horribly insecure. As a historian, you must know humans nearly didn't survive 90 years ago; it was touch and go. We were being systematically exterminated by the Magrids and Vitrameks. Did you ever see a Vitramek, Abby?"

"I've seen pictures."

"Thankfully, that's about all that's left of them. Those disgusting, slimy, genocidal *things* vowed to kill every human in the galaxy. That was their stated goal, the complete annihilation of our species. What's more, they were succeeding before the creation of the CTF."

"You realize I teach this stuff, right? You don't need to lecture me." I said, exasperated. "And, you realize *we* eventually did the exterminating? They're the ones who got annihilated."

"Yes, it's called winning."

"But, these people you're killing now never did anything to us. They're innocent."

"Innocent is a relative term. Abby, think about this: so far, humans have explored less than a quarter of the galaxy. Do you imagine the Vitrameks and Pentoffians are the *only* alien species that'll try to exterminate us when they encounter us?"

"The way the CTF is going, I imagine every alien in the galaxy will wish us dead before long."

"That's a fair point, Professor. But, when the survival of the species is at stake, don't you think it's better to be safe than sorry? AI projections say there's a 77% chance we'll encounter another species that'll attempt to exterminate us within the next one hundred years. This species, unknown to us now, will likely have advanced technologies we've never seen before. After first contact, when they attack us, we'll need time to adapt to their unique technologies and tactics. We're expanding our borders in order to create a buffer against that invasion, which will give us the time we'll need, God willing."

"Meanwhile, you're killing millions and subjugating billions."

"The end justifies the means."

"That's a repulsive attitude; do they actually teach that crap at the CTF academy? No wonder you're all such bastards."

"The CTF saved humanity during the Freehold Wars. We won't be caught completely unprepared again."

"You didn't save anybody, Gordon, you were still chasing cheerleaders when the Freehold Wars ended, you asshole."

"Wrong! You still don't understand. The wars aren't over; they'll never *be* over. We deal with constant threats from alien species. You have no idea what we're up against out here; *there are no friendly aliens*. Your idyllic life is only possible because of the CTF. You're a Telluric citizen, Abby, act like one. Now, I need your help, and you're going to give it to me."

"Go to hell, Gordon."

He smiled, "Eventually, probably. Alright, I'll stop trying to reason with you, I can see you've been brainwashed by Bradley and his Tovolek and I don't have time to deprogram you. So, I'll proceed with plan B."

"How many plans do you have?"

"I don't need any more, plan B always works." He said ominously. "Ok, let's get down to business. About three months ago we confiscated a delivery of hijacked weapons intended for insurgents on the planet Klojuak. I've been tasked with stopping these weapon shipments, all around Telluric space. There's been an exponential growth in insurgencies over the last 4 or 5 years. The one on Klojuak is particularly brutal; the death toll rises daily."

"Good. Good for the Klojuaks."

"Treasonous words won't do you any favors, Professor. My point is the ship carrying the weapons belonged to your buddy, Bradley. The Tovolek bitch was on board when it was disabled and captured. Afterwards, we raided Bradley's villa on Kyntava and arrested him. We'd recently learned of his true identity, and therefore knew where to find him."

"His true identity?"

"Oh, you didn't know?" He smiled creepily again. "His name isn't Bradley. His real name is Theodore Jesper Meyers III. Would you believe he's the great, great grandson of the famous Honorius Meyers, the big wine merchant? The family owns at least twenty vineyards on Kyntava alone, plus a few distilleries. They operate distilleries and breweries on several planets. Meyers and Sons Corporation is worth 80 or 90 billion coin, and your friend Teddy used to own a three percent stake." Gordon saw the surprise on my face.

"That's correct, he was a billionaire, if you can believe that. At least on paper; his father's stock was worth a couple billion coin when he died. However, I understand the shares Teddy inherited were challenged in the Kyntavan courts by his aunts and uncles on the board of directors. Something about the legitimacy of his birth. That's why he deals arms to rebels."

"I don't believe you." I said, but I did. Teddy might simply be a successful smuggler, but his tastes were those of man born to privilege. I could believe he grew up with money.

"He does have a villa there that passed to him from his mother's family. And a vineyard with a small distillery attached. So he isn't hurting for coin. What a man like *that* is doing running around supplying rebels with weapons is a question I can't even begin to answer." Gordon admitted.

"Maybe he's seen first-hand what the CTF gets up to and is disgusted by it." I suggested.

"Teddy Bradley as a shining example of morals? That's an interesting theory, Professor, I wish you luck with it." Gordon said sarcastically. "Anyway, we had the two of them cold, and I told him he was going to get 20 years if he didn't cooperate and tell me where they'd acquired the weapons. You see, they were CTF weapons, brand new in the crates. We've been seeing more and more of that, the insurgents using our own weapons against us."

"Wow, I guess CTF security is pretty worthless. I wonder who's supposed to be in charge of that?" I asked.

Wisely or not, I couldn't help insulting and provoking him. Even scared as I was, there was just something about him that brought it out of me. Gordon smiled, but not in what you might call a 'good' way.

"Bradley told me to get stuffed, the bastard. But when I informed him what was going to happen to his Tovolek if he didn't help me, his attitude changed. I told him I'd extradite her back to her home planet where she's wanted for murder. But, you knew that, didn't you?" He smiled again, knowing I was putting two and two together.

"I know that. She's innocent, I already told you."

"That hardly matters. She's accused by a high-ranking lord, she's guilty by default. Do you know the method of execution for murderers on Nir-Kvek, Professor?"

"I've no idea." I said, "It doesn't matter."

"It might matter to your lover." He leered, "It's a particularly brutal form of crucifixion. They take the murderer into the forest and nail their hands, shoulders and thighs to a large tree using huge spikes as long as your arm. They suspend them a half meter or so off the ground." he was grinning sadistically at me again, a look almost like lust was on his creepy face.

"Stop, Gordon. I don't want to know."

"But that isn't the worst part. They have these creatures in the wild there, called gronyurs or something like that. They're similar to canines, but only about 15 or 20 kilos. They run in packs and have needle sharp teeth, but the most interesting thing about them is their tongues. Their tongues are so rough textured they can literally lick the skin off a person's body. So, a pack of these creatures eventually shows up where the crucifixion is taking place, and licks the victim's feet and lower legs, eats their feet... well, you get the picture. The murderer dies a slow and agonizingly painful death, which is the point, of course."

"And if I don't help you, you're going to send Kara back there for execution. Is that it?" I asked, sickened to my core.

The gory description was bad enough, but now I couldn't help but imagine the woman I loved being crucified and eaten alive. I looked at the crucifix on the wall again and felt myself getting faint.

"Exactly. Bradley told me where they acquired the weapons, some brothers from New Britain. But I told him that'd only save him, not the woman. So, he offered to tell me where I could find actual Reges Scientia artifacts if we'd let her go. I was intrigued, so I used our latest concoction on him." Gordon produced a syringe from his desk drawer and held it up to show me, "XR112. It's a truth serum with a remarkable side effect: The subject remembers nothing about what happened while under the effects of the drug. This stuff is the safest thing we've ever used too, only a 3 to 5 percent chance of permanent brain damage."

"You dosed Teddy with that stuff?" I wiped my clammy hands on my trousers.

"I did. He told me all about how he traveled here years ago with some old professor and discovered a big, mysterious vault underground. The professor eventually opened it and there were hundreds of ancient books inside." Gordon pressed a button on his desk, "I sent a ship here to check out his story, and we found the vault. I even kept my word, I let the Tovolek go. I even let Bradley go, which turned out to be a mistake.

That's not a mistake I'll make again; Bradley's going to prison as soon as I make arrangements."

"So, why am I even here?" I asked. "Why'd you send for me? I was happy back on Ampora, I didn't need any of this."

"I'm getting to that." Three men entered the room and stood behind me. "I figured since an old professor from Ampora had opened it before, what I needed was another old professor from Ampora. So, I set up the phony archeological expedition here. Of course, when the professors got here they were totally useless. They told me the vault was impossible to open. I brought in ancient language experts, cryptology experts, safe crackers, and code breakers. None of them could open it. In fact, they all said it was impossible."

"You still didn't answer my question, why'd you send for *me*?"

"I eventually went back and examined the roster of the Academy's faculty. I slapped myself in the head when I noticed your name. Bradley had told me all about Henry Thornwell, but never mentioned he had a daughter. It was because I never asked, of course. That's the way the drug works, you have to ask specific questions and the subject answers; they can't extemporize or elaborate. So, that's when I sent for you, Professor. You're my last and best hope."

"My lucky day."

"I thought I'd lost you when you escaped the Archeron, I thought my career was ruined. But now here you are! That idiot Bradley brought you right back to me and now you can open the vault for *me*."

"Look, Gordon, what makes you think I can open that stupid vault? I've never been here before. I just saw the thing for the first time today."

"Well, I can only assume your father told you all about that vault when he was still alive. *And* how to open it."

"I'm telling you, like I told you before, he didn't! The first I ever heard of it was from Teddy. I don't have a clue how to open it."

"Well, let's hope that's not true, for your girlfriend's sake." He said, "I tried an industrial laser, and it didn't even put a scratch in it. I don't want to use more powerful weapons on it because I don't want to risk damaging the contents. That leaves you; I need that thing open, Professor, I've gambled everything on it."

"Just because my father opened the vault doesn't mean I can. He was a celebrated puzzle solver, and an expert in ancient languages." I argued. "I can't open it."

"We shall see, shortly." Gordon said. He motioned to the men behind me. "This is marine sergeant Tolliver. He's an excellent medic. He was with us at the siege of Roumunihava. The natives had this primitive artillery that, well you don't care. It should suffice that I was wounded," he indicated his gruesome scar, "and Tolliver took excellent care of me. I had him transferred to my ship, promoted him and he's been with me for two years now. Right, Tolliver?"

"Yes, sir. Thank you, sir."

"The Admiralty wanted to give me extended leave to have cosmetic surgery. It was Tolliver who advised me to leave the scar as a badge of honor. War wounds are something to be proud of; it was some of the best advise I've ever received."

"Thank you, sir." Said Tolliver.

The two other marines held my arm still while Tolliver prepared the syringe. "Abby, I have some questions for you." Gordon told me, "I'd like to know what was discussed when Bradley and you went to meet Cyrus Baaqir. I want to know where the vessel is that brought you to Kleos Prime. I want to know how many more confederates are with you here. And, most importantly, I want to know how to open that vault. You're going to answer my questions, you'll have no choice, and you won't even remember telling me."

"Stop. Gordon, please don't shoot that stuff in me. Please." I begged. I hated myself for it, but all I could think about was he'd said there was a 3 to 5 percent chance of brain damage. He might've just been saying it to scare me, but Gods forgive me, it worked; I was damn scared. And worried about what I'd tell him under the influence of the drug.

"Tell me how to open it."

"Dammit, Gordon, *I don't fucking know*!"

"Proceed, Mr. Tolliver."

Tolliver methodically found a vein in my arm and proceeded to inject the drug into my bloodstream. There was a distinct feeling of cold as the drug circulated, and I immediately started to feel dizzy.

"The drug has been refrigerated, so you may feel some discomfort, but it'll pass quickly. The dizziness will pass quickly as well." Tolliver told me.

"Your lies during our meeting on the Archeron were infuriating. So, you brought this on yourself, Professor." Gordon said.

"Sorry. No wait... not sorry." I was in a sweat, literally. My mind was beginning to fog up, I was having a hard time concentrating.

"The fact Bradley took you to the meeting with Baaqir was baffling. The Ministry has long suspected Baaqir of, shall we say 'unpatriotic' leanings. We've never been able to make a move against him because the CTF is dependent on Dressida Research Group weapons and technologies. Cyrus Baaqir *is* DRG, more or less, which makes him practically untouchable. However, Baaqir having a meeting with Bradley, who appears to be one of the primary arms suppliers to insurgents, is very curious. Or alarming if you have a suspicious mind; which I have."

"I don't know anything about insurgencies or weapons, or any of that. Why don't you ask Teddy?"

"I did, aboard the Archeron. He wouldn't tell me anything, but I figured I had plenty of time to question him on the way here, just like you. Then, you people helped him escape. I have to admit, that surprised me. That was bold and daring; my compliments. Now, what was the meeting with Baaqir about?"

"I can't remem... ber" I slurred. "I don't even like Bak... ur."

And that's the last thing I remember from the interrogation by Gordon aboard the George Upton.

Part Eighteen Captives of the Green Shirts

Interstellar Date: 388-07-09
On Kleos Prime

I AWOKE, MY THOUGHTS shrouded in a dense haze. Wherever I was, it was freezing, the cold seeping into my bones. Groggily, I attempted to piece together my surroundings. I was in a pitch-black room, facing a wall barely discernable even though it was mere centimeters from my face. I lay curled up on a canvas cot without a blanket or even my jacket for warmth.

Each movement sent a wave of discomfort through my neck, my head, and my aching back. An unholy thirst clawed at my throat. With a slow, cautious effort, I attempted to sit up, but dizziness overcame me, forcing me back onto the cot.

As the fog in my mind receded and my eyes slowly adjusted to the dark, I began to survey the room. It was relatively large and aside from the cot I could just make out a lonely metal desk with a single chair. I stood shakily and went to the only door; it was sealed tightly. I was a prisoner.

The inky darkness was broken only by a thin sliver of light creeping in from beneath the door, a meager relief from the darkness of the room and my mood.

With no hope of getting out, I turned my attention to the rest of the room, now becoming visible. There, in the back corner, was a sight that sent alternating waves of both horror and hope through me. It was Kara, trapped within a cage resembling an animal kennel. She was bound, hand-and-foot, within the terrible little prison. It stood one and a half meters in height, spanning two meters in width and a little over two meters in depth, just enough for a person to lie prone within, as Kara had been forced to do.

Instinctively, I rushed to the cage, only to find its door firmly locked. An even greater chill coursed through my veins as I observed the state in which Kara had been left. Even in the dim light I could see she'd been beaten viciously. Bruises, abrasions and bloodstains covered her body, evidence of merciless blows from clubs and boots. Yet, more horrifying still, was the sight of her tightly gagged mouth. Her damaged and bloodied nose was making each breath a struggle and I feared she'd suffocate if nothing was done. In that moment my own brutal thirst was forgotten, and fearing for her life, I rushed back to the room's door, pounding on it with panic and despair.

As soon as the guard opened the door I started, "You have to help her! She's going to suffocate, she can't breathe. She's gagged and they've smashed her nose. Hurry!"

The guard nonchalantly said, "Take it easy, let me see. Ah, she's fine."

"She's not fine, dammit, she can't breathe!"

"Well, I'm not allowed to remove her gag. Orders."

"Sergeant, go find someone who *is* allowed to remove her gag."

He rolled his eyes at me, "Corporal. I'm a corporal. Alright, don't get your knickers in a bunch, lady. I'll be back."

He locked the door again when he left, and was gone for what seemed an eternity. Meanwhile Kara stirred, she was waking up. I went to kneel beside the horrible cage and reached my hand in. Sticking my arm through the bars, I could just barely reach one of her fingers. I grabbed it and squeezed.

"Kara, it's me. I'm here. I sent for someone to get rid of that gag. I'm sorry, I wish there was more I could do."

The door opened and a handsome young man entered. He had an insignia on his collar, so even though I knew nothing about military ranks, I guessed he was an officer of some kind. There was a different guard with him, clearly acting differential towards the younger man. The officer approached the cage and began a crude examination of Kara.

"Sergeant, can we have some light in here please? Thank you." The sergeant turned on the overhead light; now able to see her injuries better, the officer asked, "Where are the keys to this cage, sergeant?"

The sergeant handed the keys to the officer, who opened the cage door and crawled inside with Kara; it was a tight fit. He quickly undid the buckles of the gag and freed it from Kara. She gasped for breath, coughing out a shocking amount of blood and groaning miserably. She was awake, but groggy, and her bindings looked horribly uncomfortable. She was clearly in significant pain, but her eyes shone with unrelenting fury. The green shirts better hope Kara didn't get free of that cage.

"We're not supposed to remove the gag, sir." The sergeant said, "I could get in trouble."

"Not as much trouble as if the prisoner died, sergeant. Go get me a towel, a first aid kit, two large bottles of water and some pain killers from sick bay." He ordered. The sergeant stood still, looking unsure. "Now!" the officer said, and the sergeant disappeared out the door.

"I'm the duty officer, Ensign Davis. This is simply unacceptable, the way you've been treated." He told Kara. "I don't know who did this to you, but I'm going to find out. I'm sorry I can't remove your bindings completely, for now the gag will have to suffice."

"Thank you, ensign, that's kind of you." I said. "I was honestly afraid she'd suffocate."

The sergeant returned with what Ensign Davis had asked for. Davis gently tried to clean Kara's wounds, first with water and the towel, then with antiseptic ointment from the first aid kit. He handed a bottle of water to me, and I drank greedily. He put the other bottle to Kara's lips and helped her drink her fill too. She was just as thirsty as I was. He placed two pills to her lips, but she turned her head away.

"These are for your pain, they'll help." He said.

"I don't want them. I want the pain; it clarifies and focuses my anger. Every green shirt on this planet will pay for this. Except perhaps for you, Ensign. I haven't decided about you." She said, and spit out some more blood. "Yet."

Davis shrugged, crawled backward from the cage, and turned toward me. "What about you, Professor? The commander said to give you some food and water, but he didn't say what food. What would you like?" he asked me. Surprisingly, Davis seemed to actually be a decent fellow.

"Thanks, Ensign. We'd love some hot soup and maybe a roll with plenty of butter? Is that doable?"

"I believe so. Now, I have to lock you in here," he opened the door, "but I'll return with your food, some water, and maybe some blankets. It's cold in this room. They probably do that on purpose. I'll be back shortly."

After he left the room Kara said, "Try to see if he has keys on him, Abby. I need to get out of these manacles."

"I'll try. What happened to you? Why'd they beat you?"

"I didn't ask."

Davis returned with his hands full of things. The corporal from before followed him in, carrying a tray of food for us.

"I brought some blankets, the soup you asked for, some more water bottles and I'll leave these pain pills here just in case she wants them later." He told me, "I'm going to leave the door to the cell open so you can feed your friend, and maybe clean up her wounds a little. Keep your voices down, I'm certain I wasn't supposed to take out her gag. Hopefully, the commander doesn't find out I removed it. He's not forgiving if he finds fault, especially with junior officers. Good luck."

"Hey Ensign, what do you say you let my friends and I go? Surely you can see your Commander is crazy, right?" I asked him, only half joking, "Captain Bradley is apparently a billionaire, he could make it worth your while."

"Your humor is wasted on me, Professor." Davis said. "They beat it out of us the first week at the CTF Academy. You get 30 lashes every time you laugh." he smiled at me, trying to be funny. I think.

Ensign Davis left us alone. "Kara, are you alright?" I crawled into the cage with her and gave her a kiss and hugged her awkwardly. The manacles were secured tightly on her wrists and ankles. I'd have no luck trying to free her without the keys.

"I'm fine, little human." she told me, unconvincingly. "Before I passed out, they were in here going through your things while you slept. They were obviously looking for something. I can't believe Teddy actually helped them. I should be furious, but I feel sad more than anything. I never would've believed it."

"Gordon told me when they caught you at Klojuak a few months ago, they arrested Teddy too."

"What? Teddy never told me that. *Secrets again.*"

"Don't be too hard on Teddy, Gordon threatened to send you back to Nir-Kvek to be executed. Teddy told him about Kleos Prime so they'd let you go. He did it to save your life." I explained. I didn't mention Gordon threatened me with sending Kara back for execution too. I wasn't going to let that happen.

Kara said. "I got caught going to Klojuak because our reactor failed, but that was 10 or 11 weeks ago. Teddy told me he bribed the jailors to set me free. He bribes people all the time, so I never doubted it."

It took a few minutes for me to tell Kara about my most recent visit with Gordon. I explained how Teddy was given a truth serum and didn't remember what he'd told Gordon.

Kara said, "Teddy didn't remember telling them about the vault, but he told them about this planet before he was drugged. He knew why there was an expedition here all along, but he didn't tell me; or you. I don't know if I can forgive him this time, little human."

"That's all true, but he was just trying to protect you. He loves you after all."

"Of course he loves me, but not the way you think. I told you, we're close comrades that depend on each other, but we're not *in love.*"

"Alright, if you say so." I didn't believe that, but I didn't want to argue. "Gordon says he's sending Teddy to prison as soon as he can arrange it. He told the marines to throw Teddy in the brig. Where do you think the brig is on this ship?"

"I've never been on a CTF frigate before, how would I know? But, we have to get out of here and help Teddy. I can't allow them to send him to prison, he'd never survive it. Teddy's clever and able to take care of himself physically, but he's not prepared psychologically for Tellurian prison. They like to keep prisoners in total isolation, I don't think Teddy could deal with it."

"Even if we get out of this room, and somehow free Teddy, what then?" I asked.

"Hopefully, Sebastien hasn't abandoned us, and he can help us escape. Ideally, we kill Gordon first, though that might not do us much good in the long run. They'll just send someone else in his place."

"I don't think so. I got the impression this whole Kleos business is all Gordon's idea. He told me he's planning to advance his career by claiming the contents of the vault. He wants to be the youngest Admiral in history or some such crap. I don't think he's told any of his superiors about any of this, he wants it to be a big surprise."

"That's good news. So, if we kill all the green shirts on Kleos Prime, no one else knows about it?" Kara would think that way.

"I suppose that's true. And I don't think there's any way Sebastien abandoned us. He wouldn't do that."

"I hope you're right, but you haven't known him very long." she warned.

"I've known him long enough." I didn't say I'd only known her for a few hours longer than I'd known him.

I used the first aid kit to clean and disinfect her wounds as best I could, then we ate our soup and bread slowly. I'd give her a spoonful, then myself one, and so forth.

"There's something else, Kara. My memory is foggy, but it's starting to clear a little. I'm pretty sure Gordon dosed me with the same truth serum. It blocks your memory, so there's no way of knowing what *I* told that asshole." I helped her to turn onto her side so she could sleep and placed a blanket over her.

"Well, I guess it's not Teddy's fault if they drugged him. And you either, sweetling. You can't help what you say under the influence of their drugs. It's just one more reason to kill Gordon, if we needed any more." Kara told me as she closed her eyes.

I contemplated trying to call Sebastien. Gordon had foolishly let me keep my comms device. If 'Sabes' was anywhere near, like within the solar system, I'd be able speak with him. I was getting ready to initiate the call when I realized: Gordon's no fool. I literally slapped my forehead;

Gordon *wanted* me to try to call our ship. He was trying to find it, and our communication might give away the Avernus' position.

I focused my concentration on finding the combination for the vault door. Barring escape, my only option for saving Kara was to open the damn thing for Gordon. I could never let him send Kara back to suffer that horrible fate, I'd sooner die. As I studied the symbols on the vault via the photos I'd taken, I reached for my amulet to cross reference, and was shocked when it wasn't there! Gods! I'd *stupidly* left it in its notch on the vault door. Its leather string necklace was in my pants pocket.

I realized I needed to return to the vault before I could seriously work on a solution to the combination. I needed my amulet, just like my father had. I didn't have the damn thing memorized; I'd never had a photographic memory. I studied the vault photos, but without my amulet and a frame of reference, it was useless. I crawled into the cell, laid down beside Kara and went into a fitful sleep.

Three men threw open the door to our room and barged in, startling me awake. There was a sergeant and two corporals, I guessed.

"Aww, looky here. All cozied up together like genu-*ine* lovebirds." a corporal leered. "Did you make her give you a good licking, since she's all tied up?" he asked me. "What's that primitive, trash-breed cooch taste like, anyway?"

"What would you know about it? It's obvious you've never even been laid; who'd stoop that low?" I said.

The other two laughed, which enraged the corporal who'd taunted me. He grabbed me by my hair and dragged me from the cage, threw me against the wall and shoved his forearm painfully against my throat so I could barely breathe.

"Easy Belcek, if you hurt her the Commander will have your ass." the sergeant told him, "Let her loose, dipshit." Belcek released me.

The sergeant told me, "Belcek is just pissed he didn't win the raffle last night. He bought a bunch of tickets."

"What raffle?" I asked in a raspy whisper.

"For you. Winner gets first crack at you once the Commander's done. He'll give you to the crew after he gets tired of you. You're lucky Belcek lost, he enjoys hurting women."

"And you don't, sarge?" Belcek laughed. The others joined in, as if he'd told a hilarious joke. Creeps. They were probably just trying to scare me. I hoped.

The sergeant asked, "Alright, who wants to go to the head?"

"I do." I said. Kara eagerly announced, "Yes, please." The sergeant told Belcek to take me down the hall and watch me go.

He said to Kara, "Go ahead and go where you are, trash-breed. We don't have time to undo all your bindings." The three of them had a good laugh at that. I started to argue, but thankfully Ensign Davis walked in.

"What's this, sergeant? Are you mentally defective? If that prisoner soils herself in here it'll create a mess that'll have to be cleaned up. By *you*. We can't have the place filthy and stinking. Cleaning requires water, you idiot, and in case you haven't noticed there isn't a lot of water to spare here." Davis scolded him.

The sergeant's face turned red with anger. He was at least ten years older than Davis, and obviously didn't care for being chewed out by him, not to mention being called mentally defective and an idiot.

"Corporal, escort Professor Thornwell to the head, and wait *outside* till she's through. Then escort her back here. Treat her with respect, do you understand?" Davis ordered.

"Yes, sir."

When I returned to the room, Ensign Davis and the second corporal were just finishing releasing Kara from her bindings. I was incredibly grateful as I was certain Kara had to be in considerable pain from the way she'd been bound.

Davis spoke to Kara, "Alright, Kara, is it?" she nodded, "Are you going to behave? These men are armed with Z-guns and any false move will cause them to shoot you. It's quite unpleasant, I understand. We'll take you to the head and straight back here, and if you don't cause any trouble, I'll not put the manacles back on. I'll have to lock you back in this cell again, but it should be much more comfortable. Do I have your word you'll behave?"

"Absolutely." Kara agreed.

They returned a few minutes later, and Davis locked Kara back inside the little cell, but without the manacles. Another green shirt came in carrying two bowls of some kind of gruel and more water bottles. The stuff was tasteless but filling. After we ate, the other men carried away our empty bowls and left Davis alone in the room with us.

"Ensign, can I speak with the commander? I have a request to make." I asked.

"I'm not sure that's a good idea. I'm not exactly *disobeying* orders by untying your friend, but it was pretty heavily implied she was to remain secured because she's so dangerous. I think she's been very cooperative." He said and smiled at her.

"I wouldn't want to get you in trouble, Ensign, but I need to go back down to the vault. As soon as possible. Could you at least pass along my request?"

"Of course."

After he left, Kara said "I think that boy's sweet on you. He never takes his eyes off you, and every time you speak to him, I think he almost swoons."

"Jealous?" I asked, "You have nothing to worry about. He's pretty cute, but he's way too young for me. He looks like he belongs in my freshman orientation seminar."

"Tell him that."

Davis returned before too long. "I'm organizing an excursion to the vault. Commander Gordon isn't available right now, it seems an unidentified spacecraft was detected entering orbit, but it disappeared. They're frantically trying to reacquire it. But we can take a trip down to the vault, why not? I've only seen it once; I'd like to see it again. I'll be back in a few minutes."

After he left Kara continued her teasing, using an imitation Ensign Davis voice, "I've only seen it once, but I'd *love* to see it again, *with you.* That boy has it bad."

"Oh, quit it. He's being nice to us, don't jinx it. He's the reason you're not tied up in a ball right now."

"Ask him if you can have me go with you to the vault. Tell him I'm your ancient language expert and you need me to read it for you." Kara proposed.

"I think that might be a bit too much. He's already scared Gordon's going to sack him for untying you."

"Bust him. They don't sack people in the military, they bust them down a grade. I'm telling you, Abby, he's sweet on you, it won't hurt to ask. The worst he can do is say no."

When Davis returned he had four heavily armed marines in tow. He threw me a thick coat as he walked in carrying my backpack.

"Alright, Professor." he began, "We're going to the vault now. I've packed food and water, space heaters, lights and a bunch of other gear I'm not even sure we'll need. I have two vehicles waiting outside, let's go."

"But Ensign, what about her?" I asked, pointing to Kara. "We can't leave her here."

"Of course we can. We don't need her. And, she's supposed to be dangerous. No, she stays here."

"Don't you understand? If we leave her here with those guards from this morning, not to mention the ones who beat her half to death yesterday, she'll be in grave danger. Who knows what they'll do to her while we're gone? We'll be gone for several hours; she won't be safe." I pleaded.

I could see his mind was churning on what I'd said. Ensign Davis was just a kid, and a decent kid at that. He hadn't been indoctrinated yet into the brutal atmosphere which pervaded the green shirts. He was raw, and therefore not a heartless creep yet. Yet.

"I don't know. I'd be in big trouble if anything happened." he said.

"Just tell your commander I insisted. Tell him I refused to work on the vault combination unless I had her with me and knew she was safe." I argued. "If you cuff her and have all these guards carry Z-guns, surely that'll be secure enough, right? Please, Ensign. I can't leave her here." I gave him the most pathetic, damsel in distress expression I could muster.

Davis walked over to the little cell and knelt down to speak with Kara. "Will you promise not to cause trouble? I don't like the thought of leaving you here either. Sargent Dorjean was pretty mad this morning, and I don't trust him; he might come and hurt you. The Commander told some of the men you killed security officers on the Archeron; that's why you were beaten."

"I promise. Please don't leave me here alone." Kara begged. If I didn't know better I'd have thought she was a fragile, helpless little girl, not a terrifying Demon.

"If I bring you along, you'll have to be securely manacled. The guards will use their Z-guns the second you try anything. You know what those things do, right?" Kara nodded. Davis continued, "Alright, I'm trusting you. I'm only doing this to keep *you* safe. I hope you understand that."

He sent one of the men to fetch the manacles and some warm clothes for Kara. I was practically overwhelmed with gratitude. The worries I'd confessed to Davis about what might happen to Kara while we were gone were real. Most of the green shirts were obviously cruel, especially when it came to an alien humanoid like Kara, who they considered subhuman and not deserving of respect. And apparently, they now knew about her killing their comrades.

Of course, Kara didn't respect them either, and from her point of view they were enemy combatants and deserving of death. I have to admit, I was more than a little concerned with what she might try on our trip down to the vault. I had to make it clear to her how important it was I reach the vault so I could retrieve my amulet.

As the guards pulled her from the cage I slyly opened my hand and showed her my leather necklace, sans the amulet. We made eye contact, I nodded and quickly put the necklace back in my pocket. I was sure she understood my meaning, she'd witnessed me placing the amulet into its notch the day before.

The guards helped Kara into the warm clothes and fastened the manacles on her wrists and ankles. She looked comfortable and warm; it was the most clothes I'd ever seen her wear. I wore the clothes I'd come with, except Davis insisted I take one of the marines' heavy coats instead of my own lighter jacket.

I grabbed my backpack, which was significantly lighter after they'd obviously removed Kara's mortar rounds. We exited the frigate, boarded the vehicles and maneuvered our way slowly up the mountain. We crested a hill, and I could see the cavern entrance up ahead. There were a few vehicles there already, so our little group wouldn't be alone. Not that I could've overpowered four marine guards plus Ensign Davis all by myself. Besides, if Kara and I managed to escape, where would we go? Sebastien had obviously moved the Avernus and we didn't know where it was.

As we neared the cavern entrance, I noticed a large, armored vehicle parked in front of it. It was larger than the ones we rode in, and bristled with weaponry. On top was mounted a big, two barreled gun or cannon. And the gun was manned by two marines. We walked up the hill and were stopped by two more marines armed with rifles. They waved us on after seeing Davis. As we entered the cavern I saw Gordon approaching, and he didn't look pleased.

"Ensign, what in the hell are *they* doing here?" he said as he pointed at Kara and me.

"Sorry, sir. The professor wants to see the vault again. But she refused to leave her friend behind. The Tovolek prisoner was badly abused yesterday, sir. I didn't trust she'd be safe if we left her." Davis explained.

"Didn't trust she'd be *safe*?" Gordon asked. "Ensign, you realize that prisoner *killed* 5 of our men on the Archeron? She was also captured smuggling weapons to insurgents, who knows how many KIAs she's responsible for? Why do we give a *fuck* if she's safe?"

"I care." I spoke up. "The only reason I agreed to help you is to keep Kara safe. If she isn't safe you can shove that vault up your ass, Gordon!... Slathered in pepper sauce."

He glared at me for a few moments, no doubt calculating whether I was serious or not. I could tell he wanted to call my bluff, I had several other people to protect besides Kara, including myself.

"Very well, I'll keep her safe. For now. Ensign, proceed down to the vault. And you, Professor, you *will* open it for me."

"What if I can't open it?" I asked.

"Can't, won't, don't, it doesn't matter. If you don't open the thing, the Tovolek goes back to Nir-Kvek, Bradley gets charged with treason and executed, and you Professor... *you* vanish. The Academy will get a resignation letter, and no one will ever hear from you again."

"You can't do that." I challenged.

"Why not? It's done all the time to 'undesirables.' I could plant you in some filthy prison on a client world, or send you to a labor camp. Some outdoor exercise might do you some good." He laughed and some of the marines joined in.

"You're the one that's going to disappear, Commander." Kara stated matter-of-factly.

Gordon signaled to one of Kara's marine guards who used the butt of his rifle to violently strike Kara's temple, like they'd done the day before to Teddy. Her head snapped to the side, but she quickly recovered and turned to stare icily at the marine. He was shocked, I believe, that she still stood. He'd clearly expected her to crumble to the ground. He backed slowly away and lowered his rifle, either cowed or impressed; or both.

Gordon addressed me once again, "I haven't decided what to do with you yet, but Abigail Thornwell will cease to exist. If you're lucky, maybe I'll decide to keep you as my personal pet on the Upton. You'd look cute in manacles and an iron collar around your neck. Some whip marks on the backs of your legs and that cute little ass of yours would look nice too." The marines laughed some more.

"You're disgusting. You're a disgusting human being, Gordon. You're sick."

"Yes, yes, but nobody's perfect. We have time, Professor, but not unlimited time. Get to work down there. But I'm keeping your girlfriend up here, with me. I'll keep her safe, and also make sure she stays out of mischief."

As he finished speaking, he reached behind him and grabbed a Zymtal rifle from a marine. He turned, aimed, and fired it at Kara. There was a blinding flash of light, the sound of crackling electricity and a grunt from Kara. Because she'd been standing next to me, static electricity tingled across my left arm and my neck. Kara collapsed in a ball, the muscle spasms racking her and making her fight against her bindings.

"Gordon, you fucking bastard!" I shouted. "I said I wanted her kept safe, you asshole!"

"She is. That bolt of energy, while painful as hell, will wear off eventually. She'll be blind for a few hours and therefore won't cause any trouble. It's a win-win. She'll be fine here until you get back from the vault."

"What happened to the kinder, gentler Ministry of Security?"

He laughed, "You're looking at it. In the old days they'd have diced your girlfriend up and fed her to the loppa hounds."

"Why would I help you? You clearly don't take your promises seriously. How can I trust you'll let us go after I open the damn thing?"

"I don't think you can, but that hardly matters; you simply don't have a choice. You open that vault, or your friends will suffer far worse than a little shock and some temporary blindness. Not to mention what I'll do to you, *pet*." He laughed as he walked away toward the entrance.

I'd never been so angry in my entire life, or felt so helpless. Oh, I hated that man so much, I didn't think I could hate like that. I'd never experienced anything like it before. I was consumed by it, and I couldn't concentrate. I stumbled toward the stairs that led down, thinking of ways to kill him.

Ensign Davis accompanied me with two of the marines that'd come with us from the George Upton. We didn't speak for a long time; I think he could sense my mood. When we arrived at the first vertical drop there was a rope already in place. Davis went first and waited below, ready to catch me if I fell. I attached the rope to my harness, but used the ladder that was carved into the rock, which wasn't quite vertical and was surprisingly easy to descend. When I approached the bottom, Davis put his hands on my waist and helped me to the ground. I fell against him as I regained my balance, and he held me to him momentarily. I certainly got the impression Kara's theory wasn't far off. I thought the boy might actually have a crush on me after all.

"Thank you, Ensign, but you don't have to bother." I said. "I'm not as weak as I look."

"That's the last word I'd use to describe you, ma'am. I've never heard anyone speak to Commander Gordon like that before. I wish I had that kind of nerve."

"Well, you work for him. It's probably a bad idea for you to call him an asshole." I grinned; my mood was finally improving a little. My blinding anger had morphed into a simmering, bubbling cauldron of hate.

"I've only been assigned to the George Upton for a few weeks." he lowered his voice so the guards, several meters behind the two of us, couldn't hear. "I'm pretty sure everyone hates Gordon, but they fear him more. Even the marines he encouraged to beat your friend; I think they hate him too. All he cares about is getting his promotion. He talks about it constantly."

"What's your name Ensign?"

"Davis."

I laughed, but not too loud. "No, that's your father's name. What's your given name? Mine's Abby."

"Oh, sorry." He said, embarrassed. "Mine's Oliver. It was my grandfather's name; my mother's father. But my friends mostly call me Ollie."

"Then I'll call you Ollie and you call me Abby, not ma'am, alright?"

"Sure thing, Abby." He agreed, "I know you're a professor, but you're nothing like the instructors I had at the Academy."

"They were probably all CTF officers, right?"

"Not all of them. We had a few civilian teachers too. But they were all stuffy and strict; they couldn't wait to dole out demerits. Too many demerits could make your life miserable at the Academy." Ollie confessed.

"Sometimes I wish I could give *my* students demerits." I laughed, "Listen, Ollie, Gordon is a bully. Bullies are all the same, if you stand up to them, they might get angry, and they might hold a grudge, but that's the only way to ever gain their respect, such as it is. You can't let him walk all over you. If you do, he'll never stop bullying you."

"I try not to, but it's hard. My dad was sort of a bully too. He was in the military; a Marine Master Sergeant with lots of combat experience. He thought beatings and cruelty would make men out of my brothers and me. I guess it worked, I graduated 5th in my Academy class, out of 880."

"Ollie, your father being cruel to you had nothing to do with you being a good man. You are who you are in spite of that. You earned that 5th spot on your own; your father wasn't there to help you."

Ollie smiled at me, and we continued down in silence for a while. Ollie continued to assist me at the challenging spots of our descent. He was always a gentleman. Eventually he continued the conversation.

"Abby, this was supposed to be a dream post, getting assigned to the security forces. But, so far, it's more like a nightmare." He confessed, "It's not just Gordon either. I find I don't have much in common with the veterans around here. And they don't give me much respect either. I think I might've made a huge mistake asking for this assignment."

"You seemed to stand up for yourself pretty well back there with that sergeant; Dejean, was it?"

"Dorjean. Thanks, Abby. He's one of the worst, and I get the idea he hates me. He's been in the service close to twenty years, so sometimes I think to myself, 'if Dorjean hates you, maybe you don't belong here.' Is that wrong?"

"Ollie, personally, I think he's the one who doesn't belong. If the CTF had more men like you and less like Dorjean, we'd all be better off. And we'd all be safer." I told him. Dorjean and his ilk were the ones making humans the most hated species in the galaxy, in my opinion.

"Thank you, that's a nice thing to say." Ollie said, and leaned in to give me a hug. I hugged him back, not knowing if it was inappropriate or not. But, I began to wonder if there was a way for Ollie to help Kara and me out of this predicament. Perhaps he'd even help us escape.

Eventually we came to the campsite cavern, just above where the vault was located. We stopped to rest and drink some water. I dug in my backpack and found a packet of crackers. I shared one with Ollie as he sat beside me.

"Abby, can I ask you something?"

"As long as it's not how old I am." I tried to joke. "I'm sorry, go on."

"So, it was you, the Tovolek woman and the man that's in the brig. Just the three of you came all the way here. What'd you think you were going to do here?"

"It wasn't just the three of us, but yes. We came all the way here just for this vault. I was going to open it, and we'd grab whatever's in there and take off. As simple as that."

"Do you know what's in there? I mean, what's so valuable you'd risk your lives for it?"

"I was told what's in there, but I don't know for sure. It doesn't matter though; I don't think I'll be able to open that lock. Come on, I'll show you."

The two of us went down the last set of stairs and into the vault chamber. It was just as awe inspiring as it was the first time, and just as daunting knowing what everyone expected of me.

"You see, Ollie? These dials move independently. There's 17 of them, all of them with dozens of these alien symbols embossed on them. We all assume these symbols represent an ancient alien language, but no one knows for sure. With all of these dials and so many symbols there's literally trillions of possible combinations. Plus, I don't know what any of these symbols mean, so there's no way I can figure this out. It's impossible." As I talked about it, it began to seem ridiculous even to me.

"But, if it's so impossible, why does the Commander think you can figure it out? He's convinced you can open it." Ollie said.

"He heard my father opened it 23 years ago. So, he assumes my father told me a secret about how it opens. But, the reality is my father never mentioned this vault or even this place to me. The first I heard of it was about two weeks ago, believe it or not. It's crazy, I know."

"I see." Ollie said. "If you were able to open it, how'd you plan to get away?"

"We have a ship; the one that brought us here. We didn't know Gordon knew where the vault was. We thought we could sneak in here and get away while you and Gordon were on the other side of the planet."

"Well, Abby, where's your ship? Is it close? It must be if you thought you could sneak away without us finding out." Ollie asked.

"I don't know. Our partner must've taken off without us. We... " I decided I was probably saying too much, even though Ollie seemed like a good kid. "Listen, Ollie. Can you go up and get my backpack for me? I need something out of there."

"Sure thing, Abby. I'll be right back."

As soon as I heard him on the steps I hurried over to the vault. There was my amulet, right where I'd left it. I grabbed the leather string out of my pocket and reached down to retrieve the amulet, but it wouldn't budge. I frantically tried to pry it loose, but it was like it was glued in there. I remembered the camera on my comms device and pulled it out; I captured several photos of the amulet with it. I dreaded leaving my amulet here again, and my mind raced.

I heard Ollie coming back down the stairs and I knew I only had mere seconds. Then I had an inspiration. I reached down again, and this time I used my fingernail against the little fob that fit into the aperture of my amulet. I heard and felt a 'click' and the amulet sprung free and fell to the ground. I snapped it up quickly as Ollie returned with my backpack. I put the amulet in my pocket as quickly and inconspicuously as I could and hoped Ollie hadn't seen it.

We spent quite a while there, with Ollie helping me turn the dials as I took more photos. Eventually, I went and sat opposite the thing and started to think and take notes. Ollie got bored and sat against the wall while I worked, never taking his eyes off me.

I wasn't as clueless as I let on. Teddy had told me a huge clue about my amulet. He told me my father had determined the symbols on my amulet to have something to do with a Fibonacci sequence. And also, the symbols on the vault were either numbers, or at least a combination of numbers and letters.

My father also believed the aliens used a mathematical system of base twelve, commonly known as duodecimal or less commonly as dozenal. The system was relatively rare in the quadrant, but certainly not unheard of. My problem was I'm not a mathematician, I can barely do arithmetic in base 10, and I was in way over my head if the vault lock was based on a math problem in base 12. Teddy had suggested exactly that.

I studied the vault and studied the pictures of my amulet. I began trying to find symbols that were common to both. Teddy had told me, if I remembered correctly, that the vault door had two hundred symbols on it. That wasn't even close. As I looked at it now there were *far more* than two hundred symbols, probably closer to five hundred. This might actually *be* impossible.

The whole situation brought back memories of my childhood, doing homework with my father in attendance. I've always had a lamentable lack of patience, and I'd often get frustrated when busy with a complicated task, like my homework. I'd complain, and throw my hands up saying, 'I quit.' My father's standard advise was: 'When you feel overwhelmed, just start back at the beginning to find your place. Abigail, always start at the beginning, start at zero and work your way forward.'

"Start at zero." I whispered to myself. I took a fresh look at the vault door and studied it for several more minutes. At the center, on the first dial, one of the symbols was repeated. I looked at my amulet once more and noticed the identical symbol repeated there, at the beginning of the sequence. But, there was no way to line up the two symbols on that first dial in a straight line as you would with a normal combination lock. The dial itself was a circle.

However, I suddenly realized I was thinking of this whole thing, the vault, the dials, and the combination in a very human-centric way. The Hoji Mubrani weren't human, and this wasn't a 'normal combination lock' at all. Who says the symbols need to line up?

I sat and gazed at that damn door till I thought I'd burst a blood vessel in my brain. A Fibonacci sequence isn't actually a complicated equation, it's simply a set of numbers that follow a pattern. All one needed to use was basic addition to extrapolate the sequence to infinity. I was no mathematical genius but I could do basic addition. What was I missing?

Maybe it wasn't a math problem at all. I thought more about Fibonacci and the so-called golden ratio. The ratio was often depicted as a spiral, and there were many examples of Fibonacci spirals in nature. I'd had a secondary school art instructor who'd spent a great deal of time on the concept, it had nearly bored me to death.

"Start at zero." I whispered again to myself, gazing at the dials... Well, I'll be *damned*.

A few minutes later I spoke up. "Can we go now? I'd like to start back so I can check on my friend, to make sure she's alright."

"Whatever you say, Abby. We can start back any time you want. Any luck with that door?" Ollie asked.

"Not really. I still don't think it's possible, but I'll keep trying."

We ascended, slowly. The going was much harder without Kara to basically pull me up all the difficult spots. Climbing the rock ladders and hiking up the steep slopes was unbelievably exhausting. Teddy was right, the gravity on Kleos Prime was a killer. We'd been gone for hours, and imagining Kara at the mercy of those sadistic marines again was a nightmare. Gordon, I believed, was a borderline psychotic. Certainly, he was a sociopath with delusions of grandeur. There was no telling what he might do.

Ollie and I continued to chat as we climbed, and he helped me when I struggled in places. I had to stop a few times to rest, drink some water and have a snack. But eventually we made it all the way back to the top. I practically stumbled into the surface cavern, exhausted to my bones. I think the guards and Ollie were nearly as tired as I was. I couldn't see Kara immediately, and Gordon stomped over to where we were before I could search for her.

"Well, Ensign. Did you have any luck?" he asked Ollie, ignoring me. Didn't he want to know if *I'd* had any luck?

"A little." Ollie turned toward me, "Professor, please hand me the piece you removed from the vault."

"I don't know what you're talking about." I said, but not convincingly. I was shocked at the question.

"Please, Professor; I saw you put the thing in your front pocket. Remove it, or I'll have to search you." Ollie said.

I reluctantly reached into my pocket and removed my amulet. I handed it to Ollie, who quickly handed it to Gordon.

"Ah, ha. Here it is; good work ensign." Gordon said. "What else did you find out?"

"Not much, unfortunately. I'm convinced she doesn't know where their ship is hiding. But there is a ship, and she says their *partner* has it. Their plan was to sneak in here, remove the contents of the vault, and sneak away again, just like you thought. But, she still claims she can't open it."

Ensign Davis, the little shit! Of course, being 5th in his class at the CTF Academy pretty much guaranteed he was an asshole. The farcical schoolboy act had been too good to be true, but I'd still fallen for it hook, line and sinker. Gordon had planted him with Kara and me, told him to gain our trust, and we'd given it to him. At least I had.

"Ollie, you shit!" I exclaimed, "I liked you. You seemed like a decent person; I should've known better, with you in that green uniform. You go to hell too, you little bastard!"

He laughed, "Don't feel too bad, *Abby*. Everybody loves me. Girls throw themselves at me in every port. If it makes you feel any better, I kind of like you, too. Oh, and nobody actually calls me *Ollie* except my mother." The little shit walked away laughing.

"Gods, where do you find these creeps, Gordon? That kid sure had me fooled."

"They grow on trees, on every Telluric planet. Davis is sharper than most though, I like him. If this thing works out, I might make him a lieutenant. Now, tell me what this is, Professor?" Gordon held up my amulet.

"You tell me. I found it at the bottom of the vault door, started messing with it and it fell off. I thought it might be important so I picked it up. I was going to take it back to your ship and see if I could make any sense of it."

"You just found it? When you were down there with Davis? Is that what you're saying?" he asked, nonchalantly.

I nodded, and without warning, Gordon viciously backhanded me, full force, across my face with his right hand. Unprepared for something like that, I immediately lost my balance and went sprawling on the smooth floor of the cavern. His knuckles had caught me high up on my cheekbone and my eyes were watering, my sight was blurry, and my teeth hurt. My ears were ringing horribly as I tried to get back up and failed, falling back down in a heap. Traumatized, I gave up and stayed down. I'd never, ever, been physically assaulted that way, and tears came unbidden to my eyes.

"I've taken the last lie of yours I'm willing to take, Abigail Thornwell." he growled at me.

He reached to his belt and removed what appeared to be a baton of some kind, about 20cm long.

"Help her up you idiots." he said to the marines standing near. Two of them came and lifted me to my feet by my underarms. "Hold her up."

He brandished the baton in my face and asked, "Do you know what this is, Abby?"

"No." I croaked, tasting blood. I wasn't sure if he'd bloodied my nose or loosened some teeth.

"I'm not sure what the official name for it is, but on Klojuak they call it a 'pain stick.' The former military dictatorship on the planet used it to control prisoners, induce confessions and torture dissidents."

"Wha... " I started to ask, but Gordon cut me off.

"Yes, Professor, *that* Klojuak. The one your savage friend over there," he motioned to the other end of the cavern, "was smuggling weapons to. The rebels there are actually minions of the former regime. That regime had hundreds of thousands of political prisoners in concentration camps. Prisoners *we liberated*."

"I don't believe you. You lie about everything." I said. Damn, it hurt to talk.

Gordon ignored my comment, "It's fascinating technology. We messed around with something similar a few years ago but the Council of Governors found out and forbade us to use it. These types of devices are outlawed in Telluric space. Lucky for me we're not *in* Telluric space."

"You're a lucky guy, Gordon." I mumbled sarcastically.

"Very true. The thing works on the nervous system of the subject by stimulating the person's pain receptors, sending pain signals to the brain. Here, let me demonstrate."

The bastard ripped my coat open, the buttons flying, and grabbed my shirt near my waist. He pulled up on my shirt, untucking it from my pants and exposing my bare midriff.

"It works much better when applied to the skin."

"Uh, this is unnecessary, Gordon, I'll take your word for it; be reasonable." I pleaded, tears still clouding my eyes.

"I tried to be reasonable before, remember? But you thought it'd be more fun to call me names. No, the time for being friends has passed. Our conversation yesterday on board the Upton was unsatisfying. Either I was asking the wrong questions or you honestly don't know much. It's time we found out which. Sergeant?"

The marines grabbed me more securely, making sure I couldn't avoid the evil little wand. He poked the baton into my belly and triggered it. An insanely intense, brain boiling shock of pain struck my midsection, rippling out from the point of contact. It'd triggered every nerve from my pelvis to my sternum to send a signal of extreme pain to my nearly overloaded brain. Though I didn't hear it, I know I screamed, simply from the fact my throat was raw and sore afterward. The pain only lasted a few seconds, but was so intense my bladder had emptied in humiliating fashion. I never imagined pain like that was possible.

"From now on, Professor, that's what you'll get when you lie to me. Understand?" The air had been forced from my lungs as well, so I couldn't speak. I simply nodded my head weakly, gasping for air, limp in the arms of the marines.

"Now, this is the amulet your father gave you on your 16th birthday, isn't it?" he asked.

I managed to croak "Yes."

The bastard *had* drugged me, and I'd told him about my amulet. Dammit. I had no idea how much I'd told him. I had no way of knowing; I couldn't remember a thing we talked about.

"Where was it hidden? We searched you, your clothes and your backpack thoroughly and couldn't find it."

"It was in the vault chamber." I said, still trying to recover. I didn't dare lie again; I didn't think I could endure another poke from his 'pain stick.'

"Huh, I wouldn't have guessed that. Now, I'm going to ask you an important question, Professor. Of what use is this? How can we use this to open the vault?"

"I don't know. It's just an artifact my father gave me when I was young. I didn't know it came from here until recently. But my father never told me what it was, and I don't know what it's used for. I swear." I told him, hoping I wasn't contradicting what I'd told him while under the truth serum.

"What else can you tell me about it?" he fished.

"The symbols on it have something to do with a Fibonacci sequence. I don't know what, though. I haven't figured it out yet." I said, still desperate to avoid his 'pain stick,' but unwilling to confess the revelation I'd just had in the vault chamber. I couldn't have told him about it under the drug, I hadn't thought of it yet.

Gordon grinned evilly, "So, you *are* capable of telling the truth. That's the same thing you told me when you were drugged. All it took was to smash half your face in to get a little honesty out of you. This vessel you traveled here in, the Avernus, how does it's stealth device work? How do I defeat it?"

"I have no idea, I'm not an engineer. All I know is it's called a QSDM device."

"That's what you said last night. I was hoping you'd be more helpful today, with your wits about you. I researched QSDM and there's no information available. However, the ship is obviously stealthy because we've had no luck finding it. Only small snippets of indeterminate sensor data. The Avernus belongs to Cyrus Baaqir, therefore the stealth device does too. Baaqir must believe something incredibly valuable is in that vault for him to give you his ship equipped with such amazing technology. What's he think is in there?"

I'd finally recovered my breath, "We stole the ship. It was just luck it had the stealth device installed. And, Baaqir knows nothing about the vault. He hired us to search for artifacts here, we never told him about the vault."

"Interesting. What about this fellow piloting the ship, Sebastien Fowler? I looked him up on the web and in our files. He's a real man of mystery. He was convicted of murder and sent to prison, then suddenly his records just end. There's no record of him being released and nothing about him since. He's never paid taxes, doesn't have bank accounts, never held a job and doesn't own any property. He basically disappeared completely for 13 years until yesterday, when you, inexplicably, told me he's your pilot. Tell me what you know about him, and the woman, Leanna Callicenna."

"They both worked for Baaqir." I didn't see any point in lying about Sebastien, I didn't know anything that might help Gordon anyway.

"They worked for Baaqir, off the books, for 13 years? No records? That doesn't seem possible."

"I don't know for how long. I think he worked for Baaqir longer than she did. Leanna is Sebastien's fiancée, and they hitched a ride with us to escape Baaqir. They ran away to be together."

"In Baaqir's stolen ship? So, they're just along for the ride? Abby, that's ridiculous; you can't be that naïve. They ran away from Baaqir, fine. They *got* away; why are they *here*?" He brandished the baton again.

"No, don't! I don't *know* why they came along; I suppose they thought keeping the vault away from you was a good cause." I ventured.

"Where's the Avernus now?"

"I don't have any idea."

"You know these people, where do you *guess* they went?" he asked, exacerbated.

"I don't fucking *know*, Gods curse you!"

Gordon didn't like my answer. He poked the 'pain stick' into my right thigh and triggered it. I screamed again; this time I was more aware of my voice. Excruciating pain pulsed up and down my leg, but not nearly as intense as before. This time the material of my trousers was between the thing and my skin, dulling the effect somewhat, I suppose. I was aware of someone else yelling, and as the pain receded I realized it was Kara. She was somewhere here in the cavern with us, but closer to the entrance. I couldn't see her, but knowing she was near and still alive was an enormous relief. I couldn't make out what she was saying, my head was spinning and my mind was foggy.

"Jesus, someone shut that bitch up." He ordered. He held up my amulet, "*This* is the secret your father left with you, Professor. This is why I sent for you; I knew there had to be something like this, and I was right all along. You need to help me figure out how to use this thing to open that vault and do it quickly, I don't have much more time. Can you do that?"

"Maybe." I said, breathing hard. "I don't know."

"I researched the Fibonacci sequence too. After our discussion yesterday, I thought maybe I didn't need you anymore. I'm no novice in mathematics, I studied astro physics, theoretical physics and even did a semester on the theory and function of REL drive at the academy. But, lucky for you, I can't figure out how the Fibonacci sequence could possibly help open that vault. You'd better figure it out, professor. I've wasted weeks here already and I'm rapidly running out of time and patience."

"Why is that?" I asked rhetorically, "Your superiors don't know you're here, do they? You've been stalling them until you got the vault open. But you haven't been able to, and they're getting tired of you neglecting your duties, isn't that right?" I knew I was asking for more of the pain stick, but I couldn't help taunting the bastard.

"Shut up." His eyes narrowed at me.

"Where are you supposed to be, Gordon? Chasing arms smugglers, that's your official mission, isn't it? You came on this treasure hunt on your own, and if you don't bring in the loot your ass is history, am I right?" I knew I was correct from the way his face twisted up in fury.

"I said shut up, goddamn it!" he raised his hand as if to strike me again, but he stopped himself. He still needed me or I think he would've beaten me bloody. There was murder in his eyes. He took a deep breath, and seemed to calm down a little.

"You're lucky I still need your help. I warn you, Professor, if we fail here I won't be the only one that suffers. The Tovolek will die, I don't make empty threats."

He touched the pain stick to my left thigh and I screamed, "No, don't!" in anticipation, but he didn't trigger it. He smiled at me, still touching the thing to my leg, and said, "If we need to have another discussion like this, I won't be so merciful."

"Bastard." I managed to say. "You get off on causing pain; torturing people, don't you?"

"Don't be a fool; that's not what I'm here for; all I want is that vault opened. Do that, and I'll let you and the Tovolek go free. I can't let Bradley go again; he pissed me off too much on the Archeron. But he won't face the death penalty if you help me." Gordon promised as he seemed to have conquered his anger for the moment. "I can be reasonable, when I get what I want."

One of the guards picked up my respirator from the ground where it'd been thrown when Gordon hit me. I realized I'd been deprived of oxygen for too long, so I quickly replaced it on my nose. I'd been getting shorter of breath, dizzy and disoriented; now I knew why.

The two guards dragged me across the cavern and threw me down next to Kara, but didn't bind my hands. I guess they didn't consider me a threat. I still had my backpack, but they'd confiscated anything dangerous before we'd left the frigate. I wished I had my little dagger with me, but I didn't know what they'd done with it.

Poor Kara was conscious but still bound securely. She gasped when she saw me. I was bleeding from my nose, messing up the respirator, my right eye was closing rapidly, and my face felt like it'd been slammed into a rock wall.

"Ensign Davis must not have liked you as much as I thought."

"He didn't do this, but it might as well have been that little shit. Gordon sent him to act like a decent person to get on our good side. It was all fake; an act. He even stole my amulet and gave it to Gordon. How's my face look?"

"You've looked better. While I was growing up there were many fights among the children. My father would always say 'everyone takes a beating now and then, but that doesn't mean you should stop fighting.' That's some Az-Codorian philosophy to cheer you up, little human."

"Thanks, but I'm not sure that helps. So, what do we do now?" I asked. My head was starting to clear.

"It depends. The way I see it, if you can't open that vault, we need to kill these green-shirted var-luks as soon as possible. If you *can* open it, we should *also* kill them as soon as possible. And, I still think we should blow that vault to ten different hells."

"We still might be able to grab that library. Sebastien hasn't left us, I'm sure of it."

"You certainly have a lot of faith in an ex-convict, convicted murderer you hardly know, Abby. Those two are probably halfway to the Mick by now."

A thunderous explosion came from just outside the cavern, rocks and dust came raining down on us. A second explosion rang out, and there was a muddled cacophony of shouted orders and screams of the wounded. Automatic weapons fire erupted, and the sound of men running in and out of the cavern could be heard.

"You were saying?"

Part Nineteen Problem Solved

Interstellar Date: 388-07-10
On Kleos Prime

TWO MARINES CAME STUMBLING into the cavern near us, one helping the other who'd obviously been injured. The left side of his uniform was in tatters, and it looked like he had severe burns down the whole side of his body. He gritted his teeth, bravely stifling his screams, as his comrade gently laid him down on the floor of the cavern and yelled, "Medic!"

"What should I do?" I asked Kara.

"Look for a green shirt that's been injured or killed. They might have keys to these manacles. I doubt if the marines do." She told me.

"I meant should I try to help the injured soldier? I can find a first aid kit or go looking for a medic."

Kara gave me a look that'd freeze lava. "Abby, *focus*! We need to escape from here, and this is obviously our chance. Sebastien, or someone, is attacking the CTF. *That's* who we need to help! But first I need out of these manacles, so help *me*!"

Of course, she was right. It might be our only chance to escape. I hurried over to the cavern mouth and peeked outside. The huge, imposing armored vehicle I'd seen outside the cavern entrance when we'd arrived had been blown into several burning, smoking pieces. There were bodies of CTF personnel scattered everywhere. Some of them were still moving, most weren't. There were bloody body parts strewn around as well, in what was rapidly becoming a wrecked and scorched battlefield.

There was a roar above and I looked up; high above me screamed two of Teddy's combat drones, their cannons blazing and rending the ground in a wide swath as they zoomed overhead. More screaming and yelling came in their wake, but I couldn't understand a thing anyone was saying. Another two drones roared overhead from a different direction, firing several missiles at the marines who were scattering, looking for cover. Sebastien had unleashed the full complement of attack drones.

I spied a green-shirted corpse just meters away and squatting as low as I could, I hurried over to it. I was certain this one was a corpse because its head was missing. The gory scene I approached didn't make me ill (it wasn't the first headless body I'd seen recently), but I was stunned as I recognized the name sewn above the breast pocket: En. Davis.

Ok, I wretched, but only a little. It was surreal looking at a dead man I'd actually known, if only for a little while. I knelt and quickly searched the Ensign's pockets, looking for keys; there weren't any. The incredible, earsplitting sound of multiple automatic weapons firing all at once was beginning to overwhelm me. The marines were frantically shooting at the drones, the drones' cannons were dealing the CTF soldiers on the ground a horrific slaughter. One of the CTF vehicles lurched toward the cavern seeking cover, but was disintegrated before my eyes only 40 or 50 meters from where I crouched. Flaming and smoking debris scattered everywhere, including in my direction.

I dove for cover, narrowly avoiding a scalding piece of metal the size of my head that struck the side of the hill behind me. The signature scream of the drones assaulted my ears again, and yet more explosions followed. Gods, the noise! How could soldiers stand the noise of battle? I spied what I believed was another dead man a few meters away, I thought this one was a sergeant. I rushed over to search his pockets and the man moaned. His right leg was missing, it'd been shot or blown clean off, and there was a tremendous amount of blood soaking the ground; he couldn't possibly live much longer with such a wound. His face was burned on the left side, and when he turned his head toward me and pleaded, "Help me" I almost swooned from the horror of it.

There was nothing I could do for him, of course; so ignoring the gruesomeness of the act, I went through his pockets as he died. I found a large ring of keys, grabbed it, and made my way back toward the cavern. I heard dozens of projectiles screaming past my head, like supersonic insects swooping and buzzing. I lunged toward the cavern entrance and threw myself inside as I recognized the roar of the drones overhead once more. More explosions assaulted my senses, those drones were wreaking havoc.

Kara had rolled herself closer to the entrance in my absence; I rushed to her and began trying the keys. The key ring was large, full and covered in the dead man's blood, but many of the keys were obviously too large for the manacle locks. There was another tremendous explosion just outside, sending dust and debris into the cavern in a great cloud. Small rocks from the ceiling rained down upon us, and I briefly wondered how many more explosions it'd take to bring the entire thing down on our heads.

"Hurry." Kara encouraged.

At last, I found the key that fit and began unlocking her bindings. Kara leapt up, her many injuries ignored, and raced over to the injured marine from earlier. The man had died in the interim, so Kara took his rifle and sidearm, then yelled at me "Come on!"

I ran to her, "Where do we go?"

Kara handed me the marine's handgun. "What's going on outside?" she asked.

"There's drones in the air, attacking the CTF soldiers. I think, maybe, they're the drones Teddy had in the cargo hold of the Avernus. Sebastien must be behind this. There are so many dead, it's awful."

"Dead CTF soldiers are anything but awful, little human. Those are the only kind I like. If this is Sebastien's work, I'm going to give him a big, sloppy kiss. No offense." Kara declared.

"Fine by me, I might join you."

Kara looked around the cavern, searching for CTF soldiers. "Get down, stay down. If one of those marines appears, shoot him." And she left me.

She moved swiftly, as was her habit, toward the back of the cavern. The CTF had set up a lot of equipment inside, and there were crates of supplies, a few tents and even a portable head in there. I lost sight of Kara, and she's impossible to hear when she wants to be quiet. The battle raged on outside, but my anxiety centered on my immediate situation

there in the cavern. Kara had left me alone, I realized, in the middle of a
battle. I was a history professor, for Gods' sake. I released the safety on
my gun, just like Leanna had shown me, and prayed I wouldn't actually
need to use it.

I heard three quick bursts of gunfire inside the cavern. The shots
echoed around, the sound dying out and leaving only the sounds of battle
outside. Kara came from behind one of the tents and raced over to me.

"All you alright, Abby?"

"Of course. What happened?"

Kara smiled, "There were villains lurking back there. Two green shirt
officers were hiding from the battle, proving what cowards they are. I sent
them to hell to pay for their sins more thoroughly. The cavern is clear of
enemies now, I believe. Now that our flanks are secure, we can venture a
glance outside."

We crept over to the cavern mouth to have a look outside. The
battle still raged but to my untrained ears there seemed to be fewer
rifles firing than before. I could still hear the rapid, baritone staccato of
the drones' cannons, though. I was startled as a missile was fired from
our right toward a group of CTF soldiers that'd taken shelter behind
a ruined vehicle on our left. The missile impacted the wreck and there
was a spectacular explosion, pieces of men and equipment went flying
10 or more meters into the air, the resulting fireball engulfed another
vehicle not far away and that vehicle subsequently exploded. A lone
CTF soldier ran from the second vehicle entirely enveloped in flames,
screaming madly. He ran toward our hiding place and collapsed a few
meters away. Kara shot him twice to cease his screaming. The smell of the
man roasting is something I'll never forget.

Our attention was drawn back to the hillside to our right as, from
behind a boulder, out stepped a tall character completely decked out in
armor, carrying a huge rocket launcher on his right shoulder: Sebastien
Fowler. He'd donned Kara's second tactical combat suit, launched
Teddy's attack drones, and came to rescue us, the glorious son of a bitch.

He saw us and began walking toward us as if he hadn't a care in the
world. I suppose, with that suit on, maybe he didn't. He tossed the empty
rocket launcher aside and casually retrieved a fallen marine's rifle as he

neared us. The firing had ceased. Either the CTF soldiers that were still alive had snuck away to hide, or there weren't any left alive. There was no sign of Gordon and I didn't relish the thought of searching the bodies, and body parts strewn about, in order to find him. But, I wanted to make sure he was dead.

Kara and I ran over to Sebastien and grabbed hold of him in a three-way hug. "Where've you two been hiding?" he asked. Kara ducked behind a smoking wreck and addressed Sebastien.

"Just my luck, I've been waiting half my life to fight against the Tellurians and I was tied up while you were having all the fun." Kara said. "Where's the Avernus? Abby, take cover. We don't know how many CTF are still around." I hurried to join her, and Sebastien did as well.

"The Avernus is close by, just a few hundred meters above that mountain top there." He pointed to a peak behind us.

"It's in the air?" Kara asked, "You have it on autopilot?"

"Nope. Leanna's flying it." Sebastien smiled at our shocked faces. "I've been giving her lessons for months. That girl is more than a pretty face, she's as clever as a New Britain fox. Everything she attempts, she masters. Flying, shooting, cooking, she's a marvel. I wouldn't be surprised if she could give either one of us a good game of Thezra, even though she's never played it. She's probably picked it up just from watching us.' He laughed.

"What's the tactical situation? What happened to Gordon's ship?" Kara asked.

"It's a good news, bad news thing. While the two of you were in the cave another ship landed and they transferred Bradley to it. Afterward, the ship departed."

"Teddy's gone?" I asked.

"Are you sure, Fowler? He's no longer on Kleos Prime?" Kara asked.

"I'm sure. The ship with Teddy on board left a few hours ago and departed the solar system. That's when I put my plan in motion. Once we knew you two and Teddy weren't in there anymore, we took the Avernus up to a few thousand meters and fired the main gun at that frigate down there. Amazingly, they didn't have their shields on, so the plasma bolt tore right through their armor. They're not going anywhere. Not till they can repair a two-meter hole in the side of their ship. I think we hit the reactor compartment too; they've been leaking radiation."

"What about reinforcements?" asked Kara, "Are there any more ships in the system?"

"No, not that we've been able to detect. We're jamming the crippled frigate's communications, so I believe they're on their own, for now. At least until they figure a way around our jamming."

"And you just wiped out most of their manpower. Fantastic, Sebastien, I knew there was a good reason to bring you along." Kara said, and she did give him a kiss on the cheek. "Now we need to make sure none of those CTF people ever leave this place, we have to kill every last one of them. No one can ever know what was found here. And then we can rescue Teddy. Again."

"I figured we could grab what's in that vault and get the hell out of here as fast as possible. Who cares about those green shirts down there once we have the books from the vault?" Sebastien asked.

"Kara's right, Sebastien. We especially need to make sure Gordon is dead. He was in the cavern when you attacked, he's got to be near. As long as Gordon is alive he'll never stop looking for the contents of the vault. He'd hound us to the other side of the galaxy; we'd never be safe. We have to make sure none of them leave Kleos Prime, especially him." I said.

"That's a little cold blooded, Professor." said Sebastien. "Be careful what you wish for."

"She's learning." said Kara. "Abby knows what's at stake. Sebastien, we need to hunt down any survivors. And make sure Gordon is dead."

"Can we get back to the Avernus first, though? I want to get away from this battlefield." I asked.

Sebastien raised his wrist to his mouth, "Avernus, come in Avernus. Lea, do you read?"

"Avernus reads you, my love." Came the reply. Apparently Sebastien had taught her how to fly a ship but nothing about communication protocols. "Did you find Abby and Kara?"

"I did. They look like they lost a slugfest, but they're alive. Come get us, Lea. We'll jump in and immediately dust off again."

We left cover and proceeded to an open area not far from all the wreckage. Sebastien entered some commands into a control panel on his forearm, and the drones appeared hovering overhead. There were only two drones remaining out of the four Teddy had in the hold.

"Those things are amazing. Four of those pack more fire power than a battalion of marines. Look what they did to the CTF's armored vehicles. They shredded them, like a warm knife through butter. No wonder the CTF is having trouble with the insurgents, if Bradley is selling them those things." Sebastien said.

"Remember, those things belong to the CTF. They have them too; we're just trying to level the field to give the rebels a chance. Speaking of Teddy, we need to find out where that other frigate is taking him." said Kara.

"Here she comes now." Sebastien said and pointed upward.

"I don't see anything." I said.

"Squint your eyes. See there, that blurry shape just cresting the hill? That's the Avernus with the QSDM engaged." He said.

"Quenra forgive us, it's magic. It's invisible." Kara exclaimed. "I don't believe it."

"It's in a different quantum state than we are. It doesn't just confuse sensors; it actually makes you invisible. Almost, anyway. As you can see, here in the planet's atmosphere there's a distinct blurry appearance. Once you know what you're looking for, you can see it, but just barely. I imagine in space the Avernus is completely invisible when the QSDM is engaged. I'd say the tech has passed our tests." Sebastien explained. "Come on, let's hurry. The Avernus will be visible when it lands. The frigate down there might try to get off a shot or two while it is. I don't think *all* of their weapons are out of action."

The Avernus set down and clearly became visible to us. We hurried over to the ramp when it came down, and practically ran up into the ship. The ramp closed behind us, and we felt a moment of instability followed by a jolt of acceleration as the ship rapidly gained altitude again.

I gratefully removed the respirator from my nostrils; my nose had stopped bleeding, but the little bubble of the respirator was caked with dried blood, and I didn't want to know what else. I ran onto the bridge and found Leanna calmly sitting at the pilot's console. I went to her and gave her a hug.

"Thank you, Leanna. Is there anything you can't do, little sister?" I asked with a big smile.

"I'm too short to reach the top shelf in the galley." She admitted with a smile of her own. "Ew, Abby, you stink. What happened?"

"It's a long story." I said, embarrassed. I'd forgotten about emptying my bladder in my trousers.

"My love, where to now?" Leanna asked Sebastien.

"Let's just circle that frigate down there at this altitude, so we can keep an eye on it. And, let's retrieve those drones in case we need them again. So, what's the plan, Professor?" Sebastien asked me.

"Just a moment." I said. Kara had moved to the tactical position and brought up the display. "What's going on Kara?"

"We have to finish off the frigate, and make sure no one survives. The longer we wait, the longer they have to make repairs, send for help, or find a way to attack us. We finish them off and then we worry about that damn vault." She told me. "There's no heat bloom from their reactor right now, they're defenseless."

Sebastien had moved over behind Kara and was examining the tactical display as well as the sensors. "It looks to me like they've vented a lot of radiation. It's hard to tell for sure, but it looks like there's 11 survivors down there. With those radiation levels, those people won't last long. They should be evacuating that ship and the surrounding area, but they've hunkered down instead."

"That's crazy. If the radiation from their ruined reactor will kill them, why haven't they left?" I asked. "They have a few more vehicles, they should pack up some rations and get as far away as they can from that frigate."

"It's easy for us to say." Sebastien said, "There may be casualties and they don't want to abandon the sick bay. Maybe they think they can stop the radiation leak. Maybe they're simply trying to gather together as much gear as they can before they abandon ship. We've no way of knowing."

"None of that matters." Kara argued, "Our strategic situation is simple, we have to finish them off, and hope the secret of the vault dies with them. Our tactical situation is also straight forward, we must attack and finish them off before they can regroup. If even one of them survives we'll never be safe. Look at Abby's face, Gordon did that to her. He was torturing her in the cavern right before you attacked. He planned to kill us if Abby couldn't open the vault, maybe even if she could. This is war and I *know* war; I was trained to lead armies ever since I was 12 years old. It's kill or be killed. They don't deserve mercy; they haven't earned it."

"I agree. We can't allow any of them to leave Kleos Prime." said Leanna, "When we leave here we have to know that no one will be looking for us."

"Lea, I don't think we'll know that either way." Sebastien said. "Don't be so anxious to kill those people down there. Besides, we have no idea if anyone from that other frigate knew what was going on down here. Maybe they all know about the vault."

"I don't think Gordon told anyone up the chain of command about it. He was trying to pull off a big surprise when he showed up back on Titus with that library. He basically told me so." I said. "He was convinced he'd be a hero and get promoted."

"That may be true, but there's another reason we *know for sure* the rest of the Ministry is clueless about that vault." Kara explained. "Because if they *did* know about it, there wouldn't have been 30 or 40 green shirts and marines here, there would've been a battalion of marines. There would've been a couple of battlecruisers, a bevy of supply ships, portable barracks, temporary fortifications, makeshift planetary defenses in orbit and an admiral in charge. Instead of that jumped up asshole, Gordon."

"Kara's right. The Ministry would've realized what that vault could mean. They would've seized this place with overwhelming force. The fact they didn't is proof they have no idea what's here." I said.

"I suppose that's true." Sebastien agreed.

"I'm charging the main gun. Everyone take a seat." Kara said.

None of us argued with her. We all took our seats and strapped in. Leanna, who was still piloting the Avernus, took us a bit lower and stopped with the bow pointed toward the George Upton. There was a lot of activity still going on down there, and it appeared the marines that'd survived were preparing a large weapon of some kind out on the plain a short distance from their ship. Maybe a cannon, or possibly a missile launcher, but it was clear they weren't done trying to fight.

Their leader, Gordon, had foolishly assumed whatever ship we'd used to get to Kleos wouldn't dare attack a heavily armed CTF frigate. So, they were completely unprepared when Sebastien had done just that. I knew from experience (our Thezra matches) Sebastien was a bold and aggressive strategist. We were lucky Gordon had no clue who he was up against.

"Brace yourselves." Kara warned. It was impossible for me to feel sympathy for those CTF soldiers down below after the last two days I'd spent as their captive. They were a despicable lot.

There was a terrific roar, and the Avernus shuddered noticeably as the MIP cannon spit out it's lethal bolt of hydrogen plasma. I pulled my eyes up to the main viewscreen as a blinding flash painted it in hews of purple and red similar to when you stare at a star too closely for too long. I closed my eyes in caution, and as the colors faded from my eyelids I once again ventured a look at the screen. The George Upton lay in several smashed and ruined pieces; our plasma bolt had clearly impacted their weapons storage, creating a devastating explosion. The blast had pulverized every vehicle and person in sight.

Those luckless soldiers and sailors, who'd only this morning bid good day to each other, had breakfast together, perhaps even spoken with loved ones over the great distance from home, now existed only in that sea of pulverized, floating particles. Particles which hopefully, someday, may serve a useful purpose again. But in that moment I watched them float amid the dust from the vehicles, useless. In an instant, erased from existence.

I realized, in a bout of introspection, the euphoria villains feel when causing havoc and death during war, was strikingly similar to the delight spoiled, rotten children feel when they use fireworks to blow up frogs on Founders Day. That thrill of raw, sadistic emotion comes from the same horrific place in one's soul; at once satisfying and sickening. For wishing death on those people down there, I felt shame. Sebastien had warned me to be careful what I wished for; I was horrifyingly aware of what he'd meant.

Eventually, Leanna landed the Avernus just down the mountain's slope from the cavern entrance. We'd used our sensors to scan for survivors and had detected none. Kara had gotten what she wanted; we'd killed all the CTF personnel, 'as soon as possible.'

I REALIZED THERE WAS still a possibility of more CTF showing up on Kleos Prime, so time might be a factor. But I couldn't help making time for a shower, a sandwich, and some sleep; I was filthy and exhausted. I didn't see Kara during this time, I assumed she was getting some rest as well, possibly in the cabin that belonged to Teddy.

When I emerged hours later, I went to the bridge once again and found Sebastien and Leanna there. There was still no sign of Kara.

"Hello, Professor, I hope you got some rest." Sebastien greeted me. "When do you think you'll be up to hiking back down to the vault? I'd like to see it after all we've been through to get here."

"Yes, Abby. I'd like to see it too. Is the climb down difficult?" Leanna asked.

"Not difficult, but exhausting because of the gravity. First, have either of you seen Kara?"

"I saw her earlier, before you went to sleep. I thought she went to get some rest as well." Leanna said. "Was she not with you?"

"No, she wasn't." I answered. "Sebastien, have you seen her?"

"Not recently. I took off the tactical suit, and she took it down to the hold. I guess she was packing it away again. Like Leanna said, I assumed she was with you after that."

"Well, since she's not here, I suppose this might be a good time for the three of us to talk." I said.

"Talk about what, Professor?" Sebastien asked. "Don't you want to start for the vault? We can talk on the way."

"I need to know something first." I began. "I need to know what you've been instructed to do here. What's your assignment?"

"My assignment? What are you talking about?" Sebastien asked.

"Come on, Sebastien, you know what I mean. What'd your boss tell you to do here? What's his plan?"

"My boss? What boss?" Sebastien asked, but I wasn't buying it. He was one of the most clever fellows I'd ever met. I wasn't buying the dumb act.

"Cyrus Baaqir. He sent you to Kleos Prime with us for a reason. What'd he tell you to do?"

"Abby, I shot Mr. Baaqir so we could escape, don't you remember?" Leanna asked. "We barely escaped with our lives."

"Leanna, little sister, I love you. I do. And you two had me fooled for the longest time, but I figured out what's been going on. That shooting in the shuttle bay was staged. I remember thinking at the time the trickle of blood at the corner of Baaqir's mouth was just like in a stage play. And that's exactly what it was, wasn't it? A fake. There were blanks in the gun, and Baaqir had a capsule with fake blood in his mouth."

"Why would we go to all that trouble?" Sebastien asked.

"Because Baaqir wanted you to go to Kleos Prime with us, and he wanted us to trust you. I have to say, it worked like a charm."

"Professor, you have a wild imagination." Sebastien said, desperately trying to maintain the ruse.

"You shot him and stole his ship. After that, there's no way we'd think you were still working for him. I've been thinking about our escape from the Archeron; Baaqir could've shown up in the shuttle bay with 50 armed men. He could've easily kept us from leaving. But, he showed up all by himself. Why? That seemed pretty dumb to me at the time, and Baaqir is anything but dumb. It didn't add up." I explained.

"What about those green shirts we killed, was that staged too?" challenged Sebastien.

"No, that was obviously real. But Baaqir showed his hand during that as well. He must've sabotaged the surveillance feeds, and that's why no CTF reinforcements showed up. And that's also why there was no reward posted for me. The CTF had no idea I was involved in the escape, because Baaqir had suppressed the surveillance feeds somehow; it's the only explanation. Baaqir allowed us to arrive at the shuttle bay before the rest of the green shirts or the marines even knew what was happening."

"You're too smart, Abby." Leanna smiled.

"And you, Leanna, remember when you told me you didn't think you could ever leave Baaqir, even if you loved Sebastien with all your heart? And Sebastien, after getting to know you, and the kind of man you are, I don't think there's any way you'd betray Baaqir after all he did for you. Your defining characteristics are *honor and loyalty*."

"When'd you figure it out?" Sebastien was smiling now, too.

"I guess it was a lot of things all added together that convinced me. When you told the story about Damon being in Coula with you. You said you gave Baaqir one condition when he was getting you out of that place, he had to get your friend out too. I knew you'd never betray a man that helped your *friend* that way. Your honor wouldn't allow it." I smiled back at them. "Then Teddy discovered Baaqir hadn't offered any rewards for us. For shooting him and stealing his yacht? That didn't add up either, so I was suspicious as hell."

"So, you were suspicious all along?" Leanna asked me.

"I guess so, a little. Finally, that bastard Gordon called me naïve for thinking the two of you were just along for the ride coming here. I hate to admit it, but he had a point. So, what's the plan, why *are* you here?"

"Alright, Abby, you got us." Sebastien admitted. "Baaqir doesn't consider Bradley trustworthy, to put it mildly. He thought Bradley might double-cross him. My instructions are simple: Ensure Baaqir's interests are looked after. The original deal was exclusivity when it comes to artifacts. That's it. I'm supposed to hold you all to the deal."

"Baaqir doesn't have to worry about Teddy anymore; Teddy's not here. And, Baaqir's side of the deal was to provide a stealth device for us to... "

"To get to Kleos Prime." Sebastien interrupted me. "And he did, he let us take the Avernus, which is equipped with a QSDM device. Baaqir discovered the Ministry of Security was here, but the possibility of obtaining ancient artifacts from an advanced civilization was too much to pass up. He asked me if I'd go with you to protect his interests."

"No offense, but this was a dangerous trip; you were risking your lives. Why would you agree to that?" I asked.

Sebastien just shrugged, "When Baaqir asks, I don't say no. I consider it a part of my job. I'm the one that asked Leanna to come along. I thought the story of us running away together would help gain your trust. I realize we were deceiving you, Abby, and I apologize. I hope you aren't too angry. The truth is, I really have thought about running away with Lea before, but she always says no."

"Only because I don't wish to hurt Mr. Baaqir. Otherwise I would've said yes long ago." Leanna explained, smiling at Sebastien lovingly.

"I'm not angry, I'm actually sort of impressed; the whole time we were trying to convince you to come to Kleos Prime with us, it was your assignment all along. I don't think Teddy or Kara suspected at all. So, you're just here to make sure we sell the library to Baaqir? Not to take it away from us?"

"There's no double-cross, Abby. I'm supposed to make sure you hold up your side of the deal, that's all. Baaqir provided the Avernus, and sent me to assist you against the CTF. I think it's turned out pretty well, don't you? We're here on Kleos Prime, the CTF is neutralized and all that's left to do is open the vault and empty it. Now, let's go get those books for Baaqir and get the hell out of here. I'm sick of this place."

"Not so fast, Sebastien." I said, "It's no sure thing I can open that vault. Plus, I don't know if I'm comfortable letting Baaqir have the library; I don't trust him. In our original plan, Teddy, Kara, and I were coming here to make sure the CTF didn't acquire artifacts that might lead to advanced weapons. I still think that's an excellent goal. How do I know Baaqir won't share the library with the CTF? He manufactures most of their weapons, after all."

Surprisingly, Sebastien laughed. I looked over at Leanna and she was giggling too. I failed to understand what I'd said that was so funny.

"What? What'd I say?"

"You're so stubborn you can't let go of your first impression of Baaqir." Sebastien said. "Sit down, Professor, let me tell you something."

"Alright." I was mightily confused, but I took a seat.

Sebastien began, "I'm head of security for Mr. Baaqir. That means I sit in on all his meetings, I'm privy to much of his correspondence and he shares almost all his strategies with me. I don't think I'm overstepping to say I'm his closest confidant."

"Advisor. You're his closest *advisor*, my love." Leanna beamed with pride as she said this.

"Well, that might be overstating just a bit." He chuckled, "But, he does ask my opinion on things quite often. I'm in a position to know Baaqir better than anyone. The point is, Baaqir isn't who *you* think he is, Professor."

"Alright, enlighten me, who is he?"

"He'd be furious if he knew I told you this, but the fact is, he detests the Council of Governors and their trained dogs in the Ministry of Security. For some time now he and a few of his friends in the Trade Guild have been working to curb the Council's power any way they can." Sebastien explained.

"Are you trying to tell me Cyrus Baaqir is a subversive?" I asked, incredulously.

"No, nothing as simple as that. He's simply of the opinion the Council, the CTF and the Ministry of Security have all outlived their usefulness. The Freehold Wars are over and humanity needs to move on."

"Sebastien, that sounds pretty subversive to me."

"Please, Abby, watch what you say. Words have meaning and the 's' word is dangerous. I realize it's just us talking here, but I wouldn't want you to say something like that when others were around. My point is, Baaqir would never share the secrets of that vault with the CTF. It'd be bad for business if nothing else."

"Bad for business? You mean DRG?"

"That's right. The Alliance buys most of its weapons from DRG, and they also rely on the research done by DRG at the skunkworks on KV42. If the Alliance got possession of that library, they might not need DRG anymore. Baaqir won't allow that if he can help it."

"I see. So, Baaqir's greed will keep him from sharing the library with the Alliance." I said.

"I wouldn't put it like that, but I guess that's one way of looking at it. But he wants the contents of the vault for his collection, nothing more. It's a unique cache of priceless, ancient artifacts from a lost civilization. That's honestly why he wants it. I don't think you have to worry about him sharing that library, he's not into sharing."

"I suppose that makes sense. But if he's not exactly a subversive, as you say, what's his agenda? You said humanity needs to move on. To where, exactly?" I asked.

"Well, he doesn't share *all* of his thoughts with me, the man has ten thoughts for every one we have. But, he's told me before he'd love for things to go back to the way they were before the Freehold Wars; with planets ruling themselves again, instead of the Council of Governors dictating things."

I contemplated Sebastien's explanation for a few moments. Surprisingly, I realized if Sebastien was telling the truth, it meant I'd come to almost the same conclusion about the Telluric Alliance as Baaqir: It had outlived its original purpose. The difference was I hadn't yet thought about what would become of us all *after* the Alliance had been toppled. If it *could* be toppled.

During the short time I'd known him, I'd come to trust Sebastien Fowler, literally, with my life. He'd saved it on more than one occasion. I didn't think I could hold he and Leanna's ruse against him. He was only doing his job, and being loyal to Baaqir.

However, could I trust Baaqir wouldn't share the Hoji Mubrani's library with the Telluric authorities? Baaqir's obsession with owning unique things that no one else owned was probably a benefit in this situation. While I wasn't sure he could be trusted in general, I was confident I could count on his greed, as well as his obsession.

I decided to trust Sebastien's disclosures about his boss. It was better to leave the library in the care of Cyrus Baaqir than to leave it on Kleos Prime and hope no one else ever found it. A man of his means would be able to keep it safe. And, it was possible he'd even let me study it. Maybe.

"Alright, big guy, you can relax." I told him. "If you swear he won't pass it on to the Alliance, I believe you. Baaqir can have the library."

"Abby, I swear, that's the last thing he'd do with it." He assured me. "Plus, you're liable to be fabulously rich after Baaqir pays you for that library. He'll give you a fair price."

"I honestly never even thought about that. Well, I guess all we need to do now is go and get it. Let me change into my spelunking outfit and I'll be right back."

"Can I come also? I'd like to see this vault of yours, Abby." Leanna asked.

"Lea, someone needs to stay with the ship. Let's find Kara and see if she'll stay here so you can come with Abby and me."

I went to my cabin and changed, threw some things in my backpack and went back out to the salon. Leanna was there waiting for me.

"Where's Sebastien?"

"He went below to see if Kara was down there. I knocked on all the cabin doors and she didn't answer. We aren't sure where she went." Leanna said.

It was a few more minutes before Sebastien reappeared. "She's not in the cargo hold, and the suit of tactical armor isn't either. She must be outside, perhaps she went to the vault. Leanna, please stay with the ship, Abby and I need to go find Kara, alright?"

"Whatever you say, my love. But, please be careful. Some of the CTF soldiers might've survived." Leanna warned.

"Babe, my middle name is careful."

"No it's not, it's Gregory."

Sebastien made sure I was carrying a sidearm, just in case, and my backpack was slung over my shoulder. I'd thoroughly cleaned the annoying little respirator, and donned it as we headed off the Avernus. The hike to the cavern wasn't far this time, only a few hundred meters, but it was still steep. Sebastien led the way, carrying one of the plasma rifles and alarmingly, several hand grenades. He wasn't convinced all the CTF were dead either. He'd also brought two large, empty duffel bags.

"What're the duffels for?" I asked.

"I figured we might as well start hauling those books back to the Avernus. It's a long hike down to the vault, no sense wasting a trip. You *can* open that vault, right?" he asked.

"Definitely."

"Now you sound so sure. Before, you said you didn't know. Why're you so sure you can open it now?"

"Because I already unlocked it."

He spun around to face me. "What?! You *already* unlocked it? You just told us a few minutes ago you weren't sure you could. Why'd you say you weren't sure, when you'd already done it?"

"I wasn't sure I wanted Baaqir to get his hands on those books. Now, you've convinced me he won't give them to the Alliance."

"You're something else, Abby." He said as he shook his head. "How'd you do it?"

"My father figured out the hard part. The amulet he gave me when I was young came from the vault. When he was here with Teddy, he spent weeks trying to unlock that thing. Eventually, don't ask me how, he determined my amulet contained a Fibonacci sequence."

"What in hell is a fibanacki sequence?"

I laughed, "Fib-o-nach-ee. Fibonacci was an ancient, Old Earth mathematician. He's famous for bringing modern mathematics to the continent of Europe way back before the industrial revolution. The famous numerical sequence named for him is simple, it's just a series of numbers where each one is the sum of the two previous numbers. 1+2 equals 3. 2+3 equals 5. 3+5 equals 8, and so forth all the way to infinity."

"Why's that so famous?"

"Mostly because it's a mathematical sequence that constantly occurs in nature. The sequence is often depicted graphically as a spiral. The Fibonacci spiral can be seen throughout nature, in flowers, in seashells, in tropical storms, eggshells, pinecones even the shape of the Milky Way contains Fibonacci spirals. As the Fibonacci sequence progresses, when you divide a number by the previous one, the quotient gets closer and closer to 1.618. That's known as the Golden Ratio. It's long been considered the epitome of beauty in art and architecture; as well as nature."

"I have no idea what you just said. You remind me of Baaqir when you talk like that, he makes me feel dumb too." Sebastien smiled. "But, how'd any of that help you open the vault?"

"When Teddy told me the amulet had a Fibonacci sequence on it, I assumed the solution to the vault door would be a math problem. I stink at math, so I was worried. But, it made sense it'd be math based. Math is a universal language, something ancient aliens and us would have in common. But, it turns out there's something else we have in common."

"What's that?"

"An appreciation of beauty. The solution to the lock was based on the Golden Ratio but it wasn't a math problem; it was an art quiz. I lined up the symbols on the dials in the sequence on my amulet, using the shape of a Fibonacci spiral, all the way out to the 17th dial. It created a big spiral, and once it was lined up perfectly I heard a click and the door was unlocked. Simple." I explained. "I owe it all to my secondary school art instructor Mrs. Getty. I didn't even like that class."

"I wouldn't exactly call that simple, *Doctor*. I just heard you explain it and I'm still confused, but congratulations, amazing job. So, did you see all of those books?"

"I couldn't open it. There was a green shirt ensign watching me. So, I spun the dials again to make sure it was locked, but I can open it when we get there. I can't wait." I said with genuine enthusiasm.

We entered the cavern and searched the area inside. Unsurprisingly, there were several dead bodies. However, they'd been stripped of their weapons and stacked neatly against the wall. The weapons had been gathered and sorted as well; a stack of various guns not far from the bodies. Obviously, Kara had done this, probably making sure they were all dead as she went.

"Kara!" I yelled. "Kara, where are you!?"

"Abby, let's not make so much noise. At least until we know what's going on." Sebastien admonished me. "The way I see it, we have two choices. We either stay here and wait to see if she shows up. I, personally, don't like just waiting around; it's too passive for me. Or, we start climbing down to the vault. Either choice has drawbacks. We could split up, one head down and the other stay here, but I don't like the idea of leaving you alone. What's your preference?"

"I say we start down; I don't have good memories of this cavern. I want to get back down there when I have some time to enjoy it."

"Well, let's get going then, I hate wasting time."

We started the long descent, both of us excited for what waited below. The temperature was starting to fall, as night began above. Believe it or not, I was wearing the coat Ensign Davis had given me, the one Gordon had ripped the buttons off of. I assumed my own light jacket had been inside the George Upton when we destroyed it. I'd taken a length of rope and tied the coat closed like a character from a John Steinbeck novel.

We'd been descending for about 30 minutes when we turned a corner and were confronted by a horrifying scene. Ahead, there was a man in a tattered and ripped uniform pressed against the wall with his hands above his head. On the ground beside him, two more men in uniform lay motionless. Sebastien held his hand up, signaling me to stop. He cautiously approached the chilling scene.

"This one's still alive." Sebastien told me as he indicated the man against the wall. He bent down and checked the other two for a pulse. "These two are gone. Abby, I think you better get over here."

Wearily, I walked over beside Sebastien and gasped in shock. The man hanging on the wall was none other than Percy Gordon. He'd been gagged with overlapping strands of rope, and been nailed to the wall using metal rock climbing anchors; like the ones Kara used.

This, too, was obviously Kara's work. She'd nailed his hands to the rock wall, wrapped rope around his neck and fastened the ends to the wall with more anchors. She'd secured his waist the same way, so Gordon was suspended 30cm or so above the path, feet dangling. The gruesome spectacle was an intentional homage to the Nir-Kvekian method of crucifixion Gordon had described to me. I suppose Kara thought it'd be 'poetic justice.'

Upon closer inspection it became evident his arms and legs had been broken in several places; there were bones protruding through his skin and tattered uniform. Suddenly, he opened his eyes and I jumped backward in horror and shock. His formerly cold and calculating eyes bulged, bloodshot and swollen, impossibly grotesque. He tried to speak around the cruel gag, but only managed a muffled gurgle. Sebastien reached up and cut his rope gag free, and as it fell to the ground Gordon sputtered and coughed out a copious amount of blood, along with his *severed tongue*. I held down my lunch through shear willpower; horrified by the fact the battered, bloody and mangled apparition in front of us was *alive*.

"Ig bo le," Gordon managed to croak from his blood-filled mouth, coughing up yet more gore which would've covered me if I hadn't jumped away. Sebastien wasn't as lucky, and his coat was baptized with the stuff.

"Should I try to get him down? I doubt if he'll survive anyway, and we can't very well carry him up to the top with the condition he's in. I could put him out of his misery." Sebastien asked me, brandishing his knife.

"Leave him where he is." Kara ordered as she approached from below us on the path. She wore the tactical armor, was armed with a rifle, and had Sur-rok at her hip. "I put him there for a reason. What's the matter, Gordon, you didn't like the snack I provided? Oh, well, I guess you go hungry. Don't blame me."

"Kara, what'd you do? Gods, this is disgusting." I said.

"Yes, Kara. Was this necessary? Couldn't you have simply shot him?" Sebastien asked her.

"This is no more than what he'd planned for me. It's too good for him, actually. He won't last long enough to truly suffer. I surprised him and his two guards down at the vault. He was trying to open it using this," Kara tossed my amulet at me. "He wasn't having any luck. Not much of a puzzle solver, eh Percy?"

"Fu ae bi. Ig on." Gordon sputtered.

"His brain is probably fried by now; he's been here without a respirator for hours." Kara said. "He wasn't much of a genius before the lack of oxygen. He was also carrying this." She tossed my little dagger to me.

"He didn't know the secret to opening the vault like Abby does." Sebastien said. "She can open it. So, why are these guys up here and not down by the vault?"

"When I surprised them down there, I broke Percy's legs and I made his men drag him up this far. I was going to take him all the way to the top, but I got sick of his whining, so I shot those two and nailed his Telluric ass to the wall." Kara explained. "Hey Gordon, I bet you wish you'd treated me a little better, huh? I told you, a hundred-fold, remember? Did you say Abby can open the vault?"

"She already did." Sebastien answered. "I knew it all along, she's a damn genius."

"That's great, sweetling, I guess you're just as smart as your father after all, huh?"

"I wouldn't say that. If it wasn't for what he figured out all those years ago I would never have been able to unlock it." I said. "Did you find out what happened to Teddy?"

"After he was properly motivated, Gordon told me where he sent Teddy. It's a prison on Balmora." Kara said. "We need to go after him."

"If it's where I think, it's a pretty famous place. It's called Kristoffea Maximum Security Prison. It's where the Ministry of Security puts people to rot. The whole place is solitary confinement in tiny concrete cells. A four-inch window and a hole in the floor for doing your business, that's it." Sebastien told us.

"Well, let's go. We're wasting time." Kara urged. "Let's get back to the ship."

"Aren't you forgetting something?" I asked, "We still have to go down and remove the books from the vault. Sebastien brought some duffels, I have my backpack, we can make a good start carrying those books to the Avernus. Just think, all of the collected wisdom of an ancient civilization captured in writing. It could change everything." I said, excitedly.

"No one's going down to the vault. We don't have time." Kara declared.

"We have plenty of time, it won't take long." Sebastien said. "Just a few trips with all of us helping."

"I told you, Abby. I told you what I planned to do. That library is too dangerous to be allowed to leave here. If the Tellurians ever get their hands on it, the galaxy is done for. I had to do it." She said.

"What are you talking about, Kara?" Sebastien asked. "Had to do what?"

"She's going to blow it up. Destroy it, isn't that right?" I asked her. "She's taken a nuke down there and she's going to set it off!" I told Sebastien.

"Not *a* nuke, *two* of them. I set them on a timer to detonate in about... " She checked a chronograph on her wrist, "an hour and 24 minutes from now. I figure 16 kilotons should erase that damn vault from existence."

"Damn you, Kara! What've you done? Everything we've gone through was for nothing! That library might've brought universal peace, for all you know. We couldn't be sure what was in it until we examined it. It's the greatest archeological discovery of all time!" I yelled at her, "You had no damn right to destroy it without talking to us first!"

"We did talk about it. I told you what had to be done." She argued. "I'm blowing it to ten different hells, just like I said."

"You told me?! Are you fucking serious? So, my opinion, Sebastien's opinion, didn't matter? I told you we *shouldn't* destroy it because of its historical value. We never agreed either way. You had no right to just take it upon yourself to blow it up. Damn it! Can you disable the bombs?"

"No. Not remotely. Abby, whatever's in that library didn't do those genius aliens of yours any good. They were wiped out anyway. If there was a formula for universal peace written down in there, your aliens didn't read it. This is the only way to make sure the CTF doesn't get their hands on it. We'd never be able to hide the library forever, sooner or later it'd fall into the wrong hands. This way we know for sure. *Problem solved.*" She argued.

"There's still time. If we hurry down we might make it in time to shut those bombs off. There's a chance at least." Sebastien said.

"No." I said. "It's at least a two-hour hike from here. You'd be incinerated, and I'd have to explain to Leanna why I didn't stop you. It's over, let's get out of here while we can."

"Get out of here while we can is a good way of putting it." Kara agreed, "There's another CTF ship on the way. We need to be gone by the time it arrives."

"How do you know that? We were jamming their comms; I don't think they could've called for help." Sebastien said.

"Think about it. You destroyed his ship, killed all his men, and stranded him here. Logically, he and his buddies here should've been up top scavenging for supplies and trying to find a way to call for help, right? The only reason they would've been wasting their time down there trying to open the vault is if they already knew a rescue ship was on the way. That's the only explanation."

"Damn it! I can't believe it; we were so close." said Sebastien. "I'll never be able to explain this to Baaqir."

"Baaqir? What's he got to do with it?" Kara asked.

"You'd know this stuff if you'd lowered yourself to talk to us." I said. "Baaqir's fed up with the Alliance, and hates the Ministry of Security. We were going to sell the library to him, and he would've kept it out of their hands."

"Ha, you think you can trust that guy?" asked Kara. "Abby, a historian should know better. Even if he did manage to keep it away from them, what would happen when Baaqir dies? Who'd insure the library didn't fall into the wrong hands then? Forever is a long time; this is a permanent solution."

"You should've talked to us, Kara. You disrespected and disregarded the rest of us. It's not the first time either. You did the same thing with Haney." I exclaimed. "That isn't how you treat your friends and partners."

"What do we do with him?" Sebastien asked as he pointed to Gordon.

"He got a good kicking, had his arms and legs broken, got nailed to a wall, and now he'll die. Can you think of anything else you want to do to him, Abby?" Kara asked. "Maybe hit him a few times with that wand of his? It's around here somewhere. In about... 79 minutes he'll be getting a 10,000-degree sauna."

"I just want to get out of here so I don't have to look at him anymore. So long Percy, it wasn't nice knowing you." I said. "Alright, we better get going or we'll end up fried like him."

We started the slow climb back to the surface and I could tell Sebastien was silently fuming. Clearly, he was incredibly frustrated with Kara. But, I think he was angry at himself also, thinking he should've seen it coming and done something to stop her. I knew the feeling. Kara had told me straight out what she thought should be done with the vault. She'd been crystal clear; I simply hadn't guessed she'd go so far. But, I should have after the stunt she'd pulled with Haney. Kara was a woman of action, self-assured and a no-nonsense decision maker. I knew all of that but still hadn't guessed what she was capable of. The destruction of the Hoji Mubrani library was my fault, in a way of thinking. I was sick to my stomach as I thought about the loss to posterity.

We came to the cavern at the surface, and Kara began gathering weapons from the pile she'd made earlier.

"We don't have time for that now, Kara. You've made sure of that. We only have about 35 minutes till detonation, going by what you said before." Sebastien told her.

"I'm going to collect all of the weapons I can carry, because they will be infinitely valuable to the insurgents I deliver them to. Those insurgents are killing CTF soldiers, and I'll give them all the help I can." She declared.

Sebastien and I looked at each other, and I shrugged. I went over to the pile and grabbed a couple of rifles and a bandoleer of ammo. Sebastien grabbed some things also and we started for the Avernus. I figured there was no use in pouting.

Sebastien called Leanna and told her to prep the ship for departure. She started asking questions, but he just told her we were in a hurry so she stopped. We were trudging downhill, but it was still hard going over rough terrain since we were weighted down with guns. I arrived at the Avernus exhausted, physically, and emotionally. I was trying not to scream or cry at the loss of the vault. The vault *my father* had discovered! I was also trying to get over my anger at Kara but failing miserably. The more I considered what she'd done, the more angry I got.

"Get us up into orbit, Lea." Sebastien said, "We need to get clear of this place quickly."

"Alright, if you say so." said Leanna.

We all got strapped into seats on the bridge, Leanna took off and placed the Avernus in orbit. Sebastien studied the sensors closely, checking for any targets in or near the system. He pronounced it all clear.

"What's going on?" Leanna asked. "Is anyone going to tell me?"

"While I slept, without asking any of us, Kara took two of those nukes down to the vault. She's set a timer to detonate any minute now. She's destroying the vault, Leanna." I said, not able to disguise my anger and frustration.

"Oh, my." was all Leanna could say.

"You'll thank me one day, Abby. You'll see it was the right thing to do." Kara said.

"That might be true. It may end up being the right thing to do. That's not what I'm upset about. I'm upset the person I love thinks so little of me and my opinion she'd go behind my back this way. That's not how you treat someone you care about. That vault was discovered by my father, it was his legacy to me. Now it's gone. You had *no right.*"

As I said that last sentence, the side of the mountain containing the vault bulged out momentarily, then collapsed. Soon, a cloud of dust rose and expanded up and outward. From orbit it could be mistaken for a volcanic eruption, but to me it was far more cataclysmic than that.

The deed was done, the vault was gone. Talk about anticlimactic, the destruction of all that knowledge in the blink of an eye, and the four of us were the only ones who knew, possibly the only ones that'd *ever* know. The death of that ancient civilization, described in my father's 8000-year-old codex, was finally complete. And we'd been the instruments of destruction.

We sat in silence, our thoughts to ourselves. Kara was the first to leave her seat and head back to the cabins. I suppose she needed to remove her armored tactical suit. I don't imagine she'd rested at all while I had; she'd been too busy.

After a few minutes of silence Sebastien spoke, "I suppose we should get the hell out of here, just in case Kara was right about a rescue ship being on its way. Any suggestions about where to go, Professor?"

"I guess that depends; what are you going to do now?" I asked him. "Are you going straight back to the Archeron or heading to MK141 instead. Are you going to take the job Damon offered you?"

"Well, I don't think Mr. Baaqir will be too angry we aren't bringing any artifacts for him. Disappointed, for sure, but not angry. I'm sure he'll want Leanna and I to resume our positions, and I can't leave for a job with Damon unless I have Baaqir's blessing. I still owe him that much. If I had a choice, I suppose I'd take Damon's offer. What he's doing there is exciting, and I'd love to be part of it. It'd be an adventure."

"That's exactly what I thought you'd say." I managed a chuckle. "What about you, Leanna? Would you prefer MK141 or the Archeron?"

"I'll go where Sebastien goes. He's my adventure." She smiled.

"Lea, you know the professor won't accept that sort of answer. Abby wants to know what *you'd* prefer."

"Well, life is good on the Archeron, there's everything you could want right there whenever you want it. But, truthfully I was beginning to get bored there. A chance to start new with Sebastien, in a wild sort of place like MK141, might be fun." She admitted.

"Sebastien, let's set a course for MK141. We can visit Damon again, and I need some time to figure out what I'm going to do."

"No problem." He said, as he set a course for the Mick, engaged the REL drive and the dark mode, and pronounced we'd arrive in a few days.

I remained on the bridge, unable or unwilling to venture back to my cabin in fear of a confrontation with my lover. I simply had no idea what to say to Kara. There was too much, too many emotions. Where would I even start?

After a while, Sebastien went to the comms console and transmitted a message that sounded like gibberish to me. When he finished I asked, "What was that?"

"A coded message for Baaqir. I briefly explained what happened at Kleos, where we are and where we're heading. He'll respond in a couple of hours, I believe."

"Have you been doing that this whole time?"

"I have. Are you angry with me?" he asked. "I'm just doing my job."

"No, not angry. A few days ago, I might've been, but I feel like so much has happened now my perspective has completely changed. Teddy's in prison, or at least on his way. I'm furious and beyond disappointed in Kara. I feel like you and Leanna are my only friends at this point. I suppose I should be disappointed you were secretly working for Baaqir all along, but I'm not. It didn't change anything that happened, and in a way your loyalty to him is sort of reassuring. Does that sound crazy?" I asked.

"Not at all, Professor." He assured me. "So, what're *your* plans? Do you have any idea what you'll do now, where you'll go?"

"None. I guess I have some soul searching to do."

Eventually, I excused myself and went to my cabin. I opened a bottle of Cordson's and poured myself a large drink. I had no idea what I should do now that my adventure was over. I didn't know for sure if I could return to the Academy. There'd been no rewards posted for me after our exploits on the Archeron. It was conceivable I could just show up back on Ampora and go to work. There'd be questions, but I could just claim sickness the way Kara had suggested.

Theoretically, if Gordon had kept the Kleos Prime expedition a secret from his superiors, everything that'd occurred on Kleos Prime was unknown to anyone except our little group. So far there was no evidence to the contrary. That was a stroke of luck only a degenerate gambler could seriously appreciate.

No, the more I thought about it, the more I knew I'd never be happy again being a simple history professor. My eyes had been opened on my trip to Kleos, about the Alliance's depredations and the Ministry's oppression of my fellow citizens. Whatever I did, I'd have to be involved in fighting the Tellurian power structure in some meaningful way. I could never return to my previous existence knowing what I knew.

As I poured a second drink, the expected knock on my door came.

The door opened a crack, "Can I come in?" Kara asked.

"Of course."

Kara came and sat beside me. "Abby, sweetling, I just wanted to tell you how sorry I am for what I did. You're absolutely right, I knew what that vault and the library inside meant to you. It was discovered by your father, and for you it was a link to him. I acted selfishly, but I hope you know it wasn't because I don't respect you. Please don't think so. I respect you so much, I do. I think you're the most intelligent and caring person I've ever met, and I love you. Please, can you forgive me?"

"I honestly don't know." I said, as I pondered how to proceed. "All of that is easy to say now the vault is destroyed, and you've gotten your way. You seem to have a habit of just doing what you want, then asking for forgiveness. You have strong convictions, are decisive and courageous. All of those qualities are what drew me to you when I first got to know you. However, I'm beginning to realize none of those qualities lend themselves to a partnership. You clearly don't like to ask anyone's permission or even their opinion. But I can't be your silent, submissive partner, Kara."

"Of course, you need us to be equals, I understand. I'll try harder to be a better partner. I've been partners with Teddy for years, and that's seemed to work pretty well."

I chuckled, "Kara, you call Teddy master and play the role of bodyguard, but it's obvious to anyone that's around the two of you he defers to you about anything important. I was right when I said he'd be lost without you. You're the leader of the partnership, you only let him think he is. Gordon told me Teddy was the grandson of some famous wine merchant or something. Is that true?"

"Teddy's big secret." Kara smiled, "The way I understand it is Teddy inherited stock and a seat on the board of Meyers and Sons. It's a huge corporation that owns a bunch of vineyards and distilleries. It's his family's business, but he didn't get along with his family, especially his aunt who's the chairman of the board. So, he quit and he reinvented himself as Teddy Bradley, importer, exporter, and smuggler. I can't blame him, who wants to be trapped behind a desk every day?"

That hit a little close to home for me. "I suppose some people like to play things safe. Teddy met you and decided adventure was more fun. I think I agree."

"Oh, he'd already quit Meyers and Sons before he ever met me. Teddy's seat on the board is a point of contention, so his stock has been tied up in the courts ever since he left. The coin he lives on comes from our successful business, just like he said."

"I see. He needs you, Kara, any fool can see that. There's got to be a way for us to get him out of that prison. We just need time to think."

"You're probably right about Teddy and me. In truth, the arms dealing and helping the insurgents we do are mostly my idea. It didn't take much to convince him, but without me he might never have started dealing weapons. So, we have to save him from that horrible place because he'd never be there if it wasn't for me. You see, if I wouldn't have been captured at Klojuak, literally none of this would ever have happened."

I thought about that for a moment, "I guess that's true. Gordon would never have found out about Kleos Prime; Teddy would never have introduced himself to me, the secret of the vault would never have been revealed, and you and I would never have met. *And*, the vault wouldn't have been *destroyed*." I couldn't hide the vitriol in my observation.

"That's why I felt so strongly about destroying the vault, because if it ever *would've* fallen into the wrong hands it would've been *my fault*. I hope you can eventually forgive me." She stood but bent down and kissed my forehead before she left my cabin.

The conversation with Kara hadn't given me any closure. We'd skirted the tension between us and devolved into talking about Teddy. I should be frustrated and angry, but instead I was relieved. The fact was I just didn't know what to do, or how to save our relationship. So, delaying any serious discussion gave me a reprieve of sorts.

After a few more minutes, when my glass was empty, I went back to the bridge to see what was going on. I found Leanna, Sebastien and Kara all speaking amiably. Thankfully, Sebastien wasn't holding a grudge against Kara.

"So, what's your plan for helping Teddy escape this time?" Sebastien asked Kara.

"You took out that frigate back on Kleos Prime because Gordon wasn't a true naval officer, just a jumped-up secret policeman. A real captain wouldn't have left his guard down like that with a hostile ship in the vicinity. He underestimated the Avernus and didn't understand the capabilities of the QSDM device. A frigate underway and on its guard is a different story; they'd cut us to ribbons. Even if we could catch it before it gets to Balmora, which we can't. That means we have to break him out of the Kristoffea prison. For that I'll need a heavily armed assault force. We have the weapons in the cargo hold, I just need the soldiers." Kara explained.

"There's always mercenaries available. Sometimes they're pretty good, sometimes not. But they're always expensive." Sebastien said. "Or you could try to recruit some of the insurgents you know."

"Many of those mercenaries moonlight as bounty hunters. I have several bounties offered for my head now, so I don't know if I'd be smart to trust mercenaries." Kara confessed. "And those insurgents wouldn't be interested in such a risky attack deep in Alliance territory. The odds of success are too low."

"Well, we're on our way to MK141." I offered. "What about those pentoffians you made friends with? That Kutta fellow didn't seem like the backstabbing type to me."

"Abby, that's brilliant!" Kara agreed enthusiastically. "Kutta and 15 or 20 of his most trusted men would be perfect. We find out which cell block Teddy is in, we bust in there at night and get away as quickly as possible. It's never been tried before, so it could work. Sebastien, are you in? The Avernus would come in handy during our getaway, the CTF is liable to be annoyed. The QSDM would help immensely."

"Annoyed doesn't cover it. They'll send everything they have after you. No one has ever broken out of Kristoffea, let alone broken *into* it. You're crazy." But he smiled as he said it.

My friends and I traveled to MK141 with new purpose in mind and renewed resolve. Kara was intent on saving her Gal-vek from prison. Sebastien and Leanna were dreaming of starting a new life on the Mick with Damon Offerton as their patron. How they could get Baaqir to go along with it was a mystery. As for me, my new life had already begun. I was no longer a simple history professor, instead I'd been converted to the cause of freeing the galaxy from the tyranny of the Telluric Alliance. My life up until that point seemed like a distant memory, my future an exciting adventure.

Part Twenty Machiavelli was an Amateur

Interstellar Date: 388-07-18
One Week Later, on board the Archeron

"I HAVE AN APPOINTMENT with Cyrus Baaqir," I told the guard at the 1st class lift. "Dr. Abigail Thornwell."

"Oh, yes, I see your name here. Are you familiar with the layout of this section? I could escort you to his suite if you'd like." The guard offered.

"No, thank you. I know the way."

He stepped aside and let me enter the lift. The music in the lift was orchestral and lovely, and it continued in the corridor as I walked down toward Baaqir's suite.

I'd left my friends back on the Mick and hired a ship to bring me to the Archeron. I was fortunate the luxury liner hadn't yet started its long trip back to its primary wharf in the New Britain system. If it had I could never have caught up to it in time for my purpose.

I'd told everyone I was traveling back to Ampora to settle my affairs, and I *would* do that, eventually. But first, I had some important matters to discuss with the man himself.

When I reached suite 13's door, it opened without my having to knock. A burly security guard I didn't know greeted me and ushered me inside. The place was just as lavish, just as beautiful as I remembered. A young man in a purple suit and yellow tie, carrying a notebook, appeared promptly.

"Greetings, my name is Stanislaus Doncic, I'm Mr. Baaqir's executive secretary. Can I take your jacket, Doctor?"

"No, thank you."

445

"Would you like a drink? We have an excellent wine cellar, or I can offer you ale, or nearly any spirit you wish. What can I bring you?"

"Fruit juice, please." I told him. He looked surprised, but simply nodded and left.

I waited next to the beautiful fountain, admiring the fish from afar this time. There were a few guards spread around, but none tried to converse. When Stanislaus returned with my drink I was disappointed it wasn't the juice from Grovia Leanna liked.

"It shouldn't be long now. Mr. Baaqir is finishing up an important call. He has an extremely busy schedule today." The boy passive-aggressively warned me not to waste his boss's time.

A few moments later his comms buzzed, and he ushered me down the hall. I guessed the meeting wasn't going to take place in Baaqir's private quarters this time. We entered an expansive office with more fine art, and Baaqir sitting behind a huge, dark wood desk. He was dressed in a grey suit, with a white shirt but no tie, and stood politely as I entered the room.

"Thank you Stan, that will be all. I'll call you if we need anything." He said. "Please, make yourself comfortable, Abigail. It's lovely to see you again."

I sat in a plush leather chair in front of his desk; and searching for a coaster, but seeing none, I liberated a tome from the bookshelf behind me and placed my juice on it.

"Thank you for seeing me. I'm pleased to see you again, Mr. Baaqir. I must say, there were times since our last meeting I didn't think that'd ever be the case. I believe I may have judged you rather hastily before, and for that I apologize."

Baaqir eyed me skeptically for a moment. He stood and retrieved a decanter from the bar behind him, poured himself a generous portion into a tumbler and turned back to me.

"This is excellent apple brandy from Grovia. Would you care for some? I can add a splash to your disappointing juice if you'd like?" he offered.

"Certainly, thank you." I said. "How'd you know I was disappointed in the juice?"

"Stan was unaware of your preference for the juice Leanna likes. He poured you some of the more traditional recipe, I noticed. You were bound to be disappointed in it."

I took a swallow of the juice with the brandy added. It was much improved.

"Thank you, this is much better."

Regarding me with a hint of mirth on his misshapen face, Baaqir said "I must admit, Abigail, I was quite surprised to hear from you. After the debacle at Kleos Prime I thought it highly unlikely I'd ever hear from any of you again. I hate to say I told you so, but I did tell you the Tovolek was not to be trusted."

"Yes, you told me so. And, I admit you were at least partially correct. Kara has a single-minded hatred for the CTF, and stubbornly sticks to her own council about how to deal with them. She didn't ask for our opinions about what she'd planned; she just went forward on her own. We were caught by surprise, and perhaps we shouldn't have been. I'm sorry for that. In her defense, I believe she did what she thought was right."

"Disastrously, I'm afraid. We may have discovered amazing things examining the contents of that vault. In my opinion, it's a disaster on par with the destruction of the library at Alexandria, on Old Earth. Sebastien informed me you'd left their group and were heading back to Ampora to settle your affairs. I assume that means you aren't returning to the Academy to teach. Is that a fair assumption?"

"That's true. I've decided to pursue other opportunities."

"Such as?"

"We'll get to that, eventually, but first I have an important favor to ask of you. Forgive me for jumping right to business, but it's urgent. Are you aware Captain Bradley's been sent to prison?"

"Of course."

"Mr. Baaqir, if I may be blunt, I'd like you to arrange for his release, with all charges dropped."

Baaqir chuckled briefly. "Why, in the nine circles of hell, would I do such a thing?"

"Not only that, but if possible, I'd also like you to do something about those bounties offered for my friends. I believe Sebastien and Kara are still wanted by the authorities."

"Not anymore. You needn't worry about those bounties; I've already taken care of them. Stanislaus filed a report with the Ministry of Security almost a week ago detailing a terrorist attack aboard the Archeron. My personal security staff, led by Mr. Fowler, dispatched over twenty armed militants in a firefight. Tragically, several brave members of the Ministry's contingent on board were killed during the action." Baaqir explained. "I assured the Minister himself those bounties were requested erroneously by an over-zealous officer who lacked knowledge of the facts."

"They believed that?"

"Of course, why shouldn't they? If I say that's what occurred, who will dare dispute it?"

"I see. So, all of those bounties have been revoked?" Baaqir simply nodded. I told him, "That's wonderful, thank you."

He smiled and confessed, "There's no need to thank me, I simply couldn't allow a bounty to hang over Fowler's head. I need him back here to resume his duties now the Kleos mess has concluded. But this other favor, Abigail, about releasing Bradley; I'm not sure how it would benefit me. In my opinion Kristoffea might be the perfect place for him. I assure you I didn't fabricate the terrorist story to help Bradley or his Tovolek."

"Her name is Kara. Mr. Baaqir, at this very moment, Sebastien, Leanna and Kara are on their way to Balmora. They intend to attack the prison in order to free Bradley. They've hired a group of militia to assist in the assault."

"Sebastien didn't mention this plan to me." He said. "How peculiar."

"Probably because he knows that you, like me, wouldn't approve. You know as well as I do they're almost certain to fail. Some of them are bound to be killed in this foolish attack. I knew it was unlikely I could talk them out of it, Kara has her mind made up and she's impossible to reason with when she's so determined. So instead, I came here, to you. If Bradley is released, the prison attack becomes unnecessary."

"Excellent reasoning. However, what makes you believe I can accomplish something like that?"

"You've done it before. You secured a pardon for Sebastien and his friend, Damon Offerton. It must be done quickly. His release needs to be accomplished in time to call off the assault. They could be planning on attacking the prison in the next few days."

"And *why* would I do such a thing? Besides the obvious fact I'm fond of Sebastien and Leanna, what do I have to *gain* from expending so much political capital?"

"Teddy's continued supply of weapons to insurgents helps your business, doesn't it?" I reasoned. "Plus, won't the Ministry be upset about one of their frigates being destroyed? Won't they eventually question Teddy about it?"

"Bradley has been useful, to an extent, but there are plenty of arms dealers that *don't* use *my* ships to smuggle weapons. As for the lost frigate, I'm certain the Ministry is incensed. But, Sebastien told me Bradley was gone from Kleos Prime before the frigate was destroyed. Therefore, his testimony would be entirely circumstantial. There is no hard evidence connecting me to the frigate's demise. In short, Abigail, I'm not convinced." Baaqir responded, frustratingly.

"A wise man once told me the Ministry of Security doesn't necessarily need evidence to detain people."

He smiled, "This wise friend of yours has a point."

"Besides, I didn't come here empty handed. I have valuable information to exchange. Information I don't think you're aware of. My voyage to Kleos Prime was not a complete waste."

"Abigail, it's extremely unlikely you possess information I do not." he stated, as if humoring a child, "However, if you did, I'd certainly be interested."

"Are you aware of the fighting on Furanix Prios?"

"Of course. The CTF's latest endeavor. What of it?"

"While we were on MK141, Damon Offerton had us over to his villa. His wife is Furanill, did you know?"

"I did not. Offerton is a government official there, isn't he? He's a clever man, and has done well for himself. Abigail, what about the fighting?"

"Offerton's wife has a relative, I believe she said an aunt, who's in the diplomatic service for the Furanills. She said the Furanills have been in negotiations with the Laprows for years, trying to obtain technology and weapons from them. The reason that seems pertinent is, apparently, the Furanills handed the CTF a significant defeat during the initial invasion. We were told the Tellurians were forced to withdraw from the system to regroup and send for re-enforcements. The last we heard, the fighting had resumed and the Furanills were still having success."

Baaqir had been sitting back in his chair relaxing, with an amused expression on his face for the entire conversation. That is, until my revelation about the Furanill diplomacy. My recounting of what was said on MK141 concerning Furanix Prios had brought him to the edge of his seat, and an air of excitement now prevailed in his office.

"Abigail, let me be sure I'm hearing you correctly. You believe the Furanills were *successful* in gaining weapons or technologies from the Laprows?"

"I think it likely. There's no other explanation for their success against the CTF, is there?"

"If that's the case, it represents a significant departure from their historic position of neutrality." He said, almost to himself. "That could mean a whole new strategic situation for the CTF. That *is* information I was not aware of, and therefore tremendously valuable. You do tend to surprise me, Abigail."

Baaqir pressed a button on the interface atop his desk. Moments later, the young man, Stanislaus, appeared through the door.

"Stan, get in touch with Governor Njoku's office, it's urgent. The Council is in session on Titus, so he can probably be reached at his office there. His assistant's name is Margaret DeLaurent, tell her to contact me immediately. I mean immediately, within the next 30 minutes. Be clear." Baaqir told the boy, who turned and left.

Baaqir addressed me again, "Governor Njoku is *from* Balmora, and he owes me favors. I, personally, have no influence with a prison on Balmora. Particularly one under the control of the Ministry of Security. So, this is a totally different situation from Sebastien's. But, as a member of the Council of Governors, Njoku has the authority to commute the sentence of almost anyone. If Bradley's been charged with treason, it becomes political and there may be nothing Njoku can do. However, anything else, up to and including murder should be no problem."

"Thank you Cyrus, that's wonderful. You're probably saving my friends' lives."

"Cyrus? Abigail, I have over 11 million employees, from refuse collectors to scientists, to high-level executives, and not one of them calls me Cyrus." He stated flatly.

"I'm not an employee, though. Next, I have another favor to ask of you." I began, but Baaqir's comms buzzed.

"Margaret? Thank you for your prompt attention. Listen, I have a favor to ask of the Governor." He paused to listen for a moment, "Yes, it's quite urgent... A grievous miscarriage of justice has occurred. I need a man released from Kristoffea prison, immediately... Yes, today... He's a personal friend of mine... Exactly... No, I don't want him spending another moment incarcerated... Yes, his name is Theodore Bradley, A.K.A Meyers, A.K.A Taki Ruhbar... Ah, I see... Well, he was arrested because of a personal vendetta, but he's completely innocent... of course, I agree. The charges are the invention of a devious officer... completely... I understand... Thank you, Margaret. I'll await your call to confirm." Baaqir signed off.

"A.K.A. Meyers?" I asked. "Ruhbar?"

"Abigail, did you seriously think I was unaware of Bradley's true identity and aliases? I should be insulted."

"Do you think they can free him?"

"Certainly; it's as good as done. He's been charged with smuggling weapons and entering a restricted zone. Njoku should have no trouble getting him released. I've expended a huge amount of political influence, and shall have to do Njoku several favors in return. But, alas, that's how the system works, I'm afraid."

"That's wonderful, I knew I could count on you. Now, the next favor I need should be simple. It's about Sebastien and Leanna. I want you to let them go, tell them it's alright for them to move to MK141."

"Where is this coming from?"

" Offerton has offered to give Sebastien a job with a substantial salary and a bright future. He wants to take it, but he'd never leave your service unless you give him your blessing. He's a man of honor and he feels he owes you too much to let you down. Leanna feels the same way, she'd like to move there too, but she'd never consider disappointing you. I think the two of them love you, believe it or not. You should hear the way they speak about you."

"The three of you have become fast friends, haven't you? Interesting; I didn't foresee that. Sebastien must be quite fond of you, to confide his wishes to you that way."

"It's mutual, I'm very fond of them too. Cyrus, they're in love, and all they want is a chance to be together. With your enhanced perception, you must understand that." I pleaded.

"I appreciate your sentiments, I honestly do. This might surprise you, but it's something I've given a great deal of thought to. I've known of their love affair for quite some time, it's difficult to hide thoughts and feelings from me, especially when you're around me all the time. I can't say I approved of the match, at first. There's a significant age difference and they seem so different. I assumed it was simply a sexual obsession. But, over time I've come to understand it's more than that. Did you know he's taught her to shoot?"

"She told me. After she supposedly shot you. He's also taught her to fly the Avernus." I chuckled.

"Ah, yes. My ship. Another benefit of calling off their foolish assault on the prison is I might actually get my ship back in one piece. Sebastien told me you'd seen through our little drama in the shuttle bay. What gave us away?"

"Oh, I didn't figure it out all that quickly. I thought it was odd when you showed up alone in the shuttle bay but when Leanna shot you I believed it completely, so you fooled me. You fooled all of us, none of us would've guessed Sebastien and Leanna were still working for you."

"You did, though, eventually."

"It wasn't until much later that I pieced it together. After I got to know Sebastien, I got suspicious. On MK141 he told me the story of how you got a pardon for Damon Offerton in addition to him. I figured that was too big a debt for Sebastien to ignore. A lot of other things didn't quite add up either, but the main reason I figured it out was the kind of man Sebastien is. He's too loyal to you to ever go against you. Leanna too."

"Abigail, I think you may have missed your true calling. You would've made an excellent counter-intelligence officer for the secret police. No offense." He chuckled.

"None taken. But you haven't answered me yet. Will you let them go to MK141, with your blessing?"

"*If* I were to agree, provided they bring the Avernus back here where it belongs, do you have something to exchange for this *second* favor?" he smiled. I think he was enjoying our meeting, bartering like free-trade-zone merchants.

"Absolutely. This one I think you're really going to like. Palladium."

"Palladium? What do you mean?"

"MK141 is in deep financial difficulties. They've had a recent influx of refugees and immigrants. They lack water and have borrowed extensively to invest in terraforming. However, recently they've had a bit of excellent news. The asteroid belt on the outskirts of their system was discovered to contain rich palladium deposits. Enough to solve their financial problems. Except Offerton fears a full-scale mining effort would bring the attention of the CTF. He's afraid the CTF might sweep in and seize the palladium without compensating their government for it."

"A reasonable fear. That's precisely the sort of thing the CTF has become notorious for. What's on your mind, Abigail?"

"DRG uses mass quantities of palladium, don't they?" he nodded at me, so I continued, "And, you also have mining companies under the umbrella of your investment corporation, isn't that true as well?"

"My investment group owns several mining concerns."

"So, it's simple. One of your mining companies goes to MK141 and leases the mineral rights to the palladium, then they can extract the ore and sell it to DRG. DRG then ships it back to the factories here in Telluric space. You'd be beating the CTF to the palladium, preventing them from simply seizing it; and it'd secure a vital source of currency for the government of MK141. In the process it'd also secure a source of palladium for DRG. It'd be a great deal for everyone involved. Wouldn't it?"

"Abigail, you've surprised me yet again. You worked this whole interstellar deal out in your head, involving a free planet's government and multiple business conglomerates, all before you ever even talked with me or Damon Offerton, didn't you?"

"Well, yes, I did. But, it makes perfect sense, doesn't it?"

"Yes, it does. And here I thought that diplomatic passport you're traveling under was just for show."

"How'd you know about that?" I asked. Baaqir simply smiled indulgently and continued the discussion.

"You've given me yet another valuable piece of information. Two tremendously valuable tips in one day. You are amazing, Doctor Thornwell. Do you realize I sometimes go many months without being surprised by anything? I take a sort of pride in it. But, it seems like every meeting I have with you I get another surprise. Or two." He chuckled again. "A new source of palladium would be extremely valuable. Your plan for MK141 is inspired, it's a good deal for me, and protects the government there from being a target of the CTF, I believe. Excellent, just excellent." He beamed at me.

His comms buzzed again. "Yes? I see... very good, Margaret, that's very good news, thank you. Tell the Governor it's much appreciated, and I owe him one... Yes, we must. The next time I'm at Balmora, absolutely. Goodbye."

"Good news?"

"Well, that just depends on how you look at it." Baaqir smiled at me. "Captain Bradley is being processed out of Kristoffea in the next few minutes. Whether or not that's good news for the rest of the galaxy is a question for debate. He'll be a free man shortly, though."

"Thank you, Cyrus. That's amazing; you're amazing. I knew we were going to be *great* friends, from today onward. I need to get in touch with the crew of the Avernus and let them know about Teddy. After that, I have another topic to discuss with you."

Baaqir pressed his 'Stan' button again. "Stan, can you get in touch with Sebastien Fowler on secure comms, please. And hold my call to the board meeting on Dressida, I have more business to discuss with Dr. Thornwell."

"They won't be pleased, sir. They've been holding up the meeting for you, there's a long itinerary." Stan's voice came from the comms on Baaqir's desk.

"Let them wait. If any of them need to use the WC, tell them that's approved."

"I'm Dr. Thornwell now?"

"Well, I suppose you're not going to be teaching anymore, so a different title just seems appropriate. Now, what is this other business?"

"Well, there's... " I started to explain, but the comms buzzed again.

"Yes, is this you Sebastien, my boy?"

"Yes, sir, it is. What's going on?"

"I'm sitting here in my office with a friend of yours: Dr. Thornwell. We've just been having a nice discussion about your future my friend, but first we have some interesting news. Doctor?"

"Hello, Sebastien." I said, "You can forget about the prison attack you're planning. It's not necessary anymore. Captain Bradley is being released as we speak." I giggled; I couldn't help it.

"What? How? I mean, that's great, but I don't understand. What happened?" Sebastien asked.

"Mr. Baaqir pulled some strings for me, and he's gotten Teddy a pardon, like he did for you. So, call off your assault. You can simply pick Teddy up on Balmora when you get there."

"And, Sebastien, afterward bring my ship back here to the Archeron. Straight away, no more detours. We can discuss your new job on MK141 when you get here. Dr. Thornwell will be here waiting to see you. Over." Baaqir clicked off the comms.

"I will?"

"Surely you can spend a few days here as my guest while we wait for them to bring my ship back? I find your company stimulating, Abigail. I'll arrange a cabin for you and a deposit account for your stay. It's the least I can do for the information you've given me. Tell me, I'm curious why you assumed I'd be interested in the diplomacy between the Furanills and the Laprows. The palladium I can understand, I'm a businessman after all. But why the other?"

"When we were on MK141, I heard Teddy explaining to Mrs. Offerton that Laprow technology is completely different than Tellurian technology. So much so we hardly understand it. I started thinking about your QSDM device. It's Laprow technology, isn't it?"

"Why, Abigail, that's a provocative accusation. Again, I should be offended." Baaqir smiled his crooked smile, clearly enjoying himself.

"It's like nothing the CTF possesses, completely new. Completely different, isn't it?"

"You have an astounding intellect, Abigail, absolutely astounding. This is privileged information, of course, and I must ask you to keep it in this room. Three years ago, some operatives of mine were able to hijack a Laprow scout ship. We discovered a device on board that was unlike anything we'd seen before. We've had the device at our research facility since then and have been able to duplicate it, with great difficulty. The QSDM device is the result of our efforts. We've been unable to expand on our small success however, because quite frankly, our physicists and researchers still don't quite understand it."

"They don't understand it? Truly?"

"My people theorize that human brain function is so different from Laprow brain function we literally *can't* think the same way they do. Perhaps our technology is just as confounding to them, who knows? But, the fact is we've had no luck trying to adapt the strange technology for other applications. So, you see, if the Laprows have sold or given technologies to the Furanills, it would provide my operatives with another possible source for 'research,' to put it frankly." Baaqir confessed.

"Thank you for being honest with me. I appreciate it. Oh, I almost forgot, curse me. There are members of the faculty from the Academy being held somewhere by the green shirts. Gordon told me he had them in custody, but not where. We have to try to free them and send them home, their families are probably getting worried. Can you help with that?"

"I'll have my people make inquiries, but I can't promise anything. If they were being held secretly, which is what it sounds like, it may be difficult to locate them. But, we'll do what we can."

"Thank you again. You're being extremely helpful today. Before I get to the other reason for my visit, I'd like to ask you a couple of questions. You don't have to answer, of course. But I hope we can continue to be honest with each other."

"Hmm, why do I sense these questions may be uncomfortable for me?"

"Possibly. The fact is, I need to be able to trust you completely before going any further."

"Alright, fair enough. Now I'm intrigued."

"When you came to Ampora years ago and met with my father, you weren't there simply to discuss archeology and his codex, were you?"

"I was there for some serious Trade Guild business too. I told you. But I didn't want to miss the chance to meet Henry Thornwell. Why?"

"To be honest, I've a hunch you'd met him before. Possibly more than once. I think you and my father belonged to the same organization, a secret organization which was in great danger at the time. You were there to assess the possibility of getting arrested, and how to prevent it."

"Another surprise, Abigail? I'm not confirming your insinuation; my theoretical involvement with Dectus Artiga has been speculated on before. Let me just say I was certainly sympathetic to their cause. But, honestly, I'd never met your father before that day." Baaqir contended, "I will say, however, I discovered we had much in common during our meeting. And I thought your father was quite a gentleman."

"Thank you, I appreciate that. But, I still think you had ties to Dectus Artiga."

"Abigail, that's quite a leap of logic simply from what I said about meeting your father. Are you sure you don't have any cerebral augmentations?" He teased good naturedly. I took it as a good sign.

"It wasn't such a huge leap after what Sebastien told me. While he was trying to defend you, he explained your dissatisfaction with the Council of Governors and particularly the Ministry of Security. He told me you and some friends in the Trade Guild are trying to curb the

Council's power. If that's true, it's an easy leap to think you once belonged to Dectus Artiga."

Baaqir's demeanor changed. "Where is this going, Abigail? These are delicate and dangerous matters. Matters which Sebastien should know better than to discuss openly. It's a good thing I consider you a friend."

"You have nothing to worry about. Sebastien and I are friends, and he is completely loyal to you. I'd told him plainly I wouldn't open that vault because I didn't trust his boss. He was simply trying to explain why I should trust you."

"How successful was he?"

"Moderately. But I still have questions, so I came here to ask them. If I'm correct you belonged to Dectus Artiga, or even just sympathized with them, I have to ask: Do you really think it's possible to undermine and overthrow the Council of Governors? Is that your aim? And, how could it be done, exactly?"

Baaqir stood, walked around his desk to be closer to me, and leaned against it. He focused his gaze, looking me in the eyes. I was uneasy, not knowing what he'd do or say. I'd just, basically, asked him if he was a traitor.

"Abigail, if I were to take you into my confidence by answering these questions of yours, I'd be assuming you can be trusted *absolutely*. Until now, we've had a stimulating meeting and I believe it's been beneficial to us both in equal measure. To be honest, I've enjoyed it immensely."

"As have I."

"But *these* questions steer our conversation in a very different direction. You can leave now, and we'd part friends. But if you stay, there is a certain degree of responsibility you'd be accepting. Are you absolutely certain you wish me to answer? There is no way to *unhear* what I say." Baaqir warned cryptically.

I wasn't sure what the threat was, but I was positive he'd just threatened me. I felt a knot growing in my stomach, not necessarily fear, but something close to it. Regardless, I'd come too far, gone through too much to turn tail and run; I simply had to know. So I gathered my nerve and plunged forward.

"I just travelled thousands of light years to hear your answers. Yes, I'm sure. I want to know; I *need* to know."

"Very well, in for a pfennig, in for a guilder, as they say. The answer to the first question is absolutely. The answer to the second is yes. To answer the third, I need to explain something. I not only think it's possible to overthrow the council, but inevitable." He poured himself another drink, topped off mine, and continued.

"Abigail, there is a secret so enormous, so *dangerous* the Council would do anything to keep it quiet. Simply put: The Telluric Alliance is on the brink of economic collapse."

"How is that possible?"

"The debts accumulated during the Freehold Wars have only festered and grown since. There are no less than 12 Telluric planetary governments in default as we speak. Several others are nearly to that point, including your Ampora. My exalted position in the realm of finance means I'm one of the privileged few that knows the true extent of the crisis. The council has been attempting to prop up those struggling alliance members as best they can, mostly through the CTF pillaging neighboring planets. But I believe it's hopeless; there's only so much plunder they can get their hands on. The crippling debt and the ponderous entitlement outlays the planetary governments are responsible for mean it's only a matter of time until the crisis comes to a head and can't be covered up any longer."

"I see. *That's* why you turn a blind eye to Bradley smuggling weapons." The situation was beginning to clarify in my mind. "Those insurgencies cost the Alliance billions of coin to fight, thereby accelerating this financial crisis you're talking about. You're attempting to facilitate the collapse of the Alliance, aren't you?"

"Abigail, you *should* have been an analyst for the Ministry of Security. You have a knack for seeing into the heart of matters using only a handful of facts to guide you. That's quite a rare gift."

"Thank you. But, if their wars are bankrupting them, why don't they just stop?"

"They can't. Don't you see? They've become dependent on the plunder from these 'client' worlds to prop up the planetary governments.

If they stop the plunder, several planets wouldn't be able to meet their obligations. It's a Catch-22. What would happen hypothetically, on Ampora, if suddenly the people's government assistance ceased?"

"There'd be riots. Oh Gods, you're saying the plunder from these 'client' worlds has been paying the rent on my apartment all this time?"

"That's an oversimplification, but not entirely baseless. Abigail, the riots would be fruitless. What happens next? I'll tell you: *revolution*. Of all the things that may be said of the Council of Governors, foolish isn't one of them. They're well aware of the endgame, but are at a loss in how to prevent it."

The reference to the Joseph Heller novel, one of my favorites, was incredibly apt. The Council of Governors had set a course that could only lead to ruin.

"I have another question for you; a tremendously important one, the *most* important one. *What comes after*? What are your intentions after the fall of the Alliance? There has to be something in it for you when all is said and done." I asked the critically important question I'd gone there to ask. My future depended on Baaqir's answer.

"Ahh, I think I understand. You don't believe in my altruism, eh?" he asked, smiling broadly. "Never mind, it doesn't matter. Besides being brilliant, you are simply one of the most interesting people I've ever met, Abigail. And, since honesty has been today's overriding theme, let me be completely candid with you. The dissolution of the Telluric Alliance would leave a tremendous power vacuum in the human occupied region of the galaxy. And *that* is precisely what I seek."

"I should say so. The various planets would be thrown back to the pre-war system of every planet fending for itself. Those planets in difficult financial positions would quickly become dependent on those planets that aren't. Certain planets would inevitably ascend to prominence, and I'm assuming Dressida would be among them." I theorized.

"Once again you show yourself to be insightful and prescient. You assume correctly, Doctor. I've made certain Dressida is in a strong position. My power and influence would expand exponentially in a post-Alliance galaxy; I won't deny it. Other financially viable planets, such as Titus, Astraea and Theta Barriso would have prominent positions as well. But, I plan for Dressida to lead the way into the future." Baaqir confessed. "In fact, I shall *insist* upon it."

"And you'd lead Dressida, correct?"

"Ahh, I see what you're thinking. No, I have no political ambitions, Abigail. I don't have a face for politics." He laughed, "Instead, I foresee a scenario where I'm a sort of shepherd, helping to secure a prominent place for Dressida among the community of planets. The important thing to remember is the Council of Governors will be dissolved, the CTF broken up and split among the various planetary navies, and the Ministry of Security will be dismantled completely. I'd insist on *that* above all."

"Thank you for being honest with me today, I can't tell you how much it means to me. It sounds like you have a definite vision in mind; I expected no less. As for that QSDM technology of yours, I assume you won't be selling it to the CTF. You're going to keep it for yourself and Dressida, correct?"

"Abigail, never in my life have I felt so transparent. You're right again; I feel no need to share my newest technologies with the Alliance. I actually began the process of withholding technologies a couple of years ago." He admitted. "That's one reason I was distressed to learn your Captain Bradley knew about my QSDM. He's too well informed for my comfort."

"So, you think this financial crisis is going to come to a head sooner rather than later?"

"I do, but I must caution that no one can see *exactly* what will become of the human settlements in the future, not even me. I simply believe we can do better than what we have now, which is for all intents and purposes a police state. You're a historian, you know what happens in police states, Abigail. Chairman Mao murdered tens of millions of his own people on Old Earth hundreds of years ago. Director Baltevous imprisoned, starved, and worked millions to death on Froncesa, simply because they refused to join his twisted religious vision."

"I agree completely. For now, Cyrus, I believe our goals align well. Like you, I think the Telluric Alliance has outlived its usefulness. So, what would you say if I told you I want to take you up on your job offer? Does the offer still stand?"

Baaqir burst out laughing and poured us another brandy. He called Stan into the office and told him to draw up a contract.

"Now, how much did we agree on before?" he asked, "It was two hundred thousand, right?"

"It was three hundred, and I believe you said I might even be able to talk you into four hundred." We both laughed. "But, I'll settle for three hundred on a couple of conditions."

"Conditions? Abigail, don't press your luck."

"It has nothing to do with luck. I've decided I want to help with the toppling of the Alliance. I actually decided before I came here today. So, I want to be more than just your artifact expert. I want to be involved; I want to be useful to the cause. I have a lot to contribute, I believe."

"I agree. This meeting has convinced me of that. You have instincts and brains, which is a wonderful combination. Don't worry, Abigail, I'll find plenty for you to do. First, you must have a title. Let's see... how about Director of Research? You'll be employed by Dressida Financial Holdings on the books, but work directly for me. Sound ok?"

"That's sounds fine, but why do I need a title?"

"Corporate politics mostly. You'll be working with others eventually, and you'll find corporate vultures are all about titles."

"I don't want to step on any toes, plus I know nothing about DFH."

"Abigail, it's just a title. At first you'll learn by working closely with me, but in time I hope to place people under your direction. Trust me, an impressive title will come in handy." He chuckled. "This is going to be a terrific partnership, I'm stupendously excited. Before our meeting started today I'd never have guessed where it would lead. You're a wonderful tonic for me."

"Hold on, Cyrus. I haven't finished with my conditions. I must be allowed to travel and visit my friends any time I wish, that's non-negotiable. I'm looking forward to trips to MK141 to check on the terraforming progress and visit with Sebastien and Leanna. And, I must be allowed to host visitors any time I want, as well."

"Your Tovolek, I presume?"

"Her name is Kara. Please, I understand you aren't fond of her right now, considering what she did on Kleos Prime. That's entirely fair, because I'm still trying to decide if I'm going to forgive her myself. But, I have a hunch I'll eventually forgive her, because I love her. She's dangerous, yes. She's unpredictable, yes. She has a horrible temper, and a haughty attitude that irritates me. All of those things are true. But I think about her all the time, and I miss her terribly, and I'm only human. She may be my 'time borrowed from heaven.' So, I want you to be cordial with her when she comes to visit. And, I want you to speak of her with respect when talking with me. Can you do that, please?"

"Time borrowed from heaven, eh? As you wish. I can't very well alienate DFH's new Director of Research on her first day, can I?" He smiled.

"Thank you. Now, there is one more thing I'd like to bring up, if you have the time."

"Please, go on, Doctor. I'll make the time."

I reached inside my shirt, brought out my amulet and tossed it on Baaqir's desk. He picked it up and began to examine it.

"Sebastien mentioned this; it's the amulet your father gave you? Made of the same alloy as our vault, I presume?"

"Exactly."

"It's fascinating. These markings are in the language of our ancient aliens? The Reges Scientia?"

"The Kafo Codex referred to them as the Hoji Mubrani. That's ancient Galbrodi for 'Priests of Science,' according to my father."

"What's on your mind, Abigail? This is a beautiful piece, one-of-a-kind and has an incredible backstory. Are you offering to sell it to me?"

"I'm afraid not; I'll never part with it. However, maybe I'm crazy, because those nukes Kara set off collapsed half of that mountainside. And, I've read that nuclear detonations create temperatures of hundreds of thousands of degrees within a few meters from ground zero... But, I've been wondering, what do *you* think the melting point of that alloy is?"

Baaqir slowly fixed his gaze on me, smiled devilishly and said, "Abigail, you certainly do amuse me."

THE END

Glossary of Characters, Places & Terms:

Ampora:

Home world of Abigail Thornwell, member planet of the Telluric Alliance. Ampora's surface is 80% water, and the citizens subsist on the copious amounts of seafood harvested as well as produce from massive agricultural enterprises on the ocean's floor.

Archeron, The:

Fabulously luxurious passenger liner operated by Aries Starlines. Passenger capacity of over 11,000. Home/headquarters for Cyrus Baaqir while away from Dressida.

Argonaut, The:

Oscar McTavish's colonial barge, the first of many enormous colony ships to leave the Old Earth system intent on establishing interstellar human colonies. The Argonaut carried 50,000 human colonists to the planet that would come to be known as New Earth.

Astraea:

Telluric Alliance member planet. Astraea was one of the first planets successfully terraformed by human colonists and is renowned for its beauty. Two of the 4 moons are also colonized. The planetary system's total population exceeds that of any other Telluric system.

Avernus, The:

Cyrus Baaqir's personal luxury yacht. The Avernus has state of the art technology, including stealth capability and a very powerful plasma cannon on par with much larger ships designed for battle.

Az-Codor:

Kara's family's hereditary fiefdom on the planet Nir-Kvek. Kara is the rightful heir, but her paternal uncle has usurped the lordship.

Az-Furat:

Kara's mother's family fiefdom on the planet Nir-Kvek. Kara's immediate family escaped to Az-Furat when the coup occurred in Az-Codor. Kara's maternal uncle is Lord here.

Az-Codor, Ka'rra Corda Az-Mur:

Pont-jar of Az-Codor, also known as Kara the Demon. Native of planet Nir-Kvek, heir to the lordship of Az-Codor fiefdom. Partner of Teddy Bradley.

Az -Codor, Zu'rra Corda Az-Van:

59th lord of Az-Codor, Kara's father. Killed by his brother in a successful coup. The brother subsequently claimed the lordship of Az-Codor.

Baaqir, Cyrus:

Wealthy and powerful businessman from the planet Dressida. Hereditary lord of the region known as the Kress. Controlling partner of Dressida Research Group (DRG), one of the most prolific weapons manufacturers in Telluric space. Baaqir also controls the giant finance and banking corporation Dressidian Financial Holdings (DFH) with assets in the tens of trillions. An avid antiquarian and collector of ancient archeological relics, he becomes an eager partner in the Kleos Prime endeavor.

Balmora:

Telluric Alliance member planet. Home of Kristoffea Prison, the legendary maximum-security prison of the Ministry of Security.

Bastar, Huru:

Ancient ruler of Galbrod. Huru Bastar is believed to be the author of the famous Kafo Codex.

Beddan:

The capital city of EV765. Location of the notorious red-light district known as 'Edonismo Boulevard.'

Bendix, Yoshi:

Young crew member on the Tito. Engineering apprentice. Reluctant witness to the mutiny on the Tito which cost Ernie Snyder his life.

Benoa:

Telluric Alliance member planet. Benoa is 60% covered in tropical rainforest, and is host to an astounding abundance of flora and fauna, with millions of unique animal and plant species. Biologists and botanists flock here to do research.

Benotts:

The indigenous people of the Planet Benoa. After human settlers quickly outnumbered the *humanoid* Benotts and began to take over the administration of the planet, many Benotts departed to find new homes. The original settlers of MK141 were Benott refugees. Small in stature but hardy and resilient, the Benotts who remained on Benoa have been subjected to systematic racism and segregation from the human population, more or less living as second-class citizens on their own planet.

Betrads:

Non-human species from the planet Erestis 3, their planet was overrun by the CTF, and Betrad refugees were scattered throughout the quadrant. Tall, thin, and intellectual in nature, Betrads are excellent administrators and scholars.

Bimmel, Daniel:

Abby's school friend and study partner, Daniel tried to pursue a romantic relationship. Abby tried to make it work, but in the end she broke it off.

Caffarra:

Plant cultivated on the planet Vitrallum. The leaves, when harvested and processed correctly, have narcotic effects. Caffarra is widely used medicinally but is also used recreationally.

Calad 4:

Free planet near Telluric space. Calad 4 has never been targeted by the CTF because of the Caladrians long standing alliance with Humans, dating back to the first few Human settlements. Humans and Caladrians coexisted peacefully for over a hundred years before the Freehold Wars started, and Caladrians actively supported the Telluric Alliance during the fighting, some Caladrians even enlisting in Telluric regiments. Recently, the growing number of Caladrians turning to piracy has strained relations, as well as CTF patience.

Caladrians:

Humanoid species from the planet Calad 4. Technologically advanced, friendly to Humans and excellent soldiers, they are tall, powerfully built and highly intelligent. They made excellent collaborators during the Freehold Wars, and now dangerous pirates. Many Caladrians who would have volunteered to join Telluric units during the wars now turn to piracy.

Callicenna, Leanna:

Cyrus Baaqir's personal body servant. Rescued by Baaqir from an orphanage on Dressida which was run by the fanatical religious sect known as the Followers. Leanna was abused and tortured by the priestesses at the orphanage because of her half Lirannian heritage.

Celestia:

Human inhabited planet initially colonized by the religious sect known as Mormons. The planet is a theocracy and fanatically isolationist wanting nothing to do with the rest of the human settled worlds. Because of this, Celestia never joined the Telluric Alliance, and travel to and from the planet is very restrictive.

Cerante Minta:

Home world of the vendor Evetta Abby meets on the Archeron. Another client world annexed during the Freehold Wars, it has a diverse population which includes humans and many alien species. One of the least racially restrictive worlds under the dominion of the Telluric Alliance.

Codex of Kafo:

Ancient book of poems and observations believed to have been authored by Lord Huru Bastar, ruler of the planet Galbrod over 8000 years ago. The codex is written in the ancient, forgotten language of Galbrodi in a stylized format, with allusions, metaphors and vague references. Henry Thornwell, who deciphered much of the codex, came to believe it contained the history of the galaxy as well as predictions of the future.

Common Tongue:

The primary language used throughout Telluric space. It's a mashup of several different Old Earth languages, slang terms, various alien words and phrases as well as new words adopted over the years because of wide-spread usage.

Council of Governors:

The political embodiment of the Telluric Alliance. Created to set strategy and direct the actions of the CTF during the Freehold Wars, the Council is made up of 2 representatives from each Telluric Alliance member planet. Originally, the representatives were appointed by the planetary governments, but over time the appointments have become more and more the purview of the Council themselves. Consequently, the Council has developed into an 'old boy network,' with political favors and financial concerns overriding other considerations. The Council of Governors acts as the de facto legislature for the entire Telluric Alliance because 'Telluric' law has been deemed to take precedence over planetary law.

CTF:

Acronym for 'Combined Telluric Fleet,' the military arm of the Telluric Alliance. Theoretically, the fleet answers to the Council of Governors, however some believe the CTF acts with impunity more often than not.

Bradley, Theodore J, AKA Teddy, AKA Theodore Meyers:

Smuggler, entrepreneur, ship owner and Captain. Once a partner of Henry Thornwell, now partner of Kara Az-Codor.

Dartok:

Mythological creature in the Tovolek culture. A Dartok is a supernatural creature that is revered by the people. They live in the mountains and appear to inflict retribution on evil doers. If someone has been wronged, they call upon a Dartok to avenge them.

Davis, Oliver:

Ensign Davis is a member of Commander Gordon's staff on the George Upton. Even though a green shirt, Davis is kind to Abby and Kara.

Dectus Artiga:

Activist group dedicated to revealing the truth behind the actions of Telluric authorities. Meaning 'Freedom through Truth' in Lirannian, Dectus Artiga was one of several groups that attempted to hack into

Telluric databases and expose their abuses. Labeled a terrorist organization and hunted down mercilessly by the Ministry of Security, they were all eventually killed or imprisoned.

Dekstra Minor:
Colonial world of Titus, headquarters of a very dangerous, rival criminal syndicate of Teddy Bradley's.

Dementov, Gregor:
Ill-fated head of the Archeron's security contingent.

DFH:
Cyrus Baaqir's investment group, Dressida Financial Holdings. DFH is the largest financial institution in the Telluric sphere of influence when measured by total value. DFH's value exceeds 28.5 trillion Telluric coin.

Dressida:
Home world of Cyrus Baaqir, Sebastien Fowler, and Leanna Callicenna. Member planet of the Telluric Alliance and home to the fanatical, nature worshiping religious sect known as the 'Followers.'

DRG Corp:
Dressida Research Group. Huge arms manufacturer controlled by Cyrus Baaqir's investment corporation, DFH. DRG makes a large variety of weapons for the Telluric Alliance. The company has facilities throughout Telluric space. Including the preeminent 'skunkworks' research facility in the entire quadrant, located on the highly secure planetoid KV42 near Dressida's territorial boundary with Titus.

DRG Multi-Phase Plasma Rifle:
The very newest small arm meant for the marines. The weapon is so new it hasn't even been issued to the troops yet. But Teddy has 1000 of them in his cache.

Dulose:
Another Telluric colonial world. Once terraforming had begun, hundreds of ancient cities belonging to an extinct civilization were found. Dulosian artifacts became all the rage for a time, but eventually Dulose tourism died down.

8 Kiloton Tactical Nuke:

Teddy has ten of these in his cache, capable of being dropped from the air or shoulder launched using a specialized launcher.

Elatus 6:

Situated outside of Telluric space, the Elatus system contains 3 inhabited planets populated by the species Laprow. Laprows are avian, nearly 3 meters tall, highly intelligent and technologically advanced. Their cities are said to be the most beautiful in the quadrant. Early interstellar travelers, they nevertheless didn't colonize aggressively, being content in their own star system. Laprows and Humans have coexisted for centuries without hostility, one of the very few alien species able to say so.

EM85 Electromagnetic Guass Rifle:

Standard issue assault weapon of Allied Marines. Deadly at close range and also capable as a sniper rifle, the EM85 is a superior infantry weapon.

EM-1700 Varga-Type Anti-Ship Missile:

A newer generation anti-ship missile, capable of penetrating electromagnetic shielding. The Tito is equipped with these. Manufactured by DRG, of course.

Erestis 3:

Telluric 'client' world where Sebastien Fowler's brother was stationed for a time as a marine. He admitted to participating in atrocities against the indigenous population while there.

EV765:

Free planet whose largest moon, Jett, is host to a large space port. EV765 is also a popular destination for hedonistic, debauched tourists because of its notorious red-light district.

Followers, The:

Fanatical religious order from the planet Dressida. They worship nature, and are fierce proponents of a 'pure' form of humanity.

Fowler, Sebastien:

Head of Cyrus Baaqir's personal security detail. A former convict, he was freed from prison at the direction of Baaqir, then educated and trained in many forms of combat to prepare him for command. Also, an accomplished pilot.

Fort Eversun:
Capital city of MK141, the 'Mick.' The city center consists of an upscale business district, fine dining, luxury hotels and shopping. But the city center is surrounded by slums in every direction. The population boom from refugees has created an infrastructure crisis on MK141.

40mm High-Impact Photonic Mortar:
Light infantry artillery weapon. Can be carried by a single marine with ammo carried by a few others. Highly mobile and deadly.

Freehold Wars:
Common vernacular used to describe the series of conflicts that humans fought against various hostile alien races. The Freehold Wars lasted nearly 80 Telluric standard years and caused billions of deaths. The Telluric Alliance was victorious, and in the process devastated several alien worlds and cultures.

Froncesa:
Telluric Alliance member planet. Because of overpopulation many citizens immigrate to new 'client' worlds.

Furanills:
From the home world Furanix Prios, furanills are tall, lightly built humanoids. Civilized and tech savvy, they do not intend to capitulate to the CTF if they try to invade. Damon Offerton's wife Mariella is a furanill.

Furanix Prios:
Free planet outside Telluric space. Home to the humanoid species the Furanills. Proud and independent, the people of Furanix Prios secretly plot to defend themselves against the CTF, attempting to acquire weapons and tech through diplomatic efforts.

Galbrod:
Planet of the Kafo system, ancient home of Lord Huru Bastar, supposed author of the famous Codex of Kafo. The codex is alleged to contain volumes of historical information about the entire galaxy as well as predictions of the future. Henry Thornwell became semi-famous for deciphering much of the codex.

Gal-vek:

Tovolek term, similar in meaning to liege lord, or feudal lord. Teddy Bradley is Kara's Gal-vek.

George Upton, the CTS:

Commander Gordon's frigate, named for one of the founding fathers of the Telluric Alliance. George Upton served as a Governor for the planet Titus for over 30 years.

Gordon, Percival:

Commander, CTF security forces. Captain of the CTF frigate George Upton. Megalomaniacal commander of the security force guarding the expedition sent to Kleos Prime.

Graf-tuk:

A mythical creature of Tovolek lore, much like a Dragon on Old Earth.

Grovia:

Telluric Alliance member planet, known for its agriculture. The planet is lush and green and feeds billions and billions of people. Grovia is particularly renowned for its fruit.

Goz 5:

Telluric colonial world on the outer reaches of Telluric space. The moons of Goz 5 host infamous forced labor camps for political prisoners.

Haney, Volstad (Trick):

Crewman on the Tito. Pilot and navigator, participated in the mutiny and murder of Ernie Snyder.

Hartha:

Tovolek slang for a prostitute, or a shameless woman.

Hastings, Gabriel Thomas:

U.N. Astro-Physicist who invented the REL drive, starting the era of human interstellar travel. A statue of him stands in Central Park in the city of New York on Old Earth.

Hermes, The:

Aries Starlines ship, predecessor of the Archeron. Smaller and not quite as luxurious, capable of carrying up to 8,500 passengers. Still in service.

Hoji Mubrani:

'Holy Scientists' in Galbrodi. The legendary civilization whose demise is chronicled in the Codex of Kafo. Henry Thornwell and Teddy Bradley traveled to Kleos Prime in search of traces of their existence.

Hollora:

Newly conquered 'client' planet, home world of Baaqir's blue-skinned twins. Considered a 'primitive' world by Telluric standards, Hollora has rich mineral deposits, thus making it a CTF target.

Hovenop:

Home world of Wa' L'kyne Tubau, Telluric 'client' world strategically occupied and annexed early on during the Freehold Wars even though the residents were never combatants. The planet is home to two different non-human species; the musculux and pomes.

Humans:

Dominant species in the quadrant, founders of the Telluric Alliance, technologically advanced, expansionist race.

I-Web:

The interstellar internet. A vast set of physical relays positioned throughout Telluric space through which digital data bases, personal communications, live feeds, government programs and a thousand other information-based services can be accessed. Strictly controlled, censored, and monitored by the Ministry of Security.

Ixion:

Telluric colonial world famous for its agriculture. The produce from Ixion is renowned for its variety and abundance because of the planet's year-long growing season.

Jaxx, Venson:

Premier of MK141. He has made Damon Offerton his trusted, right-hand man.

Jijia:

Free planet, outside of Telluric space. The Jijians are deeply religious, worshipping a deity called Quadda. Peaceful and kind, Jijians are humanoid in appearance. An agrarian society, and relatively backward technologically, they have yet to fall prey to the CTF and perhaps won't.

Jijians:

Humanoid species from the planet Jijia outside of Telluric controlled space. They are devoutly religious, peaceful, and unfailingly kind.

Jovell 2:
One of the newest 'client' worlds of the Telluric Alliance. Kara's seamstress friend aboard the Archeron is originally from here. The indigenous population is systematically being displaced in order to make room for human immigrants.

Kaart:
Capital city of the Planet Dressida. Leanna Callicenna grew up in a 'Followers' orphanage in Kaart.

Karmarinski Brothers:
Benny and Orlo, smugglers and arms dealers that sometimes deal with Teddy Bradley, as well as Cyrus Baaqir. They are from the planet New Britain and are very unscrupulous businessmen/gangsters.

Katapan:
A large beast of burden originally from the planet Talvia, similar in size to an Old Earth elephant. Several Telluric worlds raise them for food, the meat is rich in nutrients and widely praised for its delectable flavor.

Kator:
Star near the frontier of Telluric space. Location of an enormous region of asteroid belts that are very rich in resources, known as the 'Reaches' of Kator.

Kinians:
Violent, non-human species from the planet Vanu Kina. Quadrupeds, carnivorous and even, allegedly, cannibalistic. Known to have eaten humans in the past.

Kleos Prime:
Uninhabited, desolate planet on the outskirts of Telluric controlled space. Believed to be the location of valuable, ancient artifacts.

Klojuak:
Client planet of the Telluric alliance, currently involved in a bloody insurgency. Kara was captured smuggling weapons to the rebels there.

Krag Aft:

A particularly foul Tovolek expletive. There's no exact translation into the common tongue, but even an approximation would most likely result in this book being banned, so.

Kremins:

Humanoid species native to the planet Temorin 4. Relatively frail physically, Kremins thrive as merchants and bankers, as well as diplomats. Their planet is easily one of the wealthiest outside of the Telluric sphere, with a high standard of living even compared to Telluric planets. Cleverly, the Kremins have avoided being a target of the CTF by partnering with many human corporations, intermingling Kremin finances with human.

K2-7a Fighter Drones:

Jet fighter drones, completely automated. Capable of Mach3 plus in multiple atmospheric conditions. Armored and heavily armed, these drones lend deadly support to troops on the ground while also being capable of air-to-air combat against manned ships or other drones. Manufactured by Pentar Dynamic Systems on the planet Titus, a competitor of DRG corp.

Kutta, Kuttoriff:

Pentoffian militia officer on the planet MK141. He befriends Kara and helps the crew of the Avernus.

KV42:

Planetoid located between Dressida and Titus. Home to DRG's famous 'skunkworks' research facility. Much of the Tellurian's lethal weaponry was born here. The smallish planetoid is so heavily defended it's said it would be easier to storm CTF headquarters on Titus itself.

Kyntava:

Sometimes home base of Teddy Bradley, member planet of the Telluric Alliance. Known for its excellent and prodigious wine regions, Kyntavan wines are rightfully renowned throughout the quadrant.

Laprows:

Avian species from the Elatus system. Highly intelligent, technologically advanced, they have been able to live peacefully as the Humans' neighbors for centuries. Some believe it's because of their disinterest in expansionism, as they keep to their own planetary system.

However, there are those who speculate the humans fear Laprow technology.

Liranna:

Free planet outside Telluric space, with a mix of human and lirannian for a population. Welcoming and friendly to human immigrants, which has so far spared it from the CTF.

Lirannians:

Humanoid species from the planet Liranna. Small in stature, very pale skinned with delicate features, most people find Lirannians quite beautiful. Leanna Callicenna is half Lirannian. Semi-technologically advanced, without the capacity for interstellar travel until first contact with humans. The lirannians have welcomed human travelers and refugees for centuries. They are friendly toward humans (who have brought with them useful technologies), but very distrustful of the human authorities. They fear the CTF, but are fiercely independent and would likely fight desperately if attacked. So far, their friendliness toward human immigrants has spared them from the depredations of human expansionism.

Magrids:

One of the principal combatants against the CTF during the Freehold Wars. Magrids are a semi-humanoid species (one head, bi-ped, but little else in common physically) originally from the planet Torra in the Tempra system. Interstellar travelers and prolific colonizers, the Magrids claimed several planets also claimed by human colonists. Technologically advanced and well organized, the Magrids delivered many significant defeats to the humans during the wars. They are one of the main reasons for the creation of the Telluric Alliance. They've been hunted to near extinction, with only a handful of survivors left on their ruined planet and a few, scattered colonial worlds.

Malcolm, Delbert (Del):

Older crew member on the Tito. Engineer, training Yoshi Bendix. Old friend of Teddy Bradley. Tried to save Ernie Snyder, but was locked up by mutineer Jorra Norassa.

Mahad, Luewer:

Famous artist from the doomed planet Renticula. Only three Mahad paintings are known to have survived the natural disaster that wiped out the civilization on Renticula, and Cyrus Baaqir owns one, 'The Tempest,' declared by him to be absolutely priceless.

Marmo:

Telluric Alliance 'client' world. Marmoans are considered 'humanoid,' but not human. Sebastien Fowler's grandfather was half marmoan.

McTavish, Oscar:

Captain of the first colonial vessel to leave the Old Earth solar system. The 'Argonaut' landed on the planet that would become known as New Earth, with fifty thousand settlers.

Ministry of Security:

Created by the Council of Governors during the Freehold Wars out of concern about several near catastrophic espionage failures. The Ministry is responsible for internal security within the Telluric Alliance, as well as gathering information about external enemies. The Ministry was given authority over the CTF's military police force, and has systematically gathered more and more power to itself over time. The Ministry now has almost unchecked authority in Telluric controlled space.

MIP Cannon:

Magnetic-Induced Phased Plasma weapon, firing a bolt of superheated hydrogen plasma. The Avernus is equipped with a powerful one.

MK141:

Free planet outside of Telluric space, known by the locals as 'The Mick.' The government is sympathetic to those resisting the CTF, and routinely provides refuge to them. But the planet's population is relatively small, and has no military, so people taking refuge on MK141, as well as the local population, are under constant threat from the CTF. 'The Mick' has very little arable land and limited water, so the population struggles to feed itself. However, mineral resources are abundant, and terraforming efforts are under way.

Musculux:

Non-humanoid species from the planet Hovenop. They are short (roughly half the height of humans) with green, scaly skin and bulbous eyes. They have two legs and four arms and are the administrators and intellectuals of Hovenop.

Nemea 2:

World of origin of Cordson's whisky, Abby's favorite. A colonial world of the planet Kyntava, Nemea 2 is part the Telluric Alliance, although not an independent member.

New Britain:

Telluric Alliance member planet. Location of massive shipyards operated by Cyrus Baaqir's corporate empire. New Britain is one of the most productive manufacturing centers in the quadrant because of its relative proximity to vast amounts of mineral resources within several asteroid belts nearby, known as the Reaches of Kator.

New Earth:

The first Earth colony, it was crippled by faulty terraforming and mismanagement when newly colonized. The ecosystem never fully recovered, and now the planet is more or less abandoned with only a few mineral harvesting operations still under way. A population of nearly 300 million at its peak has now dwindled to less than 20 million.

New Gotah:

One of several planets annexed from the Pentoffian Empire when they surrendered. Much of the huge Pentoffian population was forced to evacuate to make room for human immigrants. The system holds vast mineral deposits and sits astride the axis of the former Imperial defense array. The CTF has established New Gotah as the hub of their occupation of the Empire's former territory, placing numerous military bases here in order to ensure the Pentoffians never rise up to threaten the Telluric Alliance again. The planet is also where the tactical nukes Teddy Bradley has in his weapons cache were manufactured.

Nir-Kvek:

Free planet outside the dominion of the Tellurians. Home world of Ka'rra Az-Codor. Dominated by a violent pre-spaceflight, feudal civilization which shuns advanced technology in favor of their traditional way of life.

Norassa, Jorra:
Crew member on the Tito. He leads the mutiny against Ernie Snyder. He also attacks the Avernus attempting to capture the crew for the bounties.

Offerton, Damon:
Sebastien Fowler's friend, government administrator on the planet MK141. Offerton was in prison with Fowler when they were young.

Offerton, Mariella:
Damon Offerton's wife. She originally came from the planet Furanix Prios, but emigrated to MK141 when young.

Old Earth:
The planet of origin of the human race. Remains politically independent from the Telluric Alliance, and maintains only cursory diplomatic relations with the rest of humanity. An early colonization era political figure, Plester Orgensk, famously referred to all of the people leaving Earth as 'Rats, deserting a perfectly fine ship.'

Olustra:
Minor combatant versus the Telluric Alliance during the early years of the Freehold Wars. Now a client world of the Tellurians. Significant because of the lengthy and costly rebellion which occurred there. The rebellion lasted nearly twenty years.

Orah:
One of the many deities in the polytheistic religion of Ampora known as Gremism. Orah is the moon goddess responsible for the tides, and therefore an important deity on a planet 80% covered in water. Orah's good graces mean plentiful food and calm seas. Orah is Abigail's favorite deity.

Parzok, Ghaz:
Pirate Captain from the planet Runivia. She and her crew attempt to capture Teddy Bradley and the crew of the Avernus for the bounties. Teddy supposedly had a fling with Ghaz years ago.

Pelios:
Capital city of Ampora and home of Abigail Thornwell. Location of the Amporan Academy of Sciences. Pelios boasts a population of over 90 million.

Pentoff:

Alien world, home of the Pentoffians, one of the primary adversaries of the Telluric Alliance during the Freehold Wars. After years of war the Pentoffian Empire was forced into a humiliating surrender to the Tellurians.

Pentoffians:

From the planet Pentoff, major combatants during the Freehold Wars. Accused of several atrocities before and during the wars, legendarily vicious and ruthless warriors. Red, leathery skinned and yellow eyed, many humans think they have the appearance of devils or demons.

Pioneers:

Euphemism for the humans being sent by the Resettlement Bureau to homestead newly conquered 'client' worlds, replacing the indigenous populations.

Pithra 4:

Former Pentoffian colonial world devastated during the war. After nearly a year under siege the planet's defense shielding finally gave way and the planet was famously bombarded from orbit by a fleet of CTF battlecruisers. The surface of the planet was so decimated that ancient ruins from a lost civilization, buried for centuries under kilometers of rock, were exposed. The actual death toll from the siege and battle of Pithra is classified, but the Pentoffians accused the Tellurians of genocide as a result. They claim 5 billon Pentoffian colonists were killed. The CTF has never confirmed or denied the claim.

Plavic, The:

The pirate Ghaz Parzok's flagship. Parzok makes the mistake of attacking the Avernus. A 'Plavic' is a Runivian bird of prey.

Pomes:

Non-humanoid species from the planet Hovenop. Reptilian in appearance and quite strong for their size, they are the manual laborers of Hovenop. Less intelligent than the musculux, they have a subservient position in affairs of state.

Pont-Jar:

Title given to a female heir to a lordship on the planet Nir-Kvek. Kara Az-Codor is the Pont-Jar of Az-Codor. The male equivalent is Pont-Var.

PPRs:

Pre-Portioned Rations. Dehydrated single serving meals produced mostly for military consumption. However, PPRs are often stocked on civilian space vessels because they take up little room and are good for years if stored properly.

Prockfora, Ricklan:

Leader of the rebels during the famous twenty-year rebellion on the planet Olustra during the Freehold Wars. A master of guerilla warfare, Prockfora nearly regained the Ulans' independence.

Progg:

CTF slang for insurgents, or rebels. The origin isn't known for sure; some think it's derived from 'progressive.' Others believe it's loosely based on the term 'Prockfora,' the name the rebels on the planet Olustra called themselves, after their original leader Ricklan Prockfora during the Freehold Wars.

Pruitt, The:

Another of Teddy Bradley's ships. Designed for speed and smuggling. Baaqir forces Bradley to sign over the Pruitt as collateral before agreeing to support the expedition to Kleos Prime.

QSDM Device:

Quantum State Disruption Manipulator. Baaqir's secret stealth tech developed at the DRG Corp. Skunkworks on KV42. It's possible the tech was stolen.

Quenra:

Tovolek deity. Quenra is the Goddess of the night, and sits in judgement of those who die at the hands of their enemies. If one has shown loyalty and valor, Quenra lets you pass into heaven with your comrades. If not, you are cursed to wander the land of the living in a state of confusion and fear.

Ran-Butra:

The castle keep of the Az-Codor dynasty. Kara's family has held it for centuries, and it's considered one of the most formidable castles on the planet Nir-Kvek.

REL Drive:

The Relativistic Laser Drive, or GTH Drive, after the man (Gabriel Thomas-Hastings) who invented it on Old Earth. The REL drive is what makes interstellar travel possible. The drive, coupled with an enormous amount of energy augmented with laser-induced annihilation, literally bends space/time enough to allow spacecraft to travel great distances in far less time. The only limit is it requires incredibly accurate navigational charts of the space to be traveled through. These star charts often take years to complete, making exploration of the Galaxy still somewhat arduous.

Renticula:

Home world of the famous artist Luewer Mahad, painter of Cyrus Baaqir's favorite, priceless piece of art, 'The Tempest.' The semi-primitive, pre-industrial civilization on Renticula was destroyed by a massive volcanic event centuries ago, and there were no survivors.

Resettlement Bureau:

Agency created by the Council of Governors to repopulate newly conquered worlds with humans. They recruit 'pioneers' from Telluric controlled planets.

R-Type Armor-Piercing Anti-Ship Missile:

Basic anti-ship missile, somewhat outdated because of its antiquated targeting system, but still very dangerous at close range. Ghaz Parzok's ships employ these.

Runivia:

Free planet outside Telluric space. Home world of the pirate Ghaz Parzok and her crew. Runivia is multi-species but generally friendly to the Telluric Alliance. But, clearly, not all Runivians are. Birthplace of the ancient board game Thezra, considered the preeminent test of a strategic mind.

Runivians:

Humanoid species from the planet Runivia. Heavily built, muscular with blunt features and narrow eyes. Runivians appear primitive to humans, but are quite clever and tech savvy.

Sanguinem Cerebrum:

Deadly, bioengineered virus developed by the Pentoffians during the war with the Telluric Alliance. 'Bleeding Brain' killed tens of thousands of Tellurian soldiers but failed to turn the tide of the war. Henry Thornwell contracted it and died of the disease following a long, grueling battle.

Sart-mek:

The harvest festival on Nir-kvek, the biggest holiday on the Tovolek calendar.

Santorian Trap:

In the mythology of the Delponic people of ancient Dekstra Minor, Santor was the lord of the dark and the night. He was a very clever semi-deity and discovered the secrets of the light, so he went to the sun goddess, Shichka, and made a bargain. He promised not to reveal her secrets if she made him lord of the dark. Thereafter he could do as he pleased during the night, and he delighted in playing tricks on the Delpons and making them fear him. But, he could only manifest himself in the dark and so was forever denied the warmth and grace of the light. The trap was that if he revealed the secrets of the light, he could then enjoy it, but he would forever surrender his dominion over the dark, losing all of his powers as a deity.

Snyder, Ernest (Ernie):

Ship's engineer and leader of one of Teddy Bradley's smuggling crews. One of Bradley's most trusted men. Killed by mutinous crew members of the Tito.

Talvia:

Wild, untamed alien world near the Pentoffian frontier. Big game hunters flock here to test themselves against the myriad ferocious, indigenous animals. Zoos on many Telluric planets are filled with Talvian wildlife.

Telluric:

Meaning 'of earth,' it's the name the humans decided to give to their Alliance during the Freehold Wars. Synonymous with the term 'human' in the post Freehold Wars quadrant.

Telluric Alliance:

The alliance formed near the beginning of the Freehold Wars in order to defend the human race from hostile alien species. Most of the quadrant's human inhabited planets joined the alliance with a few notable exceptions, Old Earth and Celestia being the most notable.

Telluric Coin:

Official cyber currency of the Telluric Alliance. Universally accepted throughout Alliance space and most neighboring systems.

Telluric Standard Year:

Unit of time based loosely on an Old Earth year. The Telluric Standard Year consists of 13 months of 28 days each. Each day is 24 hours, calibrated to Old Earth's rotation. The months of the TSY are Unu, Du, Tri, Kvar, Kvin, Ses, Sep, Ok, Nau, Dek, Dek-Unu, Dek-Du and Dek-Tri, though dates are normally written numerically. The year, counted from the advent of interstellar travel, is written first, then the month, and then the day. For example, the day interstellar travel was invented by Gabriel Thomas Hastings would be written as 1-01-01, or Year 1, Unu 1st. The date of Abby Thornwell's boarding of the Archeron was 388, Ses 16th. Or 388-06-16.

Temorin 4:

Free planet populated with a humanoid race called the Kremins. Friendly toward travelers and merchants from other planets, and skilled diplomats, the Kremins thrive as independent commercial investors and businessmen. Temorin 4 is an important financial center for those trying to avoid Telluric banks.

Theta Barriso:

Telluric Alliance member planet. One of the preeminent banking and finance centers in the Telluric sphere of influence. Telluric coinage is minted here, including the 50g gold coin known as the Auric. The Council of Governors guarantees the weight and purity of every Auric minted.

Thezra:

Two-person strategy game played on a board with 48 pieces, 24 per person. The game is ancient and originated on the planet Runivia. Although a two-person strategy game, it has few other similarities to the Old Earth game Chess. Thezra games between masters often take many days to finish. It is considered the preeminent strategy game in the quadrant.

Torrad:

Home world of the Magrids, one of the principal adversaries of the CTF during the Freehold Wars. The planet was beautiful and produced abundant food before the CTF got through with it, but lacks many other resources. This led the Magrids to explore and colonize extensively, bringing them into conflict with humans. Torrad is now a scorched and ruined wasteland, with large areas so saturated by radiation and poisonous chemicals the planet may never be safe for habitation again.

Thornwell, Abigail:

Professor of History at the Amporan Academy of Sciences, daughter of Archeologist Henry Thornwell.

Thornwell, Henry:

Abigail's father. He was an archeologist and professor, noted for being the man to decipher the Kafo Codex. The codex was written in the ancient language of Galbrodi as a sort of epic poem. Henry Thornwell believed it was a record of galactic history and set forth predictions of the future. Possibly even foretelling the apocalyptic end of the galaxy.

Tito, The:

One of Teddy Bradley's small, fast ships used for smuggling.

Titus:

Telluric Alliance member planet. Seat of power for the Alliance, location of the Council of Governors meeting chambers, headquarters of the Trade Guild, and CTF headquarters.

Tovoleks:

Inhabitants of the free planet Nir-Kvek. Kara Az-Codor is a Tovolek. They have a low-tech, war-like feudal society dominated by an Emperor. But power is decentralized, with the regional lords operating as virtual monarchs within their own borders.

Trade Guild:

Consortium of powerful corporations and important businessmen who own a virtual monopoly on interstellar trade. Closely aligned with the Telluric Alliance, the guild jealousy guards their monopoly with a fleet of heavily armed ships tasked with 'enforcing' trade laws which exist primarily to benefit the Trade Guild itself.

Tubau, Wa' L'kyne:

From planet Hovenop, a Telluric 'client' world. He works for the Trade Guild as a customs inspector, and sometimes spy.

Ulans:

Semi-humanoids from the planet Olustra. Minor combatants during the early years of the Freehold Wars, the Ulans are mostly remembered for their valiant rebellion fought against the Tellurians. The rebellion lasted twenty years and was quite costly to both sides. The Ulans now live a peaceful existence as clients of the Telluric Alliance.

Vanu Kina:

Wild, primitive, pre-interstellar planet outside Telluric Space. Famous for its extremely war-like non-humanoid population. Kinians are quadrupeds, carnivorous and allegedly cannibalistic. The planet is violent toward strangers, famously killing and eating the first humans to land there.

Var-luk:

Tovolek slang for a coward. Considered a vile insult on the feudal world Nir-Kvek. Similar to 'filthy coward' in the Human common tongue.

Vindiac 4:

Another primitive, alien world. The Vindiac system lies within the Telluric sphere of control and hosts several ongoing human mining and drilling operations. The natives try to stay clear of the humans as much as possible, but are nevertheless frequent victims of 'cleansing' campaigns.

Ving, Tasha:

Owner of the club Tasha's aboard the Archeron. Also, a friend of Kara Az-Codor, and customer of Teddy Bradley.

Vitrallum:

Another Telluric colonial world, origin world of caffarra leaves, the intoxicating agent in the cheroots Abby buys.

Vitrameks:

Alien species from a distant star system known as system Q-88. Vitrameks are oxygen breathing cephalopoids, and originated on the 2nd planet in system Q-88, however the vast majority of Vitrameks migrated to other planetary systems long ago. Prolific colonizers, and fiercely territorial, Vitrameks are believed to be the first serious instigators of the Freehold Wars. They attacked human settlements without warning, and with the intention of extermination. They never coordinated efforts with other species fighting against the humans, but were nevertheless, quite effective. The vicious strategies employed by Vitramek armies against humans lead to the near extinction of the Vitrameks once the humans gained the upper hand in the war. Once boasting a population of almost 100 billion, estimates now theorize a Vitramek population of less than 10 million. The true number is impossible to guess because the Vitrameks still alive have all been forced into hiding by roving, mercenary teams of exterminators, and sport hunters.

Windrites:

Humanoid race from the planet Winthra. Windrites are intelligent, and tech savvy. Well known for their engineering prowess and serious nature. Windrites are short in stature compared to humans, but physically are quite similar. Windrites have small nostrils and earholes with no ears or noses to speak of. Windrites are not militaristic, and their rather advanced technological capabilities don't extend to weapons technologies.

Winthra:

Free planet not far from MK141. Winthra is home to a thriving industrialized civilization renowned for its quality technologies and engineering. The humanoid citizens of Winthra, known as Windrites, are intelligent and serious minded.

Zymtal Rifle:

Known as a Z-gun, an anti-riot weapon widely used by police and security forces in Telluric space. Named after the inventor, the rifle is a laser-enhanced non-lethal stun gun. It renders the target both blind and paralyzed for up to two hours. Has been known to cause death accidentally from time to time.

Zymtal, Yosef:

Inventor of the non-lethal Zymtal rifle, an anti-riot stun gun used on many planets in the Telluric sphere of control. Though theoretically non-lethal, the Z-gun's effects are quite unpleasant, causing blindness and paralysis lasting hours. There are documented deaths caused by Z-guns, usually victims who suffered from heart or respiratory conditions, seizure maladies such as epilepsy, or general poor health.

Don't miss out!

Visit the website below and you can sign up to receive emails whenever P.W. Schuler publishes a new book. There's no charge and no obligation.

https://books2read.com/r/B-A-ZEBBB-OXNPC

BOOKS 2 READ

Connecting independent readers to independent writers.

About the Author

The author is a retired Air Traffic Controller, husband and father of two. Motivated by a life-long passion for reading, and a fascination with classic Science Fiction stories by authors such as Isaac Asimov, George Orwell and Robert Heinlein, he relishes the opportunity to entertain like-minded readers.

Printed in the USA
CPSIA information can be obtained
at www.ICGtesting.com
JSHW020154160224
57266JS00004B/97

9 798223 500100